Other Books & Stories
by Lynn Bohart

Mass Murder

Inn Keeping With Murder

Your Worst Nightmare

Something Wicked

Also published in the anthology of short stories:
"Dead On Demand"

GRAVE DOUBTS

By
Lynn Bohart

Published by Little Dog Press

ACKNOWLEDGEMENTS

At the time I started writing *Grave Doubts*, I worked in a small hospital in Central Oregon. I began the concept for the story by thinking it would be fun to kill someone in a saw mill – for literary purposes only, of course. Fortunately, I knew people who worked in the lumber industry back then, and they were incredibly generous to a "newbie" writer. So my thanks go to both Rosboro Lumber and Seneca Sawmill for allowing me to tour the facilities and learn something about the complicated timber industry. Although I had not yet published even one short story at the time, I was treated with great respect. I also wish to extend special thanks to accomplished author, Elizabeth Engstrom, who inspired me to write and in the process, became a good friend. Thanks, too, to my friends at McKenzie-Willamette Hospital back in the day when I first started writing *Grave Doubts*. So much of the story is based on the hospital and my experiences there. My deepest appreciation to my current writer's group - Tim McDaniel, Michael Manzer, and Lori Church-Pursley - who read every word and gave me detailed feedback and told me when things weren't working. Thanks, too, to my beta readers, Liz Stewart and Valerie O'Halloran, who give me such great support. I also extend my sincere thanks to Sharon Hu, Lab Services Director at Valley Medical Center, Erin Browder, RD, CD, CDE, Diabetes Education Program Coordinator at Valley Medical Center, Rod Cornutt at Rosboro Lumber, and Rich Sweeney at Renton

Printery, who verified all of the technical information. I also extend my thanks to my friends and fellow writers on Facebook, and to my daughter for putting up with my obsession with crafting the perfect murder.

Dedicated to my daughter.
I love you to the moon and back.

Cover photo(s): John Bohart
Photo manipulation: Chris Glidden &
Mia Yoshihara-Bradshaw
Cover Design: Jaynee Bohart

CHAPTER ONE

The hawk rested quietly on the branch of an old oak, gazing imperiously down on the gravesite below. Fresh graves produced tender morsels of food. And the hawk, with its keen eyesight and superior reflexes, would wait patiently until dinner poked its head above ground.

But the hawk's vigil was interrupted as a lone, dark car pulled up to the cemetery entrance. The predator's eyes rotated in their sockets like small, opaque marbles as they fixed a steady gaze in the direction of the intruder. They watched the car wind its way up the hill, past the mausoleum, past the bank of rose bushes, and past the small sign that led to the new burial site. The car crested the hill and turned smoothly onto the service road that ran along the top of the property, its tires rolling and popping across the gravel. Finally, it stopped behind a bank of large bushes with a cluster of pine trees stood nearby. The driver's side door opened, and a dark figure emerged to quickly cross the road and slip into the bushes that overlooked the grave. There, the figure stopped to peer through thick foliage at the gravesite below.

In the same way a sentinel waits for the enemy, the hawk renewed its vigil and focused its gaze on the newly turned earth surrounding the gravesite. Perhaps a worm would wiggle its way through the rich soil, or a beetle would scuttle across the mound of dirt looking for cover. But the bird's meal was postponed a second time when another car pulled onto the cemetery grounds. The hawk shifted its weight impatiently and twisted its head in short, sharp movements as it watched the second car climb the hill and turn at the makeshift sign pointing to the grave.

The second car parked along the road just below the gravesite. It was several seconds before the door opened and a woman emerged dressed in a long wool coat. She crossed the road and then stopped when she reached the stairs that would lead her to the gravesite. She waited there, staring at the steps as if they created a barrier she couldn't overcome. Finally, she lifted her chin. With a deep sigh, she began to climb, one slow step at a time.

When she reached the top of the stairs, she paused again to survey the area set up for the funeral. Then, she slowly weaved her way through the empty chairs to where the open grave sat waiting for its occupant. The woman gazed into the deep hole, her face a stone mask, while the hawk watched patiently from above.

A minute went by. Then two. Finally, the woman wiped her eyes and retreated to the protection of the large oak tree, unaware that she was being watched by not one, but two pairs of prying eyes.

CHAPTER TWO

Twenty-nine cold and lonely steps led to the uppermost level of the old cemetery. Lee had counted them twice before trudging to the top, her purse and spirits dragging behind. Even on a good day, she hated cemeteries. They reminded her of the overgrown one in which her father had been buried almost twenty years earlier. On that hot July day, she'd watched the one person she loved with all her heart lowered into the ground with her mother standing by, tearless and stoic, one hand looped through the arm of her second husband.

Now, here she was again – on her birthday. She'd come to bury a friend in a cemetery where the persistent rain created sticky veins of mold in the stonework and layered furry clumps of the stuff on the rooftops of all the buildings. After a rain, like today, the afternoon sun could lift the putrid aroma of mildew off the ground like steam. It was all so depressing. Even the surrounding wrought-iron fence made the rows of blackened headstones look like they'd been herded onto this tree-covered butte and held hostage. No wonder cemeteries found their way into so many bad Hollywood horror movies.

Lee waited patiently under the protection of an old oak tree, savoring the solitude. The last few days had been tortuous. She and her daughter had found Diane, dead from an apparent overdose of insulin. The grotesque images of her friend's lifeless body sprawled across her living room floor with her index finger curled limply around an empty syringe and her blue lips parted in a final exhale, had taken up permanent residence in Lee's mind. They paraded their way through her consciousness during the day and subjected her to a terrifying ordeal at night. More than once Diane had spoken to Lee in her dreams, pointing a crooked finger in her direction.

"You're no friend of mine!"

Each time, those five final words slammed Lee into a foggy wakefulness, usually tangled in her own bed sheets. Her lack of sleep since Diane's death had created an intermittent buzzing in her ears, and she thought longingly of her bed at home.

Lee served as the Vice President of Marketing and Development for a community hospital in Central Oregon, and Diane had been her Executive Assistant for the past four years. Although the two women had been polar opposites in personality, eventually their love of antiques and old movies had drawn them together as cautious friends. But it had been Diane's wicked sense of humor that had finally brought Lee out of a self-imposed emotional exile. In Diane's company, Lee laughed, and laughed often. It had felt good.

But only hours before Diane died, the friendship had ended with a bitter argument about Diane's new boyfriend. The police had quickly ruled Diane's death a suicide, leaving Lee to wonder how much she may have been the cause. The guilt was mind-bending.

Coming to the graveyard early today was her attempt to deal with the demons eating their way through her sanity, but it didn't seem to be working. The tightness in her chest was testament to the fact she was nearing a breaking point. When a twig landed at her feet, she flinched, her nerves and senses on alert.

She lifted her eyes to search the branches above her and found a hawk perched in the tree, its graceful head and watchful eye pointed in her direction. Lee felt vulnerable under the bird's gaze and was about to grab a rock, when the glint off something metal at the top of the hill caught her attention. It came from a strip of large bushes where the road wrapped around the crest of the hill. There, a bank of shade trees created a canopy that cast everything below them in deep shadow, nearly obliterating the faint outline of a parked car. As Lee watched, something moved within the bushes, raising the hairs on the back of her neck.

Whoa! Was she being watched? She'd thought so the night she and Amy had found Diane, but that had just been nerves. Or was it? Perhaps the car on the hill belonged to a cemetery worker, or a family member. More likely it was a reporter, come to cover the burial of a suicide victim. The callousness of *that* thought lit a small fire in the pit of her stomach, extinguishing the sudden chill.

She decided to ignore the intruder while she waited for the funeral to begin and turned toward the highway below. The cemetery was built in stair-steps, starting with the chapel and mausoleum at the lowest level. Diane would be buried near the top of the hill, surrounded by tall pines and several oak trees. It was late afternoon, so the highway was busy. The cars streamed in both directions, reminding Lee of industrious little ants going about their business, oblivious to the fact that someone was being buried on the hillside above. How she wanted to be among them, going anywhere but here. For a moment she thought about leaving, but just then the hearse appeared, eliminating her chance of escape.

The car carrying Diane's coffin pulled through the arched columns and moved slowly up the hill, followed by a black limousine and a procession of vehicles. The hearse parked off to the side, and four men in dark suits unloaded a long cedar box. While the rest of the cars parked along the road where Lee had left her Pathfinder, the pallbearers carried the casket in solemn ritual to a pedestal waiting under a small green tent. Engines died. Doors opened and closed. People emerged and climbed the stairs in muffled silence. Some took the chairs placed there earlier, while others huddled to the side in small groups. Everyone spoke in hushed tones, cushioning the air with their strained whispers.

Lee spied Andrew Platt, Vice President of Operations from the hospital. She was about to step behind the tree to avoid him, when he waved and headed in her direction. Lee braced herself for a numbing string of vague condolences. Andrew wasn't a bad guy, just boring. He also lived under the thumb of the hospital CEO, a not-so-comfortable place for someone who had applied for the CEO's job when it was vacant. Lee thought that right now Andrew's signature monotone delivery might just drive her over the edge.

"Hey, Lee," he greeted her with a furrowed brow. "How 'ya doing?"

There it was. Five words spoken without a note of inflection. How did he do it?

"I'm okay," she mumbled with little inflection of her own.

"It's gotta be tough," he shrugged. "Suicide. Shit," he shook his head. "I don't suppose anyone saw this coming. I mean, did you notice anything different about her? Anything that would have telegraphed something like this?"

His facial muscles were twisted with concern, but Lee cringed. She didn't want to speculate on why Diane might have made the ultimate decision to end her own life. She had trouble believing it, even though all the evidence seemed to point in that direction.

"No, I didn't. Actually, her life was pretty good."

"Hmmm," he looked at the ground in thought. "I wonder why,

then. Why would she do it? Suicide is so…I don't know, desperate. Diane must have been really hurting…emotionally, I mean. Too bad. She was a good person." He paused. "Too bad," he repeated with a sigh, shaking his head again.

"Yes, it is," Lee replied.

God, she thought, would this day never end? She finally tried to finish the conversation by making a half turn away. Andrew took the hint, placed a reassuring hand on her shoulder and moved on.

Lee remained by the tree, allowing the other mourners to fill in the space between her and the grave. Soon, a voice cut through the muffled whispers. The minister had moved into position just in front of the casket, and the mourners closed ranks. Lee was quickly sandwiched between a tall man dressed in a gray suit and a large woman wearing a horrid feathered hat. The minister began the eulogy, his voice rising and falling with a practiced cadence.

Lee glanced up to the disappearing blue sky above, holding back tears. Dark clouds had assembled off to the east and were beginning to make their move to blot out the sun. The breeze had also picked up, whistling a discordant tune through the trees. Soon it would begin to rain, making Lee wonder if you could hear raindrops through a wooden casket. She reached up to wipe away a tear, condemning herself for complaining about Diane's boyfriend the night she died. Why hadn't she just let it go? Why had she let that Neanderthal come between them? But suddenly, her thoughts were interrupted.

"What a waste," the woman next to her hissed in a conspiratorial tone. "You have to be weak-minded to turn to suicide," she said, leaning into Lee. She flicked her head with a smug look, flapping the feathers of her hat in the breeze.

Lee stared at her open-mouthed, briefly entertaining the thought of using her fist to wipe away the woman's sanctimonious expression. But just then, the mourners mumbled "Amen," and the graveside service ended. People began to move in a multitude of directions. Lee found herself in the middle of the crowd, unable to go forward, unable to go back. She remained there, as motionless as a boulder in the middle of a stream as people separated around her, some heading for the stairs, some heading to say good-bye to the family.

A few people from the hospital acknowledged her, but she merely nodded in return. Her eyes were focused now on the casket, which would appear and disappear in momentary glimpses. All of a sudden, a young man passing too close slammed into her shoulder, throwing her off balance. Her leather pump skidded in the damp grass. She would have landed on her butt had someone not grabbed her elbow and whip-lashed her quickly back onto her feet. Lee erupted in a giddy sigh of relief, only to freeze in place as she stared into the face of the man she detested.

"You want to be careful, Lee," Bud Maddox's voice hummed.

Maddox had been Diane's boyfriend and drew an artificial smile across the dark, heavy features that crowded his face. Lee twisted her wrist trying to break away, but he held her firmly.

"We've already lost one member of your staff," he murmured. "Don't want to lose you, too."

Lee finally yanked her hand free, wiping the clammy feeling off onto her coat.

"I'll be fine."

His funhouse smile lingered a moment longer before he finally turned away. Lee rubbed her wrist where the skin felt numb. When someone touched her elbow, she visibly flinched.

"Sorry, Lee." It was her friend, Robin, from the hospital. "I got here late. You okay?"

Lee couldn't help a glance at the retreating figure of Bud Maddox before replying. "Yeah, I'm okay." She turned her attention to Robin. "I thought you were in Atlanta."

"I got back this morning and heard the news."

Robin Chang Grady was the Director of Human Resources at the hospital and served on the executive team there with Lee.

Lee rubbed her eyes, thinking she needed some aspirin. "I was planning on calling you later, anyway."

"You look exhausted."

Lee sighed. "I'm just getting a headache."

"This can't be easy," Robin remarked, placing a reassuring hand on her arm. "I'm sorry I couldn't be with you at the service earlier. How are you really? They said you found her."

Lee paused before responding. There was no way to describe how she felt about being the one to have found her friend dead from an apparent suicide. There were no clever phrases. No comforting words. So, what could she say?

"It was pretty awful," she finally whispered.

"Lee, why don't you come over for dinner tonight? Alan's making some weird casserole he tried at a Boy Scout rally, but I promise a great dessert. It's your birthday. You shouldn't be alone."

The warmth that was a natural part of Robin's personality came through in her voice. But Lee wondered how Alan really felt about the invitation. As a Eugene police detective, he often worked long hours. The couple rarely entertained in the middle of the week.

"C'mon, Lee. Alan's the one who wanted me to invite you," Robin said, as if reading Lee's thoughts. "He insists."

"Okay," Lee replied. "Amy is heading back to Corvallis, and I could probably use the company. Is six-thirty okay?"

"Perfect. Just promise to humor Alan and ask him for the recipe."

The flicker of a smile crossed Lee's face. "You realize I don't cook much anyway, so it won't make a difference. Can I bring anything?"

Robin squeezed her arm. "Just a smile."

"I haven't had too many of those lying around lately."

"I know. See you at six-thirty."

Robin turned and headed for the stairs. Lee watched her leave. Perhaps a night with her friends was a good idea. When she heard her name a second time, she turned to find Diane's sister approaching.

"Lee," Carey repeated, stepping forward. "Thanks for coming."

Carey had disengaged from well-wishing mourners, but her mother still clung to her arm. Carey was a younger and softer version of Diane. While Diane's face could have been chiseled from granite, Carey's was that of an angel, with rounded cheekbones and a full, bow-shaped mouth. Yet, today, deep shadows rimmed the rich, hazel eyes that reminded Lee so much of Diane. And the corners of Carey's mouth drooped, as if her grateful smile had just finally given up and gone home. She had attempted to fix her hair by pulling it back with a couple of clips, but in the end, the normally loose brown curls looked like someone had trampled them with heavy boots. Her husband stood in the background, arms folded across his chest, the tall pines reflected in his metallic sunglasses.

"I wanted to thank you for taking care of things the other night," she began. "This has been a difficult few days, and I haven't had a chance to call you."

She stopped as if the strain would overcome her. Lee was about to say something, when Carey reached into her purse and pulled out a small, carved onyx bird, not much larger than a golf ball.

"I've started going through Diane's things and thought you'd like to have this. I know you were with her when she bought it. Think of it as my way of saying thank you." She placed the small bird into the palm of Lee's hand.

Lee recognized the bird as one of Diane's favorite possessions. As her fingers closed around the familiar dark figurine, a faint rush of energy seemed to flow through the palm of her hand and up her forearm. The tingling sensation warmed her muscles, bringing them back to life. Lee stared with wonder at the bird, forgetting for a moment that Carey was still there.

"You know, if you'd like to stop by next weekend, we'll be going through the condo. There are several things I think you'd like. In fact, I thought about bringing her old camera, too," Carey chattered nervously. "Diane said you have a collection of old clocks and cameras. Vern will just get rid of it. She said you always tried to get her to upgrade to a digital camera," Carey attempted a short laugh. "But not my sister." She dropped her head and quickly wiped away a tear. "Anyway, I thought maybe you'd like to have it, you know, as a way to remember how you guys used to argue good-naturedly."

The reference to arguments made Lee inwardly flinch. She didn't think she was ready to go back to the spot where she'd found Diane dead, but then heard a distant voice say, "Thanks, Carey. I'd like to stop by. I need to return her key anyway."

"Great. You were a good friend to Diane, Lee. She didn't have many." Carey's mouth opened and then snapped shut as her eyes darted toward her husband. "Anyway, I'll see you next weekend."

Carey turned and helped her mother descend the steps. Her husband remained poised at the head of the stairs, turning his attention on Lee. He was a hard-looking man with close-cropped blonde hair, a square face, and firm jaw. His scrutiny made Lee nervous, and she gave an awkward smile in response. He merely turned and followed the two women down the stairs.

Lee kept the bird in the palm of her hand and turned her attention to the grave. She was alone now, except for two men in dark suits who stood off to one side, presumably waiting for the workmen to lower the coffin to its final resting place. The tent flapped gently in the breeze.

Lee moved up to the casket and stared with sadness at the sleek lines of the sculpted box. She imagined Diane lying in repose within and wondered if Carey had chosen Diane's favorite lavender linen dress. Linen wouldn't be heavy enough for winter. Then, again, Diane wouldn't be feeling the cold anymore.

A plaintive cry made Lee look up to where the majestic form of a bird hung in the sky, caught by an air current like a perfectly weighted kite. It was the hawk. Lee watched the bird drift aimlessly in circles until it suddenly tipped one wing and dived for the ground. With a whoosh, it skimmed directly over the coffin before it lifted up and over the treetops. Lee watched it disappear, her heart pounding.

She didn't believe in omens, but the bird's bizarre behavior heightened the desolate feeling in her soul, and she huddled more deeply into her coat. When a cool breeze burrowed under her collar, she turned to face the wind, allowing the cool air to run its fingers across her cheeks and eyes, giving her the feeling that she was flying, too. She closed her eyes and tried to relax. She was so lost in the moment that she barely heard the familiar, throaty voice that whispered past her ear.

"Leeeee..."

Her eyes popped open and she whipped around, half expecting to find Diane standing behind her. Her entire body shivered with a chilly frost. With trembling fingers, she pulled up the collar of her coat. In the distance, she saw the hawk and wondered if what she'd heard had been only the call of the bird. As she watched the hawk sail across the tree tops, she allowed her eyes to scan the vista before her. When her gaze fell on the eerie silhouette of a woman standing motionless between two trees just above the gravesite, Lee paused.

The woman was dressed all in black. Although afternoon shadows had captured the hillside, she wore sunglasses and a large hat. Storm clouds had gathered behind her, and the crisp breeze entwined the woman's dark hair with a long black scarf draped around her neck, drawing invisible patterns in the air. She looked absolutely ethereal, as if she might float right off the ground. Lee couldn't help but stare, transfixed, wondering who she was.

In return, the woman seemed to watch Lee. It wasn't until the sound of laughter erupted on the road below, that Lee's attention was drawn away. A straggling group of mourners stood chatting by their cars. Someone had made a joke. But their laughter died as suddenly as it was born, leaving a hollow sound in its wake.

Lee turned back, but the woman in black was gone. And the onyx bird in her hand had begun to glow an eerie, luminescent red.

CHAPTER THREE

By the time Lee left the cemetery, a light rain had begun to fall. In Oregon, rain was like a neighbor you saw too often on the street. You recognized it, accepted it, but tried to ignore it. Most people didn't even carry umbrellas.

She stopped at the store to get cereal for her morning's breakfast and then entered the west side of Eugene and the University of Oregon campus where the pizza parlors, bookstores, and shops formed a small city within a city. Despite the drizzle, students filled the sidewalks and lingered at the corner Laundromat chatting and smoking, book bags thrown over their shoulders, with various dogs in tow.

Lee lived just south of campus in the University District. It was an old, affluent part of the city. Here the pace was slow, and the architecture was an eclectic mix of Craftsman and Victorian styles. Most homes enjoyed wide front porches and sloping front lawns, while trees stretched their branches across the streets in leafy canopies. One could almost picture a time when a horse and carriage was the main form of transportation and the favorite form of entertainment was a stroll after dinner. When Lee selected a home here, it had been as much a strategic move as one of taste. Lee hoped her daughter, Amy, would enroll in the School of Education at the university. But the strategy hadn't worked; Amy had enrolled at Oregon State University in Corvallis instead, some thirty miles to the north.

Lee approached her white, two-story bungalow, noticing that her brother's blue Mazda was parked out in front. As she prepared to turn onto the side street and into her driveway, a car swerved away from the curb in front of her, cutting her off. She slammed on her brakes, and everything on the front seat flew onto the floor. Lee directed a string of expletives at the retreating sedan before pulling into the narrow dirt drive at the side of her own property. She retrieved her few groceries, dumped them back into the bag, and hurried up the walkway towards the front door. As she rounded the corner of the porch and up the front steps, she almost collided with her brother. He was coming down the steps with her antique typewriter tucked under one arm.

"Whoa, where do you think you're going with that?" she snapped, ducking under the eaves of the porch to stay dry.

Patrick gave the machine a quizzical look and then looked back at Lee. "I'm off to rehearsal." With a brisk nod, he continued past Lee and down the steps.

"Patrick, stop!"

Patrick stopped. Lee moved down the steps behind him, careful not to leave the protection of the overhang. Patrick stood just beyond it, sheltering the typewriter with his jacket. The light rain glistened off the auburn curls on his head.

"I repeat, where do you think you're going with my typewriter?"

He turned around slowly, his boyish grin revealing a slightly crooked set of polished white teeth.

"I need to borrow it for a play I'm doing. Six weeks, tops."

"Did you ever hear of asking?"

The reddish brows that framed his deep green eyes creased for a moment as he considered the question. "Nope," he glimmered. He skipped up onto the step with Lee. "Do you mind, really? I mean, it's not as if you ever use it."

She sighed. "Okay, but only if I get an acknowledgement in the program."

"Deal. I'll even include your middle name," he offered.

"Lee *is* my middle name."

"Then I'll include your first name."

"I'd have to kill you first," she threatened.

"Whooo," he mocked. "Scary."

Lee frowned at her reference to murder.

"Hey, it was a joke," he defended himself. "Don't go all serious on me."

"Never mind," she deflected the comment. "I'm just tired."

"Well, you do look as if you haven't slept in a week."

"Shit!" she muttered, going back up the steps. "I'm going inside."

"Hey, you're the one who said you were tired."

She turned back. "I just came from Diane's funeral."

Patrick frowned. "Sorry. I forgot." He came to stand next to her. "You okay? I could stick around awhile."

"No," she replied, reaching for the door. "Amy is still here, and I'm going over to Robin's for dinner."

"Going to see Detective Grady, are you?"

She turned to him with a narrowed glance. "I said I was going over for dinner."

"Yeah, but you really want to talk to Alan." Patrick's green eyes sparkled, undeterred. "You don't think Diane killed herself. How could you? Diane was the toughest broad I ever met. I used to think she was a man with tits."

"Patrick!" Lee stared at her brother.

"I don't mean she didn't have feelings, but she always acted with such purpose, such focus. You know what I mean? I picture people who kill themselves as being, I don't know, kind of lost. Like you."

"What's that supposed to mean?" Lee demanded.

"Lost, you know, cut off from the rest of the world. When was the last time you had a date?"

"What does that have to do with anything?"

"When was the last time you took a vacation?"

"Who the hell cares?" she snarled.

"When was the last time you did anything for yourself?"

He snapped this last question like a wet towel, and she responded by opening the door and attempting to close it in his face. He pushed it open and followed her around the base of the staircase and down the narrow hallway to the kitchen.

"You know, Roger what's-his-name wasn't such a bad guy," Patrick prattled on behind her. "He really liked you."

"No," she spat. "He liked you." She threw her keys onto an old roll-top desk that sat against the wall in the big farm-style kitchen. "He spent more time watching soccer matches with you than he did with me."

"So? He liked sports. What's wrong with that?"

Lee placed the bag of groceries onto the white-tiled counter and pulled down a glass from the cupboard before going to the refrigerator. "I'll tell you what's wrong with that." She grabbed a liter bottle of cola, while she talked over her shoulder. "I don't like sports. That's what's wrong with that. 'Good guy' Roger, as you put it, didn't like anything I like. That's why I stopped seeing him. He was a bore." She poured herself a drink and took a long gulp.

"You have to be kidding. You think he was a bore because he didn't like Cary Grant movies and the junk you buy at yard sales? Give the guy a break!"

Patrick snorted with self-righteous indignation. That was so like Patrick, Lee thought. He never assumed he might be wrong.

"You know, it wasn't yard sale junk that he didn't like. He thought valuable antiques, like that typewriter, were dusty and smelly."

"Okay, I get it. He wasn't your type. But I don't think they're dusty and smelly," he said, patting the typewriter lovingly.

"Good thing," she said with a smile. "Or you'd be looking somewhere else for your stage prop."

"Never!" he grinned. "You are my antique dealer-of-choice whenever I need some piece of lost art or treasure."

Lee chuckled despite her mood and returned to her drink in hopes the caffeine would refuel her engine and wipe away the headache.

"What's this?" Patrick asked.

Lee turned to find him holding a card that had arrived in her mailbox the day before without a stamp.

"A poorly crafted condolence," she grunted.

"Pretty strange if you ask me," he said, reading the inside copy. "What do you think this means...'things aren't what they seem'? Sounds like either a threat or a clue."

Lee walked over and snatched the card from his hands. "No, it's a poorly crafted condolence, like I said. Now go back to your play." She waved the card in his face and then went back to the counter. She was reaching up to put away the cereal when Patrick continued.

"Hey, Lee. Can I ask you a question?"

"Ask," she replied without enthusiasm.

"Do you think Diane all of a sudden hit a wall that night and decided that life just wasn't worth living, found a needle to inject enough insulin to send her to bye-bye land and then dropped dead on her living room floor, knowing that you or someone else she cared about would find her that way?"

Lee stopped with her hand still on the shelf. "That's more than one question."

"C'mon, Lee. Even Diane wasn't that callous."

Lee turned and leaned against the counter, feeling fear welling in her chest. She crossed her arms hoping Patrick wouldn't notice that her composure was all but fractured.

"What do you think?" she asked, her voice cracking.

He paused before responding. "I think someone might have helped her."

Tears plopped over the rims of Lee's eyes before she could get a hand up to catch them.

"Dammit, Patrick! You don't know anything. You've spent too many hours on stage cooking up make-believe characters in make-believe lives. This isn't make-believe. This isn't the theater. People kill themselves. People you think would never kill themselves, kill themselves. It happens. Shit happens!"

He shrugged his broad shoulders and backed towards the door, while she struggled to compose herself.

"You keep working on that, Lee. Give it a few weeks, and you might even believe it. Meanwhile, thanks for the typewriter. I really need it."

A moment later, the front door closed and Patrick was gone. She used her sleeve to wipe away the tears and moved over to the table to pick up the strange card Patrick had held. Lee glanced at the illustration of an angel floating above the clouds, harp tucked neatly under her elbow. The card had arrived on Saturday without a postmark, addressed with slanted, curvy handwriting she didn't recognize. She opened it to read the handwritten verse again.

Little do we know
When once we chance to dream
Death may be the final blow
But things aren't always what they seem.

The roar of an engine brought her to the kitchen window just as Patrick's Mazda disappeared up the street. She stood there watching the retreating taillights.

Patrick was right. He was always right. She didn't think Diane had killed herself. In fact, she had openly challenged the police the night she'd found Diane, but they had the bottle of insulin and a suicide note, and they hadn't listened. Patrick was also right about her dinner plans. It wasn't Robin she wanted to talk to; she hoped that Alan could help her understand why the police had accepted just a few pieces of evidence to support their finding of suicide.

The sound of thunder rolling down the stairs made her leave the window to finish putting the groceries away. A moment later, her daughter's voice boomed behind her.

"Mom, I'm ready to go. Did Uncle Patrick leave?"

"Yeah, he's gone."

"Are you going to be okay?" Amy said with concern.

Lee glanced over her shoulder. "Sure, I'm fine. But it's raining again. Do you have to go now?"

"I have a class tomorrow morning."

"You could leave first thing tomorrow." Lee reached for a top shelf, bumping into a large German Shepherd that had appeared quietly by her side. "God! I'll be glad to see King Kong leaving."

Lee pushed the dog aside and grabbed for a cupboard door. As she put the groceries away, she glanced back at Amy leaning against the kitchen doorway, her long legs crossed at the ankles. At five-foot-eight, Amy shared her father's height, but had gotten Lee's dark, curly hair. Lee tried to commit to memory every detail of this child she was beginning to lose. The heart-shaped face and the fact she rarely wore make-up made her look younger than a second-year college student. Yet, even now, dressed only in a baggy T-shirt and jeans, casually leaning against the wall, Amy could have been posing for a magazine, she was that pretty. If it weren't for the severe asthma she'd inherited from her grandmother, she would be perfect.

"How was the funeral?" Amy inquired carefully.

Lee's muddled brain attempted to form a concrete thought.

"Um, it was okay."

She grabbed a can of soup to put it away in an effort to derail the conversation, but before she could change the subject, she bumped into the dog again.

"Why don't you just load this eating machine into the car right now?"

"Actually, I need to talk to you about Soldier," Amy replied. She slapped her leg and the dog lumbered over. "I need to leave her here for a while."

Lee turned to her daughter. "You what?!"

"Maddie called. She tried to get the apartment manager to make an exception and allow us to keep a pet, but no such luck. They won't even allow birds. Can you believe that?"

Amy whined in hopeful exasperation, but Lee's expression wasn't meant to be encouraging. She merely tilted her head to one side and arched her brows as if to say, "So?"

"She won't be here long, Mom. I've already made a few calls. It shouldn't be hard to find her a home."

Lee dropped into a kitchen chair, still holding the can of soup between her hands. She took a deep breath, trying to focus her thoughts through the deepening headache and sleepless haze.

"Why did you get this dog in the first place, Amy?"

"I told you, Maddie thought we would be able to stay in the house we lived in this summer, but the guys who rented it last semester had made a deal with the landlord so they could have it when they returned this fall. So, we had to move into this apartment. We thought if we paid an extra cleaning deposit, they'd let me keep Soldier. But, it's small and doesn't have a yard, and they won't make exceptions. Everything else is already rented, Mom." She threw her mother a desperate look. "I don't want to give her away, but I don't know what else to do."

"I won't have a dog, Amy. You know that." Lee concentrated on not moving a muscle, hoping it would reinforce her point.

"Mom," Amy came and sat across from her mother, her favorite charm bracelet tinkling as it hit the tabletop. "It's not as if you have to keep her. I'll be back on Saturday. She'll keep you company."

"I don't want company!" Lee snapped, inadvertently pounding the can of soup on the table. Amy's charm bracelet bounced a short melody in response.

They both froze. Lee dropped her eyes and drew her clenched fists into her lap. Amy kept silent, pulling the animal to her side.

"I'm sorry. I'm pretty wound up," Lee apologized.

She looked up at her soon-to-be nineteen-year old daughter and then down at the dog now resting its head on Amy's knee. The black mask that extended down the dog's muzzle softened her face, but Lee knew better. Soldier had been trained by a military man as a security dog and had failed a crucial test. She'd been unable to identify with a human being strongly enough to provide the required protection. The trainer had a choice to either put the dog down, or find it a home. Her soft-hearted Amy had offered a home. Now Lee had visions of her daughter's throat being ripped out by mistake.

Lee shifted her gaze to a mug sitting on the table from breakfast.

"I love this mug, you know," she said aimlessly.

Amy had given it to her for Valentine's Day. Lee reached for the mug, absently tracing the two interlocking hearts stenciled on its side. Her world was falling apart, pushing her emotions to the edge. She had just lost her assistant and close friend. Now, she was losing her daughter. She needed to get a grip. Gymnastics had once been her vehicle of choice to blot out personal conflicts. Back then, dusting her hands with chalk and heading for the parallel bars was all it took. In fact, Patrick had once accused her of using athletics to fill the gaps in her life. He'd been partially right. She hadn't dated much back then. She always said she was too focused on the sport. It wasn't until she'd been injured and had to give it up that she'd met and married Brad. After Brad, there was Amy. Now, there was only work.

Lee got up and took the mug to the sink to give her time to think. She put it under the faucet and turned on the water to rinse it out. When the old pipes stuttered, something inside her snapped, and she slammed the flat of her hand against the curved spout with a strangled curse. Amy remained silent as Lee's anguish filled the room. Lee held her breath, staring into the old, ceramic sink, wincing at the tears that threatened to explode. A full thirty seconds passed before she exhaled.

"Okay," she whispered. "The dog stays until Saturday. That's all."

"Thanks, Mom," Amy agreed, jumping up to give her mom a hug from behind. "I know it's been a tough day. You need to get some rest." She kissed her mom on the cheek. "I've got to get going. I'm meeting Maddie for dinner."

Amy left the kitchen, running up the stairs with the dog right behind her. Lee continued to stare into the sink, focused on the small water bubbles that gathered around the strainer. The phone rang three times before she actually heard it. Forgetting she'd unhooked the phone in the kitchen the night Diane died, she reached for that one first only to slam it down before hurrying into the hallway. She just caught Patrick before he hung up.

"Hey," he said. "Sorry about before. I didn't even wish you a Happy Birthday."

Patrick couldn't stand conflict. He was almost always the one to apologize first, sometimes showing up in awkward places in order to do it. He'd once appeared at her office in the middle of an important meeting, intent on assuaging his guilt over a disagreement. She had to let him off the hook now, or he'd be on her doorstep when she got home from Robin's that night.

"Don't worry about it," Lee said. "I shouldn't have snapped. I'm just really tired."

"No problem, and I'll take good care of the typewriter. And I hope you have a nice dinner. You deserve a break. Then get some rest."

"Okay," she smiled. "That's just what Amy said. I'll talk to you tomorrow."

She hung up just as Amy came down the stairs.

"I'll call you when I get back to Corvallis."

Lee perked up and turned to find Amy with a box of folded clothes in her arms.

"I'm going over to Robin's for dinner."

"Good idea. I left a little something for you upstairs," she said shyly. "I'm sorry I won't be here tonight. I mean, for your birthday and all."

Lee smiled, hoping to camouflage her disappointment. "That's okay. We'll do something next weekend."

Amy brightened up. "Absolutely. I'll call you when I get to campus, so turn the answering machine back on." Amy leaned down to give the dog a kiss on the nose, letting her dark curls flop into her eyes. "I left the dog food in the kitchen." She grabbed her purse off the hall table and turned to her mother. "I love you, you know."

"I know," Lee replied, blinking back tears suddenly. Her throat seemed perpetually tight these days, and she swallowed to relieve the pressure. Amy opened the front door and stepped onto the porch.

"You have your inhaler?" Lee stopped her, already knowing the answer.

"Yesssss, Mom," Amy replied, twisting the corner of her mouth.

"Well, don't get used to the idea of leaving this dog here."

Amy smiled. "I won't. By the way, there are a couple of bags of clothes upstairs for the thrift store."

Lee just nodded as Amy ran down the steps and started across the lawn.

"Hey," Lee stopped her again. "You originally said there were two reasons why this dog flunked out of security dog school. You only gave me one."

Amy turned back, the hood framing her face. "It seems she was a bit hard to call off, as they say."

An impish smile appeared, deepening Amy's dimples. For a fleeting moment, she looked exactly like her Uncle Patrick. Then she dashed for the street, the jingling chime of the charm bracelet fading as she reached her car. Lee watched her pull away from the curb, finding it difficult to breathe.

She continued to stand in the doorway long after the car was gone as if Amy might change her mind and come back. When Amy didn't come back, Lee crossed her arms over her chest trying to hold in the sob that struggled to get out.

How could it be that her daughter was old enough to be in college? Lee still remembered the smell of the baby powder she used to smooth onto Amy's skin after a bath, and how she laughed every time Lee touched the bottom of her tiny little foot. Lee remembered staring at that foot, wondering how a foot could be that small. It was like a perfectly made miniature of the real thing. Now, Lee wondered how that foot had grown so big it could walk away on its own.

With a deep sigh, she looked down at the dog standing quietly by her side. "Don't get any ideas. I'm not a willing partner in this."

The dog whined and placed its head beneath her hand. Lee grimaced, but didn't push her away this time. As a brisk breeze wound up outside, Lee glanced once more to the street. A handful of dried leaves had begun to chase each other down the sidewalk, pushed on by an invisible force. She closed the door under the watchful eyes of a large, black bird perched on the telephone wires above her property.

CHAPTER FOUR

A hundred small water jets pounded the knots out of Lee's neck and shoulders, sending tingles of pleasure down her back. Moments later, she toweled off and dressed in her favorite lime-green chenille sweater, faded jeans, and black flats, before surveying herself in the oval mirror that hung next to the vanity. If she thought the image would lighten her mood, she was disappointed. The high cheekbones, a gift from her Norwegian grandfather, helped support the visage, but the whole image lacked energy. Even pinching her cheeks only succeeded in creating red blotches that stood out in contrast to the shadows that dulled her normally clear blue eyes. Only the dark curls that had been cut to frame her face seemed to add any vitality to the image in the mirror. Lee stared for so long at the haggard reflection, that the image blurred and she no longer recognized the person staring back. Just the hazy outline of a woman she didn't really know - a mother, a sister, an ex-wife, an ex-friend.

You're no friend of mine!

The last words Diane had ever said to her seared her mind, and she closed her eyes, willing the tears to retreat. Finally, when she opened them again, her tear-soaked gaze came to rest on a picture reflected on the wall behind her. In it, she and Patrick were perched on the lap of a department store Santa when they were very young. Patrick was two years older than she and sat tucked in the old man's elbow, eyes twinkling, his hand outstretched to snag a curl of the man's fake beard. The expression on Patrick's face never changed. She saw it then as she saw it now. To him, life was a bit of a lark, something to enjoy, but not take too seriously. On the other hand, at some point in her own life, Lee had retreated to an inner sanctuary where few people were allowed. Even Patrick.

Lee sighed and shook her head to dispel the conflicting images. She reached over and picked up the onyx bird from where she'd placed it on the counter earlier. The head was polished as smooth as an oil slick, and the beak was carved like a fishhook. Reflections from the light over her mirror made the chiseled eyes seem as if they were alive, keeping track of her every movement. The lamp on the counter had also warmed the onyx. It was comforting, and somehow familiar. She'd been with Diane the day she'd bought the figurine in a second-hand store in Yakima, Washington, near the Indian reservation. They'd been browsing for antiques. Diane found the bird tucked behind a dusty old watering can, along with two other stone sculptures. Although the other figurines were of the same quality, it was the bird alone that had attracted her, prompting her to take it to the old Indian behind the counter.

Quick to recognize a potential buyer, the old man had waxed eloquently about Indian totems and how they represented the physical form of an individual's spiritual guide. The man had taken Diane's hand in his leathered palm and turned it over as if reading her fortune. With a curious glance at Lee, he'd claimed it was Diane's totem and even offered to lower the price. Lee sniggered in the background, thinking this guy should have been selling used cars. To her surprise, Diane had shelled out the required fifty dollars and taken it home. Cupped now in the palm of her hand, Lee wondered why Carey had picked this one item out of all of Diane's belongings to give to her. She replaced the figurine on her makeup table and finished getting ready.

Fifteen minutes later, she was back downstairs, anxious to get to Robin's. She placed a ceramic bowl filled with dry dog food in front of Soldier. The dog sniffed at the bowl and then turned up her nose.

"What's that supposed to mean? You're not getting anything else."

Soldier sat down, her German Shepherd ears standing straight up like two exclamation points. The message was clear. She wanted something else. Lee looked into the bowl and wrinkled her nose.

"It is pretty pathetic, I suppose, but you have no choice."

The dog whined and slid her paws forward until she lay on the floor, her big black nose pressed against the bowl. Frustrated, Lee yanked the bowl away and added warm water. When she replaced it, the dog rose and began to eat.

"Jeez. Is that really what you wanted? You communicate better than most four-year olds."

Soldier consumed the meal quietly. When the dog had finished, Lee snapped her fingers.

"C'mon, time to go outside."

She led Soldier onto the back porch and then let her out into the backyard. She watched her sniff her way around the withered rose bushes and rhododendrons until the doorbell rang. Letting go of the outside screen door, Lee left the back door to the house open, thinking Soldier would bark if she wanted back inside. Lee was surprised to find Carey standing under the porch light.

"Hi, Lee. Am I disturbing you?"

Carey still wore her funeral dress under a light raincoat, but had removed the gloves and hat.

"Of course not," Lee replied. "I'm going out for dinner soon, but please, come in."

Carey stepped inside and Lee offered her a cup of tea.

"Just a glass of water, if you don't mind."

Lee hung Carey's raincoat on an antique coat tree by the stairs before going to the kitchen. As she filled a glass with water, the screen door slammed. She turned in time to see Soldier pad down the hallway toward the front room with only a cursory glance in Lee's direction. Smart dog, Lee thought. She threw some ice into the glass before following her.

Carey stood looking through the front window toward the street. The sun had dipped below the trees, washing the sky in hues of dark gray. The soft light from a faceted Tiffany lamp cast a warming glaze across Lee's collection of antique clocks that lined the walls on either side of the window, their ticking creating a soothing white noise in the background. Next to the clocks was an oak bookcase that held about fifteen of her antique cameras. Soldier sat behind Carey waiting for acknowledgment.

"Here you go." Lee offered the glass of water.

As Carey turned, the spill from the lamp caught the area under her left ear lobe, illuminating a large bruise. The mark was visible for only a moment and then gone. Lee pretended not to notice as Carey took a long drink.

"Please, sit down, Carey."

Lee gestured to an overstuffed white chair, and Diane's sister sank into its comforting embrace as if she'd just returned from a long journey abroad. She closed her eyes for a moment, while Lee sat on the edge of the flowered sofa. An awkward pause filled the room until Carey opened her eyes to stare at the glass in her hands.

"I just have to talk to somebody," Carey said, still staring at the glass. "Vern couldn't care less about all of this. He thinks I'm crazy."

"You mean about Diane's death?"

"Yes. I just can't believe she killed herself."

Her voice trailed off, and she paused, looking at Lee with a frozen, haunted expression.

"I know this will sound stupid," she continued, "but I think Diane would have died before she would have killed herself."

Lee smiled despite the gravity of the statement. Lee slid down onto the sofa, curious now to hear what Carey had to say.

"I don't know if you knew this or not," Carey began, as she placed the glass on a side table, "but we had an aunt who committed suicide when we were in high school. Diane loved her very much. But instead of being sympathetic, Diane was really angry at her. She felt life could never be that bad. That's why I don't think she'd ever do such a thing."

Another long pause filled the space between the two women. Carey seemed to be calculating her next move.

"But, if she didn't kill herself, Lee, then how did she die?"

The expression on Carey's face – the rounded, innocent eyes and lifted eyebrows – reminded Lee of a child. Diane had often said her sister couldn't make a decision to save her life. Lee suspected she was right and considered whether she should be honest.

"I don't know how she died," Lee admitted.

Carey stood up and crossed to the fireplace, gazing into the cold, black chamber. Soldier lay on the floor in front of the antique chest that served as a coffee table, her eyes following Carey with a calm acceptance. Some dogs were like that, Lee thought, instinctively knowing friends from enemies.

"The police think it was suicide," Carey said to the empty fireplace. "So does my husband. Vern doesn't have much imagination I'm afraid, and can't conceive of anything else."

Carey continued to stand with her back to Lee, both hands resting on the mantle. Outlined by the rich wood of the fireplace and the warm tones of the wall sconces, she could have been a nun in prayer, all dressed in black. Lee watched her for a moment, contemplating the two sisters. Carey was shorter than Diane, and her brown hair had a natural curl to it, while Diane's had been bone straight. Carey's voice was feather light, as if she couldn't quite get enough air into her lungs to support it. On the other hand, Diane's voice had carried the heartbreak of a torch singer. Lee had tried to get Diane to sing on occasion, and once, when they'd had a little too much to drink, she'd succeeded. Diane had thrown a silk scarf around her neck, raised a shoulder and broken into, *"Whatever Lola wants...Lola gets."* The two had peeled off in a fit of laughter, knocking over a bottle of red wine and staining the cream-colored carpet in Diane's condo. It was one of the reasons Diane had recently pulled up the carpet and had the hardwood floors refinished.

"I guess I can't blame Vern," Carey said softly. "Suicide is bad enough. But if Diane didn't kill herself, the alternative is chilling. Vern thinks people who commit suicide are quitters. Now he doesn't want his name associated in any way with Diane's."

"That seems rather harsh," Lee responded.

"You don't know my husband." Carey lifted her chin to the ceiling as if to gain strength from heaven. "Diane wouldn't have been surprised. Vern is very opinionated. He likes things...a certain way. If they deviate, even to a small degree, he gets, well, upset. You'll have to agree, suicide is a severe deviation." She paused again and let her eyes drift back to the fireplace. "He won't even let me talk about it at home."

"You can't talk about your own sister's death?"

"No." Carey turned a saddened face in Lee's direction. "He says Diane was a loser. That she was always a loser. She got divorced and then in desperation dated a married man. To Vern, suicide was just the logical result of an already failed life."

Tears suddenly filled her eyes and she restrained a sob. Lee got up to put a sympathetic hand on Carey's shoulder.

"You don't think of her that way, do you?"

"Of course not." Carey gulped.

"Carey, do you know of anyone who would want to hurt Diane?"

This close, Lee saw that Carey wore heavier than normal face make-up, especially around her eyes where it was a shade lighter than her skin tone. It made her skin almost translucent. Lee thought it was meant to cover her grief...or something else.

"Let's face it," Carey began, "Diane didn't have a lot of friends, but those she did have were very close, like you." She smiled and the corners of her mouth creased into thin folds. "But I don't know anyone that would want to..."

"Kill her?"

Carey just nodded and looked at the floor. When she looked up again, her face looked stricken. "My God, Lee, who would kill my sister? It's really unthinkable. I mean, women like Diane aren't murdered."

"I know. I can't think of a reason why anyone would kill her."

Lee silently wished she hadn't used those words.

"Yet, I can't think of a reason why she would kill herself," Carey almost pleaded. "I just don't know what to think."

Lee dropped her eyes as a feeling of remorse washed over her. The fact that she and Diane had argued about her new boyfriend only hours before her death was something she hadn't shared with anyone. Although she had reasoned away any real responsibility for Diane's suicide, the guilt still lay across her shoulders like a suffocating blanket. The repeating nightmare only punctuated her self-imposed torture.

Carey looked up, her brows knit with deep suspicion. "What do you know about her boyfriend, Bud?"

Lee looked up as if Carey had read her thoughts. "Not much. I mean other than he's married and seems like he's naturally oily all over."

Even though the thought of Bud Maddox made her feel as if someone had just walked across her grave, Lee was glad to throw attention on someone else.

"He gives me the creeps," Carey agreed. "I never could understand what Diane saw in him. Vern wouldn't even allow him in our home. It's been hard these last few months. It drove a wedge between us, and I…" she choked back tears again and went to sit in the chair.

As Carey leaned sideways to wipe her eyes, Lee got another glimpse of the bruise on her neck. When she looked up, Lee looked away.

"I just keep thinking that I never had the chance to say goodbye," Carey sniffled. "It was like I lost the last few months with my sister."

Lee sat down again, considering Carey's loss and feeling very selfish for having focused only on herself these past few days.

"Do you know anything about his wife?" she asked.

Lee shook her head. "No. No one's ever seen her that I know of. Had Diane ever met her?"

"No," Carey said. "Definitely not. In fact, she mentioned once that Bud had never shown her a picture of his wife, so she didn't even know what she looked like. I think Diane was very conscious of the fact Bud was still married and didn't feel right about it. But she said he'd told her he would be getting a divorce. She was convinced that Bud was in love with her. I can't think of any reason why he would harm her, can you?"

"No," Lee replied with reluctance. "I guess you can't accuse a guy of murder just because he comes off as insincere."

"If someone did kill Diane though, I want to know who it was. I want them to pay for it." Carey's eyes lit up as she spoke. "I've looked through the house. I probably don't know what to look for, but I looked through some of her personal papers wondering if I'd find something...I don't know... unusual. Like if she was working on something suspicious, or if she was investing in something risky, or..." she shrugged her shoulders. "But all I found was normal bills and receipts."

"What about life insurance? Did she have any?"

"Yes. I thought of that. I thought maybe she'd taken out a large policy recently and made Bud the beneficiary." Carey laughed as if the thought had been stupid.

"Don't laugh. I think more people have been killed for life insurance than you realize."

"Yes, but she only had two policies. One our parents took out when we were babies. It's only worth about $1,500. And another one when she worked for a time at the university. It was for $25,000."

"Who gets them?"

Carey hesitated, her eyes studying the floor. "We do."

Lee blushed. "Oh, I'm sorry."

She waved away Lee's apology. "Don't worry. I would've asked the same question. It's not as if we can't use the money, either. Vern's business is suffering, and he's too stubborn to branch out into anything else. We've been struggling for quite a while. I have to admit that $25,000 looks like a million to me right now, but I could never have hurt my sister. Not for anything."

A strained silence stretched between them.

"Carey, I never asked you how you were notified. I should have called you myself that night."

Carey sat back with a forlorn expression. "I was home alone. The boys were out, and Vern bowls down at Willamette Lanes every

Thursday. A Sergeant Davis came over to tell me. I didn't want to disturb Vern, so I went over to my mother's and stayed with her that night."

Lee was beginning to form a picture of Carey's husband, and it wasn't pleasant. She glanced up when the clock chimed six o'clock. Carey noticed and stood up.

"Oh, I'm sorry, Lee. You said you were going out. I've stayed too long."

"Not at all." Lee got up. "I'm only going over to a friend's for dinner."

Carey went into the entryway and reached for her coat. "I'd better go anyway. I was supposed to be out picking up pizza. Vern will wonder where I am. Thanks for your time, Lee. It was good talking to you."

"I'll try to stop by this weekend. Amy will be down. I think she'd like to come over, too."

Carey hesitated for a moment as if she wanted to say something else, but turned to leave. Lee caught her as she reached the door.

"Carey, do you happen to have the suicide note?"

"Yes. The police let us have it."

"Could I look at it?"

"I suppose so. Why do you want it?"

"I don't know. Just to answer some questions of my own. Would you mind?"

"Not at all. I'll drop it off." She gave a brief smile and left.

Lee watched Carey walk to her car, wondering why she had asked for the suicide note. What did she hope to learn? She had gone along with the initial ruling of suicide, convinced it was the right thing to do. Now, both Patrick and Carey had expressed the same belief Lee had secretly harbored – that Diane hadn't killed herself. If Lee started asking questions, where could it lead? And how would she know if she found anything of value?

There was one thing Lee did know. In the four short years she and Diane had worked together, two seemingly opposite personalities had become closer than most sisters. They had become two halves of a very imperfect whole. Now, half of the whole was gone, leaving something terribly wrong in its place. And Lee wanted to know why.

CHAPTER FIVE

By 6:15, Lee was ready to go. Light rain shrouded the streetlights, turning Alder Drive into something out of eighteenth-century London. Lee popped open an umbrella and hurried down the front steps and around the corner of the house towards the garage, avoiding the large bushes that crowded the walkway. Coming from California, Lee had often complained to Diane that everything in the Northwest was either situated on a hill, wet, or both. Her cynicism only raised snide remarks from her friend.

"At least we know when the seasons change up here," Diane would reply in her deep Lauren Bacall voice. *"In California, the only way anyone knows the season has changed is when Wal-Mart revamps its store display."*

Despite Diane's obsessive attention to detail, Lee missed her. She missed the quirky mannerisms that accentuated her extreme moods and the carefully chosen words delivered in carefully crafted phrases to make a point only Diane cared about. It was all the things others disliked about Diane that Lee had grown to understand and appreciate. Diane *had* been a pain in the ass – picky, obstinate, even small-minded at times. Yet, Lee had been able to ignore that. Underneath all of her obsessive and irritating traits, Diane had also been one of the most generous people Lee had ever known. More than that, Diane had found something worthy of friendship in Lee. *"A glimmer of hope,"* Diane used to call it. And for that, Lee would be forever grateful.

Lee swallowed to relieve the lump in her throat as she climbed into the car. She backed out of the driveway, making a crisp right turn onto Alder Drive. She noticed the tan sedan that had cut her off earlier that day was parked across the street with its motor running, the exhaust sending plumes of gray smoke into the cool night air. As she passed, Lee glanced into the driver's side window and was startled when a pale, ghostly face floated into view staring at her, its identity obscured by water streaming down the glass. The disembodied image gave her a sudden chill, and she pressed down on the accelerator. The Pathfinder jumped ahead, and the sedan flicked on its headlights. A moment later, Lee saw it pull away from the curb, going in the opposite direction.

Lee hit the freeway on-ramp now anxious to be with her friends. It took her only a few minutes to cross over the Willamette River into Springfield, a small neighboring community where her hospital was located. Red-tipped smokestacks from the Weyerhaeuser paper plant billowed drafts of white steam against the blue shadowed Cascade Mountains that rimmed the valley. Although many high tech companies had moved into the Willamette Valley, there was still plenty of evidence the timber industry owned this part of the Northwest.

Lee exited the freeway and followed Marcola Road north to the open countryside. The rain was moving south, leaving behind patches of stars peeking out from behind a bank of clouds that threatened to overtake the moon. Lee sped on, crossing the Little Mohawk River before passing the golf course on her right.

Alan and Robin lived on five acres where they kept two horses, a goat, and a few chickens. At well over six feet tall, Alan was a bear of a man and an imposing figure. He'd served on the Eugene police force for twelve years and earned a reputation for being a no-nonsense kind of guy. Yet, he also had a gentle side that Lee found intriguing. While Robin owned the horses and loved to trail ride up in the hills, Alan owned two rabbits, which lived in the garage and were often allowed into the house.

Robin greeted Lee at the door dressed in black muslin pants and an Asian print tunic top. Her thick black hair was cut to her shoulders and bounced back and forth when she walked. She led Lee into the kitchen where Alan was just removing a Mexican casserole dish from the oven. The strong scent of cheese and onions made Lee realize she hadn't eaten all day.

"I hope you're hungry," he smiled. Dressed casually in brown pants and a long-sleeved brown shirt, he looked a little like a giant teddy bear.

"I'm starving, and I brought the wine," she announced, producing a bottle from her leather bag.

"Terrific," Robin exclaimed as she grabbed a corkscrew. She

poured the wine and handed a glass and an envelope to Lee.

"Happy birthday, Lee. I'd sing, but Alan said he'd divorce me if I did."

Alan turned from the counter where he had just placed the casserole. "You should thank me for that," he grinned.

Robin slapped her husband's butt. Lee's laugh was short of being lighthearted, but her smile was genuine.

"Birthday celebrations aren't high on my list of priorities right now." She ripped open the card, read it quickly and looked up at Robin with a tearful smile. "Thanks."

Robin saved the moment by pouring a glass of wine for her husband, then grabbing a glass for herself before drawing Lee into the dining room.

"Well, you deserve much more than a card. When this has all settled down, I'll take you up to Portland for a day of shopping and lunch. How are you doing?"

"It's been tough," Lee admitted, sitting in a high-backed chair across a walnut dining table.

"I've been thinking of you all day," Robin sympathized. "I'm sorry I had to miss the church service. How was it?"

"Actually, it was good. Carey read a poem Diane wrote as a child. It was very touching."

"I saw Bud at the graveyard," Robin grimaced. "Was he at the service, too?"

Lee's jaw clenched and she set her wine glass down with a rigid hand. Bud Maddox reminded her of something prehistoric, with his dark, penetrating eyes and heavy brows. She pondered everything she didn't like about the man before realizing she hadn't answered Robin's question.

"Yes. Bud was there," she squeezed the words out, lifting her finger to the rim of the glass. "Although he never approached the family that I could see. I'm sure they wouldn't have had much to say to him."

"I never did understand that relationship," Robin said, echoing Lee's thoughts.

Lee got up to look over a short wall that set off the sunken living room. She watched what was left of the rain float past the flood lamps outside the sliding glass doors that led to the deck. She and Robin had spent many a weekend summer afternoon sipping Margaritas on that deck, but now nothing was visible past the railing.

"God," Lee finally sighed in exasperation, "I hope I never get that desperate."

"Do you think that's what it was - desperation?"

"Maybe she loved him," Lee said, thinking the rain looked like fairy dust against the blackened backdrop of the night. "I'm sure she believed she did, although I can't imagine why." Lee grew silent as she turned inwards. Her final argument with Diane had been about this very subject.

"You okay?" Robin asked.

"Bud was at the funeral with another woman," she said after a moment. "He was discreet. They didn't hold hands or anything, but I'm sure other people noticed. It was rude, to say the least. I think she works in the Emergency Room."

"What a turd!"

"I agree," Lee whispered, staring at her hands.

"I can't imagine what it must have been like…I mean…to find her," Robin commiserated. "I've never been around a dead body. It had to be awful."

The comment brought all movement in the room to a stop. Even the overhead fan seemed to pause. It was several long seconds before Lee turned. When she did, her voice was barely above a whisper.

"It *was* awful. It was the most awful thing I've ever had to do. I sat on the floor next to her until the police arrived, wishing with all my might that she'd just open her eyes and be okay. But she didn't. I stayed to answer questions and finally watched the police cover her up and search the house for any clues. They opened drawers and looked under pillows as she lay at their feet with a sheet over her head." Lee took a deep sigh. "I had to watch one officer photograph her from every angle and then lift the syringe out of her hand and place it into an evidence bag. And when another officer found a note in the paper tray of the printer, they all converged into a tight little ball like a group of sixth graders with a dirty picture. And when they finally let Amy and me leave, all the neighbors stood gawking at us in the parking lot as they watched the coroner load her dead body into a van." She paused, sucking air in through her teeth. "I watched it all. And it was awful."

Robin got up and put her arm around Lee's shoulders. "I'm sorry, Lee. I'm really, really sorry."

Lee realized she was trembling and clasped her hands into a ball in front of her. Just then, Alan called from the kitchen.

"I think we're ready. You girls want to help carry this stuff to the table?"

÷

Forty-five minutes later, Alan and Lee sat in front of an imposing stone fireplace that reached all the way into the beamed ceiling, while Robin prepared dessert. A blazing fire cast a warm glow across a silk embroidery that covered one full wall. Although Robin had been born in the United States and barely spoke any Chinese, her parents had emigrated from Hunan Province when she was very young. She kept her heritage alive through books and collectibles.

Everyone had been polite during dinner and avoided the recent tragedy, focusing instead on Alan's culinary talents. Now, waiting for dessert, Lee struggled with how to broach the subject with him.

"What are you thinking, Lee? You look like you're twisted in knots," Alan interrupted her thoughts.

As Lee sat slouched in a big pillow chair, she felt like a child waiting for Alan to read a story rather than someone about to suggest something that sounded like it came from a cheap crime novel. Alan shifted his weight on the stone ledge of the fireplace, crossing his huge arms on his knees while he waited for her to respond.

"Let me guess," he decided to answer his own question. "You don't think Diane committed suicide."

Lee looked up with surprise. "I didn't know I was that easy to read."

"Most people are when they're grieving. You've probably been stewing about this all weekend." He dropped his chin and looked at her under raised eyebrows. "So, what makes you think she didn't kill herself?"

Lee took her time in answering. She figured she had one chance to make an impression without sounding stupid.

"Three things."

Alan's eyebrows arched. "Three things? Okay, what are they?"

"First, Diane would not, and I repeat NOT have left a suicide note with typographical errors in it. Second..."

Alan held up a hand. "Hold on. What typographical errors?"

"The police showed me the suicide note that night. I noticed the mistakes immediately. Diane had me trained. Someone had left the apostrophe out of the word don't, and there was a misspelled word.

She didn't write that note."

Alan's eyebrows curled into a question this time. "An apostrophe? You've got to be kidding."

Lee sat forward to defend her comment. "I know they sound like small mistakes, Alan, but believe me, they wouldn't be to Diane. This was a woman who called the phone company once to report an error on their Government Listings page. She was habitually correct when it came to grammar. If that was her last note—she would have read and reread it a hundred times to make sure it was perfect."

"Hard to prove," he countered, shaking his head.

"I'm not trying to prove anything, Alan. I only know what I know about Diane. I'm not exaggerating. I worked with her for four years. I was her boss. I knew this woman."

He eyed her carefully. "I don't doubt that." He rubbed his hand back across head. "Second?"

Lee took a breath. "She wouldn't have used the kind of syringe they found next to her body."

This time his eyebrows raised his hairline an inch. "How in the world do you know that?"

"Diane had a diabetic cat and had small syringes at her disposal. The one found on the floor was much bigger than the ones she used for the cat."

Robin called in from the kitchen. "Anyone for ice cream?"

Alan continued to watch Lee. After a moment he shifted his attention to Robin. "No, Hon, I don't think so."

"Diane was never comfortable giving the cat injections," Lee continued, ignoring Robin. "She didn't even like having the syringes in the house, but she was forced to. I know for a fact the syringe found next to her body wasn't the kind she used for the cat."

Alan looked at his hands, contemplating her comments. "If she was going to kill herself and didn't think she had the necessary syringe, all she'd have to do is go out and buy another syringe. They're fairly easy to obtain."

"Why would she buy one if she already had a box-full?"

"I don't know. But we know for sure she had insulin in the house," Alan shrugged.

Alan relayed this last piece of information as if delivering the final statement at a college lecture. No question. Pure fact. Lee felt a defeat she didn't want to admit, making her gaze into the fire. To fill the space, Alan pulled out his pipe and slipped it into his mouth. He tapped his pockets, searching for the tobacco. Robin interrupted the silence by entering the room with a tray filled with plates of apple pie topped with whipped cream. She looked at the two mute figures.

"Don't tell me...we're talking about Diane." She extended a plate to Lee.

"Do you mind?"

"Of course not." She approached her husband, and he lifted a plate off the tray. "I think we all need to talk about it. I mean, let's face it, it's a stretch to think she killed herself."

Lee looked up with a jerk. "What?"

Robin put the tray down, took her own dessert, and sat on the sofa.

"Why?" Alan inquired, putting the pipe down and lifting his fork.

"Because suicide just wasn't Diane," Robin said. "You didn't know her very well, Alan. It'd be like you offering to wear a tuxedo. Know what I mean?" She raised an eyebrow to emphasize her point. "The whole hospital is buzzing about it."

"They are?" Lee jumped.

"Yes, I've been getting text messages all day. C'mon, Lee. Diane had a reputation. And it wasn't for her easygoing personality, if you know what I mean." Robin settled back into the sofa, letting it engulf her small frame. "She was a perfectionist and a bit of a snob. And she wasn't exactly popular for it. Suicide would've been a weakness she would never have shown to anyone. It's certainly not how she would have wanted people to remember her." Robin paused to take a bite of pie.

"I agree," Lee said almost dumbly.

Alan turned to Lee as he used his fork to cut off a piece of his own dessert. "You said there were three things that made you think she didn't kill herself."

"The third was her cat, Sasha. Since her divorce, Sasha was the center of Diane's world. She doted on the thing. She always left the cat at the vet's when she went out of town and only reluctantly let me take care of it the few times when the vet didn't have room. The cat had to have shots twice a day and be fed at regular intervals. Otherwise, like any diabetic, it could go into a coma."

Robin looked up from her dessert. "What happened to the cat?"

"Amy took it to the emergency clinic. It's still there. I'm not sure who will take her. I don't think Carey's husband would allow Carey to have a cat." Lee put her pie down untouched and turned to Alan.

"You see Alan, that's what I mean. The cat was due for her shot at six that morning. Amy and I didn't find Diane until almost six that night. Sasha had missed two shots and was in a bad way. Diane would never have risked Sasha's life. I'm telling you, Alan, Diane didn't kill herself!"

Lee stopped, knowing she was beginning to sound hysterical. She sat back and took a deep breath. Robin watched her husband, her fork poised midair. Alan looked from one woman to the other, taking his time framing a response.

"The officers searched the entire house and didn't find anything, except the suicide note. They even interviewed the neighbors. There's nothing for them to act on. Nothing to prove."

"I can show you exactly where the cat's syringes were kept," Lee snapped. "The middle kitchen drawer. I showed it to Sergeant Davis that night, but he ignored me. Alan, they think this is an open and shut case of suicide. They won't investigate any further!"

"Slow down, Lee," he said, raising his hand in a gesture of peace this time. "What you're both describing are only opinions and hunches. You can't prove anything. At this point, there's nothing for them to investigate."

"What about the typos?" Lee asked, her eyes searching Alan's face for any sign of agreement.

He shrugged his broad shoulders. "She was distraught. She typed the note in a hurry. When you're about to commit suicide, you're not thinking too clearly."

Lee stood up and paced the floor in front of the big picture windows. She stopped in front of a corner curio shelf filled with carved Jade figurines. The room grew silent as they each waited. Finally, Lee turned, her feet spread apart in a firm stance.

"I don't believe it. I'll never believe it. You didn't know her, Alan. Diane once made the entire staff stay after work to help her completely reformat a sixteen-page booklet that was due by eight the next morning because she thought the margins were too narrow. The margins! No one in the office even noticed it except her. But, Diane fretted about it all afternoon until she couldn't stand it anymore. Do you understand what I'm saying?"

"Committing suicide isn't a rational act," Alan countered. "She wouldn't necessarily behave normally."

"But why would she kill herself? She had everything to live for. She had a great job. She volunteered at her church and owned a beautiful condo right on the river. And she had a new man in her life. Why in the world would she kill herself?"

Alan and Robin shared a guarded look. Then he stood and placed his empty plate on the mantel where he was pleased to find his tobacco pouch.

"Well," he began, pressing tobacco into the bowl of his pipe. "I checked the police report. They interviewed her boyfriend and asked him the same thing. He said he'd recently broken up with her and that she'd taken it pretty hard."

Alan looked at Lee, but she turned away. The room grew quiet again.

Finally, Robin broke the silence, "Personally, I think the bigger question is why anyone would murder her. That's the part I can't figure out."

"I don't know," Lee muttered and slumped back into the chair.

Robin finished her dessert and eased herself up to retrieve everyone's plates. Lee's pie remained untouched. As Robin exited to the kitchen, she paused to offer one last opinion over her shoulder.

"I don't trust Maddox. The guy is slick. If anyone killed her, I'd vote for him."

She disappeared and they could hear the rattle of dishes in the sink.

After a moment of silence, Alan asked, "Why would Robin think Maddox did it?"

"He was ten years younger than Diane," Lee replied in a despondent whisper.

"That's not exactly a motive for murder."

"It just didn't feel right."

"To you or to Diane?"

"To all of us," Robin announced as she re-entered the room.

Although Robin was small, she carried herself as if she were much taller. Lee often thought that came from being married to someone who overshadowed her the way a mountain overshadows the valley below.

"He's one smooth operator," she continued. "Technically, he's still married, but his wife lives in the Medford area. No one knows if they're estranged, but he's been pretty open about dating other women."

"But why would he *kill* Diane? He'd already dumped her," Alan asked.

The two women could only look at each other, stumped for an answer.

"You guys do criminal checks before you hire," he said to Robin as she sat down again. "Has he ever been arrested?"

"No. He was clean."

Alan returned to the fireplace. "I'm sorry, Lee. I don't see how I can help you. There's just not enough to go on."

Robin sat back and crossed her legs. "Let's face it Lee, it would be like finding a needle in a haystack, anyway. There were no windows or locks broken and nothing was stolen, right?"

"Wouldn't that prove it had to be someone she knew?" Lee looked at Alan for support.

"It could also strengthen the argument for suicide," he disappointed her.

"But you should've seen Soldier."

Alan looked up, his pipe in his right hand. "Who's Soldier?"

"Amy's dog," Robin supplied the answer. "Was she with you?"

"Yes." Lee leaned forward, resting her elbows on her knees. "Look Alan, you guys have police dogs in the department, and you know how good a dog's nose is. I read once that some dogs have the ability to pinpoint a man 500 yards away in a mild breeze."

"That's true. " Alan agreed, puffing heartily on his pipe.

"Well, Diane didn't show up for work that day and didn't answer her phone when I called. Amy had to take Soldier to the vet's that afternoon anyway, so afterwards we stopped by Diane's condo. Her newspaper was by her front door and there was a note from a neighbor. I got worried, so when no one answered the door, I used my key. Soldier ran into the living room first and was standing next to Diane's body sniffing the syringe when we finally got the lights turned on. Then, she started sniffing her way around the room, like she was looking for something. She went into the kitchen and even up the stairs." Lee finished her statement as another thought slipped into her mind.

Alan sat down again and crossed his legs. "If only dogs could talk," he said, re-lighting his pipe.

Robin had been watching Lee. "What are you thinking?"

"I just remembered that I didn't see Diane's vase on the coffee table when we found her. I was there the night before and distinctly remember the large vase with the sunflowers sitting right in the middle of the table. She brought it back with her from Italy last summer. But it wasn't there when we found the body, I'm sure of it."

"Maybe she broke it, or just moved it," Robin speculated. Robin shifted her attention to her husband who had been listening and puffing on his pipe. "What did Bud say about breaking up with Diane?"

"I'm not sure." He took the pipe out of his mouth and knocked the tobacco into the fireplace. "I didn't read much of the report, but I think Sergeant Davis said that Bud Maddox hadn't spoken to her for a couple of days."

"Where was he when she died?" his wife inquired.

"I don't think he has an alibi, but right now there's no reason to believe he needs one." The big cop looked at Lee, giving her a half smile. "You may just have to accept this one, Lee. I know it's tough."

"Yeah," Lee shrugged, anxious now to leave. She pushed herself out of the chair and reached for her purse. "I'd better be going. Thanks for the dinner. Sorry about the dessert."

"No problem," Robin consoled her, rising. "I wrapped it up for you to take home."

Lee turned to Alan. "And the casserole was really great."

He smiled and stood up, putting his big slab of a hand on her shoulder. "I'll see you get the recipe. Give this some time, Lee."

"Thanks."

Alan retrieved her coat, while Robin retrieved a paper plate wrapped in aluminum foil from the refrigerator. The three of them moved toward the front door where Robin handed Lee the pie before flicking on the porch light.

"I'll talk to you guys soon," Lee said, giving Robin a hug.

Alan opened the door, and Robin followed Lee to the car, arms wrapped around her to ward off the cold.

"Lee," Robin started, "I'm worried about you. Maybe you need some time off."

"Carey agrees with me, you know," she countered.

"Diane's sister?"

"She stopped by tonight after the funeral."

"Why didn't you mention that to Alan?"

"I'm not sure she wants anyone to know. I'm pretty sure she and her husband are arguing over it. I noticed a bruise on her neck, and I think she hides others with heavy make-up."

"You mean he's abusing her?"

"I don't know for sure, but she's nervous about this, and they're having financial trouble."

"Well, that could be what's causing the marital problems."

"It also gives him a reason to want Diane dead. They're the beneficiaries of Diane's life insurance policy."

Robin was clearly shocked. "That's a terrible thing to say, Lee. Don't start jumping to conclusions. You don't know that this *is* murder."

"I feel awful saying it, but Carey said herself they're in financial trouble, and he obviously doesn't want her talking about a possible murder."

Robin inhaled. "Wow. So, you think he may have killed Diane for the money?"

"I don't know," Lee said shaking her head. "The policy was only for $25,000."

"Should I say anything to Alan?"

"No. I don't want to get Carey in trouble. I don't think her husband knows she said anything to me. Let's just wait a while. You can answer a question, though. I thought you couldn't collect on an insurance policy if the person committed suicide."

"Most policies have a waiting period before they'll pay anything. I'm pretty sure that after the waiting period, they'll even pay on a suicide. But I can check it out to make sure. Do you really think he would kill Diane?" Robin's expression betrayed her doubts.

"I don't know. I've only met him one other time. He's pretty distant, and Carey is certainly afraid of something."

Robin cocked her head, looking at Lee. "You're not going to be able to live with this, are you?"

Lee bit her lip as she considered how she would respond. With a sigh, she made a decision.

"When my mother left my father," she began, "she convicted me to a life with a man who showed his affection by buying me a United States Treasury Bond each year for my birthday. I only got to see my real father and my brother for a week every summer. When I was a teenager, my father died, and I began to drift away from Patrick, too. So, I focused all of my energies on my gymnastics. I was good, and I had a real shot at the Nationals. But in my first year of college, an accident destroyed any chance I had at that. Then, I met Brad."

She swallowed as tears filled her eyes.

"Our marriage was a sham. I've never said that before, but it's true. The only good thing that came out of it was Amy. When he disappeared over a decade ago, I didn't care. I never lifted a finger to find out what really happened. I think I'd already shut myself into a protective box and threw away the key."

A tear plopped onto her wrist and she raised a hand to wipe her eyes.

"I'm sorry, Lee," Robin said, placing a comforting hand on her arm.

But Lee wasn't done yet.

"My friendship with Diane was different than what I have with you, or even Marion, my friend from the University. You guys are colleagues, professionals, peers. Diane was...I don't know...more like a pal. When I met her, she was as scarred and broken as I was. She told me she'd been abused by a neighbor boy when she was in middle school. Something she'd never told anyone. Her father also died when she was very young, and her mother never re-married. Everyone knows she had her idiosyncrasies. But it was more than that. She had full-blown OCD. She knew she was different. She knew people didn't like her. How could she not? Throughout her entire life people had made fun of her, criticized her, or even hated her for it. But, you know, she couldn't help herself."

Lee leaned back against the car.

"Then, she went through a bitter divorce and her husband walked away with almost everything. By the time she came to work for me, she was barely holding on. And somehow, over the course of four years, we kind of rescued each other. What most people didn't know was that Diane had a wicked sense of humor. She could make me laugh until my sides hurt. When we hung out together, it was like going to therapy. I forgot about myself and was able to just...be. It was liberating; I began to feel like that box I'd shut myself in had begun to open. And then suddenly...she was gone."

Lee shifted her weight and crossed her arms as she leveled a serious look at Robin.

"Diane didn't kill herself, Robin. I'm as certain of that as I am of my own name. And I owe it to her to find the truth. Listen," Lee continued, "I'm not mad at Alan. I might not even be mad at Sergeant Davis. It just feels like Diane is talking to me, pleading with me to clear her name," she stopped and sighed. "My God, Robin! Would a woman who keeps her shoes in individual plastic containers be likely to kill herself?"

At that, Robin finally broke a smile. "Okay," she said, squeezing Lee's hand. "But be careful. You're not a detective. And you need to get some sleep first. You look a little like the walking dead yourself."

Lee laughed. "Thanks. Only a friend could get away with that." She gave Robin a quick hug. "I'll see you tomorrow."

They said goodbye, and Lee got into the car and pulled onto Marcola Road, overwhelmed by having confessed so many of her inner truths. The sky had cleared, and she cracked the window, hoping the fresh air would relieve the leaden feeling in her stomach.

Now that she'd given voice to her suspicions about Diane's death and why she felt so compelled to look into it, she realized the seriousness of what she was doing and the potential danger. She had no intention of trying to solve a murder, but felt driven to find one piece of information that would take this out of the realm of speculation and place it squarely into the center of an investigation. Her resources were few, and she didn't know the first thing about sleuthing. So, what *could* she do?

As she watched the night shadows pass her window, she decided that somehow, Diane would have to point the way.

CHAPTER SIX

Lee left the open country and pulled onto Highway 126, feeling the need to get home to consider her options. The Kingsford briquette plant whizzed past on the north side of the highway, its mountain of cedar chips blotting out a portion of the night sky. The strip malls flashed past in a blaze of neon light, and a moment later she was crossing over the interstate into Eugene. As she neared the turnoff for home, Diane's condo came to mind and she made an abrupt decision. With a quick turn of the wheel, she was heading north.

Diane had lived in a large complex built on the Willamette River. Lee had a key, and it was the only place she knew to look for answers. It was nine-thirty when she pulled into Willamette Oaks and parked in an empty space next to Diane's lonely Ford Escort. Diane's was the last of four townhouses facing a large, sloping lawn that fronted the river.

The parking lot was at the back of the townhouse. Although the parking lot was lit, the condo's windows were dark and this end of the complex was encased in deep shadows. A nervous chill prompted her to climb out of the car and quickly skirt the building before she could change her mind.

She came around to the condo entrance from the south side, noticing for the first time how isolated the front door was from the adjoining units. Even the small front porch was encircled by a waist-high wall topped with wooden planters. No one would have a clear view of the front door. Diane liked her privacy, and Lee remembered her mentioning how she had chosen the unit partly for this very reason. Unfortunately, that decision may have contributed to her death. The thought made Lee look anxiously behind her as she approached the door.

Lee opened the door and gingerly stepped inside, locking it behind her. She was immediately struck with how crisp the air felt.

The condo was silent except for the ticking of the grandfather clock in the corner. Lee flicked on the overhead light and then stood in the entryway, wondering if she might somehow smell the scent of death. But all she detected was the faint aroma of the rose potpourri that sat on a small antique table by the front door.

Lee ignored her impulse to turn around and leave and moved into the living room. She turned on the brass lamp that flanked Diane's dark green Queen Anne sofa and threw her purse onto a wing-back chair. She stood back to survey the room.

Carey had been there. A few boxes filled with books and loose paper sat next to Diane's fourteenth-century writing table. Another empty box sat next to the bookcase on the far wall. An antique trunk stood open in the corner, revealing Diane's neatly folded quilts. Lee couldn't help but stare at the middle of the floor, just in front of the fireplace. There was no indication of the body. The police hadn't drawn a chalk outline like they do in the movies, and of course there was no blood. There was just the oval braided carpet Diane had purchased at a discount warehouse, surrounded by the newly finished hardwood floor.

Lee forced herself to shift her gaze to the fireplace mantel where Diane's old 35mm Olympus camera sat tucked in amongst some family photos. Since Carey had offered it to her, Lee stepped over to pick it up, thinking about the many times she'd teased Diane about not moving up to a digital camera. When she lifted up the camera, the back dropped open exposing an empty interior. This made Lee pause. Diane had taken a picture of Lee the night she died. So where was the film? Lee stared at the inside of the camera until she had to rub her eyes. She was tired. Too tired. And she wasn't here to worry about the camera. She was here to find the Italian vase.

She set the camera on the chair next to her purse, and then turned to the coffee table where a cut glass bowl sat right where the urn used to be, looking quite small and anemic in comparison. A quick look around the living room confirmed the urn was nowhere in sight. For the next fifteen minutes, Lee conducted an intense search, opening cupboards and drawers. She even looked behind furniture, but everything was in perfect order, not a dust mote or a single spec of dirt in sight. And no urn.

She climbed the stairs to the second floor, but Diane's bedroom and closet were studies in perfection. Hanging clothes were organized by color and season. Plastic shoe bins, labeled by type and color of the shoes inside, were stacked on the floor in strict alignment. Large plastic bins were stacked on the upper shelf, each labeled by their contents. The closet alone was enough to indicate that an obsessive-compulsive person lived here.

The bathroom didn't offer any clues, either. The counter was bare except for a small porcelain cup. Her toothbrush, hairbrush, and hair gel were all put away. In fact, the only indications that a living, breathing person had once lived there was a full trash basket and a small piece of paper sticking out of a hastily closed drawer. Lee pulled out the sheet of paper and read the heading. It was from the hospital. Some kind of lab report. Feeling intrusive, she carefully replaced it and headed back downstairs.

She stopped in frustration when she got to the kitchen. "C'mon, Diane, help me," she mumbled to herself. "Where's the vase?"

Diane's kitchen floor was cleaner than most of the dishes in Lee's cupboards, and the counters looked downright lonely for company. Lee had never realized how sparse the condo was before. It made Lee think of her own home where she had trouble understanding the need for empty space. Every counter and wall was filled to capacity.

"I don't believe in clutter," Diane had once said. Lee couldn't help smiling, remembering her response. *"You can't believe or disbelieve in clutter, Diane. Clutter isn't a religion!"*

Diane had merely raised an eyebrow before putting a pair of scissors in a drawer where they belonged.

Lee sighed, feeling a heavy ball settle into the middle of her chest again. She knew that time would eventually lift the weight she felt at Diane's loss. But that time couldn't come soon enough.

She took a deep breath and surveyed the rest of the kitchen, trying to focus on the task at hand. Her gaze came to rest on the tall plastic trashcan that stood next to the kitchen sink. On impulse, she stepped over and lifted the lid, thinking Diane might have broken the vase and thrown it away. But she was surprised to find the container lined with a clean trash bag. When Lee had stopped by the night Diane died, she'd arrived just as Diane was putting in a new trash bag. As they talked though, Diane had tossed in an empty cat food can and chicken broth box. Even those were missing now. So where were they? According to the coroner, Diane had died between nine o'clock and midnight. So, she wouldn't have emptied the trash can a second time. Unless...

Lee ran outside to the Pathfinder and grabbed the flashlight from her glove compartment. A minute later, she was standing by the shed that camouflaged the condo's two large trash containers. This was a long shot if there ever was one, and yet, if she didn't check now, she might regret it later. According to the sticker on the side of the dumpster, the trash would be picked up the next day.

Lee held her breath and lifted both steel lids. She pushed them back with a bang, giving her an unencumbered view of the inside. Both bins were filled to the top. Crumpled brown shopping bags, white plastic garbage bags, and shiny black leaf bags were scattered across the surface of the first bin, along with old shipping boxes, and an empty stereo box. Tucked in the corner was a broken lawn chair.

Lee knew Diane used only white plastic trash bags with yellow ties, purchased at the same store. God, that woman was compulsive! Lee figured the bag she was looking for would be at, or near, the top. It was difficult to sort through everything while holding the flashlight, so Lee placed the light on the ledge and pushed up her sleeves. She balanced herself on the wheel and leaned in, carefully pulling bags and boxes out. Occasionally, she paused to point her flashlight into the depths of a bag. Several times, she pulled out a false lead. Once it was a yellow ribbon, another time it was a yellow envelope addressed to someone in number seventeen. One bag with a yellow tie string surfaced, and she turned it over. Empty cat food cans and cigarette butts dropped out. She almost gagged at the smell of rotting tuna, but the cigarette butts confirmed that it wasn't Diane's. Feeling foolish, she threw everything back in and closed the lid. She turned to the second dumpster. This time, she was a little overwhelmed to find six or seven bags with yellow ties right near the top.

She pulled each bag to the front and searched through the contents as best she could. Coffee grounds and sour milk spilled over her hands. At one point, she lost her balance and lurched forward, shoving her left hand deep into the center of a bag. Her hand encountered something gushy, which oozed through her fingers making her stomach turn. When she yanked her hand out, there was a sucking sound followed by the sound of ceramic hitting ceramic.

Lee forgot her queasiness and snapped up the bag. She stepped back off the wheel, reaching for the pavement with her left foot. Instead of pavement however, her foot landed on something that moved, and suddenly a cat shot into the parking lot with a high-pitched scream. Lee's foot flew out from under her as she twisted in mid-air and fell to the ground.

With a groan, she sat up and stretched out her back. She was breathing hard, the bag of garbage forgotten beside her. When a cool breeze wafted across the trash containers, bringing the smell of something awful with it, Lee leaned forward and rested her head on both knees, careful not to touch anything with her hands. This was crazy, she thought. What in the world did she think she was doing?

The sound of an engine caught her attention just as a brown pickup truck pulled slowly through the parking lot. The headlights swept across her as the pickup passed by, and she quickly got up. She brushed old lettuce from the front of her sweater and flicked chunks of something gooey off her sleeve. Too stubborn to leave, she ripped open the bag in her hand. Pieces of porcelain tumbled onto the asphalt, along with empty tomato sauce cans. Lee squatted in the dark, shining the flashlight onto the white, glazed pieces at her feet feeling cheated. It wasn't the urn. Maybe Diane hadn't broken it after all. Carey would probably find it when she emptied the condo over the weekend.

Lee returned the pieces of porcelain to the bag and angrily threw it back with the rest of the trash. After wiping her left arm on a paper bag to get rid of the muck, she closed the lid and marched back to the condo, heading straight for the kitchen sink where she grabbed the liquid soap and began to scrub. Her hands were covered with slime, and something green filled the underside of her fingernails. Through tears of frustration, she scrubbed them clean, dried them, and then leaned on the sink as she'd done that morning with Amy.

"I can't do this alone, Diane," she cried. "Please! Show me something. Anything!"

That's when she heard a thud in the other room.

Lee turned with a jerk. Her heart pounded so hard, she thought it might escape her chest. But she waited – waited and listened. Her ears strained for the slightest sound. There was nothing. After a long pause, she pushed her right hand along the counter, looking for a drawer handle. She never took her eyes off the kitchen doorway. With trembling fingers, she pulled open the nearest drawer and blindly searched for something she could use as a weapon. When something sharp poked her thumb, she risked a glance. The drawer was filled with cooking accessories. She grabbed a meat skewer and moved slowly forward, holding the long spindle before her like a dagger.

She inched her way across the kitchen into the small dining room, where the light from the kitchen splashed shadows across the oak table and chairs, but left the corners in complete darkness. Stopping at the end of the table, her senses reached out, searching for foreign sounds. Only the ominous ticking of the grandfather clock greeted her. She crossed to the front door and then turned and faced the living room, fully expecting to confront an intruder.

Instead, she froze, her eyes wide, her veins pulsing.

Her purse lay on the floor in front of the wing back chair, its contents regurgitated across the carpet. Along with her wallet and car keys, the small onyx bird sat upright, facing her. Lee gaped as one bird eye seemed to glint in the low light. The saliva in her mouth tasted sour, and the buzzing was back in her ears.

She had left the figurine on her vanity table at home. She hadn't brought it with her. And her purse had been thrown back into the corner of the chair. So how in the hell…?

She swallowed a lump the size of a golf ball. What was going on? Was someone else in the condo? She turned towards the front door, but it was closed and locked.

Lee moved slowly into the living room and did a quick three-sixty next to the sofa, meat skewer at the ready. As she did so, the toe of her shoe lifted the braided rug and something scraped against the floor. The noise caught her off guard, and a chill rippled down her spine. For a moment she forgot the possible intruder and reached down cautiously to lift back the rug. A thick chunk of smoky yellow porcelain, about a quarter of an inch in diameter, fell to the floor.

Lee's knees almost buckled as thoughts of imminent danger evaporated; it was a piece of the missing vase. She dropped the meat skewer on the coffee table and leaned over to pick up the piece of ceramic. Her eyes danced back and forth from the bird on the carpet, to the chipped piece in her hand. Was there a connection? As she studied the broken piece of urn, something else caught her attention.

The area rug was out of place.

Why hadn't she noticed it before? The rug usually sat in between the fireplace and the coffee table − not underneath the coffee table. Lee's head riveted back and forth from the coffee table to the fireplace, calculating distances. The carpet had been moved a good three feet. She picked up her purse and all of its contents and placed it on a side table along with the piece of porcelain. Then she pulled the marble-topped coffee table away from the sofa and lifted the entire corner of the rug. She couldn't control the small cry that escaped her lips. There was a fresh gouge in the perfectly polished hardwood floor, almost exactly where the porcelain had been held prisoner by the rug's fibers. Lee leaned over and stuck her finger into the indentation, as if the jagged edges might tell her a story. The question was – did the broken vase have something to do with Diane's death? And if so, what could Lee do with this new piece of information?

She replaced everything and picked up her purse, dropping the piece of porcelain into her pocket. Then she reached for the camera and the bird, convinced now that something besides suicide had taken Diane's life. Finally, she grabbed her coat off the back of a chair and started for the door.

She had just stepped into the entryway when something dark flashed past the large mirror on the wall, making Lee nearly jump out of her skin. When a second image flitted past her right shoulder, she spun in a circle, dropped her purse and ran for the meat skewer. She grabbed it off the coffee table and backed up to the fireplace, shaking with fear.

Seconds passed and nothing else happened. No sound. No movement. Her heart raced, drumming an incessant beat in her ears. With faltering footsteps, she finally inched forward and peeked around the corner of the sofa into the entryway. She expected someone to jump out from around the corner, but what she saw made her dizzy instead, and she dropped her defensive stance in shock.

Lying on the carpet, just in front of the mirror, was a long dark feather.

CHAPTER SEVEN

Adrenalin propelled Lee home in a blur. She couldn't remember leaving the condo or getting into her car. She couldn't even remember finding her car keys. Her heart was still racing, and she couldn't seem to catch her breath. By the time she entered the area surrounding the campus, she felt completely frayed at the edges.

She was positive she'd left the onyx bird on her vanity at home. Yet, somehow it had shown up on Diane's floor, one eye glinting in the low light. She was just as positive her purse hadn't fallen to the floor all by itself. And the feather hadn't been anywhere in the house when she'd arrived. So, what the hell had happened? There were only two explanations. Either someone had been in the condo with her all along, or...or...what? What was the second explanation?

With a sudden twist of the steering wheel, she swerved to the curb and stopped. A big truck rumbled past, throwing rainwater against the car as she put on the emergency brake. She sat with her head resting on the steering wheel for a full minute. Eventually, the adrenalin pumping through her veins began to slow, and she sat back.

Privately, Lee had always accepted the *possibility* that there were things no one could explain. But she couldn't say exactly that she believed in the paranormal. In fact, she'd attended a party once at an abandoned house in college that was reportedly haunted, and spent the entire night flinching like a school girl at suspicious noises. So, if ghosts were real, she knew she didn't have the stomach for them. Faced now with something that could only be described as *ab*normal, she wondered if she was going nuts. She had no idea how to explain anything that had just happened, but decided very quickly that she couldn't go off on tangents looking for ghosts or supernatural bullshit. What she had to do was find out what had happened to Diane.

Lee reached into her purse and pulled out the bird. She stared at it in the shadows of the car, wondering if it would suddenly become animated and fly away. But it just sat there, an inanimate object. She was conflicted what to do with it. It had been one of Diane's favorite possessions, but right now, it scared her to death. And right now, she didn't need more stress in her life. Before she could change her mind, she hit the electric window button and rolled down the passenger side window. With a flick of her wrist, she tossed it into a bush and closed the window. When her breathing had returned to normal, she put the car in gear and pulled back into traffic.

She was just passing the athletic track when she noticed a dark young man crossing against the light on the other side. Lee peered through the windshield at him. He looked exactly like a younger version of Bud Maddox, only taller. Seeing the boy brought Maddox, and everything she hated about him, to mind.

Maddox had slipped quietly into Diane's life, almost before anyone noticed. He left little gifts on her desk, took an interest in her hobbies, and generally filled the void left by her ex-husband. Before long, Diane was leaving for lunch fifteen minutes early and taking unplanned days off. She started wearing brighter colors and smiling even when the mail was late. Yet, from the beginning, Lee hadn't trusted Maddox. It wasn't that she didn't think Diane could attract someone like him. Rather, on some visceral level, she recognized Maddox for what he was – an empty well, a black hole poised to suck up the universe.

A blaring horn snapped her to attention, and Lee realized she'd stopped at a green light. She raised an apologetic hand to the driver behind her and passed through the intersection. Thoughts about Bud Maddox brought back her failed marriage and the resulting decade of isolation. She had locked out that period of her life and closed herself off from everyone else as a result. As Patrick said, she didn't date much, and when she did, there was always something wrong with the guy. At the same time her husband had gone missing, her beloved black Lab had been killed. It was one of the reasons she wouldn't have a dog in the house. But how much of her search for the truth now was a reaction to the guilt she felt for having fought with Diane the night she died? And how much of it was atonement for the way she'd handled her own husband's disappearance?

Lee made it home without further incident. She parked the car and was coming around the corner of the house just as the headlights of a car flicked on across the street. She continued up the steps and stopped to search for the front door key, barely noticing the car as it pulled away from the curb going south. As she struggled to get the key into the lock, the car made a U-turn and came back up the street, slowing as it passed. Lee turned just as the car roared to life and sped away. It was the tan sedan.

With a frown, she pushed open the heavy wooden door and slipped inside, quickly closing and locking the door behind her. She peered out the small paned window, but the car didn't return. She relaxed a bit, threw her purse and coat over a chair, pulled the mail out of the mail slot, and headed for the kitchen. Soldier met her when she slid back the door, thick tail fanning the air. Lee looked into those deep brown eyes, feeling a connection building. With a grunt, she brushed the feeling aside and turned toward the back porch.

"C'mon. You go outside."

Soldier followed her down the hallway and bounded into the yard, squatting in the grass. Lee left the screen door unlatched again and the back door open, and then returned to the kitchen. She stopped at the antique roll-top desk to sift through the mail. A moment later, the porch door slammed, and Soldier came into the room.

"How do you do that?"

When the dog didn't answer, Lee reached for a small mug hanging on the wall and proceeded to make a cup of tea. Wherever she turned, Soldier followed. After dodging back and forth several times, Lee finally issued an order.

"Sit!"

To her surprise, the dog sat.

"Well, thank you."

Why was she thanking a dog?

"Now, stay there."

Soldier sat at attention, the high-set ears standing perfectly erect. Shepherds were known for their intelligence, but right now Soldier brushed her bushy tail across the floor like every other attention-hungry canine. Lee watched her, smiling, until the microwave timer beeped. She removed a bubbling cup of hot tea and placed it on the counter before going to the refrigerator to grab the milk. As she kicked the refrigerator closed, Soldier startled her with a bark. Lee turned to find the dog sitting next to the roll-top desk where the answering machine sat. The message light was blinking. Lee gave the dog a suspicious look before flicking the playback button.

"You will never make me believe that you knew there was a message on that machine."

She continued fixing her tea while the automated recording told her there were two recorded messages and gave her the date and time of the first message. The fact the first message had been left on Thursday didn't register until a deep, familiar voice filled the room. The intrusion of that voice made Lee jerk around as if she'd been electrocuted. She dropped the milk and spoon. The milk carton fell with a splat, splashing milk across the floor and lower cupboards. The spoon clattered under the table, while the message played on. When it finished, the machine beeped three times.

Diane's message was over. The next was about to begin.

CHAPTER EIGHT

Lee sat at the kitchen table, her fingers gently massaging the muscles around her right knee as she stared in numbed silence at the answering machine. An amalgamation of thoughts whizzed through her head. Lee tried to remember the sequence of events the night of Diane's death.

She'd argued with Diane just before leaving the condominium. On the way home, she'd stopped at the mall to walk off her anger. Diane must have called and left this message while Lee was at the mall. When Lee arrived home she was still obsessing over the argument and had gone straight to bed, never checking the answering machine. The next day, Lee was more than a little angry because Diane had failed to show up for work and hadn't called to explain her absence. Immediately after work, Lee had taken Amy and Soldier to the vet's and then had gone to Diane's condo, hoping Amy's presence would serve as a buffer, because she knew she was ready for a fight.

By the time she returned home, she felt as if someone had removed her brain. She'd unplugged all the phones, hoping to shut out the world. She'd even switched her cell phone to "silent." Amy had convinced her to reconnect the hallway phone for emergencies, but Lee had purposely left the answering machine off so that she wouldn't be forced to listen to condolences from well-intentioned friends. She'd never noticed there was an existing message.

She clicked on the answering machine again so that Diane's voice filled the room one more time.

"Lee, I know you won't approve, but I won't be in tomorrow. I have a couple more vacation days coming to me, and Bud and I are going to Portland for something special. Tell Marie to make sure the newsletter gets to the printers. See you on Monday."

The anger in Diane's voice wasn't lost on Lee. She stood with her finger on the button, deciding to let the tape run through. The second message was from Amy. She'd arrived safely in Corvallis. At the sound of Amy's voice, Soldier whined.

"She'll be back this weekend."

Lee stood up to erase the tape, but paused. Maybe she shouldn't. It was the last communication from Diane and could be important. Instead, she turned out the light and left the kitchen. After locking doors and turning out lights on the ground floor, she headed upstairs to her bedroom. She turned on the hurricane lamp next to her bed and was preparing to plop down on the goose down comforter, when her knees buckled and she had to catch herself on the side table.

The onyx bird was sitting on the side table next to the lamp.

Lee felt bile rise to her throat, and she turned and rushed to the bathroom. She leaned into the sink, breathing hard. Her face was hot and flushed, and she could taste the sourness of the bile in her mouth. She took several deep breaths and then looked up into the mirror. What was going on?

On unsteady feet, she returned to the bedroom and carefully approached the bird. Again, it just sat there. There was no movement. No fractured dimensions of time and space surrounding it. It looked like any other small figurine one might pick up in a gift store. Completely innocent.

Lee moved over and sat on the bed, watching it. Another minute passed. Nothing happened. Finally, she swung her legs up and leaned back against the headboard, keenly aware of the bird next to her. Her heart still raced, but she was able to think lucidly now. So, what was going on? She'd asked Diane for help at the condo, and the bird had suddenly appeared. Right where she'd found the gouge in the floor. Then, she'd thrown it away, but it had come back. She snuck a glance at it and felt a renewed increase in her heartbeat. Maybe she was meant to keep it. Maybe even keep it close.

Okay, she thought. It stays. She just couldn't deal with it right now. If she was losing her mind, then Patrick would have to commit her at some later point in time. Right now, she was fixated on Diane's death.

She took a deep breath and tried to relax. Her mind flitted back to Diane's taped message. That was the important thing. She had to decide what to do with that. She could call Alan and tell him she had a real piece of evidence. There was no denying now that Bud Maddox had lied to the police about not having spoken to Diane for several days before she died. He must have called Diane right after Lee left that night and invited her to Portland. He must have also lied about breaking up with her; he may have even been the last person to speak with her before she died. But what could Alan do? He'd probably just say it was more circumstantial evidence. There was nothing to link Bud to any crime, and she was sure Sergeant Davis wouldn't care anyway.

Heavy breathing made Lee turn to where Soldier sat next to the bed. The dog's eyes pleaded for attention, so Lee reached out her hand. Soldier scuttled forward and laid her head on the bed so that Lee could stroke her nose. The dog closed its eyes in ecstasy while Lee's thoughts returned to Diane.

"Okay, time to lie down," she finally told the dog.

Soldier complied with a groan and placed her long snout across one of Lee's tennis shoes. Lee smiled in spite of herself. Just then, the phone rang, making Lee jump.

"Damn!" she sighed. Her nerves were shot. She answered the phone.

A familiar male voice on the line made her slump back against the pillow.

"Hey, Sis, I need a favor."

"What now?"

"What do you think about me coming to stay with you for a while?"

Lee sat up.

"Why would you do that?"

"Well, what with Amy gone and everything, I thought you could use some company."

Lee felt her whole body tense.

"Patrick, you're married. Why would you come to live with me? What about Erika?"

As soon as she asked the question, she knew the answer. She'd noticed a growing distance between the couple. Erika was a graphic artist who worked at home, while Patrick spent long hours at the theater. The couple rarely spent time together, certainly not enough to start the family Erika so desperately wanted. There was a pause at the other end of the line.

"I think sometimes women like to have time alone. You know, to sort things out."

Lee sighed. "You're splitting up."

There was another pause. Patrick's normally jovial manner had disappeared.

"I hope not, but we'll have to wait and see. For now, I think I just need to give her some space."

Lee rubbed a knot on her forehead as hard as if she were rubbing out a stain in the carpet. The last thing she wanted was Patrick hanging around the house getting on her nerves.

"I'm going to have to think about that one. Let's talk tomorrow."

"Okay, I'll give you a call tomorrow. Sleep tight."

He started to hang up when she stopped him.

"Patrick! Any chance we can have lunch tomorrow? I have something I need to talk to you about."

"Sure. I have an acting class at ten and Theory at two-thirty. What's up?"

"I'd rather talk to you about it tomorrow."

"Okay. Why don't we meet at Papa Fromo's at noon?"

"Great. See you then."

"Is everything okay, Lee?"

Lee hesitated, not sure whether to say anything, yet. Her ego was still bruised by what Patrick had said that afternoon, and it would be hard to admit he'd been right. She decided to make him wait.

"I just need some advice. See you tomorrow for pizza."

Lee hung up and allowed her head to sink back onto the pillow, contemplating her brother. Patrick was two years older than Lee, and she'd grown up idolizing both her brother, and her father, John O'Donnell. But her father had been a rogue, and a philandering one at that. So on Lee's eighth birthday, her mother had packed up their things, taken Lee by the hand, and walked out on her husband. She had also left Patrick behind, something Lee had never understood. But she suspected it was because Patrick reminded her too much of his father. She and her mother moved back to Minnesota where her mother married John Vanderhaven, a bland and unaffectionate man. Deciding this time to marry for security, she warned Lee, *Love isn't everything, Lee. There's something to be said for stability.*

In time, her mother's personality became as dull as her stepfather's. Most of what Lee remembered about those days was the silent meals around the dinner table and the smell of sour milk on her stepfather's shirt where he had a tendency to dribble his morning breakfast. Lee found herself counting the days until summer when she would spend a week with her father and brother on her aunt's farm in upstate New York.

Unfortunately, when she was eleven, her father remarried and stopped coming, sending Patrick on alone. The day after her fifteenth birthday, John O'Donnell died in a factory accident, extinguishing the light in Lee's world. What Patrick didn't realize was how much she resented his good luck for having grown up with the one man she would love forever. And that resentment would, at times, find its way into disagreements with Patrick. She did love her brother, though. She loved the way he used to put a protective arm around her when the fights between their parents got to be too much. She loved his insatiable sense of humor. And loved that he truly wanted the best for her. Perhaps having him come to stay for a while might not be such a bad idea, especially now. She'd let him know the next day.

Lee climbed off the bed to brush her teeth, careful to step over the prone dog already snoring. After finishing in the bathroom, she donned a nightgown and glanced out the window before closing the blinds. The tan sedan sat alone under the street lamp across the street, like a sentinel on guard duty. She couldn't remember if she'd ever seen the car before today. It could merely belong to someone who lived across the street. But from now on, she'd pay more attention to it, just in case.

She climbed into bed and fell asleep dreaming of a flock of birds.

CHAPTER NINE

Lee tossed and turned throughout the night, finally getting up at one point to drink some warm milk. The next morning she indulged in three cups of coffee to give her enough energy to make it to work. Not a great idea, since she'd begun to notice a constant ringing in her ears.

She arrived in her office ten minutes before the administrative team meeting scheduled for nine o'clock. It gave her just enough time to check her emails before she had to go talk about budgets and cost overruns. She turned on her computer and scrolled through about thirty emails. She saw the usual array of messages from staff, board members, and outside contacts. But one email caught her attention, and she sat down to read it.

The message had been sent from someone outside the hospital and was identified as having come from "A Friend." It read very simply:

Double, double, toil and trouble
Fire burn and cauldron bubble
By the pricking of my thumbs
Something wicked this way comes
Beware!

There was nothing more.

Lee inhaled and held her breath before exhaling slowly. Wasn't that how the odd condolence card had been signed? A friend? The ringing in her ears had now been joined by a racing heart rate. Who would send her that card and then this weird email? It must be connected to Diane's death. But how?

Lee reread the poem. Parts of it sounded familiar, but she struggled to place the entire piece. She hit the print button and put the copy on her desk just as Andrew appeared at her door.

"You coming?" he inquired.

Lee looked up. "Yeah, I just wanted to check emails."

She grabbed a notepad and pencil, and then paused. Andrew held a degree in Philosophy along with his MBA. He might recognize the poem's origin.

"Andrew, do you have any idea what this is?" she asked, handing it to him.

Andrew took it and read the lines. "Well, even though I skipped most of my English Lit classes in college, I'm sure it's from Shakespeare, although I don't know which play."

"That's what I thought," Lee agreed.

"Better ask your brother," Andrew handed back the piece of paper. "Where did you get it?"

"Uh…someone gave it to me."

She stuffed the note into her purse, when something sharp pierced her finger. She yanked her hand back, surprised to find a small droplet of blood at the tip of her second digit.

"Wow," Andrew exclaimed, looking at her injury. "What do you carry in there?" He attempted a laugh. "Get a Band Aid and I'll meet you in the conference room."

Lee watched him disappear and then pulled her purse open, looking for the sharp instrument that had just impaled her. She shifted her wallet and car keys to one side, and felt the blood drain from her face. The onyx bird peeked out from behind her wallet.

A few minutes later, she joined her colleagues looking and feeling very much like she'd just stuck her finger in a light socket. As the meeting began, she attempted to quiet the thoughts buzzing in her head by purposely looking around the room and focusing on the team members.

The group was an odd mixture of intellect, impressive credentials, and less than dazzling personalities. Martha Jackson, the new CEO, ran the meetings like a military boot camp, and the room often felt as if the oxygen had been sucked out through the air vents. Andrew sat to Martha's left. Next to him was Fran Van Sickle, the VP of Patient Services. Next to her was Robin. Lee sat across the table from

Robin. To Lee's right was the head of Information Technology, and then the Chief Financial Officer.

The meeting started with an announcement from Martha that she had a conference call at ten o'clock. Lee silently thanked God for small favors. Fran Van Sickle ran through some capital equipment requests, and then it was Andrew's turn as VP of Operations to come out from under Martha's thumb and report on the construction of the new radiology unit. His muscles tightened, making his body so rigid he could have been injected with starch. He'd just begun his report when Martha raised a stubby hand to stop him.

"What happened with Dr. Roberts last week?" she barked.

Andrew's speech faltered. Everyone could feel the reprimand coming.

"I believe Dr. Roberts had a few words with the project manager," he almost whispered.

"A few words?" Martha prodded.

"I think Dr. Roberts was unhappy about something," Andrew replied vaguely. "But I believe it's all worked out now."

"It's not worked out!" Martha slammed her pencil on the table. "He was in my office yesterday complaining that no one had consulted him about selecting the new CAT scanner. I thought you said you'd discussed it with the radiologists."

"I did. Well, I mean, I discussed it with Dr. Sinner and Dr. Boswell."

Andrew's speech disintegrated into a stutter. As Lee glanced around the table, she saw that everyone had become very interested in their notepads.

"You have to talk to Roberts, not just Sinner and Boswell. And, this time, fix it."

Andrew pretended to write himself a note. "I'll take care of it right away."

"See that you do. Let's move on," Martha commanded.

Andrew opened his mouth to say something, but thought better of it and just sat back in his seat. Lee felt sorry for him, but wondered for the umpteenth time why he didn't just leave. He'd been at the hospital as VP of Operations for over six years, but hadn't even been considered for the top spot when it became available. As someone who had always played at the top of her game, Lee didn't know what it would feel like to be so undervalued.

As VP of Human Resources, Robin chaired the Safety Committee, and it was her turn to make a safety report. Lee took the opportunity to draw circles on her notepad, glancing up once or twice just to give her friend confidence that she wasn't being ignored. The doodling helped to calm her nerves and even contemplate how the bird had found its way into her purse again. In the background, Robin began.

"The Safety Committee met yesterday," Robin referred to two typed sheets of paper in her hands. "There were two security incidents reported last month. It seems the hood ornament from Dr. Olson's Mercedes was stolen again."

This brought chuckles from around the table. Dr. Olson's hood ornament had been stolen some twelve times over the past four years. A few times it was discovered in the bushes. Once it was mailed back to him, and once it had shown up lodged in the plumbing of the men's bathroom. The entire surgical floor hated Dr. Olson, and everyone suspected someone on staff was to blame.

"The second incident happened two weeks ago. It appears that someone may have broken into the lab's GCMS room."

Robert Bask was the Chief Financial Officer and the kind of guy who didn't have the personality for much more than the numbers he spent his life with. He was tall and thin and wore wire-rimmed glasses that made him look like a character from Charles Dickens. He looked up when Robin mentioned the GCMS room.

"What's the GCMS room?" he asked, as he toyed with his glasses.

Robin referred to her notes. "It holds two pieces of equipment. The gas chromatograph and the mass spectro-phometer," she stumbled over the words.

"It's where all the positive drug screens are confirmed," Fran interjected.

Robin continued. "Some of the lab techs work around the clock, but the GCMS room is closed and locked at six o'clock. Only five people are supposed to have access to it."

Lee was thinking about the bird when she heard this, and continued doodling.

"Apparently, nothing was taken," Robin said. "However, the computer was still up and running at five o'clock the next morning when security checked, and the door was unlocked."

Lee finished coloring in a circle and looked up with interest.

"What about the technicians? Did they see anyone?" Andrew inquired.

Lee thought Andrew was making a valiant effort to appear credible again in Martha's eyes. Unfortunately, Martha continued to act as if he wasn't in the room.

"No one saw anything," Robin answered. "There is a side door to the hallway, and they think whoever it was may have come into the department the back way."

"So," Robert began, adjusting his glasses again, "we really don't know what happened. Maybe someone just left the computer on when they went home."

"And left the door unlocked?" Fran scoffed. "I don't think so."

As the executive in charge of patient care, you'd expect Fran to have the bedside manner of Florence Nightingale. Unfortunately, she was as soft and cuddly as a drill bit.

"Well, the five people who have access to it were all interviewed the next day and denied any knowledge," Robin said. "But the key to the room *is* left in a central location."

"You think one of our technicians is fooling around with the computer for personal use?" Fran jumped to the negative.

"I'm only reporting the facts," Robin replied a bit defensively.

"The trouble wouldn't be in leaving the computer on. It would only be a problem if someone were entering the lab files," Andrew offered authoritatively, sneaking a glance at Martha.

"I understand that, Andrew," Fran snapped. "Was a file left opened?" she asked Robin.

Robin checked her notes again. "I'm not sure."

Lee glanced over to see if Scott Summers was awake. He was the Chief Information Officer and in charge of all technology and phone operations. Though more content to interact with computers than people, he was a borderline genius as far as Lee was concerned, and she often wondered why he had chosen a small hospital in Oregon on which to waste his talents. This should be his area, but he was browsing through some other paperwork.

"Scott, could you find out if anything had been tampered with?" Martha inquired.

"Possibly," he said without looking up. "I can take a look. Who has access to that computer?" he asked, finally lifting his chin.

"The Lab Manager. Three lab techs and the pathologist," Robin replied.

"Which lab techs?"

"John Swain and Bud Maddox. I don't know who the third was."

Lee stopped doodling and looked up.

"Did Maddox work that day?" she asked, suddenly engaged in the conversation.

Robin shrugged, giving Lee a guarded look. "I have no idea."

"Scott," Martha Jackson interrupted, "have one of your guys check it. I doubt it's anything to worry about, but we have the Joint Commission survey this spring, and I don't want any deficiencies."

Lee sat back, staring at the outdoor print of a riverboat on the wall across the table. She had no idea if this was important information. If Bud had killed Diane, there had to be a motive. Lee had racked her brain trying to generate a plausible reason why he might have wanted Diane dead. The computer incident provided something interesting. If he was doing something illegal and Diane had found out about it...well, then.

"I understand it was a nice funeral, Lee," Martha Jackson said in the background.

Lee heard the comment a split second after Martha made it and snapped to attention with a nervous jump. Everyone was looking at her, waiting for a response.

"Yes, it was," she said, hoping she hadn't missed enough of the comment to make her response sound stupid.

"Perhaps you and your staff can put this tragedy behind you now." Jackson gazed at her with a blank expression. "You can get on with your work."

Lee clenched her fingers into fists under the table. "We've never stopped working, Martha."

"I'm sure that's true. I just meant that it must be difficult." She smiled, but there was no animation in her face. "I was wondering, in fact, if there was still time to get an article on the new Cath Lab in the next newsletter."

Lee struggled to get back on track. All Jackson cared about was the stupid Cath Lab.

"Actually, Sally's already written the article. I believe the copy is on your desk."

Jackson looked at her assistant, Miranda, who sat taking minutes. "Is that true, Miranda?"

Miranda looked up. "I have a stack of things that just arrived from Marketing. I'm not sure what's in the pile."

Miranda Gonzalez was Jackson's assistant and saw herself as the right hand to God. She took immense pleasure in the power she had over everyone else as a result. With this remark, she looked across the table at Lee knowing full well that Lee's marketing staff had delivered the materials nearly two days earlier.

Martha Jackson glanced back at Lee. "Well, now that I have the article, I'll take a look at it. You look tired, Lee. A close friend's death is difficult for anyone, but when it's suicide, it's doubly hard to accept."

Lee felt the heat rise to her cheeks at this poorly disguised attempt at compassion.

"God, I can't imagine killing myself," Fran cut in rudely. "How could life be that bad?"

"Life wasn't that bad, as you put it, Fran," Lee snarled, looking at Fran as if she were an alien life form. "And Diane didn't kill herself!"

Seven sets of eyes stared back at Lee as the room fell silent. A pin dropped squarely in the middle of the table would have sounded like an iron pipe hitting pavement. Jackson fixed a steady gaze in her direction. Finally, she spoke with measured control.

"I understood the police had ruled it a suicide."

Lee stared into those steely gray eyes knowing what she should say. Instead she replied, "She was murdered."

There, Martha's icy eyes flinched.

Martha sat back in her chair, pulling her pencil into her lap. "Did the police discover something new?"

A hot flash washed over Lee, and she sat staring dumbly at her boss, a tense silence hanging in the room.

"I assume the police are investigating this," Martha prompted her again.

"No," Lee finally whispered.

"Then I'm confused." Martha's voice was infused with renewed patience. "How do you know she was murdered?"

Robin shifted in the chair next to Lee.

"I don't know that she *was* murdered. I just know that she wouldn't kill herself."

"Jesus, Lee," Fran broke the silence. "Don't start jumping to conclusions."

"Who in the world would kill Diane?" Andrew blurted.

The room had come suddenly to life.

"The police ruled it a suicide, didn't they?" Robert asked, anxious to contribute. "They don't have any suspects, do they?"

"No. They believe it was a suicide."

"Well, then, maybe you'd better forget it," Andrew cautioned.

"I can't forget it!" she flared.

"It seems like an issue for the police," Martha's voice rose above the others as she placed her fleshy palms on the table in an effort to call a halt to the dialogue.

Lee looked at her with her jaw set. "That's the problem. The police won't do anything. They hardly even questioned Bud Maddox!"

Robin groaned, while Martha's eyebrows arched into twin peaks. "Just what does Bud Maddox have to do with Diane's death?"

"They were having an affair," Fran added salt to the wound.

Now everyone shifted. Andrew glared across the table at Fran. Although the affair was widely known among hospital staff, gossip normally didn't make its way to the oval office. Martha Jackson wasn't pleased with what she'd just heard. Her eyes seemed to shrink behind her glasses, and she leaned forward, resting her heavy forearms on the table.

"I believe your fondness for Diane is affecting your objectivity, Lee. This is none of your concern. You need to leave it to the police."

Lee opened her mouth to object, but Martha cut her off with a wave of her hand.

"Maybe a few days off would help," Martha said.

Lee thought she'd gone deaf. All the sound around her abated. Although Miranda was busily writing everything down for the record, her pen was silent. Everyone in the room seemed to hold their breath, and Lee's eyes began to burn. God, what was she doing? Why hadn't she just kept her mouth shut?

"Lee?" Martha asked.

Lee stared at her boos without really seeing her.

"A few days off, Lee?" Martha's voice seemed to echo through a tunnel. "You haven't had proper time to grieve."

This woman didn't know anything about grieving, Lee thought, and her superficial concern was pathetic. But Lee needed time to think. Perhaps she should take a few days off. Maybe then she could find out what had happened to Diane. Lee swallowed and stuck out her chin.

"I'll take you up on that offer, Martha. I think I could use a couple of days off."

"Fine," her boss replied. "If there is nothing else, I need to prepare for the conference call."

Martha Jackson got up, signaling an end to the meeting. Everyone else rose to leave. Robin turned to Lee, mouthing the words *"Call me"* before she left the room. Lee gathered up her notebook and few papers. Fran and Andrew waited for her at the door.

"Lee, have you arranged for the photo shoot at Green Valley, yet?" Fran wanted to know.

"It's scheduled for Friday night, at eleven o'clock," Lee replied without enthusiasm.

They had arranged a photo shoot at a local lumber mill to illustrate how their 24-hour Occupational Health program worked to promote wellness for more than five hundred companies in the area. Since most lumber mills ran night shifts, the Director of Public Relations had arranged for a nurse to give onsite flu shots to the employees during the graveyard shift.

"Well, it wouldn't hurt if you were there. I saw Jay Gilman yesterday," Fran said. "I think he's very excited about it."

"I'll be taking a few days off," Lee retorted. "Sally is the Director of Marketing. She'll just have to go solo without me."

"You could make nice with Gilman. He's a big client and could become a big donor. Sally is good, but she doesn't carry the weight a vice president would."

Lee felt her face begin to burn. "Martha's word is my command."

Fran touched her arm. "Lee, you were close to Diane. Everyone knows that. Take the time off. This isn't the best place to deal with your grief."

Fran's empathy took Lee by surprise. Fran would never be described as a warm personality. With her severe features and frizzy short hair, even her appearance kept you at arm's length. Then, Lee remembered a year earlier that Fran had gone through a difficult divorce. Maybe she had more empathy than Lee realized.

Lee merely nodded. "Thanks."

Fran and Andrew left Lee alone. She stared for a long moment at her notepad, not really seeing the image she'd doodled there. Her mind was a million miles away. With a sigh, she ripped off the top sheet and tossed it into a nearby trashcan, leaving behind the sketch of a large black bird perched on the branch of a tree.

CHAPTER TEN

Lee closed the door to her office and sat with her head in her hands. She would not cry. The word humiliation was not in her vocabulary. Humiliation meant you'd lost the game, the match, or the competition. In her whole career, she'd never been given a bad review, let alone a public reprimand. Now she'd been reprimanded in front of the entire executive team and forced to take time off, when it was work that kept her sane. News of this would spread like wildfire throughout the hospital, perhaps even to members of her foundation board of directors. She should have just kept her mouth shut.

With a deep sigh, she spun around to look out the window to the hills and dark clouds beyond. So be it. She would take the time off, but she wouldn't sit idle. She had something to prove now, and she would employ whatever she could to find the answers. Perhaps the time off was a blessing in disguise. She turned back to her computer to finish checking her emails before leaving. Just then, the phone rang.

"Are you okay?" Robin asked at the other end.

Lee cradled the phone to her ear as she opened emails. "Yeah, I just feel stupid."

"It probably wasn't your best move. However, you really could use the time off. Look at it as an unscheduled vacation."

"Thanks, but I have more important things to do. Will you be in your office this afternoon?"

Lee continued to skim down the list of emails as she talked. She stopped at the one with the strange poem again, allowing her eyes to skim across the words. There was a pause as Robin consulted her calendar.

"I have a meeting right after lunch which should take me up to about two o'clock."

"Mind if I come down then?" Lee asked, rubbing her eyes. "I have something to tell you."

"You're not quitting I hope," Robin asked with concern.

"No, of course not."

"Okay," Robin said, relieved. "I'll have an espresso waiting."

Lee smiled in spite of her bad mood. "Thanks. Make mine a double."

"A double it is," Robin said cheerfully. "I'll see you…"

Lee didn't hear the end of Robin's sentence, though. A noise made her look up to find Carey's husband pushing his way past Marie into her office. Lee quickly flicked off the computer screen and signaled for Marie to leave.

"Vern, what are you doing here?" she asked a bit nervously.

Vern Mathews seemed to fill the room the way helium fills a balloon. His voice wasn't much more than a snarl.

"Stop talking to my wife."

Clad in a long-sleeved, black sweater, with thick, chapped hands resting at his side, Mathews could have been an angry dockworker. Lee half expected him to slam a heavy coil of rope on the desk in front of her.

"What are you talking about?" she chuckled, trying to soften his mood.

"You know damn well what I'm talking about. Stop talking to my wife about Diane's death! It's none of your business."

"Sit down, Vern. Please." She gestured to a chair.

Mathews hesitated and then plopped into the armchair facing the desk. This man represented everything Lee hated about men. She'd spent a lifetime watching her stepfather control every moment of her mother's life, down to the flavor of her toothpaste. It took all of Lee's control not to throw this clown out, but she consciously lowered her voice.

"What are you so upset about, Vern? Carey's sister is dead. We talked about Diane, that's all."

"That's bullshit and you know it!" He sat forward in the chair, clenching his fists. "I know what you talked about. You think that bitch was murdered!"

Lee nearly came out of her chair. "There are some unanswered questions," she said through clenched teeth.

"She killed herself and left a note saying so. What the hell more do you want?"

"I want to know why," Lee pressed. "And you should, too. She was your sister-in-law."

"Diane was a pain in the ass!"

This time, Lee stood up. "I don't appreciate that."

She remained very still, allowing the electricity between them to grow. He shifted uncomfortably in the chair.

"What I meant was..." He glared at her, and then rose to his feet and leaned forward to rest his hands on the desk, his right hand resting directly on top of her letter opener. "You know what I meant. And you know what I mean about the suicide. It's hard enough to deal with people talking behind our backs about a suicide, but a murder...I won't have it." He picked up the letter opener and pointed it directly at Lee. "Don't put any ideas into Carey's head. She's my wife, and this is none of your business!"

Lee held her ground. "Diane was my employee, and my friend. So, it is my business, whether you like it or not."

His small eyes narrowed until the pupils were barely visible. "It's not your business," he growled. "And I'm not playing games here. Back off!"

Lee forced herself to maintain eye contact, although she couldn't help but feel threatened by the sharp steel pointed at her face.

"You fucking bitch," he whispered, his mouth drawn into a frown. "You're no better than Diane."

With a sudden flip of his wrist, he stabbed the letter opener into the desk and whirled around to march out of the office. The room was dense with the force of his anger, and Lee held her breath until the room pressure neutralized. Marie appeared at the doorway like a nervous bird.

"I'm so sorry, Lee," she said, her eyes wide, staring at the letter opener. "He just pushed right past me."

Lee swallowed several times before answering. "That's okay."

"Should I call security?"

"No, he's gone," she said, taking a deep breath. She pulled the letter opener from the desk and put it into her drawer. "I'll be leaving shortly anyway."

Marie was only about twenty-eight and had probably never known malice in her life. Yet, right now, her face registered real fear. Gently, Lee convinced Marie to return to her desk and then sat back down to allow the adrenalin to slowly dissipate. Her right knee throbbed, and she dug her fingers into the muscles around her kneecap to relieve the tension. Once her breathing had returned to normal, she turned off the computer and went out to Marie's desk.

"By the way," she began, taking a deep breath to control the level of her voice, "I'm going to take a few days off. I need some space." It was a lie, but she hoped it sounded natural under the circumstances. Maybe Martha's executive assistant wouldn't spread the truth about her administrative leave too quickly.

"We'll hold down the fort," Marie replied a little cautiously.

Lee recognized her nervousness. "Don't worry. He won't be back," Lee reassured her.

Jenny, her Data Information Coordinator, poked her head around the partition at the back of the office. The look on her face made it clear she shared Marie's anxiety.

"Listen, thanks for taking care of stuff around here, you guys. I know it hasn't been easy." There was an awkward pause before she said to Marie, "By the way, did you check Diane's emails?"

"Yes. I went through them the next day. There was just the usual stuff. I took care of everything."

"Great. Thanks."

Lee returned to her office to get her purse, just as Andrew appeared at the doorway again.

"I'm sorry about what happened this morning with Martha," he said, as if the whole thing had been his fault. "You okay?"

"I'm okay." She slipped the purse straps over her shoulder thinking she really wasn't in the mood for Andrew right now. "I could use some time off anyway." She moved toward the door, but Andrew just stood there, blocking her way.

"Martha shouldn't have reacted the way she did," he said obstinately. "You have a right to your opinion."

"I'm sure it sounded pretty dramatic."

"The police did rule it a suicide. I suppose they know what they're doing."

"Maybe," she said without conviction.

"You need to be careful," he pressed. "Martha doesn't like anything that reflects negatively on the hospital. I wouldn't want you to lose your job. You didn't earn that Master's degree for nothing," he tried to smile. "Get some rest," he said before leaving.

Lee watched him leave feeling completely disengaged from her body. Too much was happening, too fast. On impulse, she reached into her purse and found the bird. For whatever reason, it felt warm to the touch and gave her an immense sense of calm right now. She wrapped her fingers around it and marched out of the office.

CHAPTER ELEVEN

Vern Mathews' behavior had unnerved Lee more than she wanted to admit. Add to that the re-emergence of the bird in her purse and the strange poem on her computer, and her body was beginning to feel the strain of living in a constant state of adrenalin rush. By the time she climbed into her car, she murmured a silent prayer that she would make it safely to meet Patrick for lunch.

Papa Fromo's was a favorite student hangout right next to campus. As she climbed the wooden steps and passed through the banging screen door, the tang of tomato sauce and hot cheese triggered her Pavlovian response, filling her mouth with saliva. The sensation helped to temporarily quiet the chaos in her head. She found Patrick in a rear booth nursing a large soft drink and correcting some papers.

"Hey," he beamed, putting down his pencil. "You look remarkably well."

She smiled indulgently, knowing the lack of sleep probably made her look like the Bride of Frankenstein without the up-do.

"What are you correcting?" she said with a half-smile.

He slid the small stack of papers into a large envelope. "Essays on Goethe. Get it?" he grinned.

Lee grimaced and quickly ordered an iced tea from a passing waitress. When her fingers fumbled opening the menu, she called the waitress back and changed the order to ice water. Perhaps additional caffeine was a bad idea.

"Say, I'd like to tag along to that birthday bash tonight," Patrick said, toying with the straw in his drink. "Any objections? I'll drive," he offered.

She looked at him with a blank stare. "What birthday bash?"

"Mrs. Bates."

It took a second for her brain to engage. "Oh, I forgot. I don't think I'm in the mood for a party."

"How about just an appearance? You can't make too many friends in your business."

"I don't know, Patrick," she sighed, rubbing her eyes. "I'm just so tired."

"How about an hour? You said she's one of your hospital's biggest donors."

"She is," she sighed, rubbing her hands along her legs as if the friction would recharge her batteries.

"Well, you know her husband is also head of the Economics Department at the U and a big supporter of the Theater Department. I could score some points."

"You need to score points with the Economics Department?" Lee asked, her brain functioning in slow motion.

"No," he shook his head. "He actually funded a chair in our department. He loves his Shakespeare," Patrick rolled his eyes.

Lee nodded. "Okay, but let's make it short. Somehow I can't stand the thought of being with that group of people for too long."

"Why don't you meet me at the theater at seven?"

"Speaking of Shakespeare," she said, lighting up. "This is Shakespeare isn't it?" She pulled the strange email from her purse and handed it to him.

Patrick scanned it quickly. "It's the witches' scene from Macbeth. Well, actually, someone has combined two different sections of the play into one."

She frowned. "What's the significance of the witches?"

"There's significance to everything about Shakespeare."

"I don't need a lecture, professor, just the bare facts."

"I'll give you the Cliff Notes version, then. Macbeth is a study of man's potential for evil, and the witches embody the devil by foretelling the future." He eyed her carefully for a moment. "Where'd you get it?"

"It was in an email someone sent me. I think it's from the same person who sent me that weird card you were looking at."

His green eyes widened. "Someone is trying to send you a message about Diane."

"Apparently, and I'm too thick to get it."

"The card I read seemed to be warning you off," Patrick surmised. "While this one seems to be trying to tell you something," he said, nodding at the paper.

"Yes, but what?"

"Hell if I know," he shrugged. "Is this what you wanted to talk to me about?"

"No. Diane left a message on my answering machine."

The shocked look on his face made her hasten to explain it. "I mean, she left a message *before* she died. I just didn't pick it up until last night. She said she wouldn't be in the office the next day because she was going to Portland with Bud...for something special," she added. "It might just be the last thing Diane ever said."

Just then, the waitress arrived to take their orders. Patrick ordered pizza, and the waitress turned expectantly to Lee. She picked up the menu and waved her hand over it as if hoping something would appear by magic. Finally, she ordered a large salad. Once the waitress left, she turned her attention to Patrick.

"You know what this means?" she asked.

"I think I do," he said thoughtfully. "You told me her boyfriend-- Bud, right?--told the police he hadn't spoken to her for a couple of days."

"He said he'd broken up with her."

"So, he was lying."

She nearly reached across the table for him. "Exactly. He lied!"

Patrick watched her for a minute, before saying, "Are you going to tell the police?"

Lee slumped back in the seat. "I don't know. I had a long talk with Alan last night. He was able to reason away every argument I threw at him." She squeezed a lemon into her water and stirred it. "And Sergeant Davis, the guy in charge of the case, didn't have time for me the night we found her. It was like he'd made up his mind it was a suicide and that was it. I think it would take more than this message to get the police involved."

Patrick studied his hands for a moment and then said cautiously, "I didn't push you into this, did I? By speculating about her death yesterday?"

"No. I'd already been thinking about it. I was just having a hard time admitting it. Then Carey stopped by after the funeral and told me that she doesn't believe Diane killed herself, either." She sighed.

"The trouble is that Bud could wiggle his way out of this. He could convince the police that Diane was making up the trip to Portland."

"There would probably be some kind of phone records. How long were you at Diane's that night?" Patrick's eyes had settled into a deep sea green, and there wasn't a hint of a smile anywhere.

"About thirty minutes. I left around seven-thirty. The message was left on my machine sometime after that."

"According to the police theory," Patrick was thinking out loud, "Bud broke up with her some time later that evening, apparently right after he'd already invited her to go to Portland. That sent her into a downward spiral, and she became so despondent she decided to kill herself."

"Not only that," Lee added, "their theory depends on Diane having gone out to buy a larger syringe than the ones she already had on hand, all the time ignoring the cat she adored and forgetting she'd left me a message to the contrary."

"Maybe the police will listen now."

"The police just want things wrapped up," she said, shaking her head. "Look Patrick, I bought into the suicide theory in the beginning, just like everyone else. But I know Diane didn't kill herself. She would quit her job and move out of the state before she killed herself. It just wasn't her style."

"So, what will you do?"

Lee exhaled and took a drink of ice water. "I don't know," she said, swallowing. "I just know she didn't kill herself. I don't know much more than that."

"Well, I tell my students that every story has a beginning, middle, and an end. Directors are taught to look at the whole picture," he said, using his hands to illustrate a circle. "We begin by looking at what makes characters do what they do."

She looked at him with a wry smile. "Okay, but which characters do I need to look at?"

"In a play, every character does more than just play a part. They each have a reason for being on stage. It might only be to deliver a cup of coffee, but that simple action could establish location. Maybe they deliver a message. That action might provide information necessary to the plot."

"Patrick, you're talking about the theater. This is real life."

"What's the difference? The theater is only slightly more contrived."

She sipped her water. "So, I should look at all the players. That would include Bud, Diane and who else?"

"Anyone she had influence over, or who had influence over her."

"That would include her mom, her sister, her brother-in-law...and me." She paused, her muscles beginning to tie themselves into little knots.

"Everybody plays a part," he said quietly. "You need to know which forces are greater than others. Cause and effect. This wasn't random. If she *was* killed, there had to be a reason. One force became greater than another."

They sat looking at each other while Lee thought about what he'd said. Unconsciously, she'd begun to rub her knee, a sure sign her stress level was rising.

"Then, you need to identify the inciting moment," Patrick finished.

"What's that?" she asked, watching him suspiciously.

"It's when the play's action really begins, when circumstances provide the purpose for the rest of the action that takes place. In some plays, murder may be the inciting moment. But you're going to have to go back further than that here. What forces came together to create the *need* for murder? Remember, every character has a reason for being on stage. Get to know your characters and I bet you'll find the information you need."

"You believe me, don't you?" She squeezed the words out knowing her face betrayed her doubt.

"I don't think I could have written a play with more theatrical possibilities." He leaned forward again and placed his hand over the two of hers. "You're as stubborn as they come, Lee. If you believe this, then do something about it. Don't let this one go."

His comment caught her off guard and she pulled back. "What's that supposed to mean?"

"Just that you're probably the most stubborn woman I know. Remember Girl Scouts? When you went to that camp and jogged a six-mile hike just to prove an older girl wrong when she said you were too small to keep up. Mom said you were sent to the infirmary until your feet recovered. Yet, when Brad disappeared, you didn't lift a finger to find out what happened. You climbed into a shell. If you believe something is wrong here, convince the police to take a second look. That's what you do for a living isn't it? Talk people into doing things they don't want to do?"

84

"I raise money," she said, bristling.

"Well use a little of that magic on the police."

She pulled her hands away and shrank into the high-backed seat, feeling a flush spread across her face. The waitress arrived with their food and placed the dishes on the table. Patrick declined her offer for more drinks and picked up the pizza, watching his sister. The very air between them had gone dead.

"Lee, don't get weird on me. I'm on your side."

"Brad disappeared over ten years ago," she spat. "Why do you keep bringing it up?"

He sighed and put the pizza down. "Because it colors everything you do. It's why you never date. It's why you take a new job every three or four years. It's why you hang onto Amy so tight. And it's why you won't have a dog. There's some deep, dark secret about all of that you insist on keeping to yourself."

"I'm not ready."

"Christ, Lee, when *will* you be ready?"

Lee stared at her brother. He was so much like her father. Handsome and sharp-witted. On the surface, Patrick had it all. Women adored him, and men copied him. Yet, Patrick had lost something all those year ago, too. While Lee had lost her father and all the strength of character that might bring, Patrick had lost his mother through divorce. By the time he was rewarded with a stepmother, he'd already found ways to protect himself from getting too close to the women he loved. All except for Lee.

Lee reached for her purse.

"C'mon, Lee, don't leave. Please."

"I'll see you tonight."

With that, she pulled herself out of the booth and flew out the door.

CHAPTER TWELVE

Lee roared up the hill to Hendrick's Park, her head aching from the anger that had propelled her from the restaurant. She whirled into a parking space and stopped the car, her eyes staring straight ahead. Patrick had a right to be skeptical. When her husband disappeared, she had been uncharacteristically silent. Now, she was parading around with righteous indignation about the ruling on Diane's death, when there wasn't one real piece of evidence to the contrary. It had to be confusing. It was confusing to her. And it made her all the more angry.

She pushed open the door and got out, striking off on the path that led around the parking lot. She inhaled the crisp afternoon air hoping it would relax her, but her muscles were stretched so tight they were ready to snap. When a couple appeared ahead of her, she peeled off onto a side path that curved into a grove of trees, ending at a picnic table situated under a canopy of pine boughs.

Lee sat down, her hands clenched into fists in her pockets. She closed her eyes and took several deep breaths, but Patrick's smug face kept floating into view.

"You're as stubborn as they come, Lee. Don't let this one go," the face chided.

"Dammit!" she screamed, tears springing forth. "Dammit to hell! You don't always have to be right, Patrick!"

She stood up and kicked a dent into a metal trashcan chained to the side of the table, and then grabbed the lid, intent on sending into a tree. At the last moment, she dropped it and dropped her head into her hands, falling back onto the bench, tears running down her face and sobs rolling across her body.

"Dammit! I don't know what to do," she said, rocking back and forth. "I don't know what to do."

The tears flowed as if a spigot had been turned on. They weren't just about Diane. They were for all the disappointments in her life. The lost time with her father. The loss of her favorite sport. The fact Amy was growing up, and the fact Patrick had a way of reminding her of past failings. They were even for Martha Jackson for being so damned righteous. Then, of course, there was the fact that Diane wouldn't be there at all anymore. But most of all, she was mad at herself. She'd wasted her last moments with Diane tangled in a stupid argument. That was unforgivable. The tears brought it all out, every last poisonous vapor.

Finally, her energy spent, Lee pulled a Kleenex from her pocket and blew her nose and leaned back against the table. She looked out at the lush green park through leaden eyes, thinking she'd spent her entire life as a stubborn competitor. Patrick was right. In Girl Scouts they had nicknamed her "The Mule" because she was resolute in her pursuit to be the best. If the girls had to build a fire, Lee built the biggest. If they had to dig a hole, she dug the deepest. The summer Patrick had mentioned, she'd tried to prove she could keep up with the older girls by hiking further and faster than required, only to return to camp with blisters that bled through her socks.

Then, almost two decades later, she'd simply withered when her husband disappeared, keeping everyone at a distance, retreating to an inner place to which only she held the key. Part of her had died that day, and it was Diane and her irreverent sense of humor who had reminded Lee to smile occasionally.

The breeze rustled through the pine trees like the gentle flow of a mountain stream, and Lee looked around at the layers of verdant bushes and trees feeling a sense of calm for the first time in days. The tang of pine coursed through her system like aromatherapy, and she inhaled it deeply. When she rotated her head, the pain in her neck and shoulders was gone. Even the headache was gone.

A small bird landed on the rim of the trash can, turning its head back and forth looking at her. It hopped up onto the table and bounced back and forth as if hoping Lee would toss it a bread crumb. She just smiled and reached out a finger, but the bird bounced to one side.

Lee turned away from the bird and looked around. Hendrick's Park in Eugene, Oregon, had been the place where Steve Prefontaine, a world-class long distance runner from the University of Oregon, had died many years before in a car crash. Diane's husband had been a big fan of Prefontaine's, and Diane had told Lee once that Prefontaine was quoted as saying, *"Most people run a race to see who is the fastest. I run a race to see who has the most guts."* Diane had liked that motto, and Lee realized how appropriate it felt right now. She would need guts to finish this race, but finish it she would.

As she watched two squirrels chase each other around the base of a tree, flicking and switching their bushy tails, the small bird hopped onto the bench beside her. She studied it, wondering again about the bird in her purse and what it meant. On impulse, she reached into her purse and pulled the figurine out and placed it on the bench. She thought the little bird would fly away, but it tilted its head this way and that and then bounced sideways over to the small figurine. Lee watched in wonder, as the small creature reached out with its tiny beak and touched the onyx figurine once, twice, three times. Then, in a flurry of wings, it was gone.

Lee felt an invigorating chill flow through her body as the bird disappeared into the air. Perhaps she should be frightened by the onyx figurine, but for some reason, it gave her a strange sense of comfort. She'd asked Diane for help. Lee was beginning to believe she'd given it.

The intense crying had cleared Lee's head and she decided it was time to consider her options. She was convinced the police wouldn't budge with the little evidence she had. So, what could she really do? She didn't have the police report, the coroner's report, or the syringe. She didn't have access to Bud's background or any useful information on his relationship with Diane. But she did have access to the hospital, where both Diane and Bud had worked. Patrick had talked about the inciting moment in a mystery play - the point at which the need for murder was ignited. If Bud Maddox was involved, it was likely the story began at the hospital. And it was the one place where she had inroads.

CHAPTER THIRTEEN

Lee arrived in Robin's outer office a few minutes after two o'clock wearing fresh clothes and makeup. A matronly-looking woman dressed in a gray polyester suit was hanging up the phone. She acknowledged Lee just as Robin returned from another meeting.

"I wasn't sure you'd come," Robin said to Lee. "C'mon in. Can you hold my calls, Rosemary?"

The secretary nodded as she turned to pull a fax off the machine. Lee followed Robin into her office where her friend pushed aside several file folders on a small, round conference table so they could sit down. The large window that overlooked an outdoor courtyard washed the oak furniture in a shallow band of light. Two large Asian watercolor prints warmed the room, and a small water feature on her desk gurgled like a mountain brook.

As VP of Human Resources, Robin handled the personnel files of over one thousand employees, worked with two unions, and had earned a reputation as a tough negotiator. She was quick, clever, and didn't hold a grudge. Robin settled back and scrutinized her friend.

"That wasn't your best move this morning. You must have known Martha wouldn't want to hear theories about Diane's death. She wants her executive team to walk a straight line. What in the world were you thinking?"

Lee chuckled and shook her head as if she couldn't believe it herself. "I don't know. It's an understatement to say I'm not thinking clearly. I just couldn't stand her pathetic attempt at compassion. I'd rather she just ignored Diane's death."

"What will you do while you're off?"

Lee bit her lip and didn't respond. Robin's eyes grew wide.

"My God, you're going to try to find out if Diane was murdered, aren't you? Lee, don't. I don't know what happened to Diane, but leave it to the police."

"Diane left a message on my answering machine," Lee announced bluntly.

Robin's jaw dropped. Lee knew she was wading into deep water, but plunged ahead thinking she was going to have to get better at telling this story.

"I don't mean recently. She left a message Thursday night *before* she died."

Robin recovered her composure. "I don't understand."

"She left a message saying that she wouldn't be in on Friday. I played it for the first time last night when I got home from your place."

Robin inhaled. "How awful."

Lee leveled a look at Robin, all fear gone now for the path she was embarking on.

"Diane wasn't coming in to work that day because she was going to Portland with Bud."

Robin's eyes grew wider. "But, he said…he…oh my God, he was lying! You could tell Alan."

Lee shook her head. "I need more information than that."

"But he lied. He said that he broke up with her. The police would have to talk to him again."

"Robin, be serious. Alan's not assigned to the case. He'd have to pass the information along to Sergeant Davis, and I'm positive Davis wouldn't care. Even if they talked to Bud, he would just come up with some lame excuse, and the police would drop it again. Diane's message doesn't prove he lied."

Robin sighed. "So what are you going to do?"

Lee leaned forward slightly. "You need to promise me you won't say anything to Alan. If I'm wrong, I don't want Alan involved in any way."

Robin had been toying with the pearls around her neck as Lee spoke. "I don't know, Lee."

"Please, Robin."

Robin's graceful brows were clenched in the middle of her forehead, as if they were locked in mortal combat. Robin always followed the rules and never made grandstand plays. Lee was asking her to do something against her character, and right now there was a war going on inside her as she considered Lee's request.

"You don't have to lie," Lee cut in reassuringly. "Just don't say anything."

"What are you going to do?"

"I need to find something substantial. A reason someone might have wanted Diane dead. I need more information on the players."

"The who?"

Lee made a face. "It was something Patrick said. The players...people involved with Diane. I've already had an encounter with her sister, Carey. And her brother-in-law came to see me in my office this morning." Lee grimaced, remembering the letter opener. "He was pissed off to say the least, and he doesn't want me encouraging Carey in any murder theories."

"Maybe he killed her and made it look like a suicide," Robin offered.

"I've thought of that, but I need more," Lee emphasized. "What about the life insurance?"

"I called the hospital's agent, and I was right. Many insurance policies have a waiting period – especially for suicide. If a suicide occurred during the waiting period, then the company wouldn't pay. After the waiting period though, they would."

Lee's eyebrows arched. "Carey said that Diane took out a policy when she worked at the university."

"So, if there was a waiting period, it would have been over a long time ago."

Lee became so lost in thought about Vern Mathews and the life insurance policy, she almost missed Robin's next sentence.

"You know, you also have to find out more about Bud Maddox. He's got to be your prime suspect."

Lee stopped daydreaming and stared at Robin. Each waited for the other to speak. Outside, clouds moved in a straight line across the sky like the cheap backdrop to a school play, and a bird descended onto the branch of a tree right outside the window. Lee was only vaguely aware of it.

"That's why you're here, isn't it?" Robin asked. "To get the personnel file. It won't tell you why he might have murdered Diane. I told you, we did a criminal check on him, and he was clean."

"I need a place to start."

Now that she was moving in a positive direction, Lee was as calm as a mirrored lake. On the other hand, Robin shifted uncomfortably in her chair.

"You know I can't give it to you, Lee. It's against the law."

The wind picked up and scratched a tree branch against the

window, making them both look up. Lee noticed the bird and inwardly smiled. After a moment, Robin's demeanor changed. She sat forward, cleared her throat, and glanced at the file cabinet to her left. Lee followed her gaze.

"Do you want something to drink?" she asked. "I think I'm going to run to the cafeteria. I've been taking antihistamines, and my throat is really dry." She stroked her throat and then got up to reach into a desk drawer to find her leather shoulder bag. "I'll be back in a few minutes."

Before Lee could respond, Robin left the room. Lee recognized the charade for what it was and thought of the characters on stage. Robin had just played out her role and given Lee her cue. Although her heart raced nervously, she reached over and pulled open the drawer marked "M," quickly locating the file marked "Maddox, Bud." Before she could change her mind, she grabbed a yellow notepad from under a stack of papers and slipped the file folder in between the middle sheets. The deed was done before her conscience could disagree, but her temples pulsed, and her temperature had risen significantly. As calmly as she could, she opened the door and stepped into the outer office. The secretary looked up.

"Tell Robin I had to leave. I forgot I have to make a phone call," she lied as calmly as she could.

The secretary waved her out as she juggled another incoming call. Lee hurried down the hall, her brain on fire and not really knowing where she was going. For the first time in her life, she'd just committed a crime. By the time she walked into her office, the pit of her stomach was twisted in knots. Jenny and Marie looked up in surprise.

"I thought we weren't going to see you until Monday?" Marie stated.

Lee gaped at them. "I...uh, forgot something," she said without conviction. She'd wandered back to her office out of habit, forgetting she'd already said good-bye that morning. "I'm just here for a minute," she stammered. "I wanted to take some things home...to read."

Lee hurried into her office to mask her mistake. She placed the pad with its hidden contents on a chair next to her desk and then found a stack of professional fundraising journals lying on the floor. As she bent over to pick one up, Jenny entered behind her.

"Got a minute?" Jenny asked, moving to sit in the chair. "I

wanted to ask you about that campaign report before you go."

Lee straightened up as Jenny sat down and placed the incriminating pad in her lap. Lee froze, her eyes riveted on Jenny's lap. A tip of the personnel file poked out of the pad only inches from Jenny's fingers. Even from where Lee stood, she could read the beginning of Bud Maddox's name in bold type on the tab.

"Can this wait?" Lee blurted. "I've got an appointment."

No one could know she'd taken the file. If it was discovered, at the very least she'd lose her job. But the consequences could even be greater.

"Uh...sure. No problem." Jenny stood up again, confused. She started to leave, forgetting the pad now clutched to her chest.

"Jenny!" Lee nearly barked. "I need that pad." Lee gestured toward her hands.

"Oh, sorry," Jenny said, passing it over. Lee grabbed for it and pushed the folder back into place with her thumb.

"Thanks," Lee said, her nerves starting to fray.

Jenny walked out with a curious look on her face. Lee gathered up a couple of journals and stepped out to Marie's desk.

"Okay, I'll see you guys later."

Marie looked up, her brown eyes furrowed. "Today?"

Lee was beginning to know what it felt to be a pathological liar. "Uh, no, not today. I'm working on a couple of projects at home and may have to stop by to pick stuff up," she said vaguely. "I mean, feel free to call me if you need anything. I'm not going anywhere, just taking some time off."

Marie frowned, and Lee realized she needed to just shut up. She spun around and hurried into the hallway, colliding with Martha Jackson who was just coming into the office. With an "oof!" Lee dropped everything at Jackson's feet.

"Oh, I'm sorry, Martha," Lee apologized. She quickly stepped in front of her boss to pick up the file folder.

"That's all right, Lee," the CEO said, forced to step back. "I didn't expect to find you here. I thought you had already left."

"I thought I'd take some work home," Lee said as she patted the journals in her hand.

"Well, I came over for Mrs. Bates' address. Does Marie have it? I originally turned down the invitation for her birthday party tonight, but found I can go after all."

"Marie can get it for you," Lee said, stepping away. "I'm late for an appointment," she said quickly and left.

Once out in the fresh air, she took a few deep breaths. How did con men do this on a regular basis? She was at the car before she realized she'd forgotten her jacket in Robin's office. In her imagination, alarms were already going off inside the building as security guards converged on her office to find the personnel file. She unlocked the car door thinking that her jacket would have to remain behind to face the music alone.

"Miss Vanderhaven?"

Lee wheeled around to come face to face with a police officer.

"My name is Officer Wright."

He was a tall man with short gray hair and sharp blue eyes. His right arm was tucked in at his side, holding his cap to his chest. His left hand reached into a pocket to extract a notepad and pencil.

"I need to ask you a few questions."

"Now?" she blurted. "I'm in a bit of a hurry."

How did they find out so fast?

"It's about your assistant, Diane Winter. I met you the night she died. I was part of the response team. I was just about to come find your office, but saw you come out. Anyway, your friend's condominium was broken into last night. I was wondering if you knew anything about it."

Lee was speechless, her mind a blank. "What are you talking about? I was th... I mean...why would anyone...why would they...she's dead."

"The entire place was ransacked. Her sister is over there now trying to identify anything that may have been stolen." He paused for an awkward moment. "Your car was seen there last night. Can you tell me why you were there?"

"I stopped by to check on something, but I didn't...it wasn't me...I didn't do anything. I just checked on something."

Her mind seemed to whir in reverse. Images of the garbage dumpsters, the bird, and the dark feather clicked through her head like a child's View Master.

"You care to tell me what you were checking on?"

"I'm sorry?"

There was a buzzing in her ears and she caught herself focusing on a small gnat that flitted about the officer's head.

"Why did you go there?"

"Oh," she responded, focused now on his eyes. "I was at the

condo the night she died and I remembered that I didn't see a certain vase there that night. I just wondered what happened to it. That's all. I have a key, so I looked around for it, but I couldn't find it."

"Why was the vase important?"

He squinted in the sunlight making the skin around his eyes crease into little folds. Officer Wright finally became aware of the gnat and used his notepad to swat at it.

"It wasn't important," Lee stumbled, watching the gnat. "I mean, not to anyone but me. You see, I gave it to her," she lied. "I just wondered what happened to it. Ask Alan Grady. Detective Grady," she emphasized. "I was at his house for dinner last night, and I mentioned it to him just before I left."

The officer took a note. "Did you talk with anyone while you were there?"

Lee could hardly hear anything because her heart was pounding so loudly in her ears. For God's sake, she had just lied to a police officer.

"Did you talk with anyone, Ms. Vanderhaven?" he repeated.

"No. No, I didn't see anyone."

Lee thought of the brown truck and other neighbors who must have seen her, though. Her car would have been easy to identify.

"What time did you leave the condo?"

"I got there a little after nine, nine-thirty I think. I was there about thirty minutes, but I didn't ransack anything. I mean everything looked normal when I left."

"And you didn't see anyone else?"

"No. I..." She thought about her sojourn to the dumpsters again, but decided not to mention it. "I let myself in, looked around for the vase and then left."

A chill rippled down her back when she remembered her purse and the feather. Had someone been in the house the entire time she was there?

"Do you think this has anything to do with Diane's death?" she inquired.

The officer flipped the cover closed on his notepad and tucked it back into his shirt. "I doubt it. It was probably just someone who knew the condo was empty. Thanks for your time. If you remember anything, give us a call."

Lee was sure she should respond, but all she could muster was a mute nod. Officer Wright walked to his cruiser parked at the curb.

Lee waited until he pulled away and then climbed into her own car. As she pulled out of the parking lot, she passed a brown truck parked across the street.

CHAPTER FOURTEEN

By the time Lee arrived home, she was exhausted. The strain over Diane's death, the bird, and now her foray into the world of covert investigations had evaporated a desire to do anything that involved thought or movement of any kind. She plopped down on her bed fully clothed, thinking she'd just close her eyes for a few minutes. Almost three hours later, she awoke from a deep sleep, feeling drugged and disoriented. A quick shower helped revive her before she searched for a black pencil skirt and a blue sequined top for the party she'd promised to go to with Patrick.

As she stepped into her undergarments, she turned to stare at herself in the mirror. The image that stared back was completely unfamiliar. Her skin was sallow and the corners of her mouth sagged, making her full lips look like deflated balloons. Deep shadows rimmed her eyes, so that with a little extra eye makeup, she thought she could go to the party as a raccoon. She twisted to survey her figure, thinking that at least her body was in relatively good shape. Her stomach was flat, and she'd avoided the cellulite that plagued her mother. But as she raised an arm and watched an inch of flab respond to the force of gravity, she resolved to start working out again.

She'd always kept fit as a college gymnast. Back then, nothing felt better than tight muscles supporting a vault or pinning a perfect landing. She reached down and touched the deep scar that curved along the inside of her right knee with a vague pang of regret. A split second at the end of a three-minute routine − that's all it took. A break in concentration at the wrong moment, and everything she'd worked for--including a potential trip to the Nationals--was gone. Repairing the knee had taken three and a half hours in surgery and more than six months of painful therapy. The emotional rehabilitation had taken much longer. Now she lived in fear of ever injuring that knee again. Her fingers rested on the raised edge of the scar for only a brief moment before the mental trap door closed shut.

She finished dressing and grabbed her purse to find the onyx bird. Drawing it out, she turned it over in her hand, searching for the spot that had nicked her finger earlier in the day, but the bird was polished smooth. She didn't know what type of bird it was, but it looked like a predator, perhaps even a hawk. As she turned it over, the light from above her mirror made its eyes glow again. A chill ran the length of her spine as she remembered the real hawk watching her at the graveyard. Was there a connection?

She slipped the bird back into her purse and glanced at her watch. She had about twenty minutes before she had to leave. Lee had already set out a bottle of wine to give to Mrs. Bates as a gift, along with a signed birthday card. So, she decided to take a few minutes and flip through the personnel file on Bud Maddox.

Bud's employment was uneventful. He'd been certified as a lab technician in Redding, California over a decade ago and worked for an independent lab before moving to Medford, Oregon. Currently he lived in a nice neighborhood in West Eugene, and Lee wondered if he'd bought the home or was renting. The file also listed Emily Maddox as his wife, living in Jacksonville, just outside of Medford. This piece of news gave Lee a glimmer of hope. She knew the Foundation Director at Aurora Medical Center in Medford and made a decision to give him a call the next morning. If she could get an appointment to see him, she might also be able to find a way to look up Emily Maddox.

÷

Lee parked behind Patrick's Mazda at the University's theater just before seven o'clock and entered from the back of the house. A half-completed interior set seemed to rise from the depths of the stage. It reminded Lee of an M. C. Escher painting, with stairways going nowhere, and walls and window units sitting at odd angles. Lee took a seat half way back, pulled out a breakfast bar she'd grabbed before leaving the house, and settled in to watch her brother finish his rehearsal.

Patrick stood just in front of the stage with one foot on a small set of stairs. Dressed in Dockers, a blue denim shirt, and a sweater tied around his shoulders, he reminded Lee of a young Eugene O'Neill, sans mustache. There were two male actors on stage, one in his mid-thirties with a receding hairline, and a young man with thick, dark hair who looked like he'd just stepped out of a GQ magazine. Patrick read a few lines for GQ, imitating the inflection and movement he wanted. He did this off and on for another fifteen minutes, even getting up on stage at one point to demonstrate the blocking he wanted. Then, he called it quits and packed up his script. He turned and saw Lee.

"Hey, when did you get here?" he asked, jumping off the stage.

"Just a few minutes ago," she said, throwing the empty wrapper in her purse and standing up. "I didn't want to disturb you. You're really good, you know. Why didn't you go into acting yourself?"

He leaned over and hoisted the canvas bag full of scripts and papers that sat on the floor onto his shoulder.

"I don't act because I like to eat," he finally responded, sauntering up the aisle. "C'mon, my car is out front."

Lee grabbed her coat and purse off the chair, and they pushed their way through the doors that led to the darkened lobby.

"Let's get this over with," she said in a churlish manner.

"That's what I like! A positive attitude." He smiled as he held open the outside door.

"Shall we? Don't want to miss singing 'Happy Birthday' to the ice queen herself."

"Let's hope we're long gone before that happens."

She swung her coat around her shoulders and followed Patrick outside. He dumped his things into the back of the Mazda, while she climbed into the passenger's seat. Once behind the wheel, he fired up the engine and took off with a jolt.

"Slow down," she ordered. "We're not in that much of a hurry."

"Boy, you're on edge. You're not still mad about this afternoon, are you? I'm really sorry about what I said at the restaurant."

"No. It's just been a shitty day all around."

She slumped back in the seat as Patrick guided the car past a couple of big university buildings, then turned right to circle around campus. Within minutes, Lee was watching houses pass by her window as they drove toward the hills of South Eugene.

"So, I wasn't the only scoundrel of the day?" he tried to coax her out.

"Hardly," she half laughed, gazing out the window.

"Want to talk?"

She stole a glance in his direction and felt six years old again. Even when they were young, she and Patrick were like night and day. If Lee wanted to go left, Patrick wanted to go right. If Lee wanted ice cream, Patrick wanted cotton candy. But he'd always been there when she needed him. The thought brought a familiar pang of regret, and she turned back to watch the rain spatter the windshield.

"Martha Jackson put me on administrative leave today," she said quietly. "I'm supposed to take a few days off to grieve properly." Sarcasm dripped from her lips.

"Did it have something to do with Diane?"

"It had everything to do with Diane," she reflected. "It happened just before I saw you for lunch."

The light changed and they drove on in silence for a moment.

"I guess I wasn't in a very good place when I arrived for lunch today," she mumbled apologetically.

"I'm sorry, Lee," he said, glancing sideways at her. "Not that you couldn't use the vacation, but that's a hell of a way to get it."

"Well, I blew it." She leaned her head back against her seat and turned to look at her brother. "I told the whole administrative team today that I thought Diane had been murdered."

Patrick's green eyes flashed in her direction, accompanied by a short whistle.

"I know. I know," she deflected his reaction. "Of course the first question Martha asked was whether the police were investigating." Lee laughed cynically. "No chance there. So, I guess Martha decided that I was probably nuts and needed a vacation before I hurt myself."

"Consider it from her point of view," he said, his hands resting next to each other at the top of the steering wheel. "The police have ruled it a suicide and so far nothing points to anything else."

"Except the answering machine message," Lee reminded him.

"Yes, but does anyone know about that?"

"No," she said with resignation. "Well, no one except Robin and you. Then there's the fact that Diane's condo was broken into last night."

"What?" Patrick shot another glance her way.

"I was approached by the police today. Apparently someone broke into her condo and ransacked the place. They think it was just a burglary."

"Really?" He turned back and concentrated on his driving. "Was anything stolen?"

"I don't know. I tried calling Carey before I left the house, but didn't get her."

"Maybe if you gave them your answering machine, they'd start to connect the dots. Obviously, Bud *had* talked to Diane just before she died and apparently he invited her to Portland."

She shook her head. "I still think it'd be too easy to explain away. Besides, I don't want to raise alarms before I have to." She shifted her body so that she faced her brother. "Patrick, I need something irrefutable. Something the police can't ignore."

They were in the South Eugene hills now and Patrick turned onto a side street lined with tall pines and large homes that overlooked the city. A few blocks further, and they turned into a private lane that wound up the hill, ending in a circular drive. Half a dozen cars were wedged into the space just in front of the house. Another dozen cars lined the driveway. As they arrived, a black Mercedes was just pulling out, and they slipped into the open parking spot. Patrick turned off the engine and reached for the door handle.

"You know," Lee stopped him. "What you said today. It's true. I didn't do anything to find out what really happened to Brad. I was a coward then. I admit it." She looked at him, her eyes glistening with tears. "Maybe I can make up for that now."

He reached for her hand. "Okay, but be careful. I know I encouraged you to do this, but murder isn't a game. And there's no curtain call at the end."

Lee nodded, and they got out of the car. They were protected from the light rainfall by the canopy of trees. Lee produced a bottle of wine and a card from her large handbag as Patrick joined her. Flagstone steps flanked by wrought iron lamps led up to the huge Tudor-style house where a large arched door looked like the entrance to a gingerbread castle.

Eloise Bates was an extremely homely woman and devoid of any personality, but her family had earned millions in the timber industry, making her a good catch. Roland Bates had even less personality, but held a prominent position at the university. Together, they enjoyed a reputation as the most boring couple to invite to a campus party. Patrick and his buddy professors took great pleasure in scoring university soirees. When Roland and Eloise attended a party together, the party was automatically awarded a zero. Lee's eyes swept across the massive exterior thinking that while money can't buy love, apparently it could substitute for a lack of charm.

"Well, here we are at the Bates Motel," Patrick quipped as he looked up the hill.

Patrick often tossed off obscure theatrical references, but Lee wondered if Patrick knew how close he had come to the truth by referring to one of his favorite movies, *Psycho*.

"You probably don't know," she said, climbing the stairs, "but Mrs. Bates' mother disappeared about eighteen years ago. No trace of her was ever found. Speculation has it that her father murdered her and buried her in the backyard."

Patrick's eyes grew wide. "Gaw! You're kidding. Wouldn't that be the story?" he said in a fake Irish brogue. "I'll have to take a stroll in the garden," he winked, rubbing his hands together and sounding a bit like an Irish Boris Karloff.

Lee laughed. "You'd better be careful. If you haven't met their daughter, Pauline, I wouldn't go anywhere alone tonight. The rumors about her are even worse."

Patrick suddenly changed his posture to stand up straight, puffing his chest out. "Oh well," he murmured in a clipped, Cary Grant accent. "Not to worry. We'll take a look in the cellar and see if her mother has a few companions lying around."

Lee slapped him and smirked. "Pretty soon, you'll be pretending you're Teddy Roosevelt."

He smiled and held out his fist in front of him. Suddenly, he yelled, "Chaaaarge!" and pulled her up the final few stairs. When they got to the landing, he was just Patrick again, saying, "C'mon. As you said, let's get this gig over."

Lee shook her head, thinking that he changed character as easily as most people breathe.

"Jeez, are you even aware that you do that?" she said in awe. "You pop in and out of characters so fast, it's spooky."

He stopped to flash a wicked smile in her direction and gestured to the front door. "Please, Madame," he said, the nasal quality of his voice imitating one of his favorite actors, the late Peter Lorre. "You have only to turn the knob to discover what lies in wait. Avoid the basement, avoid rocking chairs, and by all means, avoid taking a shower."

He followed this with another evil laugh and received a second slap for his effort. Just then, a young woman answered the door and ushered them through a wide foyer to a small room behind the staircase. Lee hung up her coat and hooked her purse strap over the hanger. Then, they were led into the living room, where an imposing white marble fireplace was dwarfed by a large painting of Mrs. Bates sitting in a blue velvet chair, her hair curled into a tight cap about her head. Lee thought she looked like an older version of Lady Bird Johnson and wondered at the arrogance of having your very large portrait placed so prominently.

The room was filled with people. In front of the fireplace, the wife of the University President listened to Roland Bates, who had somehow commanded the attention of two other women as well. Martha Jackson stood in the dining room next to a table laden with food, casually chatting with two of the hospital board members from the competing hospital in Eugene.

Patrick moved into the living room, greeting a number of university professors before making a beeline for the bar. He winked at Lee as he maneuvered through the dining room, grabbing something from the table before slipping quietly out the door to the sunroom. Before Lee could settle on her own strategy, she felt a leaden hand on her shoulder and turned to find Mrs. Bates only inches away.

"Lee, I'm so glad you could come," she said in a lazy voice, her jowls trembling slightly.

Mrs. Bates was wearing a rose colored wool suit that looked like it came right out of one of Patrick's old movies, with a string of pearls wrapped tightly around her sagging neck. Eloise Bates never wore makeup, even face makeup, so that, to Lee, the deep lines in her face made her look like a dried prune.

Lee flashed her best smile. "Happy Birthday, Mrs. Bates. Thank you for inviting me. This is really a lovely party."

The older woman looked around the room with a blank expression. "It's nice to have so many friends here."

Lee produced the card and bottle of wine. "I found a bottle of Fetzer wine you might like. I know you traveled down to California last year for a wine tour."

"How nice of you. Thank you. You know, Lee," she began stiffly, taking the bottle. "I'd like to stop by next week. I have something important I want to talk about. I mentioned it to that assistant of yours, but nothing was done."

"Uh...Diane?" Lee paused. It could be that Mrs. Bates was

unaware of Diane's death. "I'm sorry. Just give me a call. I'm sure whatever it is, we can figure it out."

The doorbell rang, and Mrs. Bates excused herself to welcome another couple. Lee turned away to follow Patrick, but bumped smack into Bud Maddox who was standing behind her. He was talking with a slender, dark-haired woman dressed in crisp gray slacks and a cashmere sweater. Maddox turned as if to merely acknowledge the mistake, but seeing Lee, made the full turn with a forced grin.

"Well, well, I thought you were taking a little vacation," he said, running his tongue over his lips. "Sounds like you raised quite a stir this morning." He leaned toward her as if to share a secret. "You'd do better spending your time grieving rather than raising questions."

Lee locked eyes with him in an effort to stare him down and suddenly the room felt quite small. "At least one of us actually *is* grieving."

Maddox only returned a light laugh. The woman behind him merely stared at her.

Lee turned away and muttered, "Asshole," and then retreated back into the entryway.

She ducked down a hallway and back through the kitchen to the sunroom, where she found Patrick laughing with the bartender, a glass of Scotch in his hand. Roland Bates and another man had joined him.

Roland Bates was an odd man with a protruding stomach and a large nose. He was standing with one hand behind his back. Lee couldn't decide if he looked more like W. C. Fields or Alfred Hitchcock. The man with him was short and skinny. Together, they could have been characters from a Dr. Seuss book as they listened to Patrick talk about the Ireland he really knew little about.

"I'm telling you," Patrick leaned into them, "before the Great Plague, the Irish survived on potatoes. They ate them mornin', noon and night. Potato stew, potato pancakes, potato biscuits. They even invented the French fry, although it wasn't called that then, o' course."

The little man interrupted him. "That's just like pizza. It wasn't invented by the Italians, either."

Patrick seized the opportunity. "Exactly right! The Irish used to fry up little sticks of potatoes in a skillet, and today we have French fries."

He lifted a glass in a meaningless toast. Lee stepped to the bar.

"Give me your best white wine," she said to the bartender.

He reached for a Riesling, his eyes still watching Patrick. It was clear Roland and his guest hadn't been the only ones caught up in Patrick's story. She waited while he poured a glass. Patrick turned to her as his audience drifted back into the house. She waited until they were out of earshot.

"French fries?" she smirked. "Are you kidding?"

"You don't know it's not true," he said, suppressing a smile. He took a sip of his own drink and eyed her carefully. "Don't tell me you're bored already."

"I was bored on the way here."

His eyebrows shot up in mock complaint. "Oh, thanks a lot, Sis. I'm hurt beyond belief. Sure and you'll be tellin' me that you'll be wantin' to go home with someone else. Perhaps none other than Roland himself."

"Oh, shut up," she frowned and looked around to make sure no one but the bartender had heard the affront.

"You talkin' to me?" Patrick suddenly asked pointing at her. "You talkin' to me?"

"That's from *Taxi Driver*," the bartender shouted. "Great movie!" he said as he dried a glass.

Patrick looked at the bartender and then winked coyly at his sister.

She rolled her eyes and turned to leave. "Go look for those bodies in the basement."

"What bodies in the basement?" the bartender asked in earnest.

Not too bright, she thought. She stepped back into the kitchen leaving Patrick to make his own entertainment. She grabbed a small quiche from under the watchful eye of one of the caterers and emerged into the hallway again, where she looked around with caution, hoping to God she wouldn't run into Maddox a second time. She decided to take a tour of the house and popped the quiche into her mouth before poking her head into the guest bathroom. She raised an eyebrow at the austere white interior, marble counter top, gold faucets, and monogrammed towels. When she turned to leave, she bumped into Martha Jackson, who was heading inside.

"Oh, hello, Lee. It's an amazing house, isn't it?" her CEO said.

Lee swallowed before saying, "I haven't seen much of it yet."

She felt awkward talking to the hospital CEO in a bathroom, but

Martha Jackson seemed oblivious to the moment.

"Well, make sure you see the upstairs." Martha started into the bathroom and then stopped. "And, Lee, be careful what you say tonight." She gave Lee a knowing nod and closed the bathroom door in her face.

Lee saw the sweeping staircase leading to the second floor and decided to follow Martha's advice. She climbed the stairs and started with a French provincial bedroom at the head of the stairs and then moved on to one decorated with an ebony four-poster bed that showcased a huge kimono encased in glass. There was also a richly decorated office that sported dark leather furniture and a carpet putting green. Lee looked at her watch and was disappointed to find she'd only consumed ten minutes. She was about to return to the first floor when she noticed a set of carved double doors at the end of the hallway. She looked around for intruding eyes and then traversed the space and stepped inside. What she saw took her breath away.

The room was adorned from floor to ceiling with cats. Cat figurines crowded every shelf and bureau top. A decorative wood shelf had been installed around the room sixteen inches from the ceiling to display an enormous collection of stuffed cats. Some were obviously antiques; others were collectibles, while still others were clearly nothing more than children's toys. Cat pillows filled the center of the bed. Somebody had handcrafted a set of lampshades out of a cat print material, while a large antique bureau held several inlaid jewelry boxes with cats crafted onto the lids. A porcelain teapot arranged with flowers was painted with two cats frolicking after a butterfly, and a large coffee table book entitled *Cats* sat on an antique highboy chest. Everywhere she looked, she saw felines. She was repulsed, yet riveted, barely conscious of the music and laughter downstairs.

To her left was a small child's desk. On it were children's Valentine cards. She bent over to pick one up. The colorful image was that of a cat handing a Valentine to a mouse. Lee thought this was meant to mimic the olive branch, but if you looked at the cat's expression closely, it was much more sinister. As she studied the card, she sensed the air in the room shift and glanced up. A face stared back at her from the large mirror above the bureau.

Lee spun around and let out an involuntary, "Shit!" as she came face to face with a set of dark, glaring eyes.

"I'm sorry," Lee apologized, throwing a hand to her chest. "You scared me."

"What are you doing here?" the woman growled.

"I was just looking around," Lee said, putting the card down.

"Not in here," a thin lip curled angrily.

"I… uh…didn't know the upstairs was off limits," Lee stuttered.

"This room is."

The woman's eyes were mere slits in her head, and a narrow red mouth accented the dark facial hair that covered her upper lip. There was no question as to who she was. The resemblance to her mother was unmistakable. This was Pauline Bates. According to rumors, Pauline Bates had never married and lived at home. Lee thought she'd heard that Pauline had attended the university at one time and graduated with a degree in biology or something, but that she'd never held a job.

As the two women stared at each other, a brisk breeze pushed its way through the open balcony doors. The Bates woman brushed past Lee as if she weren't there and went to the French doors. She grabbed a door handle in each hand and stood with her arms outstretched, ready to close them. A second breeze picked up the black scarf she wore around her neck, intertwining it with her stringy black hair.

A chill jerked its way through Lee's body. The black dress. The black hair. The black scarf. It was the same image − the same woman − from the grassy knoll above the graveyard the day Diane was buried.

Lee backed away feeling as if she were trapped underwater. Her lungs just wouldn't expand. As she backed up, she bumped into a small table near the door, knocking a ceramic cat figurine to the floor. It hit the table pedestal and broke in half. Lee stared at it wide-eyed, knowing full well she'd just made a huge mistake.

"Oh…I'm so sor…" Lee began.

Pauline Bates turned in a whirl of black chiffon, her face a dramatic mask of grief. As Lee reached down to pick up the figurine, Pauline rushed forward, forcing Lee to back into the hallway. The other woman flew into a kneeling position beside the fallen figurine and picked up the two pieces, turning a dark expression in Lee's direction. The two women locked eyes for a moment before Lee mumbled an apology, turned and hurried away. She glanced back only once to see the bedroom door slowly close.

Lee descended the stairs in a state of near panic, almost running into Andrew Platt as he emerged from the coatroom behind the staircase. When she flew off the last stair, he nearly ripped the seam from his pocket trying to get his hand out to catch her.

"Whoa!" Andrew gasped, pushing the lining of his pocket back in place. "Where are you going so fast?"

"Oh! Andrew. I'm sorry. I didn't know you were here," she said breathlessly, stepping back. "Um, where's Miriam?"

Miriam was Andrew's wife, and someone Lee would normally try to avoid. She'd only met her a few times at hospital functions, but had always gone away feeling like she'd been dipped in something sticky.

"I'm sure she's off somewhere silently criticizing something," Andrew said cynically. The look on his face was a mixture of bitterness and resignation. "She never gives up, you know. She thinks we ought to live like this." He attempted a laugh, but fell short. "How's the party?"

It took several breaths for Lee to slow her heart rate down sufficiently to answer. Andrew fiddled with his pockets as he waited. She glanced to the top of the staircase half expecting to find Pauline Bates floating down the banister behind her. Andrew followed her gaze.

"Did you see a ghost? I've heard the rumors," he chuckled, leaning in to her.

"No, I...uh... just got going too fast down the steps. I'm okay. Actually, I was looking for my brother."

"Patrick? Is he here?" Andrew asked.

"Yes, perched on a blarney stone somewhere telling a story, I'm sure," she laughed, still flustered. "Have a good time."

She started to step away, but Andrew caught her.

"Have you seen Martha, yet?" he asked.

"Yes, she's here."

"Well, between you and me, I wouldn't say anything. You know, about Diane."

"Yes, I know, Andrew. Believe me, I won't say anything."

"I just don't want to see you lose your job."

The front door opened to admit a new couple and Andrew lowered his voice.

"I thought she'd have a coronary today when she heard that Bud Maddox was dating Diane."

"Well, I'd like to know the truth," Lee said, remembering her conversation with Patrick. "I owe that much to Diane."

Andrew's expression grew dark. "Lee, Martha is more ruthless than you think. I ought to know. She makes my life hell. I think you should drop it."

"I'm not sure I can, Andrew, especially when Bud is already here with another woman."

Andrew's brown eyebrows adjusted up. "You're kidding? Diane just died a few days ago. That's rather crude. Oh, wait a minute," he interrupted himself, looking over Lee's shoulder. "I see what you mean."

Lee rotated her head to glance into the living room to where Maddox and his date were sitting on an elegant sofa.

"Who is she, Andrew?" Lee inquired, scrutinizing the woman through the crowded room. "It's the same woman he was with at the funeral. I've seen her before, but I can't place her."

"That's Dr. Pendleton. She's a new Emergency Room doc. And the chair of the Ethics Committee."

"I wondered how he could score an invitation to this gig." Lee felt something connect, like the coupling of two railroad cars, but then they slipped apart. She turned back to Andrew. "I guess he's moved up in the world." Tears welled in the corner of her eyes and she looked up to the ceiling in an effort to control them.

Andrew put a hand on her shoulder. "I'm sorry, Lee. This has got to be tough on you. Maybe you really ought to take a vacation. It couldn't hurt."

Lee smiled weakly. Just then, a small severe-looking woman wearing a beaded jacket appeared out of nowhere and removed Andrew's hand from Lee's shoulder.

"How are you, Lee?" she said, her features pinched into a scowl.

Andrew stiffened as the little woman laced her hand through his elbow. Her short, dark hair was cut like a boy's, and she wore no makeup.

Lee quickly dabbed at her eyes. "I'm fine, Miriam. Isn't the house lovely?"

"It's nice," Miriam replied with a dim expression. "If you like such an eclectic style."

Miriam carried an air of forced elegance and had never made a positive remark in Lee's presence that she could remember. Andrew had begun to fidget now that his wife was there. Watching the two, Lee wondered what life was like for Andrew. Between Martha

Jackson and Miriam, it couldn't be easy.

"Well, remember what I said," Andrew said with a curt nod, and the two walked away.

She stared after them, deciding this party had to be one of the worst parties she'd ever attended. It was time to find her brother and leave. She slipped into the dining room and found Patrick leaning against the food table talking to an orthopedic surgeon and the President of the University. What they all had in common she couldn't imagine. No matter. She would let Patrick know in no uncertain terms that it was time to go.

She'd almost made it safely to Patrick's side when she was intercepted by the wife of a prominent attorney who had made one too many trips to the bar. The woman had attended their annual auction six months earlier and purchased a package trip to Hawaii that had been fraught with problems.

"Lee," she wailed a bit too loudly. Her hand reached for Lee's arm but missed, and she nearly toppled over. Lee grabbed for her elbow.

"Mrs. Bernstein. How are you?"

"I'm fine," she slurred. "I wanted to thank you for taking care of that little matter." She winked at Lee and started to sway.

Lee helped her steady herself. "I was happy to help."

"If you ask me," Mrs. Bernstein whispered, breathing heavily into Lee's face, "Joseph Putnam is a cheap bastard!"

"Well, Mr. Putnam is out of town a lot, Mrs. Bernstein. I think he left most of the arrangements up to his assistant. I'm just glad we got it all worked out."

Lee felt guilty having just blamed the problem on Putnam's assistant, a woman she didn't even know, but decided it was worth it when she noticed Mrs. Bernstein listing to one side. Lee let go of her elbow and stepped away, hoping the woman could stand on her own.

"Let me know if there are any more problems."

"Oh, I will," the other woman gushed. "Thank you, Lee." With that, she stumbled away.

Someone touched Lee's elbow and she shrank from what she thought would be another hideous encounter. When she turned, it was Patrick's boyish grin that greeted her.

"Having fun?"

"Let's get out of here," she said, moving through the living room toward the staircase.

"Whoa," he called, following her. "We just got here."

"Too bad."

Lee left her brother in the foyer and went to the guestroom where she found her coat in the closet, but had to search for her purse. She found it on the floor right beneath her coat. Suspicious, she opened it to search for her wallet, but it was there, along with the small leather wallet she used for credit cards. Nothing seemed to be missing. Perhaps someone just moved it to make more room in the closet. She grabbed it and met Patrick in the hallway.

Outside, Lee waited until they had reached the bottom steps before letting out a sigh. As she swung her coat around her shoulders, she said, "I don't ever want to go into that house again."

Patrick gave her a curious look. "Well, I have to admit that it lived up to its reputation as being a boring party, but it wasn't that bad. Besides, we were there less than forty-five minutes."

"You have no idea," she countered as they approached the car. "Bud Maddox was there."

"Well, that must have been awkward."

"To say the least. I also met their daughter."

That statement stopped Patrick in his tracks.

"You're kidding?"

"I'm not kidding, and I'll never kid about her again. She is one strange cookie."

They reached the car and Patrick unlocked the doors. As they slid in on opposite sides, he stopped to look at Lee with anticipation.

"Well, c'mon. Out with it. What happened?"

Lee started slowly. "I went upstairs to look around."

"You were spying."

"No," she said, in her own defense. "I was merely taking a tour of the house. I stepped into what I thought was the master bedroom."

"So, you were spying." he said again.

"No," she replied in exasperation. "But Pauline Bates was there. And that is one weird room."

"Do tell."

"The entire room is a shrine to the feline species."

"Cats?" he asked incredulously.

"Yes, of course cats. Hundreds of them. They're everywhere. The walls. The floor. The bed. Every surface." She looked through the windshield toward the east side of the house. "But not a live one in the place."

"So, she likes cats. That's not that strange."

"You wouldn't say that if you'd seen that room. It felt like a museum. She ordered me to get out."

"Not very hospitable, I'm sure."

"Not friendly at all, but it was the way she said it. And that's not the worst of it."

"Oh good, I thought I was going to have to fake a horrified reaction because so far, this isn't that weird."

She turned and leveled a stare at him. "She was at the graveyard."

Patrick looked confused. "Who? Pauline Bates?"

"Yes. There was a woman up on the hill overlooking Diane's grave. I saw her just before I left. She was standing alone between two trees. I couldn't see her face, but I'd swear it was Pauline Bates."

Patrick merely looked at her with a blank expression. "I'm not sure why that's significant."

Lee leaned towards her brother. "Patrick," she said quietly, "Pauline Bates has never met Diane. So, why would she be at her burial?"

CHAPTER FIFTEEN

The next morning, Lee put Soldier on the porch and headed for Medford, a two and a half hour drive south of Eugene. Lee had called ahead to make an appointment with her friend, Alvin McCauley, a professional colleague who ran the Foundation at Aurora Medical Center where Bud Maddox had worked before coming to Twin Rivers. They'd settled on eleven-thirty, and she hit the road feeling as if she was doing something useful for the first time in several days. Bud's personnel file had indicated that his wife, Emily Maddox, was a nurse in Medford, but hadn't disclosed whether she worked at the same hospital. Lee hoped to find out, along with some information about why Bud had left the medical center in the first place.

It was almost exactly eleven-thirty when she arrived in Alvin McCauley's outer office on the second floor. As she waited for the receptionist to announce her arrival, her eyes scanned the swanky color-coordinated interior and found a copy of the hospital's newsletter, *The RX*, sitting on the side table. She picked it up and flipped through it, looking for the section she knew the Foundation would use to list donor names. As Lee skimmed the page, the receptionist returned to say Alvin would see her. Lee tucked the newsletter under her arm and entered the office.

Alvin McCauley drew his tall frame out of a rolling executive chair and came around the large wooden desk to greet her with a warm smile.

"Well, I can't believe you're finally here," he said with a slight Southern twang. "It's about time."

They shook hands and Lee gave him a friendly smile. "If I'd known how elegantly you lived, I'd have been here sooner."

He offered her a plush beige chair while he draped himself into a matching loveseat. "I'm lucky," he agreed. "We moved into these offices two years ago when the new wing was built; now I'm afraid they'll have to blast me out of them. So, what brings you down here?"

Lee swallowed as the lies began.

"My brother is a theater professor at the University of Oregon, and I offered to pick up something in Ashland for him. To be honest, I just needed a day off."

"How *are* things at Twin Rivers? Is it everything you hoped for?" He used his hand to flatten some wispy strands of hair pulled across a wide forehead.

"It's never everything we hope for, is it? But I can't complain."

He crossed his long legs at the knees, exposing Argyle socks. "Well, I just remember how miserable you were in San Francisco. I guess anything would be better than that."

"Amen," she confirmed.

They continued to chat for over a half hour. Lee had known Alvin for more than ten years, but they only saw each other at conferences and rarely spent real time together. Lee became so involved in the conversation that she almost forgot why she was there. Finally, they came around to the topic of annual employee campaigns, and she thought this might be the lead-in she needed.

"We do a large annual employee campaign," Alvin was explaining. "And we've raised almost $150,000 from gift annuities and one charitable remainder trust."

"We're not having much luck with the employees," Lee admitted. "Two unions got a foothold three years ago and people are confused about their loyalties." The conversation was going exactly in the direction she'd hoped. She phrased her next question as a statement. "You must have a strong employee committee."

"We have about twenty people on a steering committee. They represent most departments in the hospital. One of the vice presidents also participates, and frankly, that has made a tremendous difference."

Lee rested her elbow on the arm of her chair. It was an unseasonably warm day for October, even in Medford, where the temperature could get over a hundred degrees during the summer. Overhead, the fan hummed as it circulated cool air from a vent in the ceiling.

"Say," she said with a twist of her head, "did you know Bud Maddox when he worked here?" Her face grew warm as if Alvin would recognize the ruse.

"Oh, sure. Bud chaired one of our sub-committees a few years ago. He and his wife were very active. I'd forgotten he'd moved to your area."

Lee's heart raced. "So, he likes fundraising. I'll have to get him involved." She sat back to ask her next question, acting as nonchalant as possible. "Does his wife still work here? I heard she didn't move to Eugene with him."

The corners of Alvin's mouth turned down. "I think so. I don't see her anymore. I think after Bud left, she switched to the graveyard shift in the ICU. Guess it's easier than sleeping alone," he said with a smile. He got up and wandered over to his computer terminal and hit some keys. "She was pretty active in our employee grants program. I assume she's on the committee if she still works here. I don't staff that committee though, so...let's see." He studied the screen for a brief moment and then said, "Well, she just made a payment last week on her annual pledge, so I guess she's still here."

"Well, it's really not important." Lee tried to sound uninterested. "Bud is kind of an enigma around the hospital. I mean...everyone knows he's married, but he seems to play around a lot. Do you have any idea why she didn't move with him?"

"I'm not really up on hospital gossip, but I heard that Bud was involved in some trouble up in the lab, an indiscretion of some kind. He left Medford when he got the job at Twin Rivers. Emily stayed here. I don't know why." He glanced at his watch. "Say, I have an appointment a one-thirty, but would you like a quick tour of the hospital and then some lunch?"

He stood up. Lee was disappointed. She had been enjoying her role as Sherlock Holmes. As she stood, she made a mental note that Bud's wife worked the graveyard shift.

"We can get a bite to eat in the cafeteria. We just had it remodeled."

They left the office and spent the next forty minutes wandering the halls of the large complex. Lee complimented Alvin on a donor wall in the pediatrics department. It was a wooden sculpture of a toy train painted in primary colors and filled with giraffes, bears, and cuddly-looking tigers. As they took the elevator to the basement for lunch, Lee made another mental note of the arrow pointing to the lab on the first floor. Over salads and vegetarian chili, they chatted about the conference they'd both attended in Dallas in September. At one-twenty, Alvin walked her to the front entrance to say good-bye.

"Thanks for coming, Lee. Don't make it so long before the next time."

"I won't," she replied as they shook hands. "It's been great. You'll have to come to Springfield."

"I'd like that."

"Can you direct me to the ladies' room before I get out of here?"

"Sure," he said, turning around to point behind him. "It's right down that hallway." He indicated a short hallway that ran past the gift shop.

"Thanks. And thanks again for your time," Lee smiled.

"No trouble. I'll get up your way one of these days."

He turned and headed back towards the hospital's entrance. Lee held her breath for a minute, waiting until she was sure he was gone. Then she headed in the opposite direction. The lab was tucked into the corner of the first floor with a small waiting room and no windows. A large black woman wearing wire-rimmed glasses and a white lab coat sat behind a counter window. She concentrated on a stack of papers. Behind her, Lee could see the blood draw stations. A tall, slender man in dirty overalls sat wedged in a chair with a wraparound armrest. A small woman hovered efficiently over his arm with a long needle in her hands. As she jabbed for the vein, he looked away, and Lee found herself holding her breath.

"May I help you?" a husky voice asked. It was the woman behind the counter.

Lee flinched. "Sorry, I don't know how you guys ever get used to doing that," she said, indicating the draw stations.

The small woman in the back now held a vial filled with dark red fluid and was attaching a label to it. The woman behind the desk glanced in their direction and back.

"Yeah, well, I think every lab technician enjoys sticking it to them, if you know what I mean." The woman chuckled mean-spiritedly. "So, what can I do for you?" Her voice purred in an insincere sort of way.

"I'm just passing through and have a friend who works here in the lab. I thought I'd stop and say hello."

"Who's the friend?" The smile faded.

Lee tried to look completely honest. "Bud Maddox. Is he working today?"

The woman's face froze for a moment, and then she laughed so abruptly she took Lee by surprise.

"No, I'm afraid not," she sneered. "No, I'm afraid you won't be seeing your friend Bud Maddox today."

She laughed some more, taking her glasses off to rub her eyes, unaware that people in the waiting room were now staring at them. Lee wasn't quite sure what to do.

"I'm sorry, I don't understand."

As the woman's chuckles diminished, she looked at Lee, her small, dark eyes taking on a beady stare. When she put her glasses back on, she picked up her pencil, tapping it on the counter as she talked.

"I'm afraid your friend don't work here no more. He left more than six months ago, rather quickly, if you know what I mean."

Lee tried to appear suitably stunned. "Fired? You're kidding?"

The unappealing grin reappeared, exposing a set of crooked, yellow teeth. "Well, they didn't actually fire him now, did they? But your little friend got caught doing something he oughtn't have."

"Well, do you know where he's working now?"

"Hah!" the woman exclaimed, making several people look around. "Hopefully nowhere, if you know what I mean. That man is trouble. Sorry, I can't help you." With a nod, she dismissed Lee and resumed her work.

Lee took a few steps away. Unwilling to give up, she turned back and approached the counter. Leaning toward the woman in a confidential manner, she eyed the woman's nametag.

"Mavis," she said, forcing the woman to look up.

Lee looked around the room as if she didn't want anyone to hear. Mavis took the bait and leaned forward.

"Bud wasn't caught...for the same thing again, was he?" Lee whispered, giving Mavis a confidential look that included only the two of them.

Mavis squinted, her expression betraying her suspicion. The two women remained locked in eye-to-eye combat for several seconds until Lee began to sweat. Finally, the corners of Mavis' mouth turned into a smile.

"My advice to you, honey, is that I wouldn't give my friend, Bud, any personal information you don't want others to know. And, I'd be careful how many people you tell about your friendship with him. Know what I mean?" The eyebrows lifted one last time, and then she turned and climbed off her stool, disappearing with her papers into a small office.

Lee sighed with disappointment and turned to leave just as a toddler behind her squealed in delight. He was standing with his face pressed against a picture window, staring at a large group of birds on the lawn outside. Lee stopped and stared with him. There had to be about a hundred birds, all shapes and sizes. They milled about on a small patch of grass outside, all facing the window. It was eerie. The boy laughed and pounded on the window, but the birds ignored him. They just stood there, as if lost. Finally, the boy's mother pulled the little boy away. A half second later, the birds took to the air en masse − as if they'd received a message of some sort that it was time to disperse. Lee left the lab feeling a familiar buzz.

As she turned a corner near the main entrance, she almost bumped into Alvin McCauley, who stood talking to an elderly woman dressed in a lab coat. Perhaps he never made it back to his office.

"What are you still doing here?" he asked in surprise.

Lee gave a nervous laugh. "I…uh…decided to get my camera and take a picture of that donor wall in the pediatrics department." She tapped her purse as if the camera were inside. "I think my CEO would love it." She touched Alvin on the shoulder as she moved past him. "Thanks again, Alvin. I've got to run. I'll be in touch."

Lee made it to the car without further mishap and climbed in, her heart racing. If anyone had said a year ago that she would be masquerading as a detective, she would have laughed. Patrick had inherited all the imagination in the family. She only had a good head for numbers and the ability to multi-task. The art of lying just wasn't in her repertoire of skills. Yet, here she was stepping in and out of character with apparent ease. Maybe she shared more with her brother than she thought.

CHAPTER SIXTEEN

Lee sat back against the car seat and began to sort through information gleaned at the hospital. Bud had been asked to leave Aurora Medical Center because of an indiscretion, but he hadn't been fired. That would explain why Robin's personnel search had turned up empty. Mavis had also clearly implied that Bud couldn't keep a secret. Hospital personnel were required to abide by a strict code of patient confidentiality, but the tone of her voice indicated something more egregious than that. Perhaps there was more to learn from Bud's wife.

Emily Maddox worked the graveyard shift, which meant she slept during the day. Since it was only one forty-five, Lee decided to waste an hour browsing through stores in the historic town of Jacksonville while she practiced her approach to Bud's wife. Besides, she needed time to unwind. The flock of birds outside of the lab had reignited her anxiety.

Lee spent the next hour and a half wandering in and out of quaint shops. At three o'clock, she called the Maddox home and asked Mrs. Maddox for an audience. It was almost three-thirty when she pulled onto Remington Street, past a row of upper-middle class homes painted in a multiplicity of Victorian colors. The Maddox home sat in a cul de sac with a short white fence encircling the front yard and a dry creek-bed running along the east side. A dark green Explorer peeked out from the garage.

Lee had called with the excuse that she was writing an article for the hospital newsletter on employee campaigns. Mrs. Maddox had reluctantly agreed. Lee hoped the questions she'd practiced in the car would lead to a conversation about Bud, but the acid in her stomach told her she lacked real confidence.

She parked the car, slipped the copy of *The RX* she snatched from Alvin's office into her satchel, and made her way up the path to ring the doorbell. A stocky woman with dark shoulder-length hair that was overdue for a dye job answered the door. She was dressed in a purple nylon running suit and clutched a wooden spoon in her hand, tipped with some kind of red sauce. Her only notable features were a large, unattractive mole in the center of her left cheek and dark eyebrows that had probably been a uni-brow in her youth.

"Mrs. Maddox?" Lee spoke in a clipped, professional manner, adding a short, but warm smile.

"Yes," the woman hesitated, eyeing her carefully.

"I'm Rebecca Moore." Lee had picked the name of a college friend hoping it would roll off her tongue more easily. "I called earlier. I'm from the hospital."

"You're doing a story?"

"That's right. Alvin told me you've been involved with the hospital's employee campaign. He suggested I talk with you about an article I'm working on." She lifted up the copy of the newsletter to illustrate her point. "I'm sorry for the short notice, but as I said on the phone, my deadline is tomorrow."

The woman was slow to react, and Lee felt the pulse in her neck throb as she struggled to maintain eye contact.

"I had originally interviewed Mavis in the lab," she added quickly, "but when I wrote it up, she really hadn't given me much."

The woman's face relaxed as a small smile crept up the corners of the rigid mouth.

"I'm not surprised by that little bit of information. Why don't you come in? I'm just in the middle of making spaghetti sauce before I have to leave for work."

She turned and headed for the kitchen, leaving Lee to step inside and close the door on her own. Lee followed her through a very beige living room and into an airy kitchen with a greenhouse window over the sink. Two large ceiling fans circulated the tantalizing smell of spaghetti sauce. Mrs. Maddox stood at a center island stirring the contents of a large green pot, the steam turning her face pink. She barely looked up when Lee entered.

"So, what do you want to know?" she asked without the customary invitation to sit down.

"I want to highlight the employee campaign," Lee said, still standing in the doorway. "I'd like to know what made you to volunteer, for instance. Why you think it's important to give back to the hospital? How you feel about some of the projects they've funded? Things like that."

Lee felt on firmer ground discussing fundraising. But a cardinal rule was to ask for the gift and then shut up until the prospect spoke. Lee forced herself to wait.

Emily Maddox eyed her as if deciding what to do. Under the scrutiny, Lee imagined she had the word FRAUD printed in block letters across her forehead and held her breath. Finally, Emily Maddox turned off the gas flame.

"Give me a minute and I'll talk with you."

She lifted the kettle off the stove and placed it on a brass trivet next to the sink. Lee glanced around at the white cupboards, countertops, and cold linoleum floor. There were no homey knick-knacks or pottery jars filled with antique utensils. Only framed floral prints that were probably purchased at Walmart and a kitchen table that looked like it came from IKEA.

"That's a lot of spaghetti sauce," Lee finally said to fill the silence. "You must have a large family." As soon as she said it, she regretted it.

Mrs. Maddox turned and leveled a blank look in her direction. "No, it's only me."

She turned back to place her spoon in the sink when something outside caught her attention. Her head came up and her body jerked, spraying spaghetti sauce across her white cupboards like streaks of blood. Without warning, she turned and burst through the kitchen door into the side yard with a strangled cry, waving the wooden spoon above her head. Lee hurried to the window just as a small Sheltie dog darted into the trees on the other side of the wire fence. Emily Maddox lunged at it, screaming as if she wanted to reach through the fence holes to snare the dog and kill it. The sheer intensity of her anger made Lee shudder. It wasn't until she became aware of her fingers resting in some of the red spaghetti sauce on the counter that Lee quickly rinsed her hand and tried to look halfway calm when Mrs. Maddox returned.

When Emily came through the door again, her face was red and twisted, her breathing labored. Lee moved out of the way and allowed her to take her position again at the kitchen window, the wooden spoon clutched tightly in her hand. Lee waited. When the woman didn't say anything, Lee tried to bring her back to reality.

"Are you okay? You scared the hell out of me." Lee tried to chuckle.

Mrs. Maddox finally looked around as if realizing for the first time Lee was still there. "Did I? I'm sorry."

She stole one more glance out the window and then she pulled herself away to sit at the kitchen table. She placed the spoon in front of her as if it were some sort of weapon she might need again. Her eyes remained focused on the spoon.

"I don't like dogs."

Lee controlled the urge to laugh. The woman took several deep breaths before looking up at Lee.

"I won't have them on my property."

If Lee was expected to respond, she didn't know what to say. The woman had obviously overreacted. The dog was on the other side of the fence. Even if it had come onto her yard, what harm could the Sheltie do? The dog probably didn't weigh more than twenty-five pounds. Lee waited. After a minute, the woman's breathing slowed and her muscles seemed to relax.

"Do you own a dog, Ms. Moore?" She spoke softly, staring at the spoon again.

"I haven't owned a dog for almost ten years." Lee didn't actually own Soldier. Amy did.

Emily Maddox rose and gestured for Lee to sit down. "Please, I've been very rude. Would you like some lemonade?"

"I'd love some. Thank you."

Lee sat at the table while Mrs. Maddox filled two crystal glasses with pink lemonade. As she handed a glass to Lee, she said, "I suppose I should explain."

Lee merely sipped her lemonade in silence. Mrs. Maddox sat down again and wrapped both hands around the crystal glass, forgetting the spoon for the moment.

"I was attacked by a large dog when I was seven. I was playing in the backyard with my brother, and a neighbor came over with a dog that was part wolf, part something else. My brother and I were fighting. You know how kids can be. We were screaming and yelling, making a lot of noise. I guess we scared the dog. Suddenly, it snapped at me, taking off the tip of my ear." She paused as her hand fluttered to the left side of her face. With some hesitation, she pulled back her hair to reveal the ragged appendage.

Lee grimaced. "How awful."

"I was deathly afraid of dogs after that. A year later, I found a little white kitten in the church parking lot. It was injured and starving, so I talked my mother into letting me nurse it back to health. I was very proud of that." She looked at Lee with deep sadness in her eyes. "I think it's what made me want to become a nurse. Anyway, the kitten followed me everywhere. It even slept on my bed."

Her lips curved into a pale smile. Then she looked down at the table and took a deep breath.

"One day, I was playing with the kitten in our front yard. It was so small," she remembered, rubbing her thumb across the outside of the glass. "Suddenly, a large dog came out of nowhere and killed it. Right in front of me." Her hands began to tremble and she put the glass down. "It grabbed the kitten right out of my hand, shook it violently once, and snapped its neck."

She paused, her breathing labored.

"The dog was so close that I could smell its breath and feel its fur against my face," she said, her eyes staring into the abyss of bad memories. Finally, she looked up at Lee, a tear in the corner of her eye. "I haven't been able to see a dog since without wanting to kill it!"

"I'm sorry," Lee whispered. "But there are dogs everywhere. How do you cope?"

"Mostly, I try to ignore them," she said breathlessly. "If I see one on the street, I'll cross to the other side. If I'm in the car, I'll just look the other way and drive past as quickly as I can. But if they come onto my property, I have to do something. I just have to."

Lee felt sorry for her. The hard exterior had vanished and the woman's outlandish display somehow didn't seem quite so out-of-place anymore. Lee felt herself wanting to reach out and share her own story.

"I had a completely different experience with a dog," she suddenly heard herself saying. "I always loved them. I grew up with dogs. Mostly large dogs." She felt the warmth rising in her cheeks again. "My husband and I owned a Labrador Retriever, named Perry." She smiled as she remembered the big black dog with its soft brown eyes and silky fur. "Brad used to fish a lot and Perry always went with him in the boat. Labradors love to swim, and Perry would often jump from the boat and swim ashore. Brad absolutely adored that dog. They went everywhere together. One day, they went fishing and didn't return before dark. I didn't worry too much because we'd fished that lake a hundred times, and Brad was good with the boat." She looked at Emily Maddox with a little smile. "And, besides, Perry was with him."

"But they didn't come back," Mrs. Maddox said, finishing her thoughts.

"No." Lee looked at her hands now encircling her own glass of lemonade. "In fact, they never came back. Brad was never found. The police found the boat hidden up a side creek about two days later. There was blood in the bottom."

"And the dog?" the woman encouraged.

Lee wiped a tear from the corner of her eye. "He was found floating in the shallows about a hundred yards from where they found the boat. He had a bullet in his head. I haven't been able to have a dog in the house since. In fact, I haven't had any pets. I never liked cats much. My daughter begged me to get one, but I never did. I guess, I felt as if I'd lost two of the things I loved most in the same day. I still have a hard time looking at a dog without thinking of Perry." An image of Soldier appeared in her mind and she realized how much she was beginning to depend on the dog.

"Did you ever find out what happened to your husband?"

"No. The police investigated but didn't find anything." She looked up at Maddox. "I've played different scenarios out in my head for almost a decade, but the dog always saves the day in my mind...and Brad comes home."

There was a long silence between them, each woman nursing memories. Finally, Mrs. Maddox spoke.

"It seems like we've both experienced some loss on that front. Why don't we go into the living room and talk about your article? Give me a minute to wipe up the mess."

Lee nodded and went into the other room, dabbing at the corner of her eyes. She hadn't meant to tell that story, but somehow the timing had felt right. And it seemed to have helped break the ice with Bud's wife.

She placed her glass on a coaster and dropped her purse onto a chair next to a wall-to-wall bookcase. The living room was as spotless as the kitchen and just as boring. Lee wandered around until she ended up back at the bookcase. A fat tabby cat sat on the piano bench nearby, waiting for attention. Lee ignored the cat while she admired an expensive ceramic figurine of a woman draped over a bench, holding a parasol. On the shelf above it was a group of photos. In one, a young Emily sat in the middle of the floor, holding a small white kitten. In another, she was in her cap and gown getting her diploma.

Bud was pictured in several photos. In one, he was clearly a teenager, with his arm around a pretty girl with long, dark hair. In another, he was probably in his twenties, and again, he was in an intimate pose with a woman. Lee quickly glanced at the other photos. In two more, Bud was with other women. She didn't find any photos of Bud and Emily, although one picture looked like it could have been taken at their wedding. In it, Bud was standing in front of a black limousine dressed in a tuxedo with a blonde man, also dressed in a tux.

Curious, Lee leaned in to study the back row of frames, letting her eyes roam across the photos. Suddenly, her heart nearly stopped. In the back corner was a small pewter frame holding a picture of Bud and Diane standing before a storefront. Bud's arm was around Diane's shoulders, and he was grinning as if he'd just had the best sex of his life.

Why would Emily Maddox have a picture of Diane? Especially a picture of Diane with her own husband?

Before another thought could cross her mind, Lee reached in and pulled the frame from the shelf and quickly dropped it into her pocket. She was just about to turn away, when something behind the frame caught her eye. When she leaned in for a closer look, she sucked in a pocket of air large enough to float a boat.

It was the onyx bird!

Feeling dizzy, she reached in with an unsteady hand to grab it just as Mrs. Maddox called out from the kitchen. Lee's hand froze about an inch from the bird.

"I'll be with you in a moment," Emily called.

Lee held her breath. Finally, she turned her head and chanced a reply. "Take your time."

She turned back to grab the bird, leaning the heel of her hand on the shelf. The shelf wobbled and suddenly tipped forward, sending everything to the floor with a crash. Lee was too shocked to move. A pile of frames lay at her feet, while the onyx bird had disappeared.

"My god, what was that?" Emily rushed into the room.

Lee just stood there as if grounded to the spot. She would have said something, but her tongue seemed to have swollen to fit the inside of her mouth. Maddox quickly made a sweep of the entire room and stopped when she saw the mess on the floor. Her cat had become startled and flown to the other side of the room, where it now sat carefully watching them.

"Agatha! What in heaven's name did you do?"

Emily bent down to clean up the mess. Lee should have acknowledged her role in the disaster, but stood mutely watching Mrs. Maddox as she grabbed two of the frames and put them on the shelf, chiding the cat as she went.

"She's done this before," she said. "Such a pest!"

Lee contemplated leaning down and taking the pewter frame out of her pocket so that she could pretend to pick it up, but Mrs. Maddox scooped up the remaining frames before Lee could move. She positioned the frames in exactly the way they'd been before, stopping at one point as if she was missing something. She paused and Lee held her breath. Suddenly Maddox turned and scanned the floor.

"There should be one more," she mumbled. She bent over to check underneath a chair. "What's this?" she asked, pulling something out. She looked at it for a moment and then turned to Lee, holding the onyx bird in her hand.

The blood rushed to Lee's head, and she felt as if she couldn't breathe.

"I...uh...I'm sorry, that's mine. It must have fallen out of my purse."

"Really?" The other woman glanced over at Lee's purse sitting innocently on the chair. There was a long pause before she said, "It's quaint. Where did you get it?"

"Uh . . . a friend gave it to me."

Mrs. Maddox handed over the bird. Lee wrapped her fingers around the figurine, feeling the warmth of its body heat her hand again. Emily Maddox glanced at Lee's other hand stuffed inside her pocket, then seemed to think of something. She turned to grab an old leather frame holding the picture of Bud and a friend in tuxedos.

"This is a picture of my husband. Did you know him?"

Her head turned back so swiftly Lee took an involuntary step backwards. Lee looked at the photo and was surprised to see Mrs. Maddox pointing to the blond man standing next to Bud.

"He used to work at the medical center. I thought maybe you'd met him," she said.

"I...don't know too many of the technicians." Lee clamped her mouth shut when she realized that she wouldn't know Bud was a technician. Silently, she prayed Emily hadn't noticed her mistake.

"Too bad." Mrs. Maddox turned her attention back to the picture. "This was taken just after our wedding. He's good looking, don't you think?" She held the photo out for Lee, once more pointing at the blond man.

"Yes," Lee replied, wondering why Emily Maddox was attempting to pass this man off as her husband. She didn't know whether she should acknowledge the mistake, or go along with the game and pretend she had never met Bud. She decided to stick with the original scenario despite her blunder.

Several seconds lapsed while the other woman quietly regarded Lee. The moisture began to form under Lee's armpits. All she could think of was getting away. She glanced at her watch.

"Emily!" she almost barked. "I didn't realize it was so late. What with the dog and all, and the…this, I really need to be going. Why don't I call you in the next few days?" She grabbed her purse, vaguely aware that she'd just contradicted the deadline she'd established when she arrived. Maddox followed as Lee hurried to the door.

"That would be fine. Let me know when you'll be back in town."

Lee attempted a smile and opened the door to step outside. "Great, I'll give you a call."

Lee backed out of the door, attempting to appear calm. As she made her way back to her car, a myriad of questions flashed through her mind. Had Emily Maddox realized she'd stolen the pewter picture frame? And why in the world was she trying to pass off the blond man as her husband? But what if the blond guy really was her husband? If he was, then who was the guy calling himself Bud Maddox at Twin Rivers Hospital?

Once inside the car, Lee turned back to the house and caught a glimpse of Emily Maddox closing the front door. Only then did the woman's last words register, raising one final question.

How did Emily Maddox know Lee was from out of town?

CHAPTER SEVENTEEN

It was almost eight o'clock when Lee pulled into her driveway. She had stopped for a quick dinner on the way home, but hadn't eaten much. She was physically and emotionally exhausted and could only think about a hot bath and bed. Whatever she thought her amateur investigation would be like, this wasn't it. Emily Maddox was as weird as Pauline Bates. Bud Maddox gave her the creeps, and Diane's death had thrown her into a deep depression. But it was the image of the onyx bird peeking at her from the back of Emily Maddox's bookshelf that had invaded her thoughts all the way home. It was frightening to think the small figurine could move around on its own. It was even more frightening to think it was trying to tell her something.

She had switched off the car lights and was rubbing her eyes when the flicker of something in her upstairs bedroom window caught her attention. She peered through the windshield, but decided it had only been a reflection from the street light behind her. She grabbed her keys, drew her purse over her shoulder and climbed out of the car just as a breeze swirled a handful of leaves around her feet. Two big birch trees at the corner of her property rustled in protest of the wind, and somewhere up the street a dog barked.

With a yawn, she began moving towards the front porch. A single bulb above the detached garage threw light halfway up the path, but dissipated quickly, leaving Lee to walk part of the way in deep shadow. The porch loomed ahead, and Lee headed quickly for the light from the front door, contemplating the last half pint of ice cream in the freezer before her bath.

She was just passing the big corner bushes, when the porch light flicked off. Lee stopped short, completely engulfed in darkness. Slowly, her fingers found her long car key and pushed it to the front. It was the only weapon she had.

She couldn't see above the bushes that crowded the porch, but strained to hear any noise emanating from the front of the house. Overhead, the trees shifted restlessly. Behind her, a bush stirred. When something moved through the bushes along the pathway, Lee panicked and turned and ran for the car.

She'd almost made it, when she heard a soft bark and snapped to attention. She'd left Soldier on the back porch with access to the backyard. She veered towards the gate and the protection of the dog. Lee reached for the gate latch, fumbling with the lever and sneaking glances over her left shoulder. Soldier was in the yard and pushed against the lower part of the gate, whining and pawing at the ground. The bushes along the walkway rustled again, and Lee nearly wet her pants. Her hand slipped. Soldier began throwing her eighty-plus pound frame against the gate, barking a high-pitched alarm. Frantically, Lee struggled to unhook the latch.

With a snap, the gate released and swung open with the full weight of the German Shepherd behind it. Lee flew backwards, landing on her back in the damp grass, her head bouncing off the ground. A cat emerged from the bushes and skyrocketed across the lawn. Soldier leapt into action, landing a big paw on Lee's shoulder as she launched herself in hot pursuit.

Lee lay there for a long moment staring up at the night sky, listening to the canine's fading bark, all thought of imminent danger gone. She tried to catch her breath, but it came in short gasps, and her heart pounded so heavily it reverberated on the ground beneath her.

What a fool she was. This was the second time in two days she had been humiliated by a cat. Perhaps danger still lurked around the corner, but at this point, she didn't care. She was drained of all incentive to move until a shadow loomed above her, and a rough tongue took a sloppy swipe at her face.

"That's it!" she announced, pushing off the grass.

Lee got up, and the dog sat down, as if waiting for the praise she was surely due.

"Just until this weekend and then back you go to Corvallis," Lee snapped, pointing a finger in the dog's face.

Lee grabbed Soldier's collar and dragged the dog back to the open gate.

"You are in the dog house," she said, closing the dog in the backyard again.

Just then, the tan sedan screeched away from the curb in front of the house and headed south. Lee took a deep breath. She didn't like that car and wanted to know who owned it. But, she wasn't about to go around to the front door. So, she picked up her purse and decided to enter the house through the back door.

She left the dog on the porch again, and used her key to open the back door. She stepped into the back hallway, closing the door behind her. She moved down the hallway to the front door and peered through the small window. No one was outside. She flicked the light switch up and down and the light flickered a couple of times. It was only a faulty switch. She'd ask Patrick to take a look.

Lee always left a light on in her dining room, which fronted the street, but the rest of the house was dark. She turned on the entryway light, and threw her purse and coat over a Shaker-style chair next to the staircase.

"Life is getting just a little too spooky," she said out loud, rubbing her shoulders to warm herself up.

To her right, the living room remained cloaked in darkness, while the hallway to her left created a murky tunnel running to the back door. She walked back down the hallway and was just turning into the kitchen, when a hand emerged from the darkened study behind her and covered her mouth with a sweaty palm.

Lee tried to scream, but all she could manage was a muffled grunt. A second hand grabbed her right wrist and spun her around, slamming her up against the wall. Suddenly, a man's full weight was pressed against her. She twisted her head to the side, gasping for air, but he was much taller and heavier, and the weight of his body forced the air out of her lungs. She was pinned to the spot and his knee was shoved into her groin.

Lee tried to get her arms free, hoping to scratch at him, but he used his shoulder to immobilize her head and then grabbed her other wrist and wrenched both hands behind her back. He used one hand to encircle her wrists like a handcuff and then leaned into her again, chuckling.

She could smell a hint of a musky aftershave under sweat and body odor and could feel the scratch of a coarse sweater against her cheek. Lee couldn't see the intruder's face, but the top of her head fit just beneath his chin. She thought he was wearing something over his head, but couldn't be sure.

Lee tried to shout, but couldn't seem to get enough air into her lungs. She tried to break free, which seemed to please her attacker more than make him mad, and suddenly, she realized it wasn't his knee anymore in her groin. Panic welled inside her, and she pushed off the wall a few inches, trying with desperation to raise her knee up to block his intent. With a sudden jolt, he slammed her backwards again, bringing his lips next to her ear.

"Ssshhh," he shushed with a deep whisper.

With his entire weight pressed against her, she was helpless. She stopped moving, gasping for air. Tears slid down her cheeks. Then she felt his hand.

"No!" she whined.

Before she could take another breath, his fingers had slipped underneath her sweater and down her jeans. Lee pushed against him again, twisting and struggling to free herself, but he only chuckled with deep satisfaction.

Keep moving, she thought. Make it difficult. But it didn't work.

His tongue slid across the tip of her ear, sending a shockwave through her entire body. She cried out, but his fingers were moving downwards, struggling to get past the elastic band of her panties.

Oh God, she thought. This wasn't happening. This couldn't happen. A loud bang sounded in the background, and Lee thought maybe her head had been slammed against the wall. But it happened again, and she realized it was something else. It was Soldier, trying to get in. The fingers faltered. There was another bang, and Soldier started to bark a high-pitched alarm, her paws actually hitting the window in the back door.

Suddenly the attacker was gone.

He disappeared into the night, leaving Lee a shrinking, sobbing mess.

She slid to the floor, shaking violently. It was a full ten seconds before she realized Soldier was still barking and pawing at the back door. She struggled to rise, using the wall to propel her into a standing position. Still gulping for air and crying, she stumbled up the hallway and opened the door. The dog bounded forward and slid to a stop long enough to stick her nose into Lee's hand. Then, she headed straight for the front door. But the attacker had slammed the door shut and Soldier threw herself at the closed front door in a frustrated attempt to pursue him. Lee had no doubt that had Soldier made it inside in time, she would have had the satisfaction of watching the dog make mincemeat of him.

Lee slid down the wall to sit on her heels and waited for Soldier to come back up the hall. When she did, Lee grabbed her collar and drew the dog close, burying her face into her fur.

"Thank you, Soldier. Thank you," she sobbed. "You're a good dog, Soldier."

Then, she just cried.

CHAPTER EIGHTEEN

The antique pendulum clock on the wall struck ten o'clock with slow, even strokes. The police had come and gone. Lee had only told them about the break-in, not the assault, feeling an intense sense of shame she couldn't overcome. Now she sat at the dining room table watching the street, her emotions shut down, but her nerves on alert. Her ears sought out every nuance of the night, magnifying the mere ticking of the clock on the wall. When the heater kicked on with a rush of warm, stale air, Lee almost came apart at the seams.

After Diane's death, she had laid awake nights speculating how someone could have killed her friend so easily. Did they pose as a delivery person? Did Diane know them? Lee tried to imagine how it was done with no mess. No noise. No alarm. Now someone had broken into her own home and violated her with such ease.

The police had found a side window broken. But although the first floor had been ransacked, from what Lee could tell, nothing had been stolen. But why? Had it been a case of attempted theft, and she'd interrupted him? Or, something even more sinister? Had the attack been the objective in the first place? The combination of fear and shame she felt now was enough to shut off the blood flow to her brain.

As the clock finished striking the hour, Patrick's Mazda pulled up to the curb. She'd called him at rehearsal and asked him to come stay the night. She went to the door and peeked through the window to watch his lanky figure emerge from the little car. The chill that had settled deep inside her soul began to lift as he ambled up the walkway. Lee flung open the door with what she hoped would be a smile, but as Patrick made it to the top step, she felt her composure break. He quickly put his arm around her shoulders as they walked side by side into the house.

"I'm glad you called. You okay?" he asked, closing the door

behind them.

"I'm okay," she lied.

"Did the police find anything? Any way of identifying who it was?"

They went into the living room, where Lee had only done a minor clean-up.

"Whoa!" Patrick exclaimed. "You weren't kidding." He went to the entertainment center and looked inside. "They didn't touch your stereo, or the TV. So why the mess?" He looked around him, then over at Lee. "They were looking for something," he said with confidence. "You don't think this had something to do with Diane, do you?"

Lee sank onto her sofa feeling very cold. She pulled her knees up to her chest and wrapped her arms around them.

"I don't' know," she rubbed her eye sockets, trying to release the headache that was forming again.

"What about the message Diane left on your answering machine?" Patrick asked. "Wouldn't Bud Maddox know about that? Diane could have told him she was going to call you that night to tell you about not going in to work the next day."

Lee stared into the fireplace the way Carey had. She felt dead inside.

"If Bud knew about the tape, why didn't he come to get it before now?" she countered. "The message has been sitting on my machine for days. Maybe this has nothing to do with Diane."

"You don't believe that." Patrick began picking papers off the floor and stacking them on a table by the fireplace.

"Maybe someone was just trying to scare me."

"And, did they?"

The sound of a car's engine could be heard passing the house, and Lee glanced nervously out the window thinking it might be the tan sedan.

"Are you scared, Lee?" Patrick repeated, holding the cushion to a chair in his hands.

She turned to look across the room at him. Patrick was so familiar. He always smelled like the peanut butter he spread on his morning toast and wore the same dark green socks whether his pants were brown or gray. In his presence, she felt invincible. His arm had been the shield that protected her from the violent arguments when her father drove off angry and alone. His smile changed rain into sunshine and made up for a mother's mood gone as bad as sour milk. But that was then. And now, was now.

"Yes, I'm scared."

They stared at each other for a moment, until Lee broke away. A long pause followed.

"All right, then." He took a deep sigh and threw the cushion into the chair. "I'll straighten up down here a bit. I'll sleep in Amy's room tonight, and I'm moving in tomorrow, whether you like it or not."

"Okay." She had hoped he would say that. "What time are you due in class tomorrow?"

"Not until ten o'clock. You go on up. I'll check doors and windows."

"The police helped me nail shut the window where the lock was broken," she said as she got up.

"Okay. Get some rest, Lee. You don't look too good."

She merely nodded and climbed the stairs as Patrick continued down the hallway to the back porch. Lee paused at the door to her bedroom, rubbing her eyes. She had only given a cursory look in here when she'd walked through the house earlier and now realized that a couple of her drawers were open. She would have to survey the room to see if anything was taken, but first things first. She started for the bathroom, stumbling over Soldier, who had come up with her. The dog had stopped to sniff something at the foot of her bed. Lee halted, a curse poised on her lips. When she saw the file folder lying open on the carpet, she stopped mid-curse, all thoughts of sleep gone.

Patrick came around the upper landing a few minutes later and found Lee sitting on her bed, staring at the folder in her hands.

"What is it?"

Lee looked up at him, but her jaws wouldn't move to allow her to form any words. Patrick stepped into the room and took the folder from her. He read the index tab.

"Where did this come from?"

His eyebrows were knit into a suspicious glare. Soldier sat at attention next to Lee, as if waiting for a command. Lee just continued to stare at the folder. Finally, she forced out six words.

"It was inside my top drawer."

"What? The folder? Why?"

"I just put it there. I suppose I didn't want anyone to know I had it."

"That's understandable--I daresay you're not *supposed* to have it. This is Bud Maddox's personnel file. Isn't that illegal, Lee?"

She dropped her head. When she looked up, there were large tears in her eyes.

"That man was in my bedroom, Patrick." The chill that flowed through her body this time felt like a cold electric current. A sob bubbled out, and she wrapped her arms across her chest as she began to shiver again. Patrick came to sit beside her.

"Lee. It's okay. He's gone. He's not here."

"It's not okay," she snapped. "Don't you get it? Someone was here. In my house. In my bedroom! He..." But she couldn't say it. She couldn't tell Patrick about the assault and what had really frightened her.

His eyes softened, and he lowered his voice. "I'm sorry. I just meant that he's gone now. You weren't hurt. But what was he looking for, Lee? Why was he here?"

She wiped her nose while tears flowed unabashedly down her face. "I don't know."

"You said someone broke into Diane's place, too. Whoever it was must be looking for the same thing. Do you remember anything Diane gave you recently that could be suspicious?"

Lee thought for a moment and then shook her head. "No. She hadn't given me anything in a long while."

Patrick was working the situation, trying to make sense of it. "Magazines? Books? Bills? Reports? Anything?"

"No."

"How about antiques? Anything with a drawer or secret chamber in it?

Lee smiled as she wiped her nose. "you've' been watching too many bad movies."

He sat back, tapping the older. "Well, there's got to be something. This wasn't a normal break-in. Nothing's gone. Not even this folder."

"Maybe that means something," she said, using her sleeve to dry her face.

"What?"

"If it was Bud, wouldn't he have taken the folder with him?"

Patrick shrugged. "Not necessarily. That could have pointed a finger directly at him."

"Yes, but since I'm not supposed to have the folder in the first place, maybe he would have counted on my silence."

Patrick tossed the folder onto the bed. "Well, we're not going to solve this tonight. You get to bed. I'll be right down the hall." He paused for another moment, gave her a half smile and left.

Lee sat for a few more minutes, feeling like a beanbag on a store shelf – dead weight. Finally, she got up and went into the bathroom and stripped bare. She took a hot shower, scrubbing every inch of her body as if she could wash away that ugly moment in time. When she finally prepared to climb into bed, she thought about Maddox, or whoever it was, filling her bedroom with his presence. With a yank, the bed sheets and blankets came off, and she threw them into the hamper.

Five minutes later, she slipped in between clean sheets, feeling somewhat free of the disgusting essence of her intruder. As an added measure to change the energy in the room, she invited Soldier onto the bed. The dog bounded up, turned in a circle once, and then stretched out and pushed up against Lee's hip. The warmth of her body felt good, and safe, even though it took nearly forty more minutes before Lee's muscles relaxed and her eyes closed.

CHAPTER NINETEEN

Lee awoke to find Patrick asleep in the big chair next to the window in her bedroom, a pillow clutched to his chest. His auburn hair lay in soft curls around his face, matched by a splash of freckles across the bridge of his nose. He looked cramped, uncomfortable, and incredibly peaceful. Lee smiled as she watched the easy rise and fall of his chest. The fact that he'd chosen to stay close made her want to hug him as tightly as he hugged the pillow. Instead, she got up and tiptoed to the bathroom.

When she emerged a little while later, the chair was empty and she heard *Oh Danny Boy* being whistled downstairs. A few minutes later, dressed in jeans and a long silk blouse, she descended the stairs wondering how she would approach the day. The horror of the night before had faded some, but not disappeared altogether. The ground had shifted. Her confidence had been broken. Lee didn't like the feeling. In competition, that's when you failed.

When she entered the kitchen, Soldier barely acknowledged her. Instead, she was focused on Patrick as he used the back of a spatula to flatten sausage into a frying pan. The dog's ears stood up like exclamation points, and saliva dripped from the corner of her mouth. As Lee pulled a mug off the wall and proceeded to make a cup of tea, Patrick looked over his shoulder.

"Pancakes or French toast?"

Lee chuckled. "You're the chef, you decide."

With a flourish of the spatula he said, "Pancakes it is!" He peeked over his shoulder a second time. "You don't happen to have any blueberries, do you?" When Lee gave him an incredulous look, he said, "I thought not." He turned down the stove, gave Soldier an encouraging pat on the head and muttered, "Just a few more minutes, kiddo."

"You can quit spoiling the dog. She's not staying, you know."

Lee placed a mug of water into the microwave.

"She's a terrific dog." He sat at the table while the sausage browned and patted his knee.

Soldier took the cue and came to sit on his foot, placing her head across his knee, where the saliva formed a wet spot on his jeans.

"Besides, it wouldn't hurt to keep her around awhile, given what happened last night."

The reminder drew a blanket of fog into the room, and Lee became silent as she stared at the closed microwave door. Finally, the microwave beeped, and Lee removed her tea. Patrick got up and reached into an overhead cupboard, rummaging around until he found a box of buttermilk pancake mix. He pulled it down and opened it to pour a portion into a mixing bowl. The two of them worked in silence. Lee went to the refrigerator to get the milk, while Patrick went to the sink to add water to the pancake mix.

As he stirred the mixture, he said quietly, "By the way, my stay here will only be temporary. I'm optimistic about things with Erika."

Lee stood at the sink, stirring sweetener into her tea. Patrick took the sausage out of the frying pan and laid it on paper towels to drain. He stirred up some of the pancake mix and spooned out four good-sized circles into a second frying pan.

"I'm sorry about you and Erika," she said into her cup. "You make such a great couple."

Patrick stood watch over the pancakes, but turned to look at her. "I think she knows that. In the meantime, maybe I can help out here."

"How?"

"I could fix your window," he said hopefully. "Then, maybe I can help you find out about Diane."

Lee looked over at him as he used the spatula to check the pancakes. Something about the whole domestic picture of the two of them in the kitchen softened her mood.

"You'll have to make up the extra bed, though. Amy will be home this weekend."

"Okay. I'll change all of your locks today, too. Just in case." He flipped the pancakes.

Lee sat at the drop leaf table and waited while he finished cooking. He piled the pancakes onto two plates, added the sausage and dropped a plate in front of her. Before sitting down, he dropped an extra sausage patty into Soldier's bowl. Hot or not, the dog gulped it down in one, swift movement. Lee grimaced, but then smiled. Brother and sister busied themselves lathering the pancakes with butter and syrup. After downing a couple of bites, Patrick looked across the table at her.

"Now, let's talk about Diane."

Lee raised her eyes as she broke off a piece of sausage and slipped it into her mouth. "Do we have to?"

"I think you need to get organized. You need to stop going off on tangents and broadcasting your theories to the world. And you need to stop hiding file folders in your underwear drawer." He smiled and his eyes twinkled.

She frowned at him. "You don't know everything I've been doing."

"I know you," he said half kidding. "Look, Lee, if you're going to do this, then really *do* it. Don't play at this. It isn't a game."

"I'm not playing a game." She felt herself get defensive.

"In a way you are," he said, cutting his pancakes into bite-sized morsels. "You have some romantic notion about finding a killer. You're going to have to be more careful."

"But, I can't prove anything," she said, putting down her fork. "And the police aren't listening."

"The police don't know everything. You said that yourself."

"I only have a hunch, Patrick," she said, leveling a stare at him. "And this is not some stage play or TV movie."

"I think you have more than a hunch. You just don't have proof."

"Then what do you suggest I do?"

The tension was beginning to build, as she knew it would, and she could feel the muscles in her jaws working.

"Be systematic about it," he replied. "Build a plan. Don't make a fool of yourself."

She dropped her eyes hoping he wouldn't know that he'd just hit a bull's eye. She *was* making a fool of herself. If he only knew what had happened in Medford between the masquerade with Mavis and the debacle with Emily Maddox, he'd be imitating her right now the way he imitated actors in old movies. Then, of course, there was the fact she had actually stolen something belonging to Emily Maddox. Add that to the personnel file sitting upstairs, and Patrick could probably look forward to living in her house permanently, while she spent time down at the county jail.

She set her fork down, picked up her plate and took it to the sink.

"Lee, what's wrong. I was only joking."

"I know. It's okay," she said, holding back a new onslaught of tears. "I'm just not as hungry as I thought. I have to get dressed." She moved towards the door, hoping to get out before the floodgates opened. "We can talk about this tonight."

"I'm sorry, Lee," she heard him say to her back.

A few minutes later, Lee stood in her bathroom applying mascara when she heard Patrick's Mazda pull out of the driveway. He hadn't meant to hurt her feelings, but he'd come too close to the truth, and her pride wouldn't allow her to admit it. Just as it wouldn't allow her to admit why she'd kept silent all those years ago when Brad had disappeared. She'd hinted about a few things to Diane. Brad's doubts about having children. His reluctance to get married in the first place. Lee's suspicion about other women and their distant relationship just before the accident.

Why couldn't she tell Patrick all of that? If perfectionism had been Diane's fatal flaw, certainly pride was hers.

After fiddling with her bangs, Lee left the bathroom and went downstairs. She'd decided to go back to the hospital. There were people there who could fill in some of the blanks. It might not answer all of her questions, but it would help. She found Soldier lying with her nose pressed against the front door.

"What's the matter, did your sugar daddy leave you?"

When Lee took her purse off the back of a chair, the dog thumped her tail. Lee grabbed her coat from the closet and stepped over the dog.

"He won't be back until tonight."

Soldier got up to look expectantly at Lee.

"Oh, don't tell me you understood what I just said."

The dog tilted its noble head.

"Not a chance. You're not that smart."

Lee leaned over, cupped the big dog's soft muzzle in her hand and pulled it to within a few inches of her face.

"Frankly, I think as dogs go, you're a good-for-nothing pooch." She kissed the dog's nose gently, grabbed her collar and shoved her toward the kitchen. "C'mon. Into your sanctuary."

She was about to close the dog in the kitchen, when she remembered the night before. Better to leave the dog out. She left the kitchen door open and headed back down the hallway.

As she passed the phone by the staircase, a thought occurred to her. What she needed was some good old-fashioned support from a completely objective source. A girlfriend, not Patrick. Someone she could trust to test her theories against. Her friend Marion was just that person.

She picked up the phone and dialed the number from memory. When a familiar voice answered, she made arrangements with her friend for lunch at their favorite Mexican restaurant. On the way out the front door, Lee checked to make sure she'd locked the door securely and then glanced across the street, relieved to see the tan sedan was gone. As she stepped off the welcome mat, her foot rubbed up against a white envelope.

Lee opened it and pulled out Diane's suicide note. She'd forgotten she'd asked Carey for it. After the incident with Carey's husband, she thought Carey had guts. She slipped the note back into the envelope and tucked it into her purse.

A moment later, she was in her car. As she slipped the key into the ignition, something black swooped down and smacked her windshield. She jerked backwards, hitting the back of her right hand on the steering wheel. Swearing, she peered out the front window, massaging the back of her wrist.

It was a bird, she was sure of it. But where had it come from? More importantly, where had it gone?

Curious, she stepped out of the car and looked skyward. There was only blue sky and a few clouds. No birds. None in the trees, either. Confused, she stood rubbing her hand, when she became aware of a rustling sound behind her. She turned around and stopped short, every follicle of hair on her arms standing on end.

Behind her, a mass of crows had gathered along the telephone wire. There were about sixty of them, packed closely together, shifting their weight, ruffling their feathers, and flexing their wings. Every eye was fixed on her.

CHAPTER TWENTY

Lee stared at the birds for a few moments, her heart thumping. It couldn't be a coincidence. Not anymore. For whatever reason, she had become a magnet for the local avian population, and she had a not-so-sneaky suspicion that it had to do with the onyx bird in her purse. She could admit to making a fool of herself. She could admit to making mistakes. But she wasn't sure she could admit to this strange phenomenon. After all, she'd just accused Patrick of seeing too many bad movies; now she felt as if she were living inside one. But since none of the live birds had threatened her in any way, at least not yet, she decided to ignore them as she turned to get into the car. With a parting glance in her rearview mirror, she left the birds behind and drove to the hospital.

She parked in a lot reserved for employees and entered the hospital from the east side, heading for the espresso bar. Two corridors converged into a spacious waiting room, flanked by sliding glass doors leading to an outdoor patio and small garden area. It was early, and the gift shop was closed, but the volunteer sales person was inside counting change, getting ready to open. The espresso bar, with its assortment of muffins, biscotti, and bottles of flavorings, sat close by.

Lee had a plan. This was the early morning gathering hole for many employees. Lee sometimes came down for a mocha latte´ or a hot chocolate. But many of the employees came as regular as clockwork, and you could almost set your watch by their daily appearance. Jack Burns, the lab manager, was one of those. In fact, he was the first in line, chatting easily with the young man who busied himself making drinks. Lee waited until Jack had paid for his specially brewed coffee and then intercepted him.

"Jack, do you have a few minutes?"

Jack Burns turned with a smile. He was built like a telephone pole with large hands and feet and was dressed in his signature bow tie and button-down collar.

"Sure, Lee. I have a few minutes. But I just spent my last farthing." He pulled out the lining of his pockets to show that he was broke.

Lee acknowledged the humor with a chuckle. "I'm not here for a donation. I was hoping I could ask you a few questions. Can we sit over here for a minute?" She indicated two facing chairs.

He looked at his watch. "I have a nine-thirty, so no problem."

Lee sat down facing the garden. Jack sat with his long legs stretched awkwardly in front of him as he sipped at the cinnamon-spiced coffee.

"What's up?"

Lee had purposely avoided caffeine that morning, but couldn't help noticing a drop of foam that clung to Jack's lips. After a moment, he used his finger to clean it off, allowing Lee to focus on why she was there.

On the drive over, she'd decided she would first try to gather clinical information to help her understand just how Diane had died. Then she would back-track with as many people as she could to determine exactly what Diane had done, where she had gone, and whom she had come into contact with on the day she died. Jack was her link to Bud Maddox and could also tell her more about the drug that had killed Diane.

"Um, I…" Lee stammered uncertainly.

"You off today?" he interrupted her, noticing her casual attire.

"Yeah, I'm taking some time off… Diane's death and all."

"Of course. I'd forgotten. How are you doing?"

"It's been hard."

She relaxed a bit now that the subject was out in the open. In the background, the light chatter from a group of nurses offset the metallic whirring of the espresso machine. Jack looked over his glasses at her, cradling the hot coffee in both hands.

"I didn't know Diane well, but I know the two of you were close." He sipped the hot liquid, keeping the cup close to his lips.

"Actually, that's what I wanted to talk to you about. I'm confused about how she died. I thought maybe you could explain a few things."

Jack lowered the cup and crossed one leg over the other, looking like a gangly giraffe, all legs and knees.

"I'll do the best I can. What do you want to know?"

Lee sat forward. She remembered how she'd felt in school when she'd been keenly interested in a subject. This felt the same way.

"I want to know how much insulin it would take to kill someone."

Jack flinched slightly. "Wow, I heard she killed herself with an injection of something. So, it was insulin." He shook his head in sympathy. "Let me see. I'm not a physician, so I'm not sure I can answer that. You should really go see Janine."

"Why don't you give it your best shot?"

"Was Diane a diabetic?"

"No, but her cat was."

He couldn't mask a look of genuine surprise. "That's a new one. Although I guess an animal could be diabetic as easily as a human. Her cat would only need a fraction of the insulin a human would use, however. How many times do they think she injected herself?"

"Just once. It was a large syringe."

His eyebrows arched. "Really? That's curious." He took another swig of coffee and the bow tie bounced up and down as he swallowed.

"Why is that curious?"

"Well," he paused, adjusting the heavy, black glasses that graced his angular nose, "when you told me she had a diabetic cat, I assumed her method of suicide was just a convenience."

"I think that's what the police assumed, too. What surprises you about that?"

"I would have thought she would use a very small syringe for her cat. Not a large one."

"She did use a small syringe for the cat."

He stared at Lee for a moment, but Lee's gaze didn't waver. Whatever he was thinking to himself, she decided to ignore it. She wasn't going to apologize anymore for what she knew to be true, or to pretend the facts weren't the facts.

"What are you saying, Lee?"

"I'm only saying that I know for a fact that Diane normally used a very small syringe to give injections to her cat, just as you suggested."

"Well, I suppose if she intended to do herself in…sorry," he shrugged. "But, if she intended to kill herself, she would probably just go out and get a larger syringe. It's hard to believe someone would inject themselves once, reload, and inject themselves again with a small syringe."

Lee frowned at his logic. "I think that's exactly what the police assumed, too."

Jack took another sip of coffee, his long bony fingers wrapped around the large paper cup. Lee slid her feet onto the floor and leaned forward with her elbows resting on her knees. It was time to go for broke.

"What would get someone fired from a position in a hospital lab?"

This time he had to gulp in order not to choke on the hot coffee. "Why in the world do you ask that?"

"I'm just curious."

He eyed her suspiciously now, placed the coffee on the table next to him and folded his large hands in his lap, lacing one long finger over a bright green class ring. He was clearly contemplating the question. Lee bit her lip, but kept silent. Jack had a kind face, with high set cheekbones and a long jaw line. Even over the thick scent of cinnamon from the coffee, there was the slight smell of a tangy aftershave. He re-crossed his legs and then folded his arms over his narrow chest. If he was conflicted about answering her question, he had finally resolved it.

"Well, you know as well as I do that we fire people for continually being late to work, incompetence, inaccuracies…things like that. But I think you want something more."

She nodded and he continued.

"Well, the lab is a complicated place. It's also highly regulated and highly confidential. There are a lot of other reasons why someone might be fired. Drug and alcohol abuse. Breach of confidentiality. Falsifying information. What are you looking for?"

"I don't know, but speaking of confidentiality, you won't say anything about our conversation to anyone, will you?"

He knitted his brows. "Not if you don't want me to. But, I have a feeling this has nothing to do with fundraising."

"No, it doesn't. I'd just prefer you didn't say anything. Okay, let's go back. I understand you'd fire someone for drug or alcohol abuse and breaking confidentiality. But why would someone falsify information?"

"Are you kidding? There are a host of infectious, sexually transmitted diseases, and terminal illnesses out there. People who have them don't want other people to *know* they have them. Spouses, employers, insurance companies. You name it. We screen it, and we find it. Not to mention drug use."

"And that information could be used against someone?"

"People are fired for drug abuse. And sometimes a person with a history of a communicable disease has a tough time getting a job. Then there's the social stigma."

"So, if someone knew how, they could use that information…I don't know…to maybe blackmail someone?"

"I guess," he smiled noncommittally. "I've never done it myself, you understand."

Lee ignored the joke because a large bird had just landed on a branch outside the window. She eyed it cautiously.

"I don't claim to know the criminal mind," he continued, "but I do know that people who do that sort of thing are incredibly creative. It would be like breaking into your house. If someone wanted to do it badly enough, they could figure it out."

His example made Lee sit back in her chair. He continued, oblivious to her reaction. He paused and looked at her a little like a parent patronizing a child.

"What does this have to do with Diane's suicide?"

"I'm not sure it does. Thanks for your time, Jack. You've helped a lot."

With an apologetic shrug, she got up to leave, but stopped when he raised his hand.

"Wait a minute. Don't give up so easily."

"What do you mean?" She sat back down, watching the bird out of the corner of her eye. It sat placidly on a branch, watching her.

"Look, I'm no dummy. There are a number of ways someone in the lab could commit a crime. I hope that none of them happen in my lab, you understand. But I assume that's what you're looking for. I like mysteries as much as the next person, so I suppose if I *had* a devious mind…" He stroked his chin and lifted his eyes in contemplation. "Okay. Here's one example of falsifying information. We have something called the Drug Confirmation Room. It's a high security area where we confirm and store positive drug screens. Only five people have access to the room."

This information had a familiar ring to it. "Who are the five people?"

"Three lab techs, the pathologist, and myself."

Now her inner bell clanged, making her ears ring as she

remembered Robin's safety report at the Executive Team meeting.

"So, how would someone do something illegal?"

"Well, that's where we actually confirm that someone is using drugs. I suppose if you knew someone had tested positively, you could blackmail them. Of course, I have no idea how much money there would be in it."

"Okay," she said, diverting her attention away from the bird, "let's say someone tested positive for cocaine use. Could that person be blackmailed by someone, say in the lab, in order to change the positive results to negative results?"

"I suppose so. They'd have to have a way to run a second test."

"Could it be done without anyone knowing it?"

"Maybe," he shrugged. "At least for a while. I think it would be discovered eventually. But that's just one example. There are probably more."

"Robin read the most recent safety committee report in the Administrative Team meeting yesterday and said the door to the GCMS room was left open a few weeks ago. Does that have anything to do with drug confirmations?"

"It's the same room." They stared at each other until his eyes narrowed. "Lee, what's going on?"

She ignored his question and leaned forward again, nearly touching his knee. "Jack, who orders drug screens?"

"Just about every major company in the area, as well as most of the small ones. We do pre-employment drug testing for all of them through the Occupational Health program and then random employer requests on employees they may be suspicious of."

"Thanks, Jack. I appreciate your time."

She rose and Jack stood this time as well, forgetting his coffee.

"Lee, I'm not sure what you're up to, but I hope you're not getting in over your head."

"So do I."

She turned away just as someone called out Jack's name. Andrew Platt approached them from the hallway.

"Lee, what are you doing here?" he asked casually. "I thought you would be…you know… taking some time off."

"I'm just wrapping up a few loose ends. See you guys later."

She turned and headed for the basement, glancing out the window as she passed. The bird was gone.

CHAPTER TWENTY-ONE

Lee took the elevator to a cold, unmarked foyer in the basement, where the white walls and the chipped linoleum floors created a glaring and depressing tunnel going off in two directions. The stale odor of paint thinner pinpointed the location of the maintenance department down the hallway to the right. To the left was housekeeping. She made a quick turn to her left and into a small suite of offices marked DIABETES EDUCATION and weaved her way to the back where a petite woman with a decades-old beehive hairstyle sat with her back to the door. Lee knocked gently on the wall to announce herself.

"Janine, you got a minute?"

The woman turned with a look of surprise, pushing a pair of red-framed glasses up her nose. Janine Fletcher was the hospital's Diabetes Education Coordinator, and it was her job to instruct patients on proper diet and the self-administration of insulin.

"Hi, Lee. I don't see you down here often. What can I do for you?"

Lee usually avoided interaction with Janine because her appearance was so off-putting. She had large round eyes accentuated with heavy make-up, made worse because she had removed her eyebrows in favor of drawing on artificial ones that arched high above her natural brow-line. The macro lenses in her glasses magnified her eyes to the point that she looked like one of those cheap Halloween masks you might buy at the dime store.

"I was wondering if you could answer a few questions for me about diabetes."

The perfectly matched eyebrows pinched together in pained sympathy. "Oh, Lee, have you been diagnosed?"

"Oh, no, nothing like that. I just had some questions."

The brows lowered and the mask expressed confusion. It was so distracting that Lee made the decision to focus on the rims of her glasses instead of making direct eye contact. Patrick had once said that actors often did this during intimate scenes on stage in order to maintain their concentration, and yet make the scenes believable. She only hoped Janine wouldn't notice.

"My assistant was found dead last week from an apparent suicide," Lee said, staring at the red plastic frames of Janine's glasses. She couldn't see the other woman's reaction, but thought she recognized a look of surprise.

"How awful," the mask spoke.

"The police say she killed herself with an overdose of insulin."

"My goodness!" This time the brows pulled the eyes open wide. Janine gestured to a chair. "Why don't you sit down? What would you like to know?"

Lee rolled out the chair from the adjoining desk and sat down. The size of the room placed her knees only inches from Janine's. Lee saw Janine at monthly manager's meetings and noticed that she often changed the color of her glasses to match her dress. Today a red skirt peeked out from underneath her white lab coat.

"Diabetics take insulin all the time, so I was surprised it could kill you. How much would it take?"

"It's like they say, too much of anything, even a good thing, can kill you. But it would depend on a number of things. Her height and weight. Was Diane a diabetic?"

"No, she wasn't. But she had a diabetic cat. That's where the police think she got the insulin."

"Oh, that's interesting. Well, let me think. There are a variety of types of insulin. Some are faster acting than others." The petite, bird-like hands pulled out a chart from a stack of papers on her desk. "There are two types of diabetes. Type 1 diabetes is where the body makes little or no insulin at all."

Janine pointed to the top of the chart labeled "Type 1 Diabetes" where an arrow pointed at a list of symptoms. It was clear she'd given this lecture many times before.

"People with Type 1 diabetes must take insulin in order to live."

"And you have to inject it?" Lee asked for confirmation.

"That's right. You can't take it in pill form. The second type is called Type 2 Diabetes." She pointed to the bottom of the chart.

"Clever distinction," Lee muttered cynically.

"Many people who have Type 2 diabetes control it with diet,

although many do take insulin."

"Is it the same for cats?"

"I'm not a vet, but I'd assume it's the same. Probably for an animal the size of a cat, you'd use long-acting insulin."

She stretched across the desk to reach into a second pile of papers where she pulled out a sheet and pointed to the top of a chart.

"This is Humalog. Rapid-acting insulin like this would be taken with a meal. You want it to mimic the pancreas to get a quick reaction." She pointed further down on the chart. "Then you'd use it in combination with longer acting insulin like Lente or Ultralente. That way you would maintain the basal level of insulin in the blood stream. Make sense?"

Lee made the mistake of turning to look directly at her and flinched at the sight of her eyes magnified so close. "I guess so," she stuttered, looking away. "The difference is in how fast the body absorbs it, right?"

"Correct. So for instance, the cat might use a pre-mixed combination like NPH, because you can't force a cat to eat. At least I know I can't force mine. So you couldn't use Humalog. You'd want to provide insulin that stays in the blood stream over say, 10 to 12 hours, in order to avoid low blood sugar reactions."

"Interesting," Lee mused. "Thanks. But how much insulin would it take to kill someone?"

Janine sat back. "Again, that's hard to say. One unit of insulin lowers the blood sugar in a person about 25 points. A person without diabetes runs a blood sugar of 60 to 110 milligrams per deciliter." She paused, recognizing Lee's confusion. "You don't need to understand that. What you need to know is that a person without diabetes would rarely drop below 60. Forty to fifty units of fast-acting insulin could probably kill a person if they didn't respond by eating," she finished.

"So…how much is a unit?"

The nurse reached for a Zip-loc bag on her desk, ripped it open, and produced a syringe encased in plastic.

"This is a 100-unit syringe. Each little line indicates two units," she said, using her fingernail to trace the short lines on the base of the syringe before handing the syringe to Lee.

Lee froze as she took the syringe into her hand. It was the same type of syringe that had taken her friend's life. Janine reached into a drawer to pull out another bag and removed a much smaller syringe.

"This is what they call a Terumo syringe. It measures in half units and is often used for children. I suppose this could be used for cats," she added with a shrug.

Lee took the second syringe and said, "This is exactly the kind of syringe Diane used for her cat. But wouldn't one this size hold enough to kill someone?"

"The small syringe will hold only up to twenty-five units."

"Twenty-five units," Lee uttered slowly. "So she would have had to inject herself twice?"

"I guess so," the nurse said. Janine took the syringes back and put them away. "I hope I've helped, Lee."

"You've been a big help," Lee replied. "Just one last question. How long would it take for someone to die from insulin?"

The other woman paused before answering.

"The right amount of Humalog could take as little as ten to fifteen minutes."

Lee felt a shock wave ripple through her body. "But that means Diane could've been able to fight back."

"Fight back? What do you mean?"

"Nothing," Lee sputtered, but she leaned forward, intent on knowing the truth. "I just need to know. Would the person be awake and alert? It's important, Janine."

Janine's body tensed, the muscles flexing across her jaw line.

"Yes, I think they'd be conscious for several minutes. Now, I need to get back to work, Lee."

Janine picked up the phone as if to make a call. The interview was over. Lee turned to exit on her own. At the door, she glanced back to say thank you, but Janine had turned and was looking directly at her. Under Lee's scrutiny, she slowly replaced the phone without waiting for a connection.

Lee smiled awkwardly and left, wondering who Janine had been calling.

CHAPTER TWENTY-TWO

Lee made her way to the car, her mind filled with the image of Diane fighting for her life. It had never occurred to her that Diane hadn't died quickly. And the knowledge that her friend's last moments may have been spent suffering, or with the knowledge that she was about to die, left Lee with a profound feeling of sadness. Since Diane's condo was near where she planned to have lunch with Marion, Lee decided to confirm a few of the things she'd just learned.

Fifteen minutes later, she was using her key to gain access to Diane's house for the second time. The first thing she checked for was the feather, but it was gone. Then she remembered the intruder. Everywhere she looked books had been pulled from shelves and tossed onto the floor. The doors to Diane's curio cabinet had been thrown open and her treasures swept from their shelves. Much of Diane's glassware had also been smashed. Lee thought anger had fueled this intruder. But why? And was it the same person who had invaded her own home, and her body?

Lee shook off a sudden chill and looked around again. Carey had obviously attempted to clean up. The dining room table was covered with lopsided stacks of linen, papers, and books. More books were stacked on the floor. A large plastic bag sat in the dining room filled with trash and broken pieces of china. Lee almost cried, knowing how much Diane had loved her grandmother's rose-patterned dishes. But an overwhelming feeling of déjà vu hit her as she stepped through the mess, remembering her own living room. Lee began to tremble at the memory of her own attacker and an intense feeling of vulnerability swept over her again. She needed to make this quick.

Lee took a deep breath and marched to the refrigerator. She found a row of little bottles lined up in the door. Lee grabbed a bottle that was only half full and turned it around so she could read the label. It was NPH insulin. Her mind whirred back to Janine's chart and the pre-mixed longer acting insulin that Janine thought would be used for cats. A quick check confirmed the other bottles were the same. One fact confirmed. Now Lee had to find out what kind of insulin had been found in Diane's body.

She pulled out her cell phone and dialed Alan's number at the police station.

"Alan, it's Lee."

"Hey, how are you doing? I heard about the break-in at your house. I called you at home, but you'd already left."

"Um…I'm okay. Nothing was stolen. Hey, listen, I was just curious about something and wondered if you'd check it for me."

"Sure. What is it?"

"I'm over at Diane's condo helping to clean up." She hated lying to Alan, but didn't want to raise any alarms. "Just to satisfy my curiosity, could you check the coroner's report to see if they determined what kind of insulin was found in her body?" She held her breath wondering if Alan would question her right to know.

"What difference does it make?"

"Call me anal retentive. I just want to know."

"I'm not on the case, Lee."

"I know it's a big favor. It would just…I don't know…it would just make me feel better."

He sighed so heavily she could hear it over the phone.

"I'll call you back."

She hung up and returned the insulin bottle to the refrigerator. Then she pulled out a chair from the dining room table and sat down to wait. Her thoughts went back to what Janine had said about how long it would have taken Diane to die. Lee began to consider the vase again. Maybe Diane had fought with her attacker, and the vase had been broken in the struggle. And the attacker had cleaned it up. Or, what if Diane had tried to fend off her attacker, but was injected with the insulin during the struggle? Lee tried to picture that in her mind. It was plausible. Then, momentarily stunned, Diane might have made an attempt to escape, and that's when the murderer picked up the vase and hit her with it.

No, Lee rejected that idea. Under that scenario, Diane would have had enough time to make it out the door, or call for help. She had to have been disabled *before* she was injected with the insulin. Click. That's how the vase was broken. Lee thought back to that night when a skinny policeman knelt next to Diane's body and fingered a large bump on the side of her head. He'd looked at the coffee table and come to the immediate conclusion that her head had hit the table when she fell. Lee was certain now that he was wrong. The bump had come from being hit with the vase. But there was nothing to prove it.

Just then, her cell phone jingled.

"The report doesn't address the insulin in her body," Alan said without greeting. "It does say they analyzed the syringe and found a small amount of insulin in it. Something called Humalog."

Lee came to attention with a jolt. Humalog was the rapid-acting insulin. Not something Diane would have had in the house for Sasha. She took a deep breath to calm her nerves.

"Lee? Are you there?"

"Yes, thanks, Alan. That helps. One more question. What does the report say about the bump on her head?"

"Lee, there's no reason to investigate. I told you."

"I know, Alan, but if it will make me sleep better, it's worth it, don't you think?"

There was another sigh and the sound of paper rattling before his voice returned.

"The coroner said she had a blunt force trauma on her occipital lobe, probably caused by hitting the coffee table as she fell."

"Thanks."

"Does this mean you'll stop worrying about this now?"

"Just for the record, Alan, Diane doesn't have any Humalog insulin in the house. She didn't use that type of insulin for the cat."

"Isn't insulin – insulin?" he asked.

"No. You would use a different type for a person than you would for a cat."

She stopped again, letting what she'd said sink in.

"Okay," he said too quickly. "I'll let Sergeant Davis know. He'll look into it."

Lee's heart fell. Sergeant Davis wouldn't do anything.

"If there's a reason to investigate, Lee, we will," Alan said as if reading her thoughts.

"I know. Thanks, Alan. I'll probably see you guys this weekend."

She hung up, but remained where she was, lost in thought. Finally, there was something concrete, something the police had overlooked. Someone had brought in the insulin used to kill Diane, along with the larger syringe. But would they actually investigate it?

She got up and wandered into the living room. There had to be more. Something she could hold up to Sergeant Davis and say, *"Here, you lazy son of a bitch! Here's the evidence you ignored."* Her eyes scanned the room, landing on the oval coffee table, taking her back to the night of the murder. She and Diane had sat side by side on the sofa, flipping through a stack of color photos.

"Look at this one," Diane had said. *"I'm telling you, you could bounce a quarter off Bud's abs. He also has one tight ass."*

She had giggled at this, while Lee kept silent.

"God, I never thought I'd get a guy like Bud. He's never satisfied. He always wants more."

"And you're more than happy to give it to him," Lee had quipped, not really in the mood to banter about Bud's sexual prowess.

"Wouldn't you be?" Diane had asked. *"C'mon, Lee, I know you don't like him that much, but you have to admit he's sexy."*

Lee had begun to retreat, tired of hearing about the man she couldn't stand. Diane was oblivious to Lee's change in body language.

"When we were in Sisters last weekend, he hinted that maybe we'd make the relationship permanent. I really thought I'd never get married again, but now..."

"Married!" Lee had snapped. *"You've got to be kidding? C'mon, Diane. You can't be serious. I know the guy is good in bed, but..."*

Diane had glared at Lee, and Lee quickly tried to back track. But the tension that had been growing over the past few weeks erupted into an ugly exchange.

"What I meant," Lee began, *"was that Bud isn't right for you – long-term."*

"Right for me? How would you know who is right for me? You're just jealous, Lee. You go home to an empty house every night and can't stand that I don't."

"That's not it at all."

"Yes, it is. I've noticed how you clam up every time I want to talk about him. You probably think I'm not attractive enough to get a guy like that."

"No, what I can't stand is finding out that you've left work early or come in late because of a hot date with Mr. Libido."

"Really? Do you have a problem with my work performance?"

"No," Lee had stumbled. "*But, you'll have to admit that you've been distracted."*

"Distracted? Maybe I'm in love, Lee. Did you ever think of that? No. Because you don't really think about anybody but yourself."

"I just want you to focus on your work," Lee had shot back." *That shouldn't be too much to ask."* Lee had stood up and turned for the door. *"I think I should go."*

"Wait," Diane called her back.

Lee turned back only to have a camera flash in her eyes. Diane had grabbed her Olympus camera off the mantel and taken a picture.

"What the heck was that for?" Lee asked, not happy.

Diane had put the camera back on the mantel.

"It has all my pictures from Sisters on it. I want to get it developed. Once I'm married, I'll put that picture of you in my scrapbook with all my other single friends."

Even now, the memory of that argument drew Lee into a tunnel of grief. Diane would never have the chance to get married again, and Lee would never have the chance to apologize. She thought about the old camera still sitting on the back seat of her car, wondering what had happened to the film and that last picture. She wiped her eyes and looked around the room hardly recognizing it as Diane's anymore. The carefully organized, pristine environment was gone.

Diane's purse sat on a chair on the other side of the room. Lee went over and picked it up, thinking maybe Diane had taken out the roll of film to have it developed. But there was no film anywhere in the pockets. As Lee threw the purse back onto a chair, something besides the voice in her head filled the room.

"What the hell are you doing with Diane's purse?"

Lee swung around to find Vern Mathews standing in the entryway.

"I...I was just making sure her wallet was still there, you know, what with the break-on and all," she lied.

"How'd you get in here, anyway?"

"I have a key Diane gave me some time ago," she said, picking up her purse.

She tried to maintain her composure and stood as tall as she could, but her height would never intimidate Mathews, who had at least four inches on her. The veins stuck out on his neck, and she began looking towards the open door behind him.

"You were trying to steal something," he said, taking several steps forward. His gaze swept the room. "What did you take?"

"I didn't take anything," Lee snapped, conscious how it must look after the place had been burglarized. "I told you, I was just checking to see if anything had been stolen."

His eyes bored into hers as the muscles in his jaws clenched and unclenched. She didn't like her odds and began to circle towards the entryway. He countered, blocking her retreat.

"I'll just take a look into your purse," he said, extending his hand.

Lee sandwiched her bag between her elbow and her ribs. "You will not. I told you I didn't take anything."

He lunged forward and yanked the purse away, catching her hand in the strap and nearly pulling her off her feet.

"I don't believe you," he snarled, shoving his big hands into the pockets. "I'll just bet that... what's this?" He pulled out the onyx bird.

"That's mine," Lee exclaimed, trying to grab it from him. "Carey gave it to me."

He kept it away from her, a self-satisfied grin slithering across his face. "Well, well, well. I did catch a thief. Perhaps I'd better call the...ouch!"

Mathews' hand jerked back and flipped the figurine into the air. Lee just barely caught it before it smashed against the coffee table. She looked over to see Mathews shaking his fingers.

"Dammit! Get out of here!" he yelled, throwing her purse at her. "Or I'll call the police."

Lee grabbed her purse and sidestepped around him, not trusting that he wouldn't reach out and snag her. But this time he kept his distance until just before she reached the door.

"Just a minute! I'll take that key," he snarled, coming forward. "We own this condo, now."

As he put out his left hand, Lee caught a glimpse of a red burn mark across his right palm. Lee reached into her pocket and reluctantly handed him the key.

"Now, get out of here," he ordered, pressing the injured hand to his chest.

She turned and fled around the building to the parking lot. As she slipped behind the wheel of her car, she looked up and saw him staring at her through the living room window. Suddenly she felt sorry for Carey. She couldn't imagine what it would be like to come home to a man like that.

As she drove away, she contemplated the incident. It seemed as if the bird had come to her rescue somehow. But what was Mathews doing there in the first place? It was the middle of a weekday. Mathews wasn't the kind of guy to help Carey out with cleaning the condo, so why would he go there? Especially when he knew he'd be alone? Perhaps he, too, was looking for something.

CHAPTER TWENTY-THREE

Lee found Marion's elegant figure draped on a wooden bench inside the door of their favorite Mexican restaurant, her long legs crossed at the ankles. Dressed in green wool pants, a pale blue sweater and an understated plaid jacket, she looked out of place in the garish "South of the Border" atmosphere.

"I'm sorry I'm late," Lee tried to smile.

The older woman stood up and took Lee by the elbow and steered her back toward the door.

"It doesn't matter," she said in her low, melodic voice. "We wouldn't get a table for another fifteen minutes, anyway. They wouldn't seat me alone, and someone's throwing a special party." She gestured toward the back of the restaurant where black balloons floated among the large fiesta hats hung along the wall. "I think it's someone's fiftieth birthday. Let's grab a sandwich at the yogurt bar and go sit across the river. We actually have a little sun to enjoy." She squinted at the sky as they emerged outside. "For a few minutes anyway," she added cynically.

Although Lee felt too jittery to eat, she let Marion order sandwiches at a small shop across the street, and then the two women strolled toward the cement bridge that arched across the Willamette River. Marion chatted easily about the university where she was a professor in the English department, but Lee was only half listening. Halfway across the bridge, she stopped to look upriver, feeling spiritually and emotionally drained. The gathering dark clouds muted the bright greens of the trees and surrounding mountains into cool blues and grays as the river rolled happily under the bridge. Lee gazed at the crisp, clear water, getting lost in its tranquility.

"How long are you going to make me wait?"

Lee looked up as if waking from a dream. "What?"

Marion raised an eyebrow and continued across the bridge. Lee grabbed a last look at the river and followed. They turned left at the end of the bridge and tromped across the damp grass to a bench a short distance from the river's edge.

"Am I that transparent?" Lee finally asked as she sat down and took the wrapping off of her sandwich.

Marion dipped her chin to look over her glasses at Lee, the sun glinting off her silver gray hair. "Not necessarily, but you sounded less than casual this morning when you called. And, you haven't said a word since we bought the sandwiches." She lifted her sandwich and took a bite, swiping a blob of mayonnaise from her chin.

Lee ignored her lunch, looking out across the river as it ambled west. This was such a peaceful setting, contrasting the chaos that battled for control of her mind. She had chosen Marion to share her thoughts with because she was one of the most intelligent and honest women Lee knew. Marion wouldn't judge Lee, nor would she judge the information. She would feed it back little by little, like dissecting a poem, until Lee saw it clearly. At least that's what she hoped. The recent encounter with Vern Mathews however, had left Lee feeling unsure of how to begin. Finally, she just blurted it out.

"I think Diane was murdered."

Marion stopped chewing and swallowed. Her pale blue eyes turned in Lee's direction. "That's a bold statement."

"Do you think I'm crazy?"

Marion eyed her for a moment and then threw back her head and laughed, her voice as rich as bell chimes. "Well, how the hell would I know? I mean, I teach English. I can diagram a sentence with the best of them. I know my seventeenth-century authors backwards and forward, and I've written some pretty mean Haiku in my time. But I have never, for the life of me, known the difference between a schizophrenic and a psychopath." She placed her hand gently on Lee's knee. "God help me, though, you don't look like either one to me."

"I'm serious, you know. I think someone killed her."

Marion dropped her hands in her lap, the sandwich held loosely between them, the wide smile fading. "I know," she said, wiping her mouth. "I could tell something was wrong when you called. I don't think you're crazy. Murder though," she shrugged. "That's a pretty big leap."

Lee twisted on the bench to face her friend. "Marion, it is hard to have a close friend die. But, then to feel, to believe, that someone purposely took that friend's life – well, it changes everything."

She shifted her gaze to a young woman walking along the river's edge with a large black dog. The girl tossed a long stick end over end into the river and the dog leaped in with reckless abandon, barking and sending up sparkles of water.

"Lee, I've never known you to exaggerate, so I can't believe this is just a hunch on your part. What makes you believe she was murdered?"

Lee thought of the onyx bird and reached over and rested her hand on her purse as she spoke. "Small things. Inconsistencies, mostly."

"Well, what about the police? Have they looked into it?"

"No. There were no obvious signs of foul play, so they didn't go any further. They accepted the suicide note."

"So, what's keeping you up at night? You look like you haven't slept much. Maybe you just need some rest."

Lee shrank from the remark, knowing that her appearance had to be off-putting to someone like Marion who was as comfortable in her own skin as a pair of old shoes. Marion wore little makeup, yet her skin was the color of peaches, and her short hair wasn't just gray, it was as rich as polished silver. Her long, lean body was weathered, but sound, leaving Lee to think that if Marion were a musical instrument, she would be a cello – not because of her shape, but the strength and depth of her soul. Feeling a sense of comfort in her presence, Lee finally voiced the one question she'd kept hidden from everyone.

"Do you believe in ghosts, Marion? Or the paranormal?"

Marion stopped with the sandwich poised an inch from her lips. She didn't say anything, but the sharp chin tilted to one side, and the straight brows knit together.

"Don't tell me you think Diane is talking to you?"

"Maybe. First in dreams and now…well, now I'm not sure how she's doing it." Lee reached into her purse and pulled out the onyx bird and handed it to Marion.

"I don't understand," Marion said, putting her sandwich on the bench and taking the bird. "What's this?"

"Carey gave it to me at the funeral. It was one of Diane's favorite possessions. I was with her when she bought it last year from an old Indian up in Yakima. He went on and on about how it was her totem."

Marion wrapped both hands around the bird as if it were a warm cup of coffee and looked up with an odd expression. "Totem? Like an Indian spirit?"

"He said it belonged to her. I thought he was just trying to get her to buy it, but now I'm not so sure. I don't even know what kind of bird it is."

Marion rubbed her finger along the crest of the bird's head. "It's a hawk," she replied with confidence. "You can tell by the hooked beak and the elongated body. But, I thought girls' totems were always things like doves or deer."

"Not according to this guy. He held it cupped in both hands, much like you're holding it now. He said she had a strong spirit and that her totem was strong. We both laughed, thinking he was joking, but he just looked at the two of us and said he was dead serious. He told Diane that one day she would need this totem and to keep it close." Lee paused, her eyes drifting to the river. "Of course, I made some snide remark, but Diane bought it, and now that she's gone, strange things have been happening."

"Like what?"

Lee sighed, watching a duck float aimlessly among the shallows of the river. "If I tell you, you might change your mind about me being crazy"

Marion smiled. "Give me a chance. There are a lot of things you don't know about me."

"Okay," Lee said. "Twice, I've left the bird at home. I mean, I'm *positive* I left it at home. And yet both times it showed up later in my purse."

She glanced at Marion for a reaction. Her friend frowned, but encouraged her to continue.

"The first time was the night after Diane's funeral, when I stopped by her condo to check on something. Just before I left, I heard a thud and found my purse in the middle of the living room floor with all its belongings strewn across the floor. Along with everything else was the bird. There was no one else in the condo. A moment later, I thought I saw something flit past the mirror in the hallway and found a bird feather on the carpet where there hadn't been one ten minutes before." Lee shivered. "Then there are the birds around my house."

"Around your house?"

Lee realized Marion hadn't moved a muscle the entire time she'd been speaking. Instead, she listened with the bird held just above her lap as if she were about to release it into the air.

"I'm beginning to feel like Tippi Hedren in *The Birds*. Suddenly, groups of birds surround my house and seem to be watching me all the time. It's like this bird is connected to all other birds and together, they're trying to tell me something. I just don't know what." She looked over at Marion who watched her quietly. "Now, do you think I'm crazy?"

Her friend unwound her fingers from around the bird and stared at it. "Do you believe in coincidences?"

Lee considered the question. If all the occurrences with the bird had been coincidences, then Diane's spirit was truly gone, and she was on her own. If they weren't coincidences, then something other than a natural phenomenon was at work here.

"I don't know. I guess I do."

"Well, I don't. Things happen for a reason." Marion handed the bird back to Lee. "Just out of curiosity, when was the last time you handled it?"

"Maybe twenty minutes ago. I was just over at the condo, and Diane's brother-in-law showed up and tried to take it back. Why?"

Marion picked up her sandwich again. "The stone was warm when you handed it to me. Very warm. As if it were alive."

The chill that emanated from deep within Lee's soul rippled to the tips of her extremities. The two women were quiet for several moments, Marion nibbling at her sandwich, and Lee watching the bird as if it might take wing. Someone whizzed along the path on roller blades behind them, leaving the running sound of wheels on pavement in their wake.

"You know, Lee, this is nothing to fool around with," Marion began again, wiping her mouth with a napkin. "If you really think there is reason to believe Diane was murdered, you need to talk to the police."

"I know," she replied.

"But you should also find out more about that bird. There's a Native American woman who works at that new age gift shop downtown called Inspirations. I don't know her name, but one of my students used her for some research last quarter on Native American mythology. Why don't you go talk to her? Take the bird. See what she says."

"That's a good idea," Lee said, growing quiet.

"What else is going on?" Marion asked, watching her out of the corner of her eye.

Lee put the bird back on the bench, allowing a long moment to stretch between them. "Someone broke into my house last night."

Marion gasped, reaching out for Lee's hand.

"You're kidding? What happened?"

"They destroyed my living room looking for something, but nothing was stolen. But Diane's condo was broken into, too."

Marion's eyes were as wide as saucers. "There's more, isn't there. I can tell from your body language. What happened, Lee?"

Lee felt herself squirm as she prepared to tell at least part of the truth.

"The guy who broke in... attacked me."

"Oh, my God!" Marion's hand flew to her mouth, and then she was silent.

"He caught me in the hallway and pushed me up against the wall. I'm sure he was going to do something," she said, remembering the warmth of his hand as it touched her skin, "but Amy's dog scared him off." Lee's entire body felt scorched, as if a flame had seared her skin. This was too painful. She needed to change the subject. "But I need to focus on Diane. A nurse at the hospital just told me it would have taken ten to fifteen minutes for Diane to die after she was injected with insulin." Lee leaned forward and rested her elbows on her knees, looking out to the river, tears forming in her eyes. "Initially, I wondered if Diane had tried to defend herself and finally just ran out of steam and died. But a large vase she kept on her coffee table is missing. I'm pretty sure it was used to knock her out first." Lee sighed, wiping the moisture away from her eyes. "Diane and I had an argument that night. I said some awful things. Things I can't take back now."

Lee dropped her head, the pain of the memory swelling in her chest. Marion reached over and put a hand on her shoulder.

"Are you sure it's not guilt that's making you think someone killed Diane?"

In between sniffles, Lee said, "No. In my heart, I know she didn't kill herself. But if I'm right, that means someone else did. I need to know, Marion."

She used the palm of her hand to wipe her face just as a little bird landed in between them on the back of the bench. Lee sat up and looked at it in expectation. Marion stopped as well. A long moment passed in which the bird hopped back a forth, but did little else.

"It's just a bird," Marion chided. "It probably just wants a snack."

Marion pinched off a piece of bread and held it out for their guest. The bird ignored the treat and hopped away.

"Come here, little guy," Marian coaxed it.

A breeze rose up and caught Marian's empty sandwich bag and tossed it into the air. It startled the small bird, and it flew off the back of the bench and landed on the lawn behind them.

"Oh, I scared it away," she lamented. Marian turned to follow the little bird and froze.

"Um...Lee..." she stammered.

Lee slowly swiveled her head to look behind them. A familiar cold chill ran the length of her spine. An entire flock of birds had assembled quietly behind them.

"My God," Marion whispered.

They both stood up and turned around to face several hundred birds. Most of them were on the ground, but many others had filled the branches of nearby trees.

"I don't think they're here for food," Lee said, as she began to move around the end of the bench in their direction.

"Lee, don't do anything!" Marion exclaimed, her voice straining.

Lee ignored her and moved carefully around the bench. Taking small steps, she inched forward until she was only a few feet from the nearest bird. These were wild birds that would normally fly away. So, why weren't they? A moment later, she had her answer.

The trailing *"keeer"* of a hawk made both women look up. High above them, a hawk circled gracefully down through the sky until it landed on a lower branch of the closest pine tree. Instantly, the flock of birds dispersed in a whirl of flapping wings. In a matter of seconds, they were all gone. Marion's mouth dropped open in shock.

"Lee, what's happening?"

Lee didn't answer. She was focused now on the hawk. Taking the onyx bird into her left hand, she turned her right hand over, offering up her arm to the hawk.

"C'mon," she whispered to it. "C'mon. I dare you."

Adrenalin pounded through her body, but she waited as still as stone until the powerful wings of the hawk unfolded. It lifted off the branch and then descended, its wings spread at full span. The big bird lowered itself onto Lee's arm in a whoosh of forced air. Lee took a step back in order to balance herself under the bird's weight. She could feel the talons digging through her blouse into her skin. The bird's head shifted back and forth, its eyes watching her, its feathers glistening in the afternoon sun.

Lee couldn't breathe. Her eyes were fixed on the hawk. Slowly, she raised her left hand and held out the onyx figurine. The large predator looked at the figurine, its head jerking in short, sharp movements. Then it pushed its beak forward until it touched the onyx bird, just as the small bird had done at Hendrick's Park. The hawk turned back to Lee, watched her for another second or two, and then pushed down on Lee's arm, lifting off like a champion diver leaving a springboard. It pulled itself higher and higher into the air until it caught an air current that took it up the river and out of sight.

Lee watched it go, tears flowing freely down her cheeks. When she could no longer see the bird, she turned to find Marion standing in front of the bench, her face as white as the hair that topped her head. They stared at each other for a minute before Marion murmured, "That was amazing."

The older woman seemed to make a decision as she stuffed her remaining sandwich into the lunch bag and tossed it into a nearby trashcan. "Okay," she said with a deep breath. "I'm in. I'll be at your house tonight. We'll map out what you've got and see what fits and what doesn't."

Lee smiled in relief, as she rubbed the spot on her arm where the bird's talons had left marks. "You mean it? You believe me?"

Marion gave a hesitant smile, showing a perfect set of white teeth. "I don't know what I believe. But I just saw an inexplicable thing. Perhaps that hawk was an escapee from the local zoo and just happened to be trained to land on people's arms, but I doubt it. Something is going on here, and I want to help. I have to make a trip to Cottage Grove after work, but I'll be back by eight. I'll bring some wine. You provide the snacks."

Lee felt as if someone had just lifted fifty pounds off her shoulders. She wiped her eyes and picked up her lunch bag. She snatched a large peanut butter cookie from the bag before sending it into the trashcan.

"I'll make some popcorn with cheddar cheese that will make your mouth water."

They laughed as they walked back toward the bridge, meandering through the rose garden that bordered the path. Most of the roses were gone, but little nameplates like Camelot and Big Ben indicated the noble plants whose color had waned. They reached the other side of the bridge and started through the parking lot.

"Okay," Marion said. "Save it for tonight. I want it all. Who knows, with two brilliant minds and a little wine…"

"And a very small carved bird…" Lee interjected.

Marion laughed. "Right, well, with all of that, maybe we can shed some light on this mystery of mysteries."

"By the way, what do you know about Pauline Bates?" Lee asked.

"Why do you want to know about Pauline Bates?" Marion's eyebrows arched in question.

"She was at Diane's funeral."

"Why would she go to Diane's funeral?"

"That's what I'd like to know. She was there though, in all her eerie splendor."

"Let me think on that one," Marion said. "I can make a few phone calls. See you tonight. And don't forget," she warned. "Go see that Native American woman. You need to find out what you're dealing with here."

With a short wave, Marion climbed into her vintage BMW and pulled out of the parking lot. Lee watched her depart feeling better than she had in days. A quick check of her watch let her know that she had time to follow up on Marion's suggestion to find out more about the bird. She backed out of the parking space and started out of the lot, just ahead of a brown pickup truck.

CHAPTER TWENTY-FOUR

Lee negotiated her way through the one-way streets of downtown Eugene until she found a parking spot a few doors down from the store called, Inspirations. She put a quarter in the meter and hurried up the sidewalk. The store's front window displayed a variety of books about channeling spirits, meditation, and UFOs. Inside, Lee was met with a discordant blend of colors, sounds, and smells. One whole corner was filled with handmade birdhouses and desktop fountains. Beaded jewelry and crystal figurines filled the glass display case, while scented candles and bags of potpourri spilled from the drawers of a large antique sideboard. Layered over all of this was a kind of woodland fairy music. The cynic in Lee wanted to laugh, but since she was about to ask questions about a sculpted bird's ability to move around on its own, she wondered if there wasn't a book or two here she ought to read.

A young woman dressed in a long tie-dyed skirt and blouse stood off to one side talking with a young man who looked like he hadn't washed his hair in a decade. His clothes didn't look much better. Lee browsed among some hand-dyed silk scarves for a moment, thinking she might actually buy one, when the boy left and the young woman approached.

"May I help you?" she asked with a light voice.

"Yes," Lee replied, still fingering a bright blue scarf. "I was told a Native American woman worked here. I don't know her name, but I was hoping I could speak with her."

The girl's brown eyes lit with recognition. "Oh, you mean Lilly. She's in the back. I'll get her for you."

The girl retreated in a flurry of bright colors to disappear behind a long green curtain at the back of the store. Lee wondered how truly native this woman could be if her name was Lilly. She remained skeptical until a short, box-figured woman appeared, her black hair hanging like two braided ropes across her ample breasts. She appeared to be middle-aged and wore a turquoise gauze dress tied at the waist with a multi-colored woven belt. A heavy silver conch necklace hung around her neck. She was clearly Native American, and Lee felt ashamed at her bias. The woman approached with a warm smile.

"I am Lilly," she said in a husky voice. "What can I do for you?"

"I wondered if you could answer some questions about the Native American culture," Lee said.

"There is not a single culture. There are many tribes," she said. "But I will try to help."

Lee hesitated before bringing out the bird. Finally, she withdrew if from her purse and held it in the palm of her hand.

"A friend of mine purchased this in a store when we were up in Yakima a year ago, near the reservation. The man who sold it to her said it was her totem. She died recently." Lee stopped, not knowing if she should say anymore.

Lilly shifted her dark, impassive eyes to the bird. She had a kind face and her skin looked like tanned, oiled leather. But her eyes held a sense of wisdom that comforted Lee. While Lee studied her, Lilly studied the bird.

"I'm sorry about your friend. American Indians feel a kinship with the earth and all of its animals," she said, still looking at the bird. "The hawk is a very proud and brave bird."

"But I'm not sure I understand what a totem is," Lee interjected.

Lee felt silly holding the bird and so placed it on a glass countertop next to them. The woman glanced over at it, but didn't touch it.

"Animal totems are spiritual symbols, or spiritual tools," she explained, glancing back at Lee. "We believe that all of nature is connected, and that animals carry the qualities of individual human beings. Each person is connected to a specific animal. That animal can serve as a channel to the greater universe. Totems, like this bird," she said, nodding at the bird, "represent the animal's connection to the person. They work with the subconscious mind; if the person can tap into the energy, the totem can convey information or qualities the person needs. We have a couple of very good books on the subject," she said, turning to find the literature.

"I don't have time," Lee blurted, stopping the woman. "I'm sorry.

I'm in a bit of a hurry. I just need to know a couple of things."

"If you are doing some kind of research, there are many qualified resources at the university."

"No, it's for something else. I just need to know how a person finds out what their totem is."

The woman minimized Lee's bluntness with a slight shrug of her shoulder. "Young people go through a ritual to discover their totem, like coming of age. The totem might be a hawk, like this one. Or it might be a bear, a wolf, or even a deer. Characteristics of the animal are reflected in that person. For instance, the bear is self-reliant and adaptable. The deer is intuitive and compassionate. And the hawk," she nodded at the bird again, "is a fearless hunter that goes after what it wants."

"I still don't understand what their purpose is. The totem, I mean, other than to reflect someone's characteristics?"

The woman studied Lee, her eyes searching Lee's face as if knowing she was struggling with a demon of some kind.

"Many people believe their totem animal gives them protection and power. If they are brave, then they become braver. If they are strong, they become stronger. You say your friend has died. Perhaps you think her totem failed her?"

"No, that's not it," Lee stuttered, thinking just the opposite. "Well, maybe," she admitted. The bird *hadn't* protected Diane, so what good was it? The woman watched her, then finally turned and reached for the bird.

"Did your friend share the same characteristics as the hawk?"

Lee couldn't help but laugh. "Yes. I mean you might say that Diane had a hawk-like personality. She could be severe and biting and…"

"Those are negative characteristics," the woman interrupted. "What were the good characteristics they shared?"

"I don't know. I don't know what the hawk's good characteristics are."

Lilly studied the bird as she spoke. "The hawk has keen eyesight and perfect balance, but it lacks patience," she said. "It is a proud bird and a predator. Single-minded in its purpose. As a predator, it knows how to survive." She cupped the bird in between both hands as Marion had done. "You say your friend bought this in Yakima."

"Yes."

"Where were you when this man told your friend the bird was her totem?"

Lee felt a chill begin to flutter beneath her shoulder blades. "Uh…I was standing right behind her."

"And you believe this man was wrong."

"I don't know."

The woman paused, cradling the bird and leaning into it as if listening to something.

"Well, you are right," she finally said, opening her hand and handing the bird back to Lee. "This is *not* your friend's totem. This is *your* totem. You are the hawk. And the hawk is you. And you need to listen to its call."

CHAPTER TWENTY-FIVE

Lee returned to the hospital with a new sense of confidence. The fact the onyx bird might be *her* totem instead of Diane's was a surprise, but not a shock. All along, Lee had felt a connection to the bird. She also believed Diane was working through the bird, pointing the way. Lee just didn't know how to read the signs.

But her goal now was to return Bud's personnel file to Robin. The fact her intruder knew she had it spooked her. The last thing she needed right now was to lose her job. And after she did this, she was heading home for a nap. She needed a clear head before her meeting with Marion later that night.

"Are you back again?" Marie asked when Lee entered the office again.

Lee hesitated. If this continued, she'd have to start keeping a log of the half-truths and lies she was telling just to keep them straight.

"I just need a phone number," she lied again. Lee slipped into her office and pretended to look for the in-house phone list. Just as she found it, Jenny interrupted her search.

"By the way, the photographer called," Jenny began, pushing a lock of hair behind her ears. "He said to tell you everything is set for that Occupational Health photo shoot at Green Valley tonight. That's the good news. The bad news is that Sally went home sick. Do you want me to cancel it?"

"What?" Lee looked up, distracted. "Um...no, don't cancel it. It's taken too long to set this up." She sighed, her mind moving in slow motion. "I'll go, I guess."

"Well, before you commit, the photographer wants someone to go out to the sawmill with him this afternoon in order to find the best place to set up for the picture."

"Shit." Lee dropped her head and sighed. "I suppose I can do it. What time?"

"Two o'clock."

She looked at her watch.

"Okay. You can tell him I'll be there. Where do I meet him?"

"Go to the east gate. James Rupert is the photographer."

"Okay. Thanks."

Jenny returned to her desk, and Lee put the phone list back. She rubbed her eyes, trying to relieve the burning sensation that kept her blinking every few seconds. Grabbing an interoffice envelope, she slipped the personnel file inside, addressed it to Robin, and marked the envelope confidential. As she dropped the envelope in her Out Box, another envelope lying in the In Box caught her eye. It was a blank, letter-size envelope with no return address. Lee's name was written on the outside in a distinctive, curvy script she now recognized. She ripped open the envelope and pulled out a black and white newspaper ad for a Maytag refrigerator. Lee flipped it over, confused. The ad had been torn from a newspaper, and the backside had only two paragraphs from a story on the state's budget cuts. She looked back at the ad for the refrigerator. It declared a huge sale on all appliances that coming weekend. The name of the store had been separated from the picture, as if whoever had sent it wanted Lee to focus on the refrigerator itself. There was nothing more inside the envelope.

Lee stepped into the outer office where Marie was pulling letters off the printer. "Marie, do you know when this arrived?" She held up the envelope.

Marie glanced up, squinting to see what Lee was holding. "Yesterday afternoon, I think."

"It didn't come in an interoffice envelope?"

"No. It came with the rest of the mail, just as you see it." Marie turned away, clutching a handful of paper.

Lee shrugged and stuffed the picture and envelope in her purse, feeling too overwhelmed to contemplate it now. Glancing over at Diane's desk, where some of her personal belongings still sat, she made a decision.

"Listen, can you guys box up all of Diane's stuff? Carey and her mother are going over to the condo this weekend to do the same thing. I'll drop it off to them."

"We'll get some boxes from shipping," Marie said with a pained expression.

Jenny popped her head around the partition. "What should we do with the boxes?"

"I can pick them up."

Jenny rolled her chair all the way into the walk space. "No, Lee. One of us will drop them off at your house."

"Don't come back, Lee," Marie said quietly. "We can take care of it."

"Thanks," Lee replied, warmth rising to her cheeks. "And, I'm sorry if I seem out of sorts. I just... well, thanks."

She started for the door when Marie stopped her. "Oh, I almost forgot." Marie handed Lee a pink telephone message. "I thought you'd like to see this. Ruth Innes called. She's back in the lab. "

Lee's mind raced. Ruth was an information systems coordinator who had worked in the lab until she was hired away by a computer software company. Lee thanked Marie and headed straight for the lab on the second floor. Her nap could wait. She wound her way through a narrow hallway and found Ruth in her old office, the phone glued to her ear. When Lee arrived, Ruth waved her in, while she finished her conversation. Lee took a chair next to the cluttered desk.

After a year in the corporate world, Ruth's appearance hadn't changed. No tailored suits or white-cuffed blouses. Instead, she wore her brown hair in a long braid down her back and a full, colorful skirt accented with dangling jewelry. When Ruth hung up, she got up and gave Lee a hug that produced a tinkling melody as the strands of necklace collided.

"Lee, how are you?

"I'm fine. When did you come back?"

"This week. Jack gave me my old job back. The for-profit world isn't all it's cracked up to be. I missed having to raise money for what I needed." She winked and motioned for Lee to sit down. "So, how are you, really? I heard about Diane."

The mention of Diane's name brought a catch to Lee's throat, something she hadn't expected. "I still can't believe she's gone."

"I wish I could help." Ruth's large dark eyes showed genuine sympathy. "I liked Diane."

Lee perked up. "You mean that?"

"Mean what? That I liked her?"

"No. Help."

"Of course. What can I do?"

Lee knew Ruth meant emotional support, and God knows she

needed it. But right now, she needed much more and threw out a careless response to Ruth's question.

"The police think Diane committed suicide. I don't." The other woman pulled back, but Lee pushed forward. "I'm trying to figure out how she died. You worked with Diane on the employee campaign for two years. You know how rigid she could be and what a perfectionist she was. Can you picture her killing herself?"

"No. The moment I heard that she committed suicide, I questioned it."

"Will you help me get some answers?"

Ruth paused as her demeanor became guarded, but the dark eyes searched Lee's as if calculating a critical move in a chess game. "Are you working with the police?"

"No. I'm on my own. They ruled it a suicide, so the case is closed."

"I see." Ruth hesitated, her hands playing with the blotter on her desk, the eyes still looking for answers. "What do you need to know?"

Lee got up and closed the door. "How would someone commit fraud in a lab like this?"

"You think someone in our lab is committing fraud?" Her face registered shock, as if Lee had challenged the integrity of the department.

"No...I mean, I don't know. I'm only trying to piece things together."

"Why do you think someone is committing fraud?"

"If Diane was killed, there has to be a reason. The only thing I can think of is that she may have stumbled onto something illegal. Something someone else would kill for. So, I'm looking at everything. But she was dating someone in this lab." She paused, knowing this might cause Ruth to retract.

Ruth opened her mouth and exhaled. "Yes, Bud Maddox. I don't know him well, but he thinks a lot of himself." She glanced through the window in the door out to the lab. "Fortunately, he's on a break right now."

"Good. Look, I need to know how things operate up here in the lab."

"Do you suspect Bud?"

Lee couldn't say yes, even though she was positive that Bud Maddox had something to do with Diane's death. But she didn't want this to appear like a vendetta against a guy she just didn't like.

"I don't suspect anyone, yet. But since she was dating Bud, and he works here, I thought I should follow up."

The other woman hesitated a moment before appearing to make a decision.

"I trust you, Lee, but we need to be careful."

"If you don't want to do this, just say so."

The other woman took a deep sigh, folding one lip under the other. "No, I want to help. But, I think I should show you instead of just telling you," she said, as if catching on to a game.

"No one can know what I'm doing," Lee said cautiously. "If asked why I'm here, remember, I'm just responding to your phone call."

"Well, I did call you. I wanted to volunteer again for the employee campaign committee."

"Okay. Good enough."

They left the office and ran immediately into one of the shift supervisors. Ruth took the lead with confidence.

"Hi, Ray. You know Lee Vanderhaven from the Foundation. The Foundation is looking for some capital equipment to fund."

"Oh, sure. Hi, Lee," he nodded to Lee. "Take a look at the backup centrifuge. It's on its last legs, and we couldn't get it into the capital budget until next year."

"I will," Ruth said agreeably.

"And don't forget the staff meeting in a few minutes," he said with a raised eyebrow.

"I won't." Ruth smiled as Ray continued down the hallway. She turned to Lee. "Things haven't changed much around here. This will be the third meeting I've attended today. At some point, I'd like to actually get some work done."

Ruth led them into the lab area, which could only be described as ordered chaos. Two long counters covered with computer screens, test tubes, microscopes, and a variety of other supplies led off toward the back wall and a bank of windows that overlooked a parking lot. Boxes were stacked on top of cabinets, while tall stools cluttered the aisles. Things were cramped and congested, and Lee saw at least two workstations tucked into corners. She imagined how easy it might be to conceal your activities here.

Ruth took her to the second aisle and pointed out a large, waist-high, round metal canister that stood on the floor. This was the backup centrifuge, and Ruth pointed to the newer model sitting right next to it. She looked around to see if any of the technicians were within earshot, and then backed up to the center of the aisle where they could speak alone.

"Okay," she said softly, "let me explain a few things. We run a lot of tests here. Medical screens are run on patients who come in for routine surgery or other kinds of treatment. We run a urine profile to determine protein levels, pH, specific gravity, things like that. During each shift, a tech will work on a batch of samples. And for preliminary drug screens, they use this machine." She indicated a bulky looking machine that sat on the counter to their left. Next to it were two plastic cups.

Lee looked at the innocuous looking piece of equipment. Someone had taped a small sign to it that said, *Drug Busters.*

"Funny," Lee said disingenuously.

Ruth smiled. "The machine indicates drugs that are present in the urine sample. If the level is above a certain threshold, the tech manually marks it as positive and takes it to a locked refrigerator. Eventually it would go to the drug confirmation room. When they're finished, the samples are placed back in a locked refrigerator in the next room, along with all other samples that came in for routine drug testing."

"I'm not sure what you mean."

"Well, drug tests are routinely done on all pre-employment physicals, as well as all industrial accidents. And because of our Occupational Health contracts, we do a lot of physicals. Look there." She pointed to a row of little plastic cups at the end of the counter that had clear plastic caps and were sealed with a thin strip of red tape. "Those are here for drug testing. The red tape guarantees the seal hasn't been broken. There's a chain of custody for most everything we handle."

"You mentioned the drug confirmation room. That sounds familiar. Where is that?"

"Right over there."

Ruth pointed to a small room partitioned off by a sliding glass door. Inside, a female technician sat at a big computer, punching in numbers. When Lee turned back, her attention was momentarily deflected by the reflection of something in the window directly above the workstation.

"What happens to the urine samples that you're not testing for drugs?" she inquired, ignoring the reflection.

"There's no chain of custody on those. The sample sits on the counter until the shift is over. Like those two there. Then they're put into a refrigerator and kept for two days."

She gestured to a refrigerator standing about five feet behind the workstation. Lee realized it was the refrigerator she'd seen reflected in the window.

"Is that refrigerator locked?"

"No."

"You mean anyone can get at those samples?"

"Yeah," Ruth shrugged. "But after two days, they're thrown away anyway."

Lee was trying to figure something out. "If the samples are just put in an unlocked refrigerator, someone could just reach in, pull out a urine sample and run another test?"

"Why would they run another test? These samples haven't been tagged for positive drug screens."

A lab tech appeared to get a clipboard off the counter, and the two women stopped talking. Ruth overreacted, saying a little too loudly, "What if the fundraising committee picked the centrifuge as their project?"

Lee was focused on the lab tech and almost missed her cue. "Oh," she uttered, "Sure."

Lee's off-the-mark reply brought a look of irritation from Ruth, but the lab tech left the area making it unnecessary to continue the charade.

"You'll have to do better than that," Ruth chided.

"Sorry, I was distracted. So, how would someone run an unordered test?"

Ruth thought a moment. "They could spike a sample with what we call a standard. If they did it with a positive standard, the sample would test positive."

"Even though the sample initially had no trace of drugs?"

"That's right."

"And then the sample would go to the drug confirmation room?"

"Not necessarily. If they were only running controls it wouldn't go anywhere."

"What's a control?"

"Quality control tests," she clarified. "Every tech has some responsibility for quality control. Routine controls are run daily."

"Could someone fake a quality control run?"

"I suppose so, although I'm not sure why they would."

"Would anyone notice if they did?"

"You mean, would they notice if someone was running something they shouldn't be?"

"Yeah." Lee felt her pulse quicken at the thought she may be onto something.

"They could probably do it undetected. The techs work on a variety of samples during their shift. And as you can see, this place is a bit like a maze, and no one looks over their shoulders."

There was a black ribbon stretched across the flat screen of the computer right next to them. Lee noticed it.

"Whose station is this?" she asked, indicating the ribbon. "Did someone die?"

"Yes. Her name was Martha Osgood. She had this station for seven or eight years."

"Wow, that's sad. What happened to her?"

Ruth's face fell. "She was killed last night…in a hit and run accident. Somebody mowed her down right in front of her own apartment. She worked the night shift and was on her way to work. I think that's probably why no one's at the computer today. Out of respect."

"No one saw who hit her?"

Lee turned slowly to stare at the refrigerator and for the second time in just a few days, she felt like someone had crossed over her grave.

"I'm told they found the car, but it was stolen. Martha was very nice. She'll be missed." Just then a woman appeared at the corner of the aisle.

"Ruth, you have a phone call. It's Mary Jacobs from the blood bank. And everyone is in the break room. Jack is just about to start the meeting."

"I'll take the call. And tell Jack I'll be a few minutes late." With a look of apology, she said to Lee, "I've got to take this call, but I'll come right back. The meeting can wait." In a flurry of colorful folds of fabric, she billowed away.

Lee was left to survey her surroundings. The reflection in the window drew her attention again. It was directly above Martha Osgood's station. Lee looked from the reflection back to the refrigerator. During the daytime, the reflection in the window was faint, but Lee imagined how crisp it might be at nighttime, set against the darkness outside. The refrigerator opened from right to the left. That way, the interior would also be reflected in the window, along with whatever anyone was doing. The newspaper ad for the refrigerator suddenly made sense. Somewhere behind her a door closed.

She looked around to make sure no one was coming back to the work stations and then moved over to the refrigerator. With a momentary heart flutter, she opened the door and glanced inside, sure that she was shattering yet one more rule of order. Leaning on the counter with her right hand, she leaned in to peer into the cold interior. She studied the labels attached to the small cups, wondering again what exactly the anonymous tip about the refrigerator meant. Was someone doing something illegal using this refrigerator? And was the messenger Martha Osgood?

Without warning, the warm flesh of another hand landed directly on top of hers. Lee jerked her hand back as a shriek erupted from her throat. A dark blue sleeve disappeared from the other side of the counter. Lee backed up against the opposite counter, wheezing like an asthmatic. She glanced to her left. She could make a dash for the main hallway. Just as she was about to move, something brushed against the lobe of her right ear. Lee rebounded to her left and bumped against the counter like the steel ball in a pinball machine. Her foot got caught under the wheel of a cart, and she would have fallen had it not been for a strong hand. She was about to say thank you, when she found herself staring once more into the leering face of Bud Maddox. He held her wrist in a firm grip, the blue sleeve of his shirt folded back against his forearm.

"I didn't scare you, did I?" he smiled. "I couldn't resist, you know. There you were, sneaking a peak into a restricted refrigerator. This is the second time I've saved you from a nasty fall."

The aroma of his aftershave lingered in her nostrils from where he had touched her ear. The smell immediately took her back to the night in her hallway, and her entire body went rigid.

"It was you," she exhaled. "You…you…" she couldn't finish her sentence. But the thought of his hand on her skin made her anger boil over. "You fucking bastard," she said in a low voice.

She wrenched her arm free, but Maddox's smile only broadened. "Well, now, we didn't get to that part, did we? I mean the fucking part. We were just warming up."

"I'll report you."

"No you won't," he smiled, leaning in. "Because if you did, I'd have to tell them about that file you had on me. The one you stole from HR. It would get you – and probably your friend, Robin – fired."

He continued to chuckle, the way a schoolyard bully laughs when his victim pleads to get his lunch money back. But Lee had finally hit her limit. She took a deep breath and leaned toward him.

"If you EVER touch me again, I swear to God, I'll kill you."

He waited a moment and then grinned.

"Gee, thanks for the warning." Suddenly, the arrogant expression was gone. "I'd be careful, Lee, if I were you. You're digging yourself into a pretty big hole around here. And there are people who don't like it."

With that, he turned and left. Lee remained where she was, her body numb. A moment later, Ruth appeared at the end of the aisle.

"What did Mr. Wonderful want?" she asked, looking at his departing figure.

Lee took a deep breath to quiet her thoughts.

"Nothing," she lied. "Can we go back to your office?"

Ruth gave her a suspicious look. "You okay?"

"Yeah, I just need to get rid of the stench left behind by that guy."

When they'd gone back to Ruth's office and closed the door, Lee sat in a chair for a moment, catching her breath.

"Lee, what happened out there? You look a little green."

Something inside her told Lee to play down the incident. "Everything about that guy makes me sick, that's all." She wiped perspiration from her forehead. "Listen, I have just a couple more questions and then I'll get out of your way. So, how would someone produce a phony report? Wouldn't you have to put it into the computer? And if you did, wouldn't that produce a record?"

"Not necessarily," her friend replied. Ruth reached into a pile of papers on her desk and produced a piece of paper, carefully putting her thumb over the name of the patient. "Here's what the report looks like. If the person had any knowledge of computer programming, it would be easy to run a phony report like this, and it would never show up officially." Ruth looked closely at Lee, her dark eyes straining to understand. "Is that what you think happened, Lee?"

Lee didn't hear the question because she had stopped breathing.

"I found a report like this in Diane's condo."

"You're kidding? Did it have Diane's name on it?"

"I didn't notice."

"You need to get that piece of paper, Lee," she said with earnest. "And find out what it is."

"Can I keep this?"

"Sure." Ruth took a marking pen and blotted out the name before giving it to Lee.

The pounding in Lee's ears was loud enough to make her feel like she was at a nightclub. She got up and reached for the door handle, but was caught off-guard by the sight of a card pinned to a bulletin board right next to the door. Her eyes locked on four-lines of verse written in familiar, cursive handwriting.

"Who gave this to you?" Lee demanded, her head suddenly clear as glass.

"Martha," Ruth replied, standing behind her. "She was an odd little woman. Meek and mild, I suppose you'd say. Most of the time you forgot she was even here, she was so quiet. But she liked to write limericks and left little notes for people in verse all the time. She gave me that to welcome me back on Monday."

"Did she ever quote Shakespeare?" Lee asked, knowing the answer.

"Yes. But usually she wrote the verse herself."

Lee stared at the card until she heard Ruth clear her throat. Lee looked up to see Maddox staring at them from across the room, a deeply satisfied grin on his face. Lee knew she should be unnerved, perhaps even scared, but something inside her had shifted with the realization that Bud Maddox was the one who had broken into her house and terrified her. With a firm set of her jaw, she stared back at the man she now believed may have killed not once, but twice.

CHAPTER TWENTY-SIX

Lee pulled in at the east entrance to the Green Valley Lumber Company a few minutes after two o'clock. After her conversation with Ruth, her mind was working overtime trying to figure out how she could regain entrance to Diane's condo to find that sheet of paper. Also fighting for her attention were images of Maddox and the death of the lab technician, Martha Osgood. It was a miracle her mind cleared in time to prevent her from driving right through the yellow guardhouse barrier, but she slammed on her brakes half a second before the grille of her car broke it in two. A young man with wispy brown hair and a thin mustache came to the passenger side window.

"Good afternoon," he said crisply.

"I'm here for a tour," she said, wondering if he'd noticed she'd almost smashed through his barrier. "I'm with Twin Rivers Hospital."

"Yes." He consulted a clipboard. "You'll be meeting with Mr. Gilman."

He directed her to the Research and Development office, before returning to the guardhouse to lift the barrier. She managed to pull forward without mishap and find the right building. She parked next to a blue Ford pickup, but sat for a moment taking a few deep breaths to regain her composure before heading up to the second floor.

"There she is," Jay Gilman offered amiably when she finally made an appearance. "Come on in, Lee."

Gilman was a small man in his early forties, with round, dark eyes and thick, dark hair. A nervous energy punctuated every gesture, as if he were inhabited by another person trying desperately to get out. He nodded to a man who stood to his left.

"I assume you know Mr. Rupert?"

"Yes." Lee greeted the photographer with a formal nod.

Gilman was already pointing to a second man who stood behind a metal desk. "This is Arthur Masterson. He's our environmental specialist."

Masterson was about thirty-five with a lock of bright red hair that flopped into a set of piercing blue eyes. He stood by passively, giving the floor to his boss.

"Arthur will take you on the tour," Gilman rattled on. "I'm expecting a phone call, and Arthur knows the plant as well as anyone." Everyone smiled and nodded. "We're very excited you'll be doing the article on our night shift. They don't get much attention. So, now we need to get you guys into hard hats."

Gilman turned and pulled two yellow hard hats from a shelf behind him and handed them over. Lee's was too large and it slipped to one side. She pushed it back up with a snap, wishing she could be anywhere but here right now. She had things to do.

"And, here," Gilman said, reaching into a drawer. He pulled out two small packets and handed one to Lee and one to Rupert. "Ear plugs – in case you need them. It gets pretty loud out there. Okay, follow Arthur and he'll take good care of you."

Lee thanked him and Gilman left. She and the photographer trailed behind their leader like a couple of kids on a field trip. They descended the stairs and sloshed across the yard, through sawdust and mud, to a building about a hundred feet away. Masterson stopped at a metal staircase that led up to an unmarked door.

"This mill only works the day shift, but the South mill runs twenty-four hours a day. If you choose the mill for the photograph, you'll go over there tonight. The two plants are identical."

Rupert towered over everyone else; he nodded without uttering a sound. Lee remembered that Sally had remarked once that Rupert preferred to deal in images rather than words. Watching him swivel his dark head back and forth taking in his surroundings, he looked like a human camera, mentally photographing his environment.

Masterson climbed the stairs and yanked open the door, releasing the dull roar of a working sawmill. The sounds of metal on metal, metal on wood, and the rattle and clank of moving chains created a crushing disharmony of noise. Lee momentarily cupped her hands over her ears to block it out and then remembered the ear plugs. She quickly opened the packet and stuffed one in each ear, before following the group onto a steel catwalk that jangled underfoot and swayed under the combined weight of three people.

Lee glanced through the steel grids to the floor below, thinking that wearing a dress would have been unthinkable. She looked out over the operating mill. It seemed that everywhere she looked, something was moving – sawing, flipping, or sorting. Conveyor belts ran in every direction. When a piece of machinery finished its job, multiple conveyor belts transported the wood or its byproducts to the next location. Lee was transfixed, momentarily forgetting the events from earlier that afternoon.

The group kept moving to a flight of stairs that led to a small structure mounted above the operation. It looked to be about the size of a studio apartment, with a front door and two windows looking out over the mill. Masterson stopped at the foot of the stairs, turned and yelled back at them.

"This is the filing room."

Rupert had to lean down to shout in his ear. "What's the filing room?"

"It's where we repair and sharpen the saw blades," he yelled. "Could be a good backdrop for the photo."

Rupert nodded. They climbed the short staircase and entered through a single door. When the door closed, the blaring sounds of the mill were partially muffled, and Lee removed the ear plugs. Masterson motioned for them to come closer.

"This is what's called a vibration-free room," he announced, his hands making a wide arc to include the entire room. "We strive to achieve precision accuracy. The higher our accuracy, the more lumber we produce. In fact, we beat our competition by using thinner saws." He walked over to a stack of ribbon-like saw blades that sat on the floor behind him. "See this saw tip? This is called stellite." His fingers touched the point of a blade where there was a color differentiation in the metal. "It's harder than steel, which means it's harder than the saw blade itself. When it's applied, it actually becomes part of the blade."

Lee took a closer look at the band of dark color where the two metals had become one. She pointed this out to Rupert, but his thoughts were imperceptible as his dark eyes clicked away.

"These are band saws." Masterson gestured to a set of blades that looked like large steel rubber bands. "The blade is wrapped around two wheels and then stretched tight with 35,000 pounds of pressure. It's important that sawdust doesn't build up down here in the gullet.

If it fills up with sawdust, the blade will heat up."

"And that's a problem?" Rupert finally joined the conversation, putting a sick of gum in his mouth.

"Think of it like a rubber band. If you stretch the rubber band and then heat it, it will become limber. If the blade becomes limber, it will move through the wood like a snake. Not good."

Masterson moved to the other end of the room, where a trap door opened to the floor below.

"Once the blades are sharpened, they're lowered back into the mill from here," Masterson pointed. "And here are the trim saws."

He turned and they moved to another machine busy grinding a more traditional round saw blade. When the sharpener met the blade, it emitted a high-pitched metallic whine and shot off a ring of sparks. Lee walked past it and poked her head into a small workroom that sat off to one side. Just then, Masterson called her back.

"Let's go back the way we came in," Masterson offered quietly.

Re-entering the mill deafened Lee's sensitive ears and she replaced the ear plugs. They crossed more catwalks until Masterson crowded them into a small room and closed the door, again shutting out much of the noise. A heavy man in overalls sat on a metal stool at the far end of the room staring at a computer. A large picture window extended the length of the room, reminding Lee of the surgical observation rooms in teaching hospitals.

"This is where it all begins," Masterson explained. "The log comes in from the yard and goes through the de-barker. The de-barker spins around the log and scrapes the bark off as it travels through. The log then comes through the head rig just outside," he said, pointing to his right. "It's sent in here, scanned and sent to the saw."

They looked out the window and saw a log as it was flipped up onto a turning chain and held. Something that looked like a short, covered bridge on wheels suddenly whizzed over it.

"Wow, what was that?" Lee asked in awe.

"That's the scanner," Masterson replied with a slight smile. "The scanner measures the log and decides how to cut each one." He pointed to where the log was now positioned between two steel pads. "Those pads are called dogs. They'll hold it in place while the log is sawed."

As they watched, the log was carried through the saws and quickly cut into three pieces. The cut timber instantly fell onto a conveyor belt and returned to the area in front of the windows. In the blink of an eye, chains picked it up and transferred it to another set of conveyors moving in the opposite direction, while a second log took its place. The whole system reminded Lee of the Matterhorn ride at Disneyland.

"Where does the junk go?" Rupert inquired, his jaws working the gum in his mouth.

"The trim ends and edgings go to the chipper. I'll take you down there in a minute. First, I want you to look over there." He pointed to the left where an operator stood at a console, monitoring the timber as it left the saws. "He's like a traffic cop. Boards that need additional cuts get diverted up here." Masterson pointed to the far left where a set of irregular cut boards were moving more slowly up another set of conveyors. "Thinner boards go straight through."

Lee looked back. The operator had stopped the conveyor and stepped out to reposition a board. He grabbed what looked like a long handled pick to move the board into its new position, reminding her of pictures she'd seen of loggers who skillfully rolled logs in the river.

"That's called a picaroon," Masterson offered, following Lee's gaze. "It has an extremely sharp tip and helps move the wood in the direction they need it to go."

"That's got to be dangerous," she mused out loud.

"Everything around here is dangerous."

As he said this, a huge set of rollers appeared suddenly out of the framework like some fiendish monster in a cheap science fiction movie and pushed a board forward.

"Jeez," Lee said in admiration. "This is pretty amazing."

He smiled indulgently. "C'mon, I'll take you downstairs."

Masterson led them through a maze of ductwork and conveyor belts and down a cement staircase until they were at the back of the building. They crossed a small open area surrounded by large metal cylinders and climbed a short set of steps onto a platform, which opened up to the yard below. A large trough, filled with small pieces of wood, shavings, and sawdust, ran from right to left about two feet off the floor.

"This is called a vibrating conveyor. The sawdust falls through those holes at the bottom and is carried off to another building. Nothing goes to waste here."

Three loud whistle bursts startled them, and an operator off to the side punched a button that made the trough begin to shake. While the sawdust fell through the holes, the larger wood products were left behind and moved forward until they disappeared over a ledge into something that thrashed and churned.

"That's the chipper," Masterson said to Rupert. "You wanted to know where the waste goes. Well, the chipper takes the waste material from the logs and does just what the name implies, makes them into chips."

Lee remembered a groundskeeper at the hospital that had gotten his hand caught in a backyard chipper the summer before. She often passed him in the hallway and felt cold when she saw his bandaged arm, imagining how it must have felt. Watching this chipper now made her think bandages here wouldn't be necessary, because there would be nothing left to bandage.

Masterson gestured for them to follow him back down the short staircase to where several lines of ductwork converged on the ceiling above. He turned to his right and led them under the pipes, around a few corners, to a metal ramp that zigzagged back up to the catwalks. The group left the building through an exit door and sloshed through the mud again to an adjacent wooden building. This building was connected to yet a third building by a conveyor chain above them. Lee thought the most important employee here had to be the guy who kept all these moving parts moving.

Masterson led them through a steel door where they found themselves in a cavernous room that resembled a large barn. In the far right corner was a huge pile of bark. A large crane sat in the middle of the room, connected to a platform above it.

"This is what we call the fuel house," he explained. "We produce our own steam on the property to heat the kilns." He pointed to the roof that was more than two stories high. "See that conveyor that crosses the building up there?"

Lee dropped her head back to see a large chain that ran across the roofline. Intermittent daylight flashed by as the chain moved and bark floated down from the roof onto the bark pile.

"That chain carries bark from the mill and drops it in here," Masterson continued. "The rake," Masterson gestured to the crane, "is hooked up to the rake carriage above." He pointed to where the crane was attached to a platform that ran the width of the building. "The rake, or crane, is powered by hydraulics and can swing from side to side. The carriage, or the bridge it sits on, rolls up and back.

And a boiler operator in the other building watches through a camera and can see when he has to move fuel around in order feed the chain."

"Feed the chain?" Lee asked with distaste. For the first time she realized there was more than one chain attached to this building.

Masterson smiled. "Look over here."

He moved over to the bark pile where a guard rail surrounded what looked like a conveyor belt that ran along the floor. It was actually a large-linked chain that sat in a shallow trough. The chain emerged from the center of the bark pile, picking up bark as it came, and moved across the floor.

"This is what's called a drag chain, and if you watch, you'll see how the big flights pick up the bark."

"Flights?"

"Those pieces of steel attached horizontally to the chain. They're indented slightly, so they're like shallow cups. They hold the bark until the chain drops into that hole."

He turned and pointed across the floor to his left. "C'mon, I'll show you."

They followed the guard rail that surrounded the length of the chain, either to protect it, or to protect people from getting caught *in* it. The railing ran two-thirds the length of the building, until it ended at a small, two foot square opening in the floor. Lee's gaze followed the chain where it emerged from the bark pile, until it dropped out of sight into the black hole.

"Where does it go?"

"The chain drops down, circles around and exits at the back of the building, where it loops around a spool and comes back in underneath the bark pile again."

She peered over the guardrail in order to get a better view of where the chain disappeared into the floor.

"What happens down there," she asked.

"When the chain drops down, the bark falls onto the boiler room chain, which runs underground to the next building. That's where the bark is deposited into the boilers."

Lee glanced to the roofline again. "So, one chain drops the bark in, another other moves it, and a third takes it out?"

"That's right."

"Amazing," she said, thinking of how efficient everything was.

"Well, I'd hate to get caught in that," Rupert said lightly, gazing into the hole in the floor.

"God, no kidding," Lee agreed.

Masterson smiled. "Yes. It wouldn't be good. Mainly because you wouldn't fit very well."

"I've never seen so many moving parts in my life," Lee quipped. "This whole place is like an accident waiting to happen."

Masterson shrugged. "Actually, we have very few accidents."

"Yeah, but when you do, I bet it's a whopper," Rupert whistled.

Just then, a loud beeping noise filled the room. Masterson took Lee by the elbow. "C'mon, we need to move."

They quickly circled around the end of the guard rail and went up a short flight of stairs. A moment later, the sound of metal wheels forced Lee to look up. The rake carriage began to move along two metal tracks in the direction of the bark pile. As the platform moved, the crane moved with it, its big scoop bucket reaching out at an angle toward the pile. The bucket slid across the bark pile, depositing bark onto the chain.

Masterson indicated that it was time to leave and led them out the door. Lee couldn't help a fleeting look back at the feed chain and shuddered. They crossed the expansive yard once again just as a giant skip loader picked up six big logs with huge, crab-like claws. It whirled around with amazing speed and disappeared behind a building, making Lee feel vulnerable everywhere she moved.

"Do you want to see anything else?" she asked Rupert, hoping to God that he wouldn't.

Rupert shook his head, pushing his glasses into place. "I don't think so."

The three returned to the office, where they removed their helmets.

"Any questions?" Masterson asked taking the helmets and putting them back on the shelf.

"No," Lee said, running her fingers through her hair. "Thanks for your time." She turned to Rupert. "So, where do you want to set up tonight?"

He rubbed his beard. "Probably that filing room. The one with the saw blades. I can do a lot with the blades in the background, and since it's a motion-free room, it won't affect the camera."

"That's a good choice," Masterson confirmed. "I'll let them know at the front gate." He turned to make himself a note. "Now, remember, you'll be going across the yard to the South Mill. I'll let the night manager know to be on the lookout for you."

"Thanks," Rupert said as he started out the doorway.

"Also," Masterson stopped him, "this back gate will be closed. You'll need to come through the front gate, off Main Street."

The two thanked him and left. Outside, Rupert said goodbye and walked off to his truck with a wave of his hand. As Lee drove slowly out of the yard, she realized she didn't relish the thought of coming back at night. The plant was a huge monstrosity that seemed poised and ready to devour her at any moment, leaving her with an inexplicable feeling of danger. And she thought she'd had enough of that lately.

CHAPTER TWENTY-SEVEN

It was three-thirty that afternoon when Lee arrived home. She had tried calling Carey twice from the car, but no one answered, and Lee was too cautious to leave a message about the lab report she hoped to find. Carey would be her only hope of getting back into the condo to find it. A leisurely shower and a nap were top on her agenda now, but she found Jenny coming up the walk carrying a bulky cardboard box.

"Hi," Jenny greeted her brightly. "We got busy and boxed up Diane's stuff. I thought I'd drop it off before I ran to the bank for the deposit."

"Come on in." Lee unlocked the door and they stepped inside. "Just put it over there." She gestured to the corner of the entryway where Jenny dropped the open box next to a plant stand.

"How are you doing?" Jenny asked, turning to Lee.

"Fine," she said, knowing her voice carried all the enthusiasm of a dead fish. "I just got back from the tour with Rupert."

Jenny's face brightened. "How'd it go?"

"That place is amazing. Scary, but amazing."

"My brother-in-law worked for McKenzie Mills a while back. He used to cringe whenever the phone rang at night because it usually meant there'd been an accident."

"Yes," Lee agreed. "It's a bit intimidating. Anyway, where are you off to tonight?" she asked, trying to be casual.

"I'm going bowling with Jim. He's trying to get me to join a league."

"Oh, right, the new boyfriend. Somehow, I can't see you bowling."

"Well, he practices every Friday night like clockwork, so he can bowl Thursday nights with the league. If I want to see him on Fridays, I go bowling. I'm not sure it's how I want to spend the rest of my life, but I'm willing to give it a chance." She rolled her eyes. "I'd better get going. I still have to go to the bank and run an errand for Marie." She started for the door.

"Jenny, hold on." Lee reached over and fumbled around inside her purse for the envelope with the suicide note. "Just out of curiosity, does this look like something Diane would have written?"

Jenny studied the note and her blue eyes clouded over. "It's the suicide note."

"Yes. Read it and tell me if you... well, if you see anything wrong with it."

Jenny's eyes skimmed the note. "There are a couple of mistakes. Plus..." she scraped her fingernail over the copy on the paper. "Unless Diane bought a new printer, she didn't print this at home." She handed the note back to Lee.

"What do you mean?"

"It's printed on an ink jet printer. Diane didn't have one."

Lee looked at the document. "How do you know what kind of printer it's been printed on?"

"Diane had a laser printer, which lays the ink on top of the paper. You can actually scrape it off."

She stuck her finger out for Lee to see. It was clean.

"This has been printed on an ink jet printer. The paper absorbs the ink. It's more professional. That's why Diane used to bring important things to the office to print. Anyway, I've got to go. I'll see you on Monday."

"Hey, by the way, doesn't Diane's brother-in-law bowl?"

Jenny paused on the bottom step. "I think he's in the same league with Jim. Diane talked about him once and what a jerk he was. Why?"

"Would you do me a favor? Ask Jim tonight if Vern Mathews bowled last Thursday."

"Sure. I'll see if I can find out."

"Thanks. I'll see you next week."

Jenny sauntered down the walk as Lee closed the door focused on one thought. The suicide note hadn't been printed on Diane's printer.

÷

At 8:45, Lee grabbed the jar of popcorn and a pan to get ready for Marion, who had called to say she was running late. Soldier lay next to the kitchen table, watching Lee's every move. Lee had finally left an innocuous message for Carey about the lab report and jumped when the phone rang, thinking it might be her.

"Hi, Mom. I've got good news."

Lee gently shook the pan as the oil crackled inside. "Is it about Soldier?" she asked.

"No, it isn't about Soldier, but I'm working on that."

Lee frowned. "What's the good news then?"

"This apartment is working out really well, and we're signing a one-year lease tomorrow."

Lee stopped shaking the pan. "A one-year lease? I thought you were coming home for the summer."

"If we want this apartment, they want us to sign a year's lease. That's pretty standard, you know."

Lee cringed. Her daughter didn't know the first thing about leases. She could hardly negotiate a turn. Lee pictured some middle-aged man with a cigar tapping the lease document with a stubby finger and saying, *"Yep, one year. That's the standard. Gotta have it."*

"And I've applied for a job at a pizza place in town," Amy continued. "They don't want to hire anyone who isn't planning on being here through summer break."

This time, Lee pictured Amy in some goofy-looking mini-skirt with a matching pizza hat, delivering bubbling hot pizza to a bunch of drooling fraternity boys. The popcorn started to smoke, and Lee quickly pulled it off the burner, turning her nose up at a cloud of acrid smoke that now filled the kitchen.

"Shit!"

"Mom, I need a place to live, and I'm only forty minutes away. It's not like you'll never see me again."

"That wasn't directed at you. I just burned the popcorn. Just a minute," she snapped.

She put down the phone and dumped the blackened kernels into the trash can, before waving a towel in the air to dissipate the smoke. She put the pot back on a cold burner. With resignation, she took the phone and went to sit at the table. The dog took the cue to move over next to her. "Amy, I just don't want you making snap decisions. If you sign a lease, you're stuck. Can you be sure Maddie will be there all summer, too?"

"Maddie already has a job at the university bookstore that runs through the summer. It'll be okay, Mom. Trust me."

How many times had she heard that phrase? The last time was when Amy had just rescued an orphaned German Shepherd. Lee sighed and patted the dog on the head. Her daughter was pulling away and it hurt.

"What kind of deposit do they want?"

"They want first and last month's rent and a $100 cleaning deposit. That's pretty standard, too. I'll need about $600."

Lee merely grunted. "Okay. I'm good for it. You can tell them you'll pick it up this weekend when you pick up the dog."

"Thanks, Mom. I'll be home around noon on Sunday."

"Not Saturday?"

"Well, there's a big party up here Saturday night with some of the kids in the Education Department. I'll be home Sunday."

"Then you're here for only half a day."

"Mom!" Amy whined, and Lee knew she was holding on too tightly.

"Okay," she cut off the complaint with a raised voice. "See you Sunday. Just make sure you come with a leash."

They hung up, and Lee went back to the stove to finish the popcorn. A few minutes later, she had a large bowl filled with plain popcorn and was starting on the butter when the phone rang again. She answered it with a cube of butter cupped in her hand.

"Hey," Patrick's voice greeted her. "I'm sorry about what happened at breakfast this morning."

After Amy's phone call, Lee was hardly in the mood to deal with her brother. "Don't worry about it."

"Well, I thought I'd bring some stuff over after rehearsal tonight. Maybe we could talk then. I'd like to help."

"I won't be here. I have to work."

"What are you doing on a Friday night?"

"We're doing a photo shoot at Green Valley Lumber Company."

"So, no date."

"Patrick! I have to go."

"What time is the photo shoot scheduled?"

She became impatient. "Not until eleven o'clock, so I'll be there late. Marion is coming over in a few minutes to help me work out some things. So, come on over, and we can catch up tomorrow."

She hung up and took a deep breath. She took the wrapping off the butter before placing it into a small pan. As it began to melt, she thought about Patrick with a twinge of remorse. Patrick, the habitual peacemaker, would probably follow her to the sawmill. Oh well, so be it. She knew she was being overly sensitive, but she'd had a lot to deal with lately. She'd apologize to him later.

The doorbell rang, interrupting her thoughts. Lee turned off the burner and placed the large bowl of popcorn on the counter, pointing a finger at the dog.

"Don't even think about it."

Marion was at the door with one arm wrapped awkwardly around an easel and the other clutching a bottle of wine. A large erase board leaned up against the door.

"Sorry I'm late, but I brought props."

"I can see that. Here, let me help you."

Lee grabbed the white board and wine and stepped back to let her inside. Marion set the easel up in the living room, while Lee hung her coat in the closet.

"I'm just finishing the popcorn. Come into the kitchen."

"Smells like charcoal," her friend teased.

They entered the kitchen to find Soldier guarding the snack bowl.

"When did you get a dog?"

"I didn't. She's leaving this weekend as soon as Amy finds her a home."

Lee went to the stove, while Marion sat at the table. Soldier abandoned the popcorn to greet the new visitor. Marion stroked her head, while her tail fanned the room in appreciation.

"She's charming. You should keep her. You could use some companionship now that Amy's gone. And some protection," she emphasized with a raised eyebrow.

"I don't think so," Lee answered. She relit the stove and played with the melting butter. "I'm not really a dog person anymore."

"Anymore?"

"I had a dog once, a long time ago. I'm not really in a position to take care of an animal right now."

"Nonsense. You just said good-bye to a teenager. What's the difference? In fact, a dog would be easier. They don't talk back."

Lee crossed to the counter to pour the butter over the popcorn just as the phone rang. Lee asked Marion to get it.

"It's someone named Jenny," she said.

"Could you just take a message," Lee asked.

While Marion wrote a note, Lee opened a cupboard to find the cheese stuff she had promised earlier that day. She grabbed an orange colored bottle the size of a small saltshaker and sprinkled it over the popcorn and then stirred it up. Then, she pulled two wineglasses out of a cupboard and asked Marion, "How are you at opening wine bottles?"

"Great, given the right tools, which I have right here," Marion said, handing Lee the note she'd written. She reached into the large square pocket of her brightly quilted jacket and pulled out a bottle opener. With a little twist of her wrist, the cork popped. "There, you see?" she said as she grabbed the glasses from Lee. "Shall we?"

Lee reached for two bowls and the popcorn and they headed for the living room.

Lee was beginning to feel energized, as if she were within reach of the finish line of an important race. By the end of the evening, she hoped they would be able to put the final piece of the puzzle in place. Then, she could go to the police.

She placed the popcorn on the coffee table and began to fill the bowls, while Marion poured the wine.

"I'd better get some napkins," Lee said, starting back to the kitchen.

"Do you have a marking pen?"

"Yeah, I'll get it."

Lee ducked into her study to find the marking pen and wrinkled her nose at the smell of burnt popcorn. She pulled up the sash window that looked onto the back porch to let in fresh air, and then rummaged through a desk drawer to find a thick black marking pen. When she returned to the living room, Marion had placed the erase board horizontally on the easel. She looked up when Lee came back.

"Well, aren't we professional?" she quipped.

"Hardly," Marion laughed as she stepped up to the board. "Did you find a pen?"

Lee handed her the marking pen, and Marion drew a line across the top from left to right. Above it she wrote the headings, "Facts, Suspicions, and Research." She drew a vertical line down the left side of the board.

"How's that look?"

Lee sat cross-legged on the sofa, a bowl of popcorn in her lap. "It's as good a place to begin as any. Let's begin with facts."

Marion lifted her glass of wine off the table and took a sip. "Okay, let's start with Diane. Tell me what you know about Diane that's significant."

Marion stood poised and ready to write. Lee considered for a moment and then began.

"Well, Diane was an absolute perfectionist, to a fault. That's a fact."

Marion looked at her with eyebrows raised.

"Believe me, it's pertinent. Just put it down."

Lee also instructed Marion to add the typos in the suicide note and all the information about the diabetic cat, insulin, and syringes. Lastly, she had Marion add a column called Crime Scene.

With her wine glass in one hand and pen in the other, Marion finished writing all of the facts on the board and then began to sit down when Lee stopped her.

"Wait! Put 'vase' under Suspicion in the crime scene row. Something fishy happened with the vase that Diane usually kept on her coffee table. It was there earlier that evening and gone when Amy and I found the body."

Marion complied. When she finished, she perched on the arm of a chair and took a swig of wine. "Did you find anything of consequence when you were there the other day?"

"I found a lab report."

Marion's eyes lit up. "What does a lab report have to do with anything?"

Lee took a deep breath before responding. "Bud Maddox works in the lab."

"So?"

"I think he might have been blackmailing people by running phony lab reports."

Marion stopped with her wine glass inches from her mouth. "How?"

The adrenaline started to pump as Lee began to explain. "I met with both the lab director and a lab technician today. What I pieced together is that someone could run phony lab reports and use them for a variety of illegal purposes."

Marion just stared at her for a moment. "And you think the lab report you found at Diane's was one of those?"

"I don't know. I didn't know what it was at the time, so I didn't read it. It was in a bathroom drawer, and her condominium was broken into the other day. It was ransacked as if someone was looking for something, so I'm not sure it's even still there. And, as you know, my house was broken into, too."

Her voice trailed away as her mind raced back to that night. Perhaps that was what Bud was looking for. Perhaps he thought Lee had found the lab report at Diane's and brought it home. That would mean he'd known she had visited the condo the night of the funeral.

"You okay, Lee?" Marion's voice pierced the haze of thoughts whirling around in Lee's head. "You look a bit green."

"Sorry," she said, shaking her head. "I just got a chill."

Lee got up to open a blanket chest next to the fireplace. She pulled out her favorite afghan. "I did find something else, though," she said, sitting down and pulling the afghan across her lap. "A chip from the missing vase. It was under a throw rug that had been placed under the coffee table."

"So, you were right, it had been broken?"

Marion turned to the board. Under Suspicion, she wrote *vase broken - by whom?* Then she drew an arrow extending into the Research column, and finally, wrote *broken chip* in the Facts column.

"Stay there," Lee continued. "There's more. The throw rug had been moved to cover up a deep gouge in the floor."

"A gouge that could have been caused by a vase being smashed on the floor?" Marion speculated.

"Exactly. The gouge in the floor wasn't there before. I couldn't prove it, but I'm positive it wasn't. Diane had just had her floors refinished."

Marion noted the information on the board, and then said, "This is pretty incredible." With her long fingers wrapped around the wineglass, she slowly sank onto the arm of her chair.

"I wasn't kidding this afternoon."

"I know. I guess I just didn't know how much information you actually had."

"You still want to help?"

The look on Marion's face betrayed her doubts. This was no longer a lark − two friends playacting at being investigators. A long moment stretched between them until Marion made a decision.

"Let's keep going. What does Pauline Bates have to do with all of this?"

The bushes near the window scraped against the glass making both women look up.

"There's a wind coming up," Lee said, standing up and crossing to the window.

She pulled the curtain aside and gazed out at the clear night. The moon shone brightly across the lawn and sounds of music drifted from across the street where a number of cars were parked. She felt relieved when she saw only a VW bus, a brown pickup truck, and a beat-up old station wagon. She frowned at the brown pickup, realizing she'd seen one just like it several times over the past few days. She paused a moment, trying to remember if she knew anyone who drove one. Finally, she shrugged and let the drapes close. At least the tan sedan was gone.

"Patrick and I went to the Bates' party the other night," she said, remembering Marion's question about Pauline Bates.

"Fortunately, I was busy and couldn't make it." Marion poured another glass of wine.

Lee twisted to look at her friend. "Have you ever been through that house?"

"Can't say I've had the pleasure," she said, grabbing a handful of popcorn.

"I'm not sure I can say it was a pleasure. I wandered upstairs and went into what I thought was the master bedroom."

"I've heard weird stories about how Mrs. Bates' mother disappeared. Was she stuffed and mounted on the wall?"

"No," Lee smiled. "But the room was filled from stem to stern with cats."

"Live cats?" Marion asked in astonishment.

"No. Figurines, stuffed animals, prints, enameled boxes, pillows. You name it. Some of the things were obviously expensive collectibles, but others were cheap, trashy looking things. I was just about to leave, when Pauline was just there, right in front of me, glaring at me. Then, she ordered me to go."

"Okay, but I still don't get how she's connected to Diane's death."

"She was wearing a black dress and a long black scarf. There was a woman at the graveyard just like that. I couldn't see her well because she was watching from a distance, and she had on a black hat and sunglasses."

"That's a pretty far stretch. A lot of women have black dresses and scarves, especially for funerals."

"I know. You just had to be there. I have a very strong feeling she was at the cemetery and that she's involved in this somehow."

"Well, I know I shouldn't be editing what we put on the board, but I think we need more than that to go on where Pauline is concerned."

Lee returned to the sofa, pulling her legs up underneath her. "She's just so weird. She actually makes the hair on the back of my neck stand on end."

Marion offered more wine to Lee. Lee waved her away.

"I did make a few phone calls today," Marion began. "I don't know that I learned anything of value. Certainly nothing that would connect her to Diane."

"How about Bud Maddox?"

"No," she confirmed. "Pauline has lived at home forever. She's never worked until recently. She graduated with a degree in economics, like her dad, but never held a job in the field. No one's ever seen her out on a date. She doesn't have any friends that she's seen with regularly. However, I found out two significant things. She volunteers one day a week at the blood bank."

Lee sat up. "The blood bank? So, she would have access to syringes."

"Well, I suppose." Marion looked doubtful again. "She also just took a job at the University and is working in the library."

Something in Lee's mind clicked. "Wait a minute. Who holds the University's occupational health contract?"

Marion looked confused. "I have no idea."

"I'll bet Twin Rivers does!" Lee announced with jubilation.

"I don't get it."

Lee was sitting forward now. "Don't you see? You guys all have to have drug tests before going to work, don't you?"

"Hell, I don't know. I've worked there for twenty years. They didn't give drug tests back then. I've never had one."

"Well, I bet new employees do. And they'd come to our hospital, our lab, for the test."

"I still don't get it."

Lee was up at the board now. She took the pen and began writing as she talked. "Bud Maddox is a lab technician." She wrote this under the heading of Facts and added *Pauline Bates - drug test?* Then she drew an arrow from the Suspicion column to the Research column. "I'll need to check this out."

"Don't you think that's a slim connection? So what if she had her blood drawn by Bud Maddox?"

"Maybe they hit it off."

Marion nearly choked on a mouthful of popcorn. "You've got to be kidding. You met her. She'd be lucky to hit it off with Andy Warhol."

"He's dead."

"My point exactly," Marion smiled grimly.

"There's got to be something." Lee's eyes lit up. "What about the cat connection?"

"What cat connection?"

"Pauline Bates is obviously obsessed with cats. Diane had a cat."

Marion rolled her eyes, "No, Lee. I don't think there *is* a 'cat connection.' After all, what could the connection be? They both had the same vet? Or, that Pauline is an animal activist and thought Diane was abusing her cat by giving it injections with the wrong size needles? I think we need to look for something else. Think. Give me some more."

Lee thought for a moment. "I told you I went to Medford. That's where Bud used to work. I found out he was asked to leave."

"He was fired?"

"Not fired, but something happened that made him leave under pressure. I couldn't find out the exact reason, but I did find out that it had something to do with a breach of confidentiality."

Marion wrinkled her forehead. "What could that mean?"

"It would have had to have been patient-related. But if he's doing something illegal now, maybe he was suspected of the same thing down there."

"Like doctoring the results of drug testing." Marion was catching on.

"Yes, just like that. There have been a few incidents recently where our night security has found secure rooms left open and computers on." Lee turned and scribbled all of this onto the board. "And there's one more thing. I'm not even sure if I should add this, but…"

"Go on. We need to get it all out if we're going to analyze it."

"I've received some very weird messages."

"Messages? From the birds?" Marion was serious.

"No. Through the mail. Two were written in verse, and one was the picture of a refrigerator. Each message was signed only 'a friend.'" She paused and leveled a solemn look at her friend. "I was up in the lab today and was told that one of the technicians was killed yesterday by a hit and run accident. Turns out she liked to write verse, and the refrigerator where they keep the lab samples was right next to her station."

Marion stopped in the middle of a sip of wine. Lee continued.

"It's certainly not conclusive, but I'd bet my last dollar there's a link." Lee sat in a wing-backed chair next to the easel. "I've been thinking a lot about this, Marion. What if Bud was doing something illegal and Diane found out about it? He might have killed her to keep her quiet. And somehow he linked up with Pauline Bates."

Marion's face appeared pale in the low light. She sat immobile in her chair, a full glass of wine held limply in one hand.

"It could have happened that way," Lee went on. "Perhaps this technician saw or heard something, and was trying to tell me about it."

"But why?" Marion asked. "Why you?"

Lee shrugged. "I don't know. Because I was her boss. Because people knew we were close friends."

Marion finally became animated again. "I don't know, Lee. It's just too fantastic. And how does Pauline Bates fit into it? Just because she's weird doesn't mean she murdered someone."

"I know," Lee answered in exasperation. "There are obviously a lot of holes to fill, but I feel like there's a picture being painted here."

"Painted by numbers, maybe," Marion offered cynically.

"Well, I may be painting by numbers, but I'm positive Bud Maddox had something to do with Diane's death. I'd stake my life on that! I had an encounter with him up in the lab today, and he practically admitted he was the one who broke into my house."

"You're kidding? Lee, you need to be more careful."

The phone rang, making them both jump. Lee got up to answer it as the sound of a truck engine flared outside and then faded away. She listened as a male voice spoke on the other end.

"Um, yes," she mumbled into the phone. "Well, okay. Fine. I'll be there. Thanks."

"What was that?"

"We have a photo shoot later tonight at one of the lumber mills. My public relations director can't be there, so I have to go. They just changed the location."

Marion looked at her watch. "What time is the shoot?"

"Eleven o'clock."

"Okay, we've got some time. Keep going. What else do you have?"

Lee explained about Vern Mathews, the life insurance, and the family's financial trouble. She finished by profiling Mathews' violent personality and abusiveness towards Carey.

"The man is a brute," Lee finished. "If he can hit his wife, maybe he could kill his sister-in-law. Maybe Diane knew about the abuse and confronted him. Maybe they got into an argument and her death was an accident of some kind."

Marion crossed her legs. "That would change things, wouldn't it?"

"Maybe, but I have one more piece of information about Mathews." She grabbed the note Marion had taken. "Jenny's phone call earlier was to tell me that Vern wasn't where he was supposed to be the night Diane died."

Marion looked suitably surprised. "Where was he?"

"He was supposed to be bowling, but he didn't show up, and he wasn't home. Carey was alone when the police called her."

"How much was the life insurance policy?"

"Only $25,000, but they're broke."

"I suppose crimes have been committed for much less." Marion stood up and wrote all of this on the board.

"I think you should add one more thing. He came to the condo today when I was there."

"You were alone with him?"

"He kicked me out and wasn't too nice about it. But the question is, what was he doing there in the middle of the afternoon on a workday?"

"What does he do for a living?"

"He's a drug rep for some pharmaceutical compa..." Lee stopped in the middle of her sentence, her facial muscles freezing into place. "Oh, my God! He represents a drug company. I never thought of that. He'd have access to the insulin and probably the syringes."

Marion looked like she'd just swallowed a spider. "I think it's time you told somebody about all of this, Lee."

Lee recovered from her surprise. "I don't have anything concrete, except maybe how the suicide note was printed and the insulin. Nothing that points directly to one person."

"What about the suicide note?"

"Jenny is positive it wasn't printed on Diane's printer. Something to do with how the paper holds the ink."

Lee went to the hallway and grabbed the suicide note off the hall table and presented it to Marion who read it quietly.

"It's the original note," Lee said. "You can see right here that there is an apostrophe missing, and she misspelled the word 'a lot'. A sloppy job by anyone's standard, but especially if you're a perfectionist like Diane."

"I agree," Marion said. "So someone printed this note on another printer and brought it with them." Marion looked up at Lee, adding, "Which means her death couldn't have been an accident."

"Right," Lee whispered.

The true gravity of what they had put together settled in the room like a fog. There was only the sound of the clock ticking slowly in the background.

Finally, Marion spoke. "I don't mind telling you this frightens me."

"I know," Lee said in a small voice. "Now that we've put it all together, it looks different than when it was just swimming around in my head."

Marion put the pen down. "I think you need to call the police. Tonight."

"I have to get ready to go to the sawmill."

"Seriously? After all of this, you're going to a sawmill tonight?"

Lee grimaced. "I have to work. There will be several other people there. I'll be fine."

Marion looked at her watch and sighed. "Okay, look, I have an early class in the morning, but we need to talk tomorrow. No ifs, ands, or buts. Tomorrow, you call the police."

"Deal. Thanks, Marion," Lee said as she stood up.

Marion held her hand up to wave off the show of gratitude.

"Don't thank me. I think I'm sufficiently scared shitless for one evening, and you should be, too." She stepped in close to her friend. "Not all of this is correct, but something's going on and you need to be careful." She looked Lee squarely in the eyes as she stepped around her to the closet. "I'll do a little more checking on Pauline Bates and the occupational health thing, but, really, Lee, it's time to bring in the police."

Lee leaned against the rear of the sofa. "I just hope they don't laugh me out of the precinct. Alan is my friend. I don't want him embarrassed."

"I think you can afford to take that chance. I'll leave the work in progress," she gestured toward the easel board. "And I'll give you a call tomorrow. We'll talk about how we can take this to the authorities."

"Okay," Lee acquiesced. "With you by my side, how can I go wrong?"

Marion only grunted and left. Lee looked back at the board. She didn't think they had nearly enough to complete the full picture, but she felt in her gut the board held at least one piece of information that could break the case open. Now if she could only figure out what it was.

CHAPTER TWENTY-EIGHT

Lee arrived at the lumber mill feeling oddly energized by the thought she might finally be close to the end of her journey. She would call the police the next day, meet with Sergeant Davis, and hopefully impart enough information to force him to launch a real investigation. And then her part in all of this could be done.

The small security building off Main Street was bathed in the light from large floodlights mounted to the top of two telephone poles. The huge lumber mill stood in the background, silhouetted against the night sky as if someone had painted it into the backdrop of a stage play. Tiny glow worms of light peeked out from various parts of the sprawling complex, and steam spewed from smoke stacks on the north side of the property. A string of railroad cars sat idle along a track framing a large empty parking lot that lay just past the gate.

Another guard sat at a small desk inside the hut. Lee rolled down her window letting in a cool breeze and tooted her horn. The guard poked his head out the door.

"May I help you?"

"I'm with Twin Rivers Hospital. We're doing a photo shoot here tonight."

He stepped to the car window, stuffing his hands into the pockets of his leather jacket.

"Right. You'll find your friends at the mill office on the south end of the yard."

"Actually, I believe plans have changed and we're going to the North Mill."

"The North Mill?"

He was young, overweight, with pudgy eyes that narrowed in confusion.

"Yes, I understand that mill isn't running tonight. Can you tell me how to get there from here?"

"Um...sure...let me grab a map." He returned to the guardhouse and grabbed a sheet of paper off his desk. When he returned, he rested the map on her open window.

"Here it is," he pointed. "You can drive around this building and head straight back. None of the log loaders are running tonight. Follow that yellow line past the log decks," he said pointing to a yellow stripe painted down the center of the pavement. "Turn left at the shavings bin, and you should be all right. Your photographer is already here, but I sent him to the other mill. You'll have to pick him up there. You should see his truck as you pass by."

His hand hesitated over the map as if he had something else to say, but he only smiled before going back inside. A moment later, the barrier lifted, and Lee drove through, eyeing the yellow stripe illumined by her headlights.

"Follow the yellow brick road," she muttered, peering out the front window.

She drove slowly and followed the yellow line. As soon as she left the security building, she was engulfed in darkness. Large buildings waited quietly in the shadows along the route. Lights appeared and disappeared in one building, as if a ghost walked from room to room with a lit candle. Stacks of lumber rose out of the darkness and just as quickly disappeared again. They were replaced by another building with the word "Laminating Plant" painted across the door.

Lee continued to follow the yellow line like the track-powered cars in an amusement park ride. Finally, she slowed to a stop in front of a building where lights blazed, and the sound of heavy machinery reached through the closed windows. Several cars were parked outside. This had to be the South Mill, but where was Rupert's truck? A hundred feet beyond was a tall diamond-shaped apparatus that was labeled on the map as the 'Shavings Bin.' She drove up to it and turned. Moments later, she pulled up to the North Mill.

The North Mill was equipped with only two small security lights, which did little more than outline the front door. Andrew hadn't explained why the photo shoot had been changed when he'd called earlier, but Rupert's blue Ford pickup sat out in front. Somehow he'd gotten the message. Lee stepped out of the car and immediately wrapped her arms around her for warmth. She wore an insulated vest, but there was a distinct chill to the air. She glanced at the sky, which was clear, but the air was dense with moisture. She hated damp cold.

A crisp breeze flooded her nose with the rich smells of sawdust, while sounds of compressed air oozed from the mill like a resting steam engine. Across the yard, the machinery of the South Mill clanked in a muffled cadence, giving Lee some comfort. She pictured the logs being grabbed, turned, and sawn as they proceeded on their merry way to becoming planks of finished lumber.

A scuffling sound from somewhere in the darkness made her freeze.

She turned and squinted into the shadows. It could have been a rodent. There had to be tons of them around here, but the hairs on the back of her neck told her it was time to go inside.

She quickly approached the steel door and pulled it open, trading the darkened parking lot for the shallow light of the mill's ground floor. Work lights were set high into the ceiling, spilling light only onto the areas directly below them. The monstrous equipment that had been so busy earlier in the day now slumbered quietly. She found a staircase leading to a familiar set of catwalks and started to climb, thinking about how much she wanted to be home and in bed.

Ping!

She stopped and listened.

Where had that come from? She strained to locate the sound's origin, but could only hear the compressed air escaping into the night outside. Perhaps she'd merely kicked a nail off the stairs. A chill rippled across her shoulders, and she grabbed the handrail to finish the climb. She was anxious now to find Rupert.

A light shone through the window of the filing room, and she opened the door with a rush. One look at the tripod and camera set up at the other end of the room, and she began to chastise herself for magnifying the sounds native to a large factory at night.

But the room was quiet. And there was no Rupert.

Shit! Where was he?

Lee wandered around for a moment, impatient to get the photo shoot over with. A thumping sound drew her attention to the small workroom off to the right. She headed in that direction. Perhaps Rupert was searching for a better place to set up, or maybe someone was working late. Either way, she craved contact with a real person.

She hurried past the open trap door and entered a workroom the size of a single car garage. It was the one she had almost stepped into that afternoon. A wide worktable equipped with a built-in anvil ran down the center of the room. Counters lined opposite walls. A pegboard hung above the counter to her left and was filled with shop tools. At the end of the left hand counter was a tall cupboard that jutted out into the aisle by eighteen inches, its door ajar. There was an office at the far end of the room, with slivers of light peeking out from behind mini-blinds.

Lee didn't know Rupert well, but didn't think he'd prowl around someone's office. She was about to retreat, when a muffled voice made her think someone was on the phone. Perhaps whoever was working late would know where Rupert was. She started up the aisle at a fast clip. Three feet from the office, a man stepped from behind the cupboard into her path.

"Hello, Lee."

Lee's hand flew to her chest. "God, Andrew, you nearly scared me to death."

"Really? I must say, that would have been far easier." A slow grin spread across his face.

"What?" she muttered.

Andrew's normally hazel eyes were liquid masses. And his mouth had frozen into a half smile. A long moment passed between them before Lee realized she was in trouble. Andrew was VP of Operations at the hospital. Why was he here for a photo shoot?

"What are you doing here, Andrew?" she whispered, feeling a sour taste in her mouth. "Where's Rupert? Where's the nurse?" Lee raised her voice, hoping whoever was in the office would hear her.

"Rupert is indisposed at the moment. And the nurse won't be coming."

Andrew hadn't moved and held his right hand behind his back.

"What do you mean?"

Lee found herself glancing at his arm, wondering what he was hiding. His dark eyes gleamed, and Lee's body temperature began to rise. This wasn't the Andrew she knew. His voice was duller than his normal monotone; it was absolutely flat. And there was no animation in his face. And then, there was that dark stare. He hadn't broken his gaze, and she was sure he hadn't blinked. She felt she was looking into the face of a complete stranger.

Just above a whisper, he said, "I have to get rid of something."

Alarms screamed in her head, and she became acutely aware of the small room closing in around her. There were no windows, only the door behind her and the one to the office. If she could make a clean break to the rear, she might get away. Her heart banged in her chest, and she felt her legs might give out at any moment.

"I don't understand," she said, stalling for time.

Andrew finally stepped forward, closing the space between them to just a few inches. His expression was anything but friendly. A voice in her head yelled, "Run!"

Lee grabbed the tall cupboard door and swung it open, slamming it directly into Andrew's face. She turned and lunged for the open door behind her.

But Bud Maddox had just stepped through the door at the far end of the saw room. Lee slid to a stop. She couldn't handle both of them. Panicked, she shoved the heavy workroom door closed and flipped the lock into place. Without thinking, she whirled around and grabbed one of the picaroons from the wall next to her, and then spun around and pressed her back against the door. Andrew stopped short, only a few feet away, a trickle of blood visible at his left nostril. He used his sleeve to wipe it away.

"You shouldn't have done that," he scowled. "Closing the door will keep Maddox out, but I'm still here."

Something slammed against the door, and Maddox called out.

"Hey, bitch! Open up."

"Go around," Andrew called out. "I'll take care of things in here."

"I don't think so," Lee threatened.

She took a step forward, holding the picaroon out and flashing the vicious tip at Andrew. But he merely smiled and brought forward his left hand. In it was a small caliber pistol. Lee looked at the pistol and then at the contemptuous look on Andrew's face.

"You killed Diane," she exhaled.

Andrew chuckled. "No, but I am going to kill you. You're going to have a nasty little accident. Through the trap door in the other room."

"What makes you think I'll willingly step through the trap door?" she asked, feeling a giddy sense of power as the adrenalin flooded her veins.

"It's that or a bullet in your head. At least you have a choice. That's more than Diane had," he said, smiling.

That was all it took. Too much caffeine. Too little sleep. And this man's arrogance. Lee snapped.

"You son-of-a-bitch!" she screamed, swinging the pick fully at his face.

Andrew jumped back and released a round of ammunition that slammed into the wall. Lee charged on, swinging the weapon back and forth like a two-handed sword. She forced Andrew backwards up the narrow aisle. As the pick swung to the left, it hooked a pair of pliers off the pegboard and sent them flying. Andrew ducked, but Lee kept swinging. Andrew couldn't get off a shot. Finally, as she came to the end of the table, she swung the pick back and it launched a small hammer on its return.

The hammer whizzed across the aisle and hit Andrew right in the face. He cried out and stumbled. With a grunt, Lee turned towards him and swung the pick all the way back in hopes she could finish the job. But she'd moved in front of the long cupboard door, and the sharp tip of the picaroon got caught in the wood, almost yanking her off her feet. Frenzied, she turned and pulled on the long wooden handle, but it wouldn't budge.

"Shall we take a walk now, Lee?" Andrew slurred behind her.

Lee stopped pulling and glanced over her shoulder. Her breath was coming in ragged gasps. Andrew had regained his footing and held his left hand up to his left eye, which was closed and bleeding. His mouth was also bleeding, and his facial muscles were twisted in pain. But his right hand still held the gun, and it was pointed at her.

"Why don't you just shoot me?" she asked, breathing hard.

"Like I said, you need to have an accident." His voice reflected the pain he was in. "Let's go."

Lee's heart raced, and the buzzing in her ears had returned. But she didn't move. She just watched him.

This horrible little man would not best her, at least not without a fight. Counting on Andrew's arrogance to blur his judgment, she turned away from him and placed her foot against the cupboard. With a loud grunt, she pulled until her muscles burned. With a crack, the door suddenly broke, releasing the pick. It shot off the wall, swinging Lee in a half circle. The pick slammed into Andrew's gun hand, cracking his wrist. The gun flew under the workbench on the opposite side of the room, and the pick slammed into the anvil, nearly shaking Lee's hands loose.

Lee steadied the weapon. Her arms ached, but she raised the pick over her head. As she did, Andrew scurried to the other side of the table, clutching his wrist. She was about to go after him, when he grabbed a ball peen hammer. Even injured, she thought, he was still a threat, and she hesitated.

She spied a door out of the corner of her eye. It was hidden by an overly large cupboard on the far wall to her left. She looked at the door, and then looked at Andrew. With only the flicker of a thought, she was through the new door in a flash and back on the catwalk. Most likely, she was on the opposite side of the filing room and prayed she wouldn't run into Maddox.

She lurched forward. The metal walkway swayed and rattled as she ran, making her cringe. But there was no way to escape quietly. She had to keep going. She rounded the back corner of the filing room and ducked under a conveyor belt where she encountered a staircase. She didn't know where it led, but gripped the handrail and propelled herself down, holding the pick in the crook of her elbow. Five feet from the bottom, the pick slipped and caught in the railing. Lee was catapulted the last few feet, landing face down in the sawdust. The pick dropped over the hand rail and out of sight.

Stunned, Lee raised herself to her knees and spit out sawdust and dirt. She glanced around a little dazed. Overhead pipes and machinery surrounded her in deep shadow. A path opened up to her left and extended back into the mill. Perhaps she could find the door she'd entered through and escape to her car. Her fingers touched the pocket of her vest where her car keys lay hidden.

The thought of safety motivated her to get up and sprint carelessly forward. She ran directly into a heavy valve that stuck out from a huge cylinder. It bounced her backwards, and a searing pain shot through her forehead. She teetered for a moment, thinking she actually saw stars. Before she knew it, she was on her hands and knees again, feeling like she might throw up.

She stayed there, trying to swallow the bile that billowed up in her throat. When it subsided, she got her left foot underneath her, and was about to push herself up, when her right hand brushed against something near the bottom step. It was the handle of the picaroon. Her fingers laced around it, just as a voice behind her sent chills to her very core.

"I kind of like you on your hands and knees in the dark," Maddox chuckled.

Every one of Lee's muscles tightened at the sound of his voice and an intense feeling of hatred swelled inside her. She remained in a crouched position, one knee on the ground, one foot planted underneath her. Then she twisted away from Maddox and toward the pick. Slowly, she drew the lethal weapon towards her, counting on the fact her movements would be hidden in the dark. She concentrated through her dizziness, trying to calculate the space available to her. She would have one chance at this. That was all. Just then, Andrew called out above and she paused.

"Bud! Where are you?"

Lee could tell that Bud was directly behind her. She secured her left foot, and then reached over slowly with her left hand, using her body to block her movement.

"We're down here," Maddox shouted back.

In a single fluid movement, Lee swung the pick around at full force. Maddox had pivoted towards the stairs, and the pick slammed into his back, imbedding itself a good six inches. He froze in place, a wheeze escaping his lungs. His reaction was hidden in the dark, but the gurgling sound that came from his throat told her she'd at least hit a lung, if not other major organs. A moment later, he toppled forward onto the stairs, his head rebounding off one of the steps with a metallic twang.

Lee stood absolutely still, panting, and feeling an odd sense of detachment. She'd just killed a person. A man she detested, but someone she knew. Yet, she had no remorse. She didn't even feel anger anymore. He was just gone.

"Bud?" Andrew called again.

It was time to go.

She had a raging headache. Blood ran down her forehead, and her vision was a bit blurry. But she knew she had to get moving.

She turned and moved forward, carefully this time, using her hands as buffers. Within a few feet, she came out into an open area with only the barest amount of light. To her right were the stairs they had taken down to the chipper. She tried to picture their short tour that afternoon, and remembered there was a ramp down there that lead up to an exit on this floor. She raised her head and squinted into the darkness. Tucked behind some large mechanical apparatus about a hundred feet ahead of her, was the faint green glow of an exit light. Her heart fluttered. She had a chance.

As quickly as she could, she made her way towards the exit. She was more unsteady on her feet than she realized, and her progress was slow. Behind her, she heard the catwalk rattle, then the stairs. Andrew would find Maddox. She had to speed this up.

The word, "Shit!" echoed behind her.

"Goddamn it...I'm coming, Lee! I'm right behind you."

Lee tried to run, but the world kept tilting. She had just about made it to the exit, when she banged her left shoulder into a conveyor belt. The noise was loud enough to alert the Fifth Infantry, so she decided to make a run for the door. She willed her legs into a lopsided gate and zigzagged around machinery until she hit the exit bar on the door. No alarm sounded, but she emerged into the foggy night, gulping down the sweet fresh air.

CHAPTER TWENTY-NINE

The fresh air filled her lungs, helping to clear her head. She was at the back of the mill. A chain-link fence ran along the property in front of her. Beyond it were two parked cars – a blue Honda Civic and a brown pick-up truck. To her left and right were more buildings and alleyways. She didn't think it made much difference, so she stumbled down the stairs and lurched to her right. She began to run with more confident strides, practically skidding around the corner.

She headed for the front of the building and her car. Low clouds had moved in, blocking the moon and bringing in a heavy mist that hung between the two buildings. The mist obscured the security light at the far end of the building, so that it glowed like the beacon from a lighthouse. She couldn't see well, but began to jog toward the light. That's when the sound of tires on gravel broke the silence, and headlights flashed across the alley. Someone had pulled up to the front of the mill. The sound of a car door slamming confirmed it.

Lee skidded to a stop. Who was this? No one else was scheduled for the photo shoot. That meant it had to be someone Andrew had called out to for help. Lee backed up against the wall of the opposite building, hiding in the shadows. Now what? She could wait until that person went inside and then run for her car. But when a door slammed from behind her, she knew her options had just evaporated. Andrew had followed her out the back door.

Her hands began searching the walls on either side of her. When her fingers looped around a door jam, her heart leapt. Lee grabbed for the door handle. To her relief, she found the door unlocked. She ducked inside, closing it behind her as quickly and quietly as possible. She moved blindly into the musty interior of a room filled with boxes and metal canisters. She groped in front of her, looking for a place to hide, her feet sliding over a dirty, cement floor. When a shadow flicked past the outside window, she panicked and began to look for another exit.

A crack of light underneath a set of barn-like doors, and the sound of a motorized conveyor belt drew her forward. Maybe someone was working in there. Lee grabbed the large metal handle of one door and pulled it sideways. The door slid open, exposing a two-story room she recognized as the fuel house. At least this was familiar territory. Masterson had said someone in the boiler room operated the crane on a twenty-four hour basis, so with luck, she might get his attention.

A blast of the fragrant fresh bark hit her as she stepped inside and bark chips continued to drop from the ceiling, landing in the huge pile in the far right corner. She searched the wall to her left for the camera she assumed the operator used to move the crane. But the crane was quiet now, positioned in the middle of the room like a dinosaur on display. A momentary panic seized her as she contemplated the possibility she was still alone out here.

Across the room was the door Masterson had used to exit through that afternoon, along with a floor-to-ceiling roll-up loading door. Both exits were closed, but her only chance of escape seemed to lie in that direction. She would have to zigzag around the crane and the end of the chain to the door. Once she made the commitment, she would be stuck. Either the door was unlocked, or it wasn't. And if it wasn't, she'd be a sitting duck in here. There was no place to hide unless she wanted to bury herself in the bark pile.

The grinding noise of the chain grated on her nerves like the dull clanging sound of a pipe organ out of tune. When Andrew suddenly laughed behind her, she whipped around with a gasp.

"Too bad, Lee. You were almost home-free."

Lee hardly recognized her fellow administrator anymore. He looked like some misshapen monster. His left eye was swollen shut and had turned an ugly eggplant color. Blood oozed from the corner of his eye and ran down his cheek, and his upper lip was swollen. Spittle glistened as he spoke, and his right arm was bent at his waist as he tried to cradle his broken wrist. But the gun was firmly seated in his left hand and pointed directly at her.

"You killed Maddox," he said matter-of-factly. "No great loss. All I have to do is create a new scenario." He attempted a lopsided smile. "Lee Vanderhaven went crazy and attacked both of us. I had to kill her. I had no choice."

"No one's going to believe that."

"Maybe not. But I'll think of something. I'm better at this than you think, Lee. Let's go," he gestured with a flick of his wrist.

Her feet didn't move. She couldn't go with him. It wasn't in her nature. She glanced behind her, wondering if she could make it to the door.

"Don't even think about it," he snarled.

Andrew had moved up behind her and was looking past her at the drag chain with a kind of reverence.

"This place is amazing," he whispered. "So efficient. The hospital ought to work this well."

"If it doesn't, it's your fault," Lee shot at him. "You're in charge of Operations."

He turned to look at her with his good eye.

"You think I have any influence over anything? Martha makes all the decisions. It's Martha this, and Martha that," he sneered. "She just wants someone to take the heat so she doesn't have to. The doctors hate her, you know. There are rumblings of a vote of no confidence. That would surprise her," he chortled. "The great and mighty Martha Jackson."

He took a step to the right and gazed again at the bark pile and chain. His expression made her skin crawl; she could see he was devising some sort of plan. Lee took a step forward so that she was further in his blind spot. It was time to take a chance. She suddenly darted toward him, and then around his back. He jerked awkwardly trying to follow her, swinging the gun to the left. But by the time he'd made a full circle, she had made a run for the door.

She skidded around the crane just as a bullet ricocheted off the bucket. She flinched, but kept running. She circled around the end of the guard rail and bounded up the few steps that led to the door. The door was locked. She banged on it frantically, and Andrew's cruel laughter rang out behind her.

"Too bad, Lee. Caught like a mouse in a trap!"

A bullet slammed into the wall right next to her, sending cement chips flying. She ducked and jumped off the steps and tried the metal roll-up door. Locked!

"Give up, Lee. I'll make it quick and easy," he shouted.

Lee turned, breathing hard. There was no exit other than past Andrew, who now stood on the far side of the guard rail. Thank God he was right-handed. Between his broken wrist and bad eye, she'd been lucky. But he was beginning to move along the guard rail, albeit slowly. If he got too much closer, her luck would run out.

She turned to her left and spied a pipe ladder mounted into the cement wall. It led to the rake carriage above. While Andrew negotiated his way around the chain, she ran for the ladder and began to climb, hand over hand. The steel rods were cold to the touch, but she made it to the top and stepped onto the carriage before Andrew could stop her.

"That won't make a difference, Lee," he called from below. "Bullets can still reach up there. Wanna see?"

He raised the gun and fired. The bullet came frighteningly close to where Lee stood, forcing her to step back. Her foot slipped over the edge and she grabbed the railing to catch herself. The entire rake carriage shook precariously. With caution, she stepped further onto it, trying to find a way to hide from Andrew. But there were breaks in the planks, and he was almost directly below her now. A lucky shot could kill just as easily as a well-placed one. She had to figure something out.

She stepped to the far side of the platform and carefully moved forward to where the planks were solid and blocked her from view. Just then, a bullet smashed through a floor plank and nicked her earlobe, sending a shock wave through her entire body. She ducked down and grabbed her right ear.

Damn! Her ear burned with pain, and blood flowed freely down her neck into her blouse. She had no way to stop the flow other than to put pressure on the injury, so she backed up against the crane and squatted down. She took off her vest, wadded it up, and pressed it against her neck and ear.

"C'mon, Lee. I hit you, didn't I?"

She waited him out. If she didn't move, maybe he wouldn't know exactly where she was. But then she glanced down and realized there was a gap between the carriage and the crane. She could see him. He had moved to the far end of the crane and was looking up at the carriage, trying to find her. He riveted his head one way and then the other, scanning the platform with his good eye.

It was eerie watching him. He shuffled around like a zombie, unsteady on his feet because he couldn't see well. Suddenly, he saw her and lurched forward, bringing up the gun. But he didn't see the base of the crane, and his right foot caught underneath it, throwing him to the ground. The gun flew out of his hand, landing on the floor and sliding under the guard rail, towards the chain. It stopped only a few inches from where the drag chain disappeared into the small opening in the floor.

Lee cursed. Why couldn't it have just gone in? When Andrew realized the gun had stopped just in time, he hooted.

"Oooooh, too bad, Lee. Did you see that? I almost lost it. But fate has saved me once again," he cackled.

He stumbled to his feet and scuttled over, crablike, to where the gun lay. He looked up to where Lee watched him, displaying a leering grin. When he turned back, he reached out with his good hand, but miscalculated the distance and bumped the butt of the gun before he could grab it. The gun tipped over the edge and into the hole.

Andrew froze, empty fingers outstretched. A full five seconds passed. Then, he threw back his head and howled. The desperation in that cry chilled Lee to the bone. She leaned back against the crane, shivering.

A moment later, she heard something that stopped her heart. Andrew was climbing the ladder. She shoved herself up, still putting pressure on her ear. The top of Andrew's head appeared at the far end of the carriage as he struggled up the ladder using only one hand. Lee's heart began to race.

She looked around again, wondering how the hell she could get off this thing. Even though the crane extended to the floor, there wasn't any way to climb down. But underneath the carriage, the two wheel tracks ran the length of the building, one on each side of the crane. The rake carriage was attached to them by steel wheels. One of the beams was about ten feet to Lee's right — in between her and Andrew. Without a second thought, she dropped the vest, ripped off her shoes and socks, and ran.

She had just thrown a leg over the railing of the platform above the cross beam, when the rake carriage shook. She glanced to her right. Andrew was standing at the end of it. She was out of time. She swung the other leg over and started to climb down.

"Where are you going this time, Lee?"

Lee looked over at him. He reached behind him, and Lee panicked. Did he have a second gun? No. Instead, he brought forward the ball peen hammer. His eyes never left her face as he began to move towards her. She had to move, too, and fast.

The beam ran to the back wall where it intersected with the rest of the structure supporting the platform. If she was lucky, she might be able to slide down one of the support beams to the floor. It would be risky, and she might break something in the process, but she had no choice.

She climbed off the railing and onto a small ledge, grabbing onto a steel pipe for balance. She placed her left foot forward onto the beam and tested it. It was solid and nearly the same width as a competition balance beam. The balance beam had been her best sport, but the memory of the accident flashed into her mind, and she momentarily panicked. *No, not this time*, she stopped herself. There was no room for doubt right now. She shut it out.

She took a couple of tentative steps forward, focusing on the beam and allowing a familiar feeling of confidence to take over.

"You won't make it, you know," he said quietly from behind her. "You'll fall. You have to. It's too narrow, too slippery."

She paused. He could be right. Her heart was pounding, and one misstep would send her into the chain below. A glance past her toes made her stomach turn. The two-foot wide chain lumbered relentlessly across the floor to cascade into the black hole, disappearing to depths unknown. It would rip and tear her flesh apart, crushing bone and marrow.

She lifted her chin and took a deep breath. She'd be damned if she would die that way. She'd once bled through her socks just to prove a point. She wouldn't give up. She would focus on the back wall, hold her arms out to her side, and keep going.

With a grace that belied the situation, she placed one foot in front of the other, toes reaching out for the beam, and began to move again. All thoughts of the noisy, sawdust filled lumber mill faded away, and she was in the middle of a competition again. She could almost hear the hushed voices of the spectators around her and the voice of her coach in training, "*Don't look down, Lee. The floor isn't going anywhere, so you don't need to check on it.*"

Time slowed, and she was alone with the beam. She was almost a third of the way across when she heard Andrew whisper an expletive. Then something slammed into her right shoulder.

She flinched to the left as the ball peen hammer spun end over end to the back wall. A cry escaped her lips, and she started to fall, the world swirling around her. But years of training kicked in, and she immediately twisted her upper torso sharply to the right and grabbed the beam with both hands as she came down. She swung under the beam, her feet coming up on the other side. Her fingers looped around the lip of the track, allowing her to anchor herself so that she could jackknife back up. In an instant, she was lying across the beam on her stomach. A moment later, she'd swung her left leg up and over, and she was straddling it. The cold steel dug into her inner thighs, and her shoulder ached, but for the moment, she was secure.

She looked up at Andrew, her breathing coming in deep gulps. He glared at her, clearly unhinged. She had bested him once again. It took him only a moment to make a decision.

He grabbed the railing and hoisted himself over it, wincing when he bumped his wrist. He lowered himself awkwardly onto the small ledge that ran the width of the carriage, his face red with the strain. Without a word, he held onto the railing and lifted his foot and slammed it down onto the beam. The beam shook, and Lee was forced to lean forward and wrap her arms around it, struggling to keep her balance.

This seemed to please Andrew, so he did it again, harder.

"What's the matter, Lee? Having trouble holding on?"

He sniggered as he did it again and again. She was forced to hug the beam in order not to slide sideways, and he began to laugh.

"Maybe one more time. What d'you think? Send you into the jaws of death below."

As Lee hugged the beam, she glanced down. The chain and the small opening in the floor were right below her. She tightened her grip and her legs circling the beam. The unforgiving steel cut into her flesh.

"Enough!" Andrew screamed. "I'm done with you. This ends now!"

Lee lifted her head to watch him. Andrew turned and extended his good hand to the pipe Lee had used for balance. Once he was secured, he turned back to her, a fierce look of determination on his swollen features. He slowly lifted his knee chest high, ready to bring his foot down full force.

This would be it. She couldn't withstand that much of a jolt. She turned away as tears slipped from the corners of her eyes. It seemed she would die in this horrible place after all. She would never see Amy again. She would never hear Patrick laugh again. This awful little man, who had killed Diane, would kill her. And for what? She would never even know.

That's when a familiar sound rose above the clanging of the chain. Her head came up with a jerk.

It was the distant *"keer"* of a hawk. But how?

"Goodbye, Lee," Andrew screamed.

Andrew yanked his knee up as high as it would go and then slammed it down – just as something swooped in front of his face. That's all it took. Just half a second.

Andrew flinched.

Then his foot missed the beam.

His hand was pulled off the pipe behind him, and with a sickening scream, he fell away from the carriage. His head hit the ledge hard, as the fleeting shadow of a bird disappeared into the rafters.

Andrew landed on his back, crossways on the chain, right in between the guard rail. Blood gushed from his mouth. He lay still, too stunned, or too broken to move. His eyes were open, but they stared lifelessly at the ceiling. Lee thought he was dead, until she saw his fingers move.

He tried weakly to roll to one side, but one of the lugs on the chain caught suddenly on his jacket and began to drag him head first towards the opening in the floor. Lee gasped, feeling her stomach lurch. Andrew's legs twitched and his hands fluttered. He knew what was happening, but he couldn't move. His head had hit the ledge hard enough to cause real damage, and his back was likely broken. He was clearly disoriented and in pain, and seemed to have trouble getting air into his lungs.

But the chain didn't care. It continued to move him inch by inch, carrying him toward the hole like a passenger on a train. Lee remembered what Masterson had said; the hole was too small. A person wouldn't fit through it. It would rip Andrew apart.

"Get out of your jacket," Lee whispered, horrified. "Please...get out of your jacket!"

But it was too late. He couldn't hear her, and he was a mere inches from that black well of death. The pounding of the chain drowned out all other sounds, as Andrew seemed to surrender to his fate. The muscles in his face relaxed, and he looked directly up at Lee. As they made eye contact, for a brief moment, he looked like the man she'd once known.

Two seconds later, his left shoulder reached the opening in the floor, and Lee shut her eyes, sobbing uncontrollably. She turned away and tried to cover her ears. But she couldn't block the sounds as the chain began to feast on its victim. The air filled with wave after wave of Andrew's terrifying screams, until the chain was satiated, and the screams suddenly stopped.

CHAPTER THIRTY

Lee remained where she was, still clinging to the top of the beam. At some point her stomach had emptied the popcorn she'd shared with Marion earlier to create a nice starburst pattern in the sawdust below. Now that her stomach was quiet, Lee rested her cheek against the cold steel, arms wrapped tightly around its hard surface. Quiet sobs racked her body, and tears rolled down her face to form little puddles on the steel surface. The thought of Bud Maddox surfaced briefly. He was dead, with a picaroon embedded in his back. Andrew was dead, too. The chain had never stopped. It had never even slowed down. The events of the last hour stunned Lee. Life wasn't supposed to be like this. Friends weren't supposed to be murdered, and people you knew weren't supposed to be the murderers.

The clanging of the chain began to numb her brain, and her thoughts drifted. Images surfaced. First hazy, then so clear they seemed real. She was on the farm where Lee and Patrick had spent the summer when she was ten. Patrick and a friend were tossing stones at an overturned bucket next to the old red barn. Lee stood behind them, laughing, pressing her legs together to control the urge to pee. Finally, she warned the boys to stay away and ran behind the barn where she pulled down her pants and squatted in the brown grass. Laughter rang out behind her, and one of the boys yelled, *"God, look at the glare off that thing."* Lee screamed and pulled up her pants too soon, wetting the denim. The boys laughed harder, and she ran away in tears to climb an old oak tree behind the house hoping to hide. Later, Patrick sauntered across the yard calling her name, apologizing. Lee squeezed her eyes shut as if that would make her invisible, but Patrick's voice kept getting closer. Finally, she knew he stood in the grass just below her, but she kept her eyes closed, willing him to go away.

"Lee, I can see you."

He sounded so close, yet so far away. Like a dream. She opened one eye to look down into that handsome face, pinched with genuine concern at the foot of the tree. Then she closed it again.

"Lee, are you all right?"

She wouldn't give him the satisfaction of replying. She'd wait until he was gone, and then go inside to change out of her wet jeans.

"Lee!"

Lee's eyes fluttered open. Remarkably, Patrick stood below her in the sawdust, just as he had so many years before.

"Are you okay?" he asked again, a steely edge of concern in his voice.

Her eyes had trouble focusing, but when she looked again, Patrick really was there. Those days on the farm were gone.

"I'm not sure." Her husky voice wasn't much above a whisper. "I don't think I can get down."

"I'm coming up," he yelled.

It seemed like an eternity, but finally the carriage rattled.

"Lee, I'm here. I'll get you off. Hold on."

She tilted her head up, resting her chin on the beam. Patrick had found a thick rope somewhere and was climbing over the railing. He lowered himself onto the beam and then leaned back against the carriage. He slipped the rope off his shoulder and tied one end securely around the beam, making several knots. Then he took the other end and tied it into a small loop, yanking on it several times to test it. Finally, he wrapped his legs around the beam, threw the loose rope around his neck and slowly began to inch forward. It took Patrick only a minute or two to come within reach.

"Okay, you're going to have to help me a bit here."

Patrick held the small loop out for her to grasp. She didn't respond. Her eyelids closed again so she could rest and listen to the chain.

"Lee!" Patrick snapped. "Look at me!"

Her eyes snapped open.

"We both need to get off this beam. You have to concentrate. Extend your hand."

She looked at him, but didn't move.

"C'mon, Sis. Do it. Reach toward me."

It took every bit of energy she had, but she finally extended her hand along the beam. Patrick slipped the rope over her wrist and pulled the loop tight, making the rough strands of the rope cut into her skin.

"Okay, I hope you won't need it, but if you fall, it'll hold you. 'Course it might separate your shoulder, but…"

He tried a smile, but his upper lip quivered.

"Okay, now slide forward."

She still didn't move.

Just then, the distant blare of sirens made them both look up. Patrick quickly relaxed.

"It's the police. I called them when I found Maddox. But it will take them too much time to find us in here, so let's keep going. You need to get off this beam. Trust me, Lee. And keep looking at me. Now, move!"

She flexed her muscles to see if they would work. Then she began to inch forward. Keeping her legs and feet tightly wrapped around the beam, she scooted forward like she would if she were climbing a rope in gym class. Once her feet slipped on the beam, yanking her to one side, and she stopped in a panic, feeling the bile rise in her throat again. Patrick froze, too. He wasn't in a position to help and could only wait until she regained her composure.

"C'mon," he chided. "You can do it. You won a medal once for something that looked much harder than this."

The remark was enough to get a rise.

"Shut up," she snapped. "The closest you've been to a balance beam was walking a straight line when you got stopped for drunk driving."

Everything seemed to work in slow motion, and it was a painful journey. But she kept moving. Her brother inched backwards. When his feet touched the carriage behind him, he sat up, straddling the beam. He reached behind him to the same handhold Andrew had used, and with a strong right hand, pulled himself up the few inches to the carriage ledge where he waited for Lee.

She continued to inch forward, the clanking of the feed chain below matching her pace.

"You're almost there," he encouraged.

When she was within a few inches, he reached down and grabbed her wrist. Just the mere touch of his hand was enough to muffle the sound of the chain until it finally died away.

"I've got you."

He pulled her gently forward until she lay below him on the beam.

"I'm going to let go of your wrist now."

"No!" she cried.

"It's okay. You're still tied off. Sit up. I'm going to slide my arm around your back. Keep your left hand down to steady yourself."

She arched her neck to look into his eyes, fear spreading across her face.

"It's okay. Really."

Her eyes never left his face as she sat up, both hands resting in front of her, her muscles shaking and exhausted. Patrick still held onto the bar behind him and leaned forward to slide his left hand underneath her right armpit, keeping contact all the time until he'd encircled her with his full arm.

"C'mon, now. I'm going to lift up. You reach over my shoulders and grab the ledge. You'll have to pull yourself over me. Think you can do it?"

Her face was only inches from his. She knew she smelled of vomit, and her makeup had all but blackened her eyes. But she didn't care. More importantly, she knew Patrick didn't care.

"Yeah, I can do it," she said weakly.

"Okay, one, two, three."

On three, he pulled her off the beam. Patrick grunted as she reached behind him and grabbed the bar. With quivering muscles, she climbed over him and up and over the railing, collapsing into a heap on the other side. In one, swift movement, Patrick was by her side. He reached out and pulled the rope off her wrist before hugging her close.

"You're okay," he whispered.

Tears flowed and she began to shiver as her body released all the tension that had kept her alive. He just held her more tightly. They didn't say a word for several minutes. Finally, her tears stopped flowing. Then the shivering subsided. Finally, she leaned her head back against Patrick's shoulder, wiped her nose and sighed.

"Andrew fell into the chain," she whispered, catching a sob.

"I know. I saw," he said. "But you're okay. Don't think about him now."

Her shoulders shuddered, and she wiped her eyes.

"And I killed Maddox." she exhaled, grabbing his arm. "I actually killed someone, Patrick. But they were trying to kill me." She started to cry again.

"I know. I found him. You had no choice," he soothed her.

Lee wiped her eyes and sat back. They were both silent for a few moments. Finally, she spoke up.

"I'm sorry, Patrick," she said softly. "Sorry about all the times you tried to get me to open up, and I shut you off."

"It's okay," he shushed her.

"No," she insisted, almost frantic. "You don't understand. I need to tell you. Brad wasn't murdered. He didn't even die. He left me," she choked out, starting to cry again. "I never told you. I never told anyone. I couldn't."

Patrick only listened, keeping his arm wrapped snugly around her shoulders.

"He was seeing another woman," she continued, feeling like a rusty gate had finally opened. "I knew he was cheating on me for some time, but I couldn't confront him." She lowered her chin and pursed her lips as her sobs subsided again. "Damn him. He cleaned out our savings. He took every penny we'd saved together, plus the money Dad left me. He told me he was taking some money out to take me on a cruise. I guess he concocted the story so people would think he'd been killed when someone tried to rob him." She laughed. "What an idiot. Why would he have all that money on him when he was out fishing?" She paused again as a painful memory surfaced. "That's why he killed Perry, you know. To make it look like murder." She clenched her right fist as it lay atop her knee, remembering the dog. "He didn't realize I wouldn't tell anyone about the money. The police assumed it was either murder or suicide. Without my help, the investigation just faded away. It was easier that way. I didn't want people asking questions. I didn't want to dredge up the rotten life we'd had together. I didn't want everyone to say… I told you so."

"Especially Mom?"

She sighed. "Especially Mom."

"For the record, I think she knows. We all suspected it. We were just waiting for you to acknowledge it. I always thought Brad was a jerk, anyway. I never thought he was good enough for you. Typical big brother stuff, huh? I was happy when he disappeared. I thought you lucked out." He lifted his hand over her head to place it in his lap.

"Who knows? Maybe I did," she said wistfully. "I just wish I'd handled it better."

"We could all second-guess our lives, Lee − God knows I could." He paused and sat back a little.

"In a way, this forced me to deal with some things I'd ignored for a long time. You know, for not having dealt with Brad. For having argued with Diane. Either I had to see this through or pay the consequences."

"That's pretty severe."

"I was paying for it with my life anyway, Patrick. You said so yourself. Something had to give."

They were both silent for a few moments. Then Patrick said, "Remember Dad's nickname for you?"

"Cricket," she said with the hint of a smile. "Mom said he named me that because I made a funny sound when I was a baby."

Patrick stole a glance in her direction. "You probably didn't know it, but he always carried a picture of you in his wallet. You must have been about six years old. He called it his cricket charm. Said it brought him good luck."

Her face reddened and the tears threatened to flow again. "I didn't know that."

"I'm sure there were moments in his life he wished he could live over again, too." Patrick reached for her hand and squeezed it.

Voices outside interrupted them as police officers searched the large facility. When two officers appeared at the big double doors with their weapons drawn, Patrick got to his feet and called down to them, telling them he was the one who had called them. Then he turned to Lee and held out his hand.

"C'mon, it's time to get off this thing."

She looked up at him, not sure her legs had the strength to stand. "By the way," she said, stalling. "Why did you come here tonight?"

He gave her a rueful smile. "Because when I was at the house, Alan called to tell you that Bud Maddox had been implicated in a hit and run. A woman was killed. She worked in the hospital lab with Maddox and the police are handling it as a homicide. I decided you needed to know right away. And," he stressed, "that you needed protection. I guess I was a little late."

Lee nodded and took his hand.

"Late or not, I'm just glad you're here," she said, as he pulled her to her feet. "And I'm glad it's finally over."

CHAPTER THIRTY-ONE

It was late afternoon when Lee emerged from the grips of a haunting dream with the ring of a familiar voice in her head. It took a moment to realize she was actually holding the phone and listening to Robin.

"The police searched Andrew's office early this morning and found a notebook with names and addresses of some local VIPs," she said, "along with deposit slips for regular amounts of cash. Ruth, from up in the lab, is helping them look for hard evidence on the hospital computers."

Lee rubbed her eyes. "Mmm..." she murmured.

"You gunna be okay?"

Lee mentally checked the bruises on her body − inner thighs, wrists, forehead, shoulder. "Yeah, I'll be okay. I just want to sleep...for another week, or so."

Robin chuckled. "Okay. I'll give you a call later tonight. Alan and I are going to a Boy Scouts spaghetti fundraiser, but we should be home by 8:30 or so. Get some rest."

Lee thanked Robin and hung up. She was tired and didn't really want to think any more about what had happened at the sawmill. By the time she had climbed off the rake carriage, the police had found someone to turn off the chain. Lee hadn't been able to stay in the building. She just couldn't. So they allowed her to be interviewed in a nearby office, while police technicians arrived and attempted to remove what was left of Andrew from the chain. It was after three o'clock in the morning when Lee finally got home and into bed. Two sleeping pills helped her relax, yet sleep was anything but restful. Not only had new nightmares disturbed her, she'd been awakened once, when Amy called around seven o'clock because she had heard a report on the news. Lee had insisted she was okay and went back to sleep. A half hour later, Marion had called and offered to come over. Again, Lee had thanked her, but said she just needed sleep.

Now, the sun that filtered through the lace curtains in her bedroom made her squint. She turned to hide her face in the pillows, but groaned when her muscles came alive with pain. Soldier stood up and rested her head on the bed, her big tail swinging back and forth. Lee opened one eye to locate the dog, whose muzzle was only inches from her face. The message was clear. She had to go out.

Lee willed her body to move, but it protested loudly. When Soldier gave a frustrated bark, Lee swung her legs out of bed with a hefty shout and hobbled to the bathroom. Then, as Soldier raced ahead of her, Lee hobbled downstairs, her legs moving as though every muscle had shortened significantly overnight. She let the dog into the backyard and then shuffled back to the kitchen where she began the arduous task of making tea.

She hadn't realized how many separate movements went into making a simple cup of tea, but reaching for the sugar actually made her cry out as the muscles along the underside of her arms stretched for the first time. She finally grabbed a couple of saltine crackers and made her way to the living room, where she collapsed into a heap on the sofa. As she spread her quilt across her lap, Soldier wiggled into the room.

"How *do* you get back in?"

Soldier sat beside the coffee table panting in Lee's direction, her eyes alight with a dog's natural enthusiasm.

"Jeez," Lee waved her hand in front of her face. "You've got bad breath." She pushed the dog away. "Okay, I get it. You're very proud of yourself." Lee paused, but the dog refused to answer. "Well, next time, I'll close the back door tight, and you won't be so smart."

She made a face, but Soldier ignored the rebuke. When the doorbell rang, Soldier went to stand at attention in the hallway.

Lee cursed under her breath as she put her tea down and pulled herself off the sofa to peek out the window. It was Carey. The dog hadn't even barked, and Lee wondered at the dog's uncanny ability to sense a friend.

"I hope I'm not bothering you, Lee," Carey apologized, watching Lee lean weakly against the open door. "I heard about what happened last night. How are you feeling?"

Lee stepped backward, jerking slightly when her muscles responded a half second after her brain gave the command.

"I'm okay. Barely," she tried to smile. "Please, come in."

Realizing she didn't have full control over her body yet, she followed Carey carefully into the living room.

"Are you sure you're all right?"

"I suppose," Lee exhaled as she lowered herself against some pillows. "I certainly wouldn't want to repeat it."

"I can't imagine what you went through. It's all so awful." Carey sat awkwardly on the edge of the wing-backed chair, twisting her purse strap as she had at the cemetery.

"Yes, but *you* must feel better," Lee offered hopefully. "At least Diane has been exonerated. She didn't kill herself."

Carey glanced at her hands as they worked the leather into a knot. "I don't know if feeling good is how I would describe it. When I was told Diane had committed suicide, I was devastated. I couldn't believe she would do something like that. Now, I'm angry because someone took her life instead."

"At least they paid for it."

"I suppose," she said, looking down." If they were the ones who killed her."

Lee looked up. "What do you mean?"

"I don't know. Something," she shook her head slightly. "Just the way the policeman described what happened to you last night. The attack on you sounded so brutal. Diane's death was so clean, so simple." Carey paused and then looked directly at Lee, her chin held high. "Thank you, Lee. You vindicated my sister, me too, in a way."

"I'm not sure what you mean."

Carey paused, losing the momentary brilliance. "I think you know that Vern and I are having trouble."

"I suspected," Lee responded.

"In his own way, Vern tried to provide a good life for us. But when his clients began to dry up, he didn't know how to regain his balance." She paused again to brush a strand of hair from her eyes. "He'd always been too controlling. It seemed like every minute of our lives had to be planned and accounted for." Carey's head dropped lower before she continued. "From the beginning, he took a sadistic pleasure in berating me in front of others, especially the boys. He'd criticize my clothes, my cooking, how I cleaned the house. Nothing was ever right. Never enough. Eventually, he was successful in getting the boys to join in. It was just teasing at first. But as they grew older, the teasing became cruel. Suddenly, I was the retard mom, or the stupid mom." She lowered her voice so that she was barely audible. "The real problem started the first time Vern slapped me. It gave him a kind of power I don't think he'd ever had. I could see it in his eyes. A week later, he did it again. But that time, he used his fist."

Carey paused for a long moment. Lee just waited.

"The last time, he grabbed my neck just before the funeral. We got into an argument about Diane's death. He was afraid I'd make a public spectacle of myself."

"I would have thought he would want to find the truth," Lee rose to Carey's defense as if it still mattered. "It wouldn't have made any difference in the end. The insurance company would have paid either way."

"Yes, but, you see, Vern doesn't know about the life insurance policy. I never told him. The policy names me as the beneficiary, and I've contacted the company directly."

"Good for you." Lee couldn't help smiling.

"Yes, and now I plan to use that money to get free," she said, lifting her chin. "I've left him, Lee. And, the boys I'm afraid. They're not mine, anymore. Maybe I'll have a chance with them when they're older." Tears suddenly appeared in her eyes. "I contacted the insurance company this morning after I talked to the police. Then I packed up my belongings and moved out. I have a little bit in savings, and my mother will help out until the insurance money arrives."

"Wow," was about all Lee could say.

Carey had found a new voice.

"I figured now was my best chance. If Vern ever got a hold of that money, I'd never see it again. This way, it can give me a new start."

"I'm impressed, Carey. I really am. Diane would be proud of you."

"You think so?" she brightened up. "I've thought so much about her the last few days and what advice she would give me. I think she would have told me to go for it."

"I know she would have."

Carey glanced over at the erase board where Marion had written Vern Mathews' name. Lee noticed the surprised look on Carey's face and was immediately embarrassed.

"We were just speculating," Lee began to apologize. "We didn't have any real theories." Her voice trailed off as Carey stood up and went to the board.

"So, Vern was a suspect."

"Not really. Like I said, we just…"

"No. It's okay," she dismissed Lee's attempts at apology with a wave of her hand. "I can see why you would have thought that."

"We were really just speculating, Carey. Looking at any possibility."

Carey smiled, diffusing the tension in the air. "Don't worry, Lee. I probably would have suspected Vern myself, if I didn't know better." She looked back at the board. "I'm impressed at how far you'd gotten. I had no idea. But why is Pauline Bates name up there?"

CHAPTER THIRTY-TWO

Lee spent the rest of the day napping and watching TV. But she was restless. Carey's last words kept popping into her head. How *was* Pauline Bates involved in all of this?

By 7:15 p.m., she was just finishing a slice of pizza when the phone rang. She grabbed the phone in the kitchen, but was met with silence on the other end.

"Hello!" she nearly shouted when there was no answer. "Hello! Shit! Now, I'm getting crank calls," she said to Soldier, slamming the receiver down.

But she couldn't stop the chill that ran the length of her spine. Soldier merely cocked her head and sat on Lee's foot.

Lee looked down at the dog and shook her shoulders to get rid of the tension the phone call had instilled. Even though intellectually she knew she was out of danger, her ordeal the night before had left her raw. She wondered if she'd ever not flinch at the thought of danger. She needed to get things back to normal, and so took a couple of deep breaths and vowed to relax.

"Okay, big girl," she said, ruffling Soldier's fur. "It's time for you to go out again."

Soldier pushed ahead of her down the hallway toward the back door. Lee moved more fluidly than she had that morning, but her muscles still fought back although with less success. Soldier bounded out onto the back porch and then used her nose to open the screen door.

"So, that's how you do it," Lee said, eying the broken latch on the screen door. "Wait a minute," she said, returning the kitchen.

She went to a cupboard where Amy had stashed a bag of large rawhide chew sticks. She grabbed one and went back to the porch and called the dog. It had begun to rain, and a blustery wind had kicked up outside. Soldier came back onto the porch and shook the water off. When she saw what Lee held, she came to attention immediately, her gaze glued on the rawhide.

"Want this?" she asked, teasing the dog.

Soldier scooted forward a couple of inches, her ears standing straight up.

"Okay," Lee said, holding it out.

Soldier grabbed it in her powerful jaws and climbed up on a bench that sat under the study window. She quickly settled down to focus on her treasure.

"I guess that will keep you busy for a while. I'm closing the back door tight this time. I have some serious relaxing to do."

Lee returned to the kitchen and downed a couple of Advil. She grabbed a last bite of pizza, before wrapping up the remaining slices and tossing them into the refrigerator. Then she made some hot tea and returned to the living room.

Lee closed the drapes, kindled a fire and settled back with the afghan spread across her lap. As she watched flames engulf the instant log, thoughts of Diane surfaced. So much had happened in just a few days, and so many people had died. Why? She still didn't know the answer to that question. Perhaps, she never would.

Her head felt heavy, and she closed her eyes hoping to relieve the burning sensation behind her eyelids. The wind outside lulled her into a doze, and the muscles in her shoulders began to relax. Before long, she was sound asleep. One by one, haunting images began to parade their way through her mind. Andrew with the ball peen hammer. Bud Maddox with his leering grin. The gruesome chain. Diane's living room, right down to the pictures on the fireplace mantle.

Lee came suddenly awake. Her heart raced, and her skin tingled. What was it about Diane's living room that had spooked her?

When she couldn't get her brain to focus, she allowed her head to flop back onto the sofa. God, she thought. She was so tired. Her body was a wreck, and she needed to stop thinking about the events of the past few days. She just wished the dull ache behind her eyes would subside.

Her head rolled to the side, and she allowed her gaze to come to rest on a silver-framed photo on the side table. Amy's shining face smiled back in a picture taken at the beach the summer she turned fourteen. Lee stared at the picture, thinking of Amy. The pendulum clock on the wall ticked softly behind her. Somewhere in the distance, a car door closed.

Lee continued to stare at the photo until the ornate silver frame began to float. Fatigue blurred her consciousness, and her eyelids began to close again. Her thoughts began to run together. Amy and the beach. Amy and the dog. Amy at school. Amy coming home this weekend to celebrate Lee's birthday.

Birthday!

Lee's eyes popped open again, bringing the silver frame back into focus.

"Shit! That was it!"

She sat up, threw off the blanket and hurried as fast as she could to the hall closet to search for her large photo album. When she found it, she returned to the sofa and opened it to a series of pictures taken at a surprise birthday party she'd thrown for Diane only a few weeks before her death. She flipped through pictures of the party until she found the one she was looking for. In it, Diane held a present up for the camera that Carey had given her.

Lee pulled the picture out of its protective sleeve and reached for the drawer in the end table. She extracted her mother's old magnifying glass. Then, she wedged herself into the corner under the direct glare of the lamp and forced her eyes to focus through the magnifying glass at the photo in her hand. Suddenly, her heart felt too big for her chest.

Lee was staring at a photo of Diane holding a small, but now familiar, pewter picture frame.

Lee dropped the photo and bolted to the hallway to grab her purse. Her fingers delved into the main pocket, pushing aside her wallet and makeup bag until she felt the cold metal of the pewter frame she'd stolen from Emily Maddox. She pulled it out and studied it.

It was definitely the one in the picture – the one Carey had given Diane. So how had Emily Maddox gotten it?

As Lee contemplated this, she took notice of the picture itself. It was of Bud and Diane standing before a western storefront in Sisters, a small town up in the mountains. Diane and Bud had made the trip with another couple from the hospital just the weekend before she died. A second chill flushed Lee's body.

This had to be a picture from the missing roll of film in Diane's camera!

Lee thought back. Hadn't Diane said she was taking the last picture on the roll when she'd taken the picture of Lee that night? So, if this picture was from the missing roll of film, how the hell did it get on a shelf in Emily Maddox's home?

"My God!" she whispered to herself. "I'm so stupid. Stupid! Stupid! Stupid! Andrew said last night that he didn't kill Diane."

Lee stumbled to the phone to call the police station. She remembered it all now, including what Diane had said that night.

"I'll put this picture of you in that teeny frame Carey gave me...or better yet, in my scrapbook with all of my other single friends.

Damn! Why hadn't she remembered the part about the frame? Why had she focused only on the part about single friends?

"I'm sorry, Sergeant Davis has already left," a brusque voice said. "Do you want to leave a message?"

"No, thanks," Lee snapped to attention.

Lee's hands trembled as she cut the phone connection. In the background, a roll of thunder punctuated her racing heartbeat. Sergeant Davis wasn't available. And Alan had gone to a scouting event. He and Robin wouldn't be home until 8:30 p.m. Lee glanced at her watch. It was just after eight o'clock. Patrick was at the theater and wouldn't be home for another hour or so. If she left now, she'd get to Alan's house just about the time he and Robin returned. And she could tell Alan what she now knew – that it hadn't been Bud *or* Andrew who had killed Diane. And she could tell Robin that it hadn't been Pauline Bates at the graveyard, either. In fact, Pauline Bates had had nothing to do with Diane's death.

Lee took the photos and hurried back to the closet to grab her coat. A crack of lightning lit up the front yard, making her jump. Her nerves were frayed, and she was shaking. She took a deep breath and then stuffed the frame and the photo from Diane's birthday party into the side pocket of her purse. There was an incessant drumming on the roof, which meant it was raining hard.

"Just my luck," she mumbled.

As she grabbed an umbrella from the umbrella stand by the door, a shadow flashed past the front sidelight. In her mindless rush to get to the car, Lee swung the door open, only to come face to face with Emily Maddox.

"Going out?" the other woman smiled.

Lee's knees nearly buckled.

"I've caught you at a bad time," Maddox purred.

Lee's mind filled with a cacophony of sound that blocked out any logical response. Diane's murderer stood in front of her, while the night disappeared behind her like a black hole in space.

"I was just leaving," Lee said in a faint voice.

"I've remembered something that might be of help," Maddox said.

Lee opened her mouth to respond, when Emily Maddox suddenly swept past her into the entryway.

"It won't take long," the woman whispered, gliding into the living room. "I'm sure you'll want to hear this."

Lee swallowed her response, cursing herself for not closing the door in the woman's face. But all of Lee's circuits seemed to have shut down. She felt like an electrical appliance someone had forgotten to plug in, and now it was too late. Lee glanced at the open door. It was her only means of escape. She could just step outside and be free of this woman. Maddox seemed to read her thoughts and turned to her.

"I have something for you," she said.

From the inside of her coat, Maddox brought something out and rolled it back and forth between her fingers like a blackjack dealer. The melodic tingling riveted Lee to the spot. It was Amy's charm bracelet.

"Where did you get that?" she gasped.

Lee couldn't help herself. She dropped the umbrella and stumbled forward, staring at the bracelet as it glinted in the low light. Tears flooded her eyes so that she could barely see.

"What have you done with my daughter?" Her whole body trembled now, and she feared she might actually collapse. "What do you want from me?"

"You have something I need. Please, close the door."

Lee leaned helplessly against the archway to the living room, her body a limp collection of bones and muscles. Everything she'd fought for in the last few days, her idea of friendship, her own pride and sanity, even justice, had evaporated. None of it mattered anymore. Only Amy. She turned and closed the door, feeling like she was shutting the door on her own life.

"I don't have anything," Lee mumbled, turning back. "I don't know what you're talking about."

"It wasn't at Diane's, so you must have taken it. Bud didn't have time to find it here, but I know you have it."

A flash of recognition blazed through Lee's mind. The photo. Emily Maddox wanted the only thing that would link her to Diane. Lee's elbow clamped down on her purse as she took a few faltering steps backwards.

"Your daughter!" Maddox stopped her. "She needs you."

Lee stopped, feeling unsteady on her feet. The colors in the room had become a psychedelic collection of shimmering crystals. Emily

Maddox reached into her pocket and produced a key, like a magician pulls a rabbit out of a hat.

"This will get you what you want. Now give it to me."

Lee moved to the back of the sofa, staring at the key dangling from the woman's gloved fingers. Attached to it was a tag, like the key to a storage locker. Lee felt her stomach rise into her gullet at the thought of Amy stuffed inside a locker somewhere.

"It's clearly marked. You shouldn't have any trouble finding the location, but you don't really have time to waste."

Lee hesitated, her mind turning over her few options. If she ran for the police, this woman would disappear into the night, and she might never find Amy. If she gave her the photo, there would be no proof that she was involved with Diane's murder. But did that matter if Lee lost Amy? If she was successful in finding her daughter, Amy could identify Bud's sister as her abductor. Perhaps Emily hadn't thought of that. The possibility motivated Lee to step in front of the sofa.

"How do I know you won't try to kill me once you have what you want?"

Emily patted down her pockets with her free hand.

"I have no weapon. You see? Nothing hidden inside." She opened her coat like a street vendor shows off his collection of watches. "Give me what I want, and I'll leave you alone. You can cry all you want to the police. They won't believe you. All the evidence they have points to Andrew and my brother. And they're both dead."

"Your wha…"

Then the last piece of the puzzle dropped into place. The eyes. The brows. Even the cocky way she held her head. This was Bud Maddox's sister. Not his wife. The implication twisted Lee's intestines into a knot. No wonder she'd looked so familiar.

"You didn't know, did you?" the other woman said. "I wonder if Diane knew. It was a good charade."

"But why?" Lee asked again.

"Because it was convenient. Because women are silly. They always want to think they're saving someone. Especially from a hopeless marriage. And Bud was very good at playing the beleaguered husband."

"But, why Diane?"

"She was a means to an end. Information is power, they say. The right information, anyway." Emily Maddox's lips stretched into a thin, knowing smile.

"The lab reports," Lee gasped. "You were blackmailing people. And Bud got the names of wealthy people from Diane."

Diane's killer began to stroll around the living room, making cursory examinations of some of Lee's collectibles.

"Oh, don't worry," she said. "Your dear friend didn't actually betray the secrets. She didn't have to. Bud was good at lifting the things he needed. Like keys. Or combinations. Or passwords. He could be very persuasive," she finished with a sly grin.

"And Andrew?" Lee asked.

"Andrew was a buffoon, a pathetic little man," she continued. "With someone like that, all you have to do is make him believe it was his idea. And he served his purpose," she said with a shrug. "He identified certain important clients, distracted certain prying eyes. And he led me to you."

"Me?" Lee nearly laughed. "So Abbot and Costello botched the job, and you're the cleanup crew?"

"No, no, no," Emily Maddox smiled with patronizing patience. "Andrew just talked my brother into taking things into his own hands a bit too soon last night. Obviously, that was a mistake. I don't make mistakes. You just give me what I want, and I'll be gone."

"I don't believe you."

"Seriously," she said, twirling the key around her finger. "The police have never caught me before, why should now be any different?"

Lee's mind whirred as she watched this horrible creature practically swagger around the end of the sofa. Then she remembered the photos on the shelf at her home. The photos of Bud with other women.

"You've killed other women," she stammered. "The other women in those photos."

Maddox drifted around the other end of the sofa, coming up on the backside.

"Oh, well, now. Nothing actually points to me. Just Bud. And as I said, he's not here anymore to contradict me." She stopped, leveling her gaze on Lee. "Now, it's getting late."

The conflict inside Lee was almost unbearable. The woman standing before her was a serial killer. Lee needed the photo to turn her in. But the threat against Amy was too real. Lee had to take a chance. She reached into the inside pocket of her handbag and pulled out the pewter frame and handed it over.

The woman exploded, throwing the photo to the ground. "Stop playing games! I swear I'll throw this key into the river on my way out of town!"

Lee let out a strangled cry. "No! My daughter is an asthmatic. Please, I don't understand." Lee was breathing hard as panic tore at her chest. "I thought that's what you wanted. You said Bud couldn't find it. I took the photo from your house…"

Lee stopped.

Her house had been ransacked, but so had Diane's. Bud couldn't have been looking for the photo at Diane's, because Emily had taken the entire roll of film. When Lee realized the truth, she thought she actually felt the light bulb go off in her head.

"You're looking for the camera."

Emily Maddox didn't smile this time. She just stood watching Lee, her features set in a grim mask. Lee finished the puzzle.

"You've done this so many times before, you got cocky. After you killed Diane, you took off your gloves thinking the job was done. But then you couldn't resist, could you? You have photos of all the women you've killed. Your trophies. And there was Diane's camera. Just sitting there on the mantle. You knew she'd gone to Sisters with Bud the weekend before, so you took out the film. That's how you got the picture in this frame. But in doing so, you left fingerprints all over the camera."

Lee paused, allowing the truth to float in the air like mist on a foggy morning. When Emily Maddox spoke this time, her voice wasn't much above a growl.

"I want the camera, Miss Vanderhaven. And I want it now."

Lee's brain was alarmingly clear all of a sudden. She knew that if she told Emily Maddox the truth, namely that the camera was in her car, she would never find Amy. She also realized that Maddox had moved in between her and the front door. She was trapped in her own living room. Her heart fluttered.

"It's not here," she bluffed.

Her intruder didn't move.

"It's in my office," Lee tried to control her voice.

"You're lying."

"I put it with Diane's other belongings. Her sister will pick them all up next week."

Lee's eyes flitted to the box Jenny had dropped off in the entryway. Maddox caught the slip and turned, eying the open carton filled with

Diane's personal belongings. Her head snapped back so fast it made Lee jump.

"Dammit! Do you think I'm kidding?" She advanced on Lee, her body as rigid as steel. "I don't give a shit about you or your pathetic little daughter. I want that camera!"

Lee backed up, her eyes on the key in Emily Maddox's hand.

"It's in my car! I swear. Please! Amy's so young."

Lee reached for the key, but Maddox held it back, watching her as if she were trying to gauge Lee's truthfulness. Suddenly, as if she'd come to some conclusion, she sidestepped Lee and threw the key into the fireplace. Lee screamed, "NO!" and grabbed the fireplace poker.

She shoved the poker deep into the burning embers, pushing the flaming log aside. The heat seared her face, but she didn't care. She would reach in with her bare hands if she had to. When she found the key, she hooked the chain with the end of the poker and pulled it out. The tag had just begun to burn, so she quickly dropped it on the fireplace stones and used her foot to stomp it out. Lee let go of the poker and leaned over to grab the key by the tag. She stood up and turned, ready to mow Maddox down on her way out the door if she had to, but the blur of a needle jumped before her eyes. She had just enough time to deflect it with her purse. The blow meant for her neck glanced off her shoulder.

Lee dropped her purse and grabbed the hand holding the syringe, driving it toward the floor. Maddox was in a rage. She reached in and gripped Lee's wrist with her other hand, twisting the skin painfully. The two women struggled, yanking back and forth, straining to gain control of the weapon. Maddox was strong and started to snarl, her lips pulled back from her teeth. The sound terrified Lee, but she held on, her knuckles turning white.

The two women spun to the right, locked so close in combat that Lee could smell the foulness of her breath. They slammed into a plant stand, sending it crashing to the floor. They rolled onto the top of a hutch, wiping it clean of Lee's collectibles.

Lee's strength began to fail, and Maddox gained the advantage. She swung Lee in a circle and slammed her into the fireplace. Lee ended up sitting on the fireplace ledge. But she wouldn't give up. She used the back of her leg as a fulcrum and pushed herself back to a standing position. Lee's muscles burned, and she was almost too tired to hold on. Maddox seemed to sense this and smiled. She swung Lee to the left. Then with all the strength she had, she whirled Lee viciously to the right again.

Lee flew sideways, but her hand held onto Emily's an instant too long. Emily was yanked off balance with a jolt. Her ankle twisted and cracked, and she crumpled to the floor with a cry, her leg tucked awkwardly beneath her.

Lee crashed into the side table, her head coming down directly on top of the steel foot of her Tiffany lamp. The table collapsed under her weight and the lamp went flying.

When it was over, Lee lay on her side, watching a blurred image of Emily Maddox sitting in a twisted heap in front of the fireplace. Lee tried to focus, but all she saw was a swirling image of the other woman still holding the syringe. Lee tried to rise, but a wave of nausea stopped her. She couldn't even get to her hands and knees. Instead, she lay on the floor watching her attacker attempt to get up. But something about Emily's leg prevented her. Both women were momentarily incapacitated. Or, so it seemed.

"I'm not finished with you," Emily Maddox snarled.

Like any good horror movie, Emily leaned forward and began to crawl painfully in Lee's direction, dragging her injured leg behind her. She was determined to finish what she came for, and Lee was out of options.

A low-grade humming began to vibrate in Lee's head, and she closed her eyes, feeling as if she might actually throw up. As the humming grew louder, a high-pitched scream brought Lee's head up in a snap. For a moment, she saw the living room clearly.

Emily Maddox was on her hands and knees, about three feet from Lee. Her eyes were focused in a glazed stare at Lee. No, that was wrong. She was staring at something *behind* Lee. That's when Lee became aware of another presence in the room. Emily's eyes were alive with an intense fire, and her mouth was drawn into a hateful grimace. Lee had seen that look once before.

Emily suddenly raised herself up and swung the syringe high above her head to strike the killing blow. Lee lifted her arm in defense, but the move was wasted. A large, gray blur sailed over Lee's head and planted a heavy paw in the middle of her shoulder as it slammed full-force into Emily Maddox's chest.

Emily flew backwards. The syringe in her hand dropped to the carpet, and her head hit the edge of the fireplace bench with the force of a cantaloupe hitting pavement. Suddenly, all was silent.

CHAPTER THIRTY-THREE

It was Monday, late afternoon, and strings of gray clouds marched across the sky in military formation. Alan leaned heavily against the porch pillar, while Lee sat on the wicker settee wrapped in a fuzzy blanket, enjoying the fresh air. She had arrived home that morning, having spent almost forty-eight hours at the hospital to rule out a possible concussion. Patrick busied himself in the kitchen making dinner.

Lee was still on pain medication for a headache caused by hitting her head on the lamp stand. And she was mentally and physically exhausted. She found herself staring at her yard, thinking about random things like cutting back the bushes and raising the limbs on some of the trees. Even though Alan had stopped by to debrief her on the police report, she was barely aware he was there. But she was keenly aware of the big dog pushed up against her ankles, snoring.

"Lee," Alan interrupted her thoughts. "Are you okay? I can come back."

"No, I'm okay," she said, shifting her attention to him. "Sorry. I'm just tired."

"Well, I'll try to make it quick. It was a neighbor kid from across the street who called the police. He happened to come out around 8:15 and saw weird lighting effects over here. He knew your brother taught in the drama department at the university and thought maybe there was a rehearsal going on."

Her eyebrows lifted. "Really?"

Alan shrugged. "I'm not sure he actually knew Patrick was your brother. Just that he was a drama professor. The point is, he got spooked and called 911 when he heard Emily scream. He knew the scream wasn't an act."

Neither of them said anything for a moment. A delivery truck rumbled by, shaking the ground around them as it passed.

"I see," Lee finally responded.

She lifted her hand and touched the large knot on the side of her head. She remembered enough to know she didn't want to think about the details. She wasn't sure she'd ever feel limber or fully mobile again.

Alan lowered his head slightly. "She was dead when the police got here."

"I know," she said as she pulled the afghan closer. "Patrick couldn't get the blood stains off the fireplace stones."

There was another long silence and Lee's eyes glazed over for a moment. A large bird of prey descended through the branches of a cedar tree to land on the lower branch of the evergreen bordering her property. She watched it float gracefully down and fold back its wings. Birds that size were rarely seen in the city, but this one didn't surprise her. She was used to them by now.

Her fingers moved to her eyes where she let them gently explore the sockets. She needed a rest as her foot gently stroked Soldier's back. The front door opened and Amy appeared. She'd come home as soon as she'd heard her mother had been attacked again. She'd never seen or heard of Emily Maddox. Dressed in faded jeans and a baggy blue sweater, she came out and draped herself across the arm of the settee. The dog wagged its tail and raised its head.

"Hey, Mom, are you doing okay? Need anything?" Amy asked, leaning forward to fondle the dog's nose.

"No, I'm okay." Lee answered a trifle slowly. "Just very tired."

Amy looked up at Alan. "Have you found out any more about what was going on? I mean, why that woman killed Diane and tried to kill Mom?"

"We talked with your friend, Ruth…at the hospital," he said to Lee. "She found something interesting on Bud's computer. Apparently, he took names off Diane's computer and kept a separate file in his own linked to the patient admission information. These were people with money and influence. When someone was admitted to the hospital matching the list he got from you guys, it linked up with the network, alerting him."

"Why did he do that?" Lee inquired.

"He couldn't always count on being the lab tech that ran tests when VIPs were admitted to the hospital. He had to have a way of knowing who they were and when they were admitted. When one was, he would come in after hours and run a sample drug test with false results. Since it was a sample test, we're told it wasn't picked up anywhere else in the system. He could produce an official looking document showing the individual had tested positive for amphetamines, cocaine, or whatever. He knew exactly the kind of people he wanted to target and used your information to build the profiles. Then, he and Andrew would wait until the opportunity presented itself to blackmail them.

"Martha," Lee said quietly to herself.

"Martha?" Alan's ruddy face twisted into confusion.

"Martha Osgood. I think she may have seen something up in the lab and tried to alert me, but she was killed before I could ever figure out what she was trying to tell me."

Alan nodded. "Yeah, a runner out early the morning she was killed identified Bud Maddox's truck near the spot where we found the stolen car that hit Martha. He must have dumped the stolen one and switched back into his truck."

"I still don't get it," Amy said, confused. "How would they blackmail people if the person they tested knew the results were false?"

"Think about it," Alan replied. "If you were running for a political office and someone threatened to leak it to the press, it would kill your campaign instantly. Or, what if your mother was in a nursing home, frail and on the verge of death? Threatening to expose the fact you had HIV might kill her. Wouldn't you pay to save her from that?"

"Even if you cleared your name," Lee continued, "the suspicions would always be there. I suppose most people would rather just try and make it go away."

"Besides," Alan interjected, "Maddox and Andrew weren't asking for exorbitant payoffs. Usually not more than $25,000. And they picked people very carefully. People with a little money, but who wouldn't be likely to have the resources or the fortitude to challenge them."

"Then all they had to do was destroy the phony report?" Lee finished.

"That's right. No evidence left behind. And the real tests were still in place, so no one was the wiser."

The porch had grown quiet except for the backdrop of rustling trees at the corner of the property. The bird, still perched among the evergreen watched them as if waiting for something.

"We found that lab report you mentioned in Diane's bathroom drawer, just where you said it would be," he said to Lee. "The report has the name of one of your donors on it. We'll probably never know where she found it, but she must have gotten suspicious and asked Bud about it. That's what started the whole ball rolling."

"But if she suspected something like that," Lee shook her head, "why would she agree to go to Portland with him? Why would she talk about marrying him?"

"Remember that he was very good at lying. He must have been able to explain it away somehow, but it didn't matter. By that time her fate was sealed."

"So, Emily Maddox was a full partner in all of this?"

"We think so. We're not sure what the relationship was between Emily and Bud. We sent a couple of officers down to Redding, where they grew up. From what they learned, Emily was older by four years. Apparently their father was a blatant philanderer, even sexually abusing Emily from the time she was very small, although she denied it. According to neighbors, she would get especially hostile every time another woman entered the picture. A couple of them even speculated that she was jealous of her own mother. When she was sixteen, one of the father's girlfriends turned up dead. He took off, but was never implicated in the murder. The mother tried to kill herself twice and was finally committed to a mental hospital. Emily spent the next few years raising her younger brother, doing God knows what to him," Alan cringed. "Anyway, the two of them have never been apart for more than a few months at a time. They eventually moved to Medford as a couple, either as a façade, or for some twisted reason I'd rather not think about."

"You learned a lot in two days," Lee said.

"Well, one of the detectives also contacted the attending physician at the institution where her mother was hospitalized," Alan said. "I guess mom talked a lot while she was there. And, we've talked to several former neighbors and church friends. For instance, one story corroborated by several people was that when Bud was seventeen, he got a girl pregnant. Not long afterwards, the girl mysteriously disappeared. Everyone suspected it was Emily who had gotten rid of her, but there was no evidence."

"So Emily eliminated Bud's girlfriends," Lee whispered.

Alan was leaning against the porch railing and watched her as if judging how to respond.

"There were suspicions in Medford, too. Two different women who dated Bud at the hospital died suspiciously. He was cleared each time, but now both the Redding and Medford Police Departments have reopened the cases. So, whether Emily Maddox killed Diane because she had uncovered their little blackmailing scheme, or just because she was involved with Bud, we'll never know. By the way, we found your driver's license in Emily's purse. I guess that's how she found you."

Lee frowned, her mind backtracking to the Bates party and her purse.

"Listen, Lee. I owe you an apology," Alan said quietly. "If I'd listened to you, maybe none of this would have happened."

She shrugged. "It's okay, Alan. In the beginning, I wasn't even sure what I believed. I probably sounded like a nut case."

"No," he said, holding up a hand. "You didn't. You knew what you knew about your friend, but I wasn't hearing it. I learned something in all of this." He nodded his head toward Lee. "To listen better. Read between the lines," he said. "Well, I have to go," he said, rising. "You'll be okay?"

"Yeah. Thanks, Alan," she said with a half-smile. "You're a good friend."

He smiled and kissed the top of her head. "Let me know if you need anything." He patted Amy on the shoulder and stepped off the porch to lumber down the sidewalk.

Amy squeezed her mom's shoulder. "I'm proud of you, Mom. You were very brave."

Lee reached a hand up and caught Amy's. "I'm not sure brave is how I'd describe it. By the way, how in the world did she get your bracelet?"

Amy curled a lip. "The apartment manager let her in. She said she was my aunt. It was too normal to sound suspicious, I guess. I never saw her. I was out with a friend. She was long gone by the time I came back. I never even knew she'd been there until Uncle Patrick told me about it."

"So her threat was an empty one." Lee squeezed Amy's hand. "I'm just glad you're okay. The thought of that woman even touching you could drive me mad."

"Well, it's all over. Now, maybe things can get back to normal around here. I'll take Soldier back in the morning, and you can get some rest. It's pretty cool though, don't you think, that Soldier saved you?" Amy patted the dog's head. "By the way, is Uncle Patrick actually moving in?"

Lee smiled in spite of herself. "For a while. He is my brother after all."

Amy smiled back. "Awesome! It'll give me one more reason to come home on the weekends. I'll go help him with dinner."

Amy turned and went inside.

Soldier got up and sat patiently by the settee, her eyes imploring Lee for attention. Lee patted the sofa. With one graceful movement the animal landed softly beside her, turned once in a circle and tucked herself under Lee's elbow. Lee draped her arm across the muscular back and rested her hand gently on one ear, thinking the dog hadn't turned out to be so bad after all.

She was lost in thought when a young man appeared on the steps in front of her. Soldier came to attention, making Lee look up. The boy was medium height, slight build, short brown hair and pleasant features. He stood hesitantly on the steps.

"I'm glad to see you're okay. That was quite an ordeal."

"You're the young man who rescued me," she guessed accurately.

He took this recognition as permission to move to the top step.

"Yes, I called for help."

"Well, thank you. I was in no condition to call them myself."

"I did look in on you before the police got here, but your dog wouldn't let me get near you." He nodded to Soldier. "So I waited outside until the police arrived. In fact, they weren't successful either, until your brother showed up. He's one protective dog," the boy said with admiration.

He seemed rather mild-mannered and a bit shy. Lee liked him immediately.

"It's a she, actually. You live across the street, I understand."

"Yes," his eyes lit up. "I live with six other guys. It's kind of a madhouse over there. I hope we don't make too much noise."

She smiled. "No. Actually, I've been surprised that you don't. I thought it was a fraternity."

"Nothing that organized," he laughed. "We all happen to be architectural students. I've drawn your house a couple of times – because of the gables." He pointed towards the roof. "It's a great old house. I've even taken a couple of pictures of it. I'll show them to you sometime."

"I'd like to see them. I was told you recognized my brother,

Patrick."

"Yes," he answered quickly. "One of the guys I live with does some designing for the theater." He shuffled from foot to foot. "Is your daughter in the theater also?"

"My daughter?" So, he had noticed Amy. No wonder he seemed so interested in the house. "No, she goes to Corvallis."

"Oh. Well, I'm sure she's glad you're okay, too," he said awkwardly. He stood a moment glancing back and forth to the door. It was obvious he hoped Amy would make an appearance. "Well," he began almost disappointed, "I guess I'd better go." His eyes searched the entryway one last time.

Lee stroked Soldier's head. She liked this boy. Maybe he could provide yet one more reason for Amy to come home on the weekends. Maybe even move back permanently.

"Perhaps you'd like to come to dinner. I think we should get to know each other better. After all, you helped save my life. I could have Amy set another place at the table."

He jumped at the chance. "I'd like that. Tonight?" His eyes shone.

"Sure. How about six-thirty? I'll tell Amy to plan on one more for dinner."

The shy smile widened into a full set of shiny, slightly crooked teeth, making him irresistible.

"I'd like that." He began to back off the porch. "I'll see you at six then." He turned and nearly fell off the bottom step.

"Six-thirty," Lee corrected him as he gained his composure.

"Oh, yeah. Sorry. Six-thirty. I'll be here."

He practically skipped to the curb and across the street. Lee watched him with a growing feeling of warmth. When he reached the other side of the street, he got into the tan sedan that had haunted her for the last several days, and the feeling of warmth she'd had for him faded. As he pulled away from the curb, he looked over and waved, then slowly disappeared up the street.

Lee sat in a daze until Amy's laughter rang like a bell from inside the house, illuminating her mistake. This boy hadn't been stalking Lee. This shy boy had driven slowly by her house every day and night hoping to catch sight of Amy. She chuckled and shook her head. One more mystery solved.

Amy appeared at the doorway. "Mom. I just talked with Maddie, and she said she's found someone who will take Soldier if we can leave her here until next Saturday. Sound okay to you?"

Lee looked down at the noble head with its pointed ears and black muzzle. Soldier's eyes were closed, and she breathed contentedly now that all the excitement had faded.

"No. I don't think that's such a good idea."

"But, Mom..." Amy started to object.

Lee merely raised her hand. "Tell Maddie...you've already found a home for Soldier." She patted the dog's head, waking her up. Soldier rolled over on her side with a loud groan.

Amy gave a broad smile. "I'll call her right back. Of course, you might change your mind when you see what she did to your desk in the study."

"Oh?"

"She must have jumped up on the bench on the porch and pushed the window up with her nose. That's how she got in the other night."

Lee smiled, remembering how she'd opened the window in the study because of the burnt popcorn.

"By-the-way," Amy added, stepping forward. "I found this on the window sill." Amy held out the onyx bird. "I wouldn't use it as a window stopper, Mom. It could get chipped."

Lee took her totem, smiling, knowing full well she hadn't placed the bird in the window.

"I'll take better care of it in the future."

Amy started back inside when Lee caught her. "Amy, we're having company for dinner. Tell Patrick to set the table for four."

Amy looked puzzled, but disappeared inside. Lee smiled to herself.

She leaned back as far as she could and rested her head on the pillow, her hand idly stroking Soldier's fur. How life had changed in such a short time. She had lost her best friend and felt an emptiness she thought would never be filled. She had uncovered a blackmailing ring and almost been killed twice. She had avenged her friend's death and could now finally deal with the loss. Although her body felt like hell, she felt stronger emotionally than she had in fifteen years. Perhaps she might even start to date again, once she healed. And, finally, she could admit that what Brad had done had been the cowardly act of a pathetic man.

As she petted Soldier, she thought of Perry, the good and loyal Labrador retriever who died in order to give her husband the freedom he so desperately craved. She grabbed a handful of Soldier's fur, fighting back the tears.

"You'd have liked Perry," she said aloud to the dog. "You'd have liked him a lot."

Soldier whined and twisted her head around to lick Lee's hand.

Overhead, a large black thundercloud had moved behind a tall tree, threatening to block out the afternoon sun. Lee brushed the tears from her eyes and looked up in time to see the hawk lift off from the branch, gain altitude and circle a few times in the sky. She watched it, marveling at its grace and strength and thinking of her friend.

Lee took a deep sigh. "Thanks, Diane," she whispered.

When the onyx bird in her hand grew warm, she glanced down. A deep burgundy fire seemed to glow from within, like the embers from a dying fire. Just then, a gray cat jumped lightly onto the railing and began weaving back and forth.

"Well, Sasha, this is your home now, isn't it?" she said, reaching out to pet the cat. "I guess it's time for your injection. We'd better go inside."

She stood up, disturbing Soldier. The dog jumped off the settee and went immediately to the door, wagging her tail. The cat followed, pushing itself under Soldier's belly like they'd been friends forever. Lee shook her head and pushed open the heavy door, allowing the animals to tumble inside and head straight for the kitchen.

As Lee stepped inside and began to close the door, she glanced back to the stormy sky. The hawk had been circling in a wide arc. Suddenly, it dipped one wing as if in salute, and sailed away over the rooftops to get lost in the thundercloud.

The End

Thank you so very much for reading *Grave Doubts*. If you enjoyed this book, I encourage you to go back to Amazon.com and leave an honest review. This will help position the book so that more people might also enjoy it. Thank you!

About the Author

Ms. Bohart holds a master's degree in theater, has been published in Woman's World, and has a story in *Dead on Demand*, an anthology of ghost stories that remained on the Library Journal best seller list for six months. As a thirty-year nonprofit professional, she has spent a lifetime writing brochures, newsletters, business letters, website copy, and more. Recently, she did a short stint writing for Patch.com, and she teaches writing for Green River Community College Continuing Education. *Mass Murder,* her first novel, is available on Amazon.com and has been endorsed by Compulsion Reads as an "excellent read." She has also self-published a book of creepy short stories and mysteries called, *Your Worst Nightmare*, and a single short story, *Something Wicked*. Look for her most recent paranormal mystery novel, "Inn Keeping With Murder," on Amazon.com.

Ms. Bohart also writes a blog on the various aspects of writing and the paranormal on her website at: www.bohartink.com. She lives in the Northwest with her daughter, two miniature Dachshunds, and cat.

Follow Ms. Bohart

Website: www.bohartink.com
Twitter: @lbohart
Facebook: Facebook @ L.Bohart/author

Made in the USA
Charleston, SC
02 February 2017